Children of Fear

Children of Fear

Des Morley

My thanks to my agent Frances Bond whose warm and patient guidance was so important to me in the development of this book.

First published in Great Britain in 1989 by
Judy Piatkus (Publishers) Ltd of
5 Windmill Street, London W1

British Library Cataloguing in Publication Data

Morley, Des
Children of fear.
I. Title
823 [F]

ISBN 0-86188-828-6

Phototypeset in 11/12 Compugraphic Times by
Action Typesetting Limited, Gloucester
Printed and bound in Great Britain by
Mackays of Chatham PLC, Kent

Author's Note

While any writer who bases his story on events of the Second World War runs the risk of discovering as I did, that the plot he so lovingly created has its parallel in actual events, it is nonetheless heartening to find that the finale of both imaginary and actual adventures had equally happy endings.

The true parallel to my story involved one of the most intrepid and daring escape stories of those dark days; the rescue of more than twelve thousand Jewish children bound for the death camps, and it was only while carrying out further research on an aspect of my half-written story, that I discovered I had been pre-empted by history.

Nevertheless, my story, the discovery by a trio of escaping Allied prisoners, that even children were not immune from the horrors of those days, is mirrored in many of the events overtaking the world today.

Let me hasten to say that I have written my novel purely to entertain the reader and I hope it does just that, but in doing so, I trust that it does not escape the reader that in any conflict, the suffering of the innocent ones is made more appalling because of their absolute inability to control their own destinies. They did not influence events; they had no voice in its beginnings; and in the final analysis, they were swept along in an enveloping tide of tragedy that they were neither able to comprehend nor restrain.

These were unhappy children – the Children of Fear. They had seen their parents dragged away, never to be seen again, and now they themselves were entering the nightmare.

Since 1944, many of the towns featured in the story have had their names changed. The towns and their new names are listed below.

Auschwitz	– Oswiecim
Breslau	– Wroclaw
Brux	– Most
Eger	– Cheb
Gorlitz	– Zgorzelec
Komotau	– Chomutov
Leutensdorf	– Litvinov
Liegnitz	– Legnica
Reichenberg	– Liberec
Sagan	– Zagan
Tetschen	– Decin

GERMANY
Berlin
POLAND
Sagan
Kottbus
Bischofswerda
Leipzig
Bautzen
Liegnitz
Gorlitz
Breslau
Dresden
Liebstadt
Tetschen
Glashutte
Teplitz
Most
Komotau
Eger
Bayreuth
CZECHOSLOVAKIA
Nuremberg
Kempten
Munich
Wangen
Friedrichshafen
Konstanz
ROUTE
walking
train
bus
tanker
AUSTRIA
SWITZER-
LAND

Bibliography

Operation 7, the plan by which Admiral Canaris, Head of German Military Intelligence (Abwehr), saved many Jews from the concentration camps by recruiting them into his organisation, is told fully in *Canaris – The Biography of Admiral Canaris* by André Brissaud, translated by Ian Colvin and published by Weidenfeld and Nicolson Ltd. It is also described in *Canaris* by Heinz Höhne, published by Secker and Warburg.

Bishop Hudal's infamous career as a Nazi-loving priest who helped German war criminals is told in *Aftermath* by Ladislas Farago, published by Hodder and Stoughton.

The story of Doctor Kockel's part in the solving of the Green Opel Murder Case, in which a German businessman was alleged to have been burnt to death, is told fully in *Dead Men Tell Tales* by Jurgen Thorwald, published by Thames and Hudson.

Anton Schmid's heroism in helping Jews and their families at Vilnyus, is fully documented in *The Murderers Among Us* by Simon Wiesenthal, edited by Joseph Wechsberg, and published by Heinemann.

The Reverend André Trocmé's efforts to save Jewish children from the Nazi horror is told in *Lest Innocent Blood Be Shed* by P. Hallie, published by Harper & Row Ltd.

Details of Sir Winston Churchill's tour of the Italian Front from the 12th to the 21st August 1944 are given in *The Second World War,* by Sir Winston Churchill, published by Cassell.

Prologue

Sunday, 30th January, 1944

The prisoner stood in the small courtyard, his hands above his head, manacled to the bars of a window. The walls of the prison were of dark, grey stone, filthy with the dirt of centuries and stinking with the odours of the thousands who had ended their lives here. The pock-marked wall opposite was discoloured by ominous brown stains, and the chain rings, thick steel let into the wall at waist level, appeared to be covered with thick rust.

The prisoner saw nothing of this, nor did he see the bright blue sky overhead. His bruised and beaten body sagged against the cruel manacles on his wrists.

The prison, a castle which had once been home for some medieval knight, was a harsh and forbidding place. The German High Command had recognised at once its value as a place of incarceration. New arrivals were struck immediately by a feeling of absolute hopelessness, and the sense of being abandoned to the last vestiges of despair.

For some time now, he had been alone in the courtyard. There was no doubt in his mind that his time had come, that in a short while the execution squad would march out and he would be chained to one of the rings opposite.

He was beyond caring. If he felt anything at all, it was the exultation of having defeated them. He would go to his death knowing that nothing they had done had broken him. He was still master of his own will.

It was quiet in the courtyard. He heard the flies buzzing

and, far away, the sound of the pigeons roosting in the high towers. He moved a little to settle his body more comfortably against the rough stone.

Then he heard them, their footsteps in a one-two cadence coming down the corridor behind the great arch. They wheeled into the courtyard, eight of them commanded by an officer in the black uniform of the S.S. At his harsh command, they took up a straight-line formation facing the opposite wall. He waited for them to unlock the manacles before chaining him to the iron rings, but nothing happened. The Germans stood immobile,waiting.

Then he heard more footsteps, three or four sets, and as the new group wheeled into the courtyard, he realised that he was not the only one to be executed. He did not look up, knowing that all he would see was another bruised body like his own. He heard the chains rasp and a soft sobbing.

A hand grasped his chin and turned his head. His ear scraped the rough stone, forcing tears into his eyes. Then in a mist he saw the sagging body opposite, and with a shock of recognition he saw the bloodied face and pleading eyes.

He heard his own voice cry out: 'Oh God, no! Please! I'll do whatever you want! Please!'

He never felt the hands that took off the manacles and led him back to his cell.

He only knew that they had beaten him.

They had used the ultimate persuasion against him – his own love and compassion.

Chapter One

Reichenberg, Germany. Sunday, 6th August 1944

In the offices of the S.D. in Reichenberg, S.S. Rottenführer Carl Hartman sat in his office at his grey typewriter, and hated his job. As a member of the S.D., the elite intelligence arm of the S.S., he should have been proud and happy. Not every corporal in the Wehrmacht gets to be a member of the Sicherheitsdienst, but on this sunny Sunday morning in early August, he would have preferred to put a thousand kilometres between himself and this particular branch of the organisation, headed as it was by Colonel Baatz. Although the Colonel was his commanding officer, he had never even seen him until yesterday.

It was yesterday that his immediate superior, Lieutenant Schäfer, had called him into the inner office, where to Hartman's immense surprise, he had found the Lieutenant standing stiffly to attention on the wrong side of his desk. In the chair usually occupied by the arrogant Schäfer, sat a lean, elegant, monocled man wearing the insignia of a Standartenführer on his immaculate black uniform.

Corporal Hartman was well aware of the fact that a Standartenführer was the equivalent of a Wehrmacht Colonel. He had felt the cold fingers of fear touch his heart, and the beginnings of bile at the back of his throat. Not since he had been wounded on the eastern front and watched the enemy advancing over the hill, had he felt such breath-catching fear. The Colonel had stared coldly at Corporal Hartman. His eyes had flickered to the Lieutenant who had stared fixedly ahead.

Corporal Hartman was suddenly aware of the fourth man in the room, a Major in the uniform of the Kripo, the Kriminalpolizei whose duties covered those areas not under the jurisdiction of the Gestapo, the S.S. or the S.D. This did not leave much, and the Kripo were considered by many of the S.S. officers to be no better than a Home Guard unit. Hartman had formed the impression that the Major was far more than that. He only had time to note the hard eyes and the tough military stance before the Colonel had spoken.

'Have the lists come through this morning?' he snapped.

'Yes, Herr Standartenführer.' The Corporal's heartbeats had eased slightly. This meeting had nothing to do with any omission of his.

'Get them.'

The escape lists, the lists of prisoners-of-war who had broken out of the camps, were circulated through every district office within hours of a breakout. The list for that day was smaller than usual. Back in his office, the Corporal had unlocked his drawer, picked up a sheet of thick official stationery, and returned to the inner office. He did not hand it directly to the Colonel, but to the Lieutenant. Corporal Hartman knew his place.

He had been dismissed then, and floating in a vast cloud of relief had gone back to his desk. But it had not ended there.

For a while he had heard the rumble of voices behind the closed door, then it had opened and Corporal Hartman had leapt to attention as the Colonel, followed by the Major, had stalked through his tiny back office and out through the back door to the car park. The Corporal had stood open-mouthed as the two senior officers had leapt into the back of a waiting car. Never, in all the months in the Security Police office in Reichenberg, had he seen an officer leave by the back door. Not even the Lieutenant, who worked there.

The procedure was for the officer to shout to the Corporal, who shouted for the driver, who drove round to the front door. Yet here were two senior officers leaving by the back door like common privates.

'Hartman!' The Lieutenant's voice had cut through his astonishment.

'Lieutenant.' The Corporal marched swiftly into the other room.

'Tomorrow, Corporal, you will dig out all the lists issued this year and make a composite list to be ready for me by Monday.' All self-possession again, the Lieutenant had lounged back in his deep chair, though Hartman noticed that he had not recovered sufficiently to light his inevitable cigarette.

'But, Lieutenant, it's Sunday tomorrow, and – ' He had stopped at the expression on the Lieutenant's face.

'Did I hear you refuse to obey an order? An order that has just been conveyed to me personally by a Colonel of the Sicherheitsdienst?'

'Of course I'll do it, Lieutenant. I just thought – '

'Enough! You will have those lists ready by Monday morning. And what is more, you will not breathe a word of this to a soul.'

'Yes, Lieutenant. I mean no, Lieutenant. I – '

'Get out.'

That is why, on this sunny Sunday morning, Corporal Hartman hated his job. He should have been out in the park with his wife and daughter, instead of typing a long list of names that had no meaning for him.

Early on Monday morning, Obersturmführer Schäfer drew on his black leather gloves, tucked his black death's-head cap under his arm, picked up the envelope containing the composite list, and shouted for Hartman to send his car to the front.

Thirty-five minutes later he was standing stiffly to attention in the office of the Major he had met for the first time on Saturday morning. The Major put out his hand for the envelope. Sullenly, Schäfer handed it across the desk, holding it so that the Major had to reach out for it.

The Kripo officer noticed the insurbordination and smiled inwardly. Who the hell did these black-uniformed apes think they were? His orders came from the highest level, orders only he was in a position to carry out efficiently and ruthlessly. With all their power, the S.D. did not have the kind of experience needed for this operation; experience that only the professional police would have. For once the scum of Hitler's death's-head units had been instructed to place themselves at the disposal of a service they usually treated with contempt, and there was nothing they could do about it.

The Lieutenant began to fidget. The Major went on reading the list, ignoring the fury that threatened to explode from the junior officer.

He looked up. 'What is it, Lieutenant?' He feigned enlightenment. 'Oh, I beg your pardon, the toilet is through there.'

The Lieutenant could take no more. He exploded. 'Herr Major, I did not come here to be insulted. The Colonel asked me to give you every assistance, and this is what I will do, but I will not be insulted.' His neck muscles bulged with fury.

The Major's eyes hardened. 'Asked, Lieutenant? Asked?' The rising inflection was a menace the Lieutenant could not ignore. His anger began to fade. He heard the Major through a mist. 'Colonel Baatz does not ask, young man.' He stood up and slammed the table with his open hand. His next words were cold and hard. 'Don't you dare speak about insults. You are part of an operation of which I am in charge. These are instructions from the highest level, and you will obey them – and me – or you will take the consequences.'

He sat down and stared at the young officer for a long moment. The Lieutenant began to regret his impetuousness. The Major went on: 'I'm not at all sure that you have the right qualifications for this job. I have a good mind to request your removal from the operation. I – we – the General and I, cannot afford to have it fail through the incompetence of someone like you.'

The Lieutenant cringed inwardly. General? That meant that this operation could even be a Führerbefehl, an order emanating from Hitler himself. For the first time in many years, the Lieutenant felt the pricking of the bubble of his colossal conceit. He was up against something he could not counter with his usual arrogance. For years his membership of the Sicherheitsdienst had allowed him to strut through life with complete disregard for his fellow men, and now this right, this freedom to dominate all but his superiors in the S.D., was being stripped from him. He was on dangerous ground, and he knew it. He had not been given enough information about the operation to know just how powerful the Major's position was. Galling as it was, he knew he had to back down.

The Major watched him, shrewdly estimating the moment when the man was at his most vulnerable.

'Well, Lieutenant?'

Schäfer realised he was being given another chance. He seized it eagerly. 'I beg your pardon, Herr Major. It will not happen again.'

'If it does, I will have no mercy.' He looked at the list again. 'It seems as though our first contact may be made at any moment. Six men went through the wire on Friday, three of them from Stalag Luft III. Those are the three we want.' He went to the ordnance map covering part of the wall opposite his desk. 'Our information is that they will walk the first part eastwards from Sagan, to meet the Breslau-Liegnitz road here.' He used his stubby forefinger as a pointer. 'They will then move into Liegnitz to catch the Leipzig train at seven-thirty.'

Schäfer watched fascinated as the Major's finger traced the thin black line on the map that was the railway line from Liegnitz to Leipzig.

The Major looked at him. 'You looked surprised, Lieutenant.'

'Why that route, Major? Surely a more predictable route would be to take the Berlin train at Sagan, and then take the Copenhagen train from there.'

The Major moved his finger downwards and tapped the map at Zurich. 'Switzerland, Lieutenant. So many of them have been caught trying to get a Swedish ship, this lot decided to go the other way. We even know they are taking the long way round; through Gorlitz. We'll take them here at Rietschen while they are still in our jurisdiction.'

'But how can you be so sure of their route, Herr Major?'

An expression almost like a smile crossed the Major's face. 'I've known for some time, three weeks as a matter of fact, that this escape was being planned. It was a simple matter to give it every assistance. Their leader is Flight-Lieutenant Robert Erskine Mason, who was transferred from a tank corps to the Royal Air Force in 1943. He is ostensibly Louis Bouvier, a skilled French artisan, travelling to Munich to join a Todt organisation doing repairs to the airport. Mason is known to be audacious and enterprising. His companions are Thomas

Hackett, an American, and Gwillam Davis, another Englishman.'

Schäfer shook his head, perplexed. 'But, Herr Major, if you know this, why not arrest them at Liegnitz?'

The Major walked back to his desk. 'I think it is time you were briefed, Lieutenant.' He sat and stared at the map on the wall. 'This project is known as Operation Geld, and has been instigated by a man at the head of a department in Berlin. Only four people in the whole of the Reich know the details of the operation. You will be told only what your orders are. Beyond that you will talk to no one, you will ask no questions and you will carry out your orders to the letter. Do I make myself clear?'

'Yes, Herr Major. Perfectly clear.'

'Then listen carefully to what you have to do.'

Chapter Two

Monday, 7th August, 1944. 3 a.m.

They saw the lights at least ten minutes before the sound of the heavy motor reached them above the soughing of the wind and the soft rustle of the leaves in the woods behind them.

Crouched in the ditch alongside the road, their heads just high enough to see along the surface of the dusty highway, the three men watched the pinpoint become two great headlights as the vehicle rumbled towards them. They heard the screech of the tracks when it was two hundred metres away.

'Tank?' The American ducked his head and looked back at the British officer crouched behind him.

The officer shook his head, the movement only just discernible in the dark. 'Not the right motor. A half-track, more likely.'

The third man, a short well-built Welshman, straightened his legs and rolled quickly towards them. 'It's a prime mover. I can see the eight-eight millimetre gun behind it.' His voice was louder now, his fear of being heard overcome by the roar of the vehicle as it thundered towards them. 'It's fully manned, too. See.'

They watched it come down the Breslau road, and as it passed them, saw the German helmets and the gunners sitting in the canvas-hooded half-track. Then the eighty-eight millimetre gun was above them, the rumble of its rubber-tyred wheels faint above the diminishing roar of its twelve ton horse.

Slowly the noise faded, leaving only the night sounds of the woods and the soft sigh of the wind in the trees.

The three men remained crouched in the ditch.

The road to Breslau stretched away to the south-east. Two kilometres in the other direction lay the town of Liegnitz, and due north of that was Sagan and Stalag Luft III. From the prisoner-of-war camp to this spot on the Breslau-Liegnitz road was just over forty kilometres, but it had taken more than forty-eight hours to make the journey.

The escape had taken months of meticulous planning. Forged papers had been updated to conform to the new documents of the Reichsicherheitshauptamt, the German central security headquarters in Berlin; civilian clothing had been hand-made from blankets, and German marks painfully accumulated over the months by the escape committee under Squadron-Leader Harry Crossley. The committee had given them a leeway of fifty-six hours to make the seven-thirty train from Liegnitz to Leipzig.

The British officer, Bob Mason, stood up first. He scrambled up the bank and looked towards Breslau. Summer was still with them, and the fields across the road from the woods were fragrant with the last wild flowers of August. He looked across at the woods, the trees washed dark now with the black of night. He stood there listening, small case in hand, his tall figure towering over Davis, the Welshman, who had moved to stand close beside him.

The American, Hackett, stretched out on the bank, content just to lie there, his tired muscles aching from the tension of the last two days. He looked up at the sky, cloudless except for a gossamer translucence on the western horizon.

Mason took off his cloth cap and rubbed his forehead. At once, his fair hair was like a beacon in the dark, topping the deep grey wool of his suit. Beside him, Davis, who was hatless, was dressed in the garb of a labourer, grey coat over woollen polo-necked jersey. Mason slapped his cap against his thigh and pulled it on, the peak low over his forehead. He took a fob-watch from his pocket.

'We've got three hours before our train leaves. If we rest in those trees until half-past six, we can get to Liegnitz before seven-fifteen. We'll go in singly from three different directions. That way, we won't have to hang about the station. We'll meet near the ticket clerk at seven twenty-five.'

He spoke quietly but firmly, in the tones of a man who was accustomed to command. He was a tall man, hard and muscular, but there was a gentleness there too, and the paradox enhanced his instinct for creating the kind of empathy that makes a tight-knit group out of individuals who are normally incompatible. He was that rare being, a natural leader, and the others felt it and respected it.

He led the way through a barbed-wire fence into the shelter of the woods. 'We'll make some slop while we have time. We won't have another chance of a meal before we get off the train at Leipzig.'

They found a small glade in the middle of a copse through which flowed a muddy stream. Each of them carried a small bag of oatmeal, cocoa and powdered milk in bags strapped around his waist. Mason took three small bowls from the case and mixed some of the brown water from the stream to a little of the powder taken from each of their rations. They sat in a tight circle, spooning the slop into their mouths.

Mason took the last spoonful and looked at his fingernails, dirtied to conform with the character he was playing.

'Dirty fingernails – dirty character.'

He smiled inwardly. The headmaster had an aphorism for every occasion, and through the years the folk in the village of Milton Turvey had come to know them through their children. Mason remembered them all, and conceded wryly that the combination of the headmaster's wisdom and his father's gentle admonitions had made him conscious of what was required of him as the Vicar's son.

Mason frowned as he looked at his broken thumbnail. He couldn't even recall his mother reproving him for the state of his hands; or for any other boyhood omission. She was a gentle, and somewhat vague writer of children's stories, and though she did not neglect him, he was gratefully aware that she was often unmindful of his minor transgressions.

Growing up in a village which straddled the Oxford Canal, Mason had all the advantages of town and country, for Banbury was only a few miles away. Yet he remembered most the quiet fields, the hawthorn and elderberry, and the gurgle and whisper of the canal in the locks.

He realised that Davis had spoken.

'Sorry, Taff. What was that?'

'That slop needs a spoonful of mine-tip to improve the flavour.'

Mason grinned. 'I always knew you Welshmen had some strange habits.'

'Sometimes I wonder what I've been complaining about all these years. One year in that bloody camp, and I'd give anything to see the tip standing proud over the village.'

Hackett took three sorry-looking cigarettes from his pocket, handed them out, and lay back on the cool turf. 'All I want is a good look at Mary Lou Watson from Mansfield, Ohio. Not to touch. Just to look. Boy.' He sighed deeply, his thin face beatific with remembrance.

They puffed silently at their cigarettes, and then buried the butts in the loose earth.

Davis stood up and stamped his feet. 'You two sleep for a while. I'll wake one of you in an hour.'

Hackett yawned, his bony face stretched tight. 'Thanks, Taff. I'm all in.' He tucked a log under his head. 'Wake me up early. Mother, for I'm to be Queen of the May.'

Mason closed his eyes thankfully, and was asleep in minutes. His dreams, triggered by his thoughts, were of his home and the people he loved. His sleep was untroubled, and it seemed as though he had slept only for a moment when he felt his arm being shaken. He opened his eyes and sat up quickly. It was broad daylight.

'Hell! We've missed the train. Taff, what's the time?'

'Shh! Quiet!' Davis gripped his arm tightly.

Mason turned his head and listened. He saw Hackett at the edge of the thicket, parting the leaves gently and peering through them across the field from where a deep baying could be heard.

Hackett looked back at the two men. He held up one finger and mouthed silently. 'One man. One dog.' He turned to watch as the baying grew fainter. He let the branch fall back into place. 'We'd better get back on the road,' he said softly. 'It's nearly time.'

Mason was still shaken. 'I thought they'd got the dogs after us.'

Davis said: 'Early morning rabbiting. He had two slung over

his shoulder. We'd better get a move on.'

They washed in the little stream, dried themselves with grubby kerchiefs, and then obliterated as much as they could of the evidence of their night in the copse. They went back through the barbed wire fence and stepped cautiously into the road. The sun was still a golden ball in the east, and the trees and fields were tinted with red. A slight breeze was lifting puff-balls of dust at their feet, and on the western horizon, dark clouds heralded the first gloomy days of autumn.

They walked towards the single beckoning church tower that was Liegntiz. They passed farm labourers who greeted them briefly. Mason replied in German while the other two merely nodded. On the outskirts of the town, they passed a column of soldiers marching to their guard duties at the local factory. Now and then a straggling, listless group of forced labourers, accompanied by their guards, trudged toward the quarries beyond the river.

They separated at the terminus where Mason boarded a tram that would leave at ten minutes to seven. He had five minutes to wait. He wedged himself between two evil-smelling labourers, and glanced out of the window. He saw Hackett just turning the corner, followed by Davis a few minutes later. Nothing in their demeanour gave him any cause for uneasiness. They appeared to be just two more inhabitants of the town going about their business.

Hackett trudged past the cathedral, turned left down a narrow street of small shops, and then right again past the bridge over the river, a small tributary of the Oder. In an occasional shop window, he saw Davis following about a hundred metres behind him. The streets were busier. He hoped no one stopped to speak to him for he was terrified as he knew Davis was, of using his limited French vocabulary, but it was the only way to carry off the subterfuge of being French artisans on their way to a factory in the south.

Their forged travel documents permitted them to travel to Munich via Nuremberg. Once in Nuremberg, however, they would wait at an address given to them by one of the escape committee. That was all they had; just the address. Whoever was to meet them, to escort them through the escape route, would keep them under surveillance for some days. They expected that. The Underground was highly sensitive to betrayal, to the possibility of infiltration by the Gestapo, and at the slightest suspicion they would be abandoned to fend for themselves. They knew that, too, and were prepared to accept the conditions dictated by circumstance. If no contact was established, then the alternative plan was to keep on southward to Stuttgart, from where they would try to make their way to Karlsruhe and the Swiss border.

Hackett walked with a slight stoop, favouring his right leg a little. The old wound troubled him when he was tired, the ache in his calf a nagging reminder of a German grenade and an aborted raid in the mountains of Yugoslavia.

Thin-faced, his black hair greying slightly at the temples, he looked older than his twenty-eight years. He knew he was not a brave man, though he possessed more courage than most. He had known fear, and he knew that in moments of danger he would experience again the gut-tearing feeling of being afraid; but he knew too that he carried within him the ability to direct his own weakness into a hatred of his enemy, and by this means turn it to his advantage.

The thing which weighed heaviest was not the fear of danger, but the knowledge that he was irrevocably altered from the person known as Thomas Hackett of Mansfield, Ohio. The boy who had kissed Mary Lou Watson goodbye before hugging his parents on the station platform, was no longer this same Thomas Hackett, OSS. He had strayed from his own identity, and it troubled him. He wanted to become again the careless college graduate who had danced to the swing bands appearing in Columbus or Cleveland.

When he first realised that he could no longer recall the emotions or relive the joy of those moments, he had cried real tears for the first time in years. Although he had wondered if other men felt the same frustrations, he had never spoken of it.

Hackett saw the station a block away. It was a grim, smoke-blackened building occupying the whole length of the street. He waited for Davis to catch up with him, and as soon as he knew that the Welshman was close, went through the door to the main hall. He looked around for the ticket office. He hesitated as he saw Mason already in the short queue.

Mason observed the arrival of the others, and nodded

slightly to Hackett. When it was his turn at the window, he pushed his papers through the half-round gap in the glass.

'Leipzig. Zweiter Klasse, bitte.'

The clerk examined the documents briefly, stamped a ticket and pushed the papers back.

'Danke.' Mason half turned, then turned back to the window. 'Von welchem Bahnsteig fährt der Zug ab?'

'Bahnsteig fünf.'

'Danke.'

Davis and Hackett watched with trepidation as Mason stood at the window. Neither realised it but the tension in their bodies built to an unbearable level before, with a collective sigh, they saw him leave the ticket office with his ticket in his hand. They waited amongst the jostling crowd, watching him stroll towards the toilet a few feet from them.

'All in order. The papers are O.K.' They heard the shake in his voice. 'Get your tickets and keep me in sight. Make sure you get into the same coach.'

Hackett grabbed his arm. 'What the hell did you turn back for.'

'I forgot to ask what platform the train left from. It's platform five.'

Five minutes later they stood at the end of platform five, their tickets to Leipzig in their pockets, feeling the euphoria that comes from achieving an objective, albeit a limited one.

Mason turned slowly, looking at each group of people, watching their reactions to each significant incident; new arrivals, loud conversation, the clang of shunting engines. No one appeared to show undue interest in the three men. A train on the opposite platform, on its way to Breslau, whistled and steamed, and slowly dragged its dozen coaches out of the station.

The bustle subsided a little, and then increased, as the Leipzig train was heard in the distance. The three men stood closer together, their contact with each other their only security against the gigantic forces ranged against them.

They watched with mounting excitement as the rumble grew louder, and the green liveried engine appeared at the bend and bore down on them. They felt the surge of humanity at their backs as they were jostled forward, pushing and shoving, forcing their way through the people in front of them. Mason felt the case pulled out of his grasp. He forced himself back, grabbing at the handle he could see between two massive bodies. He pulled it through, and looked for his companions. They were already through the door, and he forced his way on to the steps and into the carriage behind them.

The three men made their way towards the end of the corridor, only to meet a surging mass of peasants coming through the other end of the carriage. They held a place near the toilet door, the best place to be during the long journey ahead of them.

Mason found himself pushed against the carriage window. He was facing outward, and as his head was pressed against the glass, he realised that he was looking straight into the eyes of a Lieutenant of the Sicherheitsdienst. The man was three feet away from him, standing on the station platform, his hands behind his back, rocking gently on his heels as he looked at Mason. Then the man turned and strolled away towards the station exit, and Mason saw the two S.S. corporals following him.

He let out a long breath, his heart pounding with fear. He watched the officer with relief as the three men went through the big door. Then he frowned, perplexed. An S.D. officer on railway duty? He felt again the faint stirrings of trepidation, and then pushed it away impatiently. The S.D. were everywhere, like maggots in a corpse. He relaxed, oblivious of the man in a blue cap watching him from the other end of the corridor.

At that moment their engine let out a long whistle that sounded like a sigh in the distance, then the carriage jerked as the driving wheels gripped the rails.

He heard Taff's voice in his ear. 'This is it, Bob, m'boy. We've made it. Nothing can stop us now.'

'Take it easy, Taff,' he whispered. 'Speak only French from now on. Even if it's just the few words you know.'

Beneath their feet, the wheels clattered over the points and the coaches began the long climb out of the valley. The air in the carriage was oppressive with smells of sweat and garlic, and Mason pulled at the top of the window, releasing a stream of cold air into the stifling corridor, but his relief was short-lived as a large furious woman thumped his arm and slammed the window shut. She berated him in a language he did not understand. Probably Polish, he thought.

He smiled weakly at her, and apologised in German. He saw Hackett grinning at him and shrugged.

The train made five stops in the first hour, then Mason noticed that they were passing through smaller stations without stopping. He eased himself down so that he was squatting with his back to the carriage wall. Several passengers near him had done the same, some of them seated on their luggage, others stretched with their legs out. He envied those in the compartments with comfortable seats, and determined to find a place for himself as soon as the coach emptied.

He dozed for a while, and then woke suddenly as he felt a change in the rhythm of the wheels. He stood up and looked out of the window. The sun was high now, and they were passing through the outskirts of what appeared to be one of the bigger towns. He felt the wheels clatter over dozens of points, and wished he could get the map from his case to see where they were, but he knew that the incongruity of an artisan studying a map would attract attention. They passed factories and warehouses, and the coach lurched as the engine braked.

As they slowed, he heard Hackett at his shoulder. 'Gorlitz,' he said quietly. 'We've just crossed the River Neisse. We have to change here for Leipzig.'

Mason nodded, remembering. This train continued on to Dresden, but their route lay northwards through Rietschen and Kottbus. Beneath their feet, the brakeshoes screamed as their grip tightened on the wheels. The train stopped with a final jerk, and passengers grabbed cases and bundles, and pushed for the exits. Mason saw Hackett and Davis drop to the platform ahead of him and look around. He joined them and led the way, motioning them to follow him to the timetable boards. Gorlitz station was covered by a huge arch of steel and glass, soot-blackened and grimy with the dirt of decades. The timetable was lit by one naked bulb and the faded and fly-blown paper was surrounded by travellers running their searching fingers over the close print. It was Davis who found the timetable for Gorlitz – Soremberg-Kottbus – Leipzig.

He grabbed their arms as he looked at the clock above the

boards. 'It leaves in five minutes,' he said quietly. 'Platform four. Where the hell is that?'

Mason looked around for the platform indicators, but Hackett was ahead of him. 'There it is. Across the track. Quick.'

He led the way to the iron bridge that led from one side of the vast concourse to the other. A stream of passengers was already on its way to the train standing at platform four. The three men struggled through the crowd milling about at the bottom of the staircase. They hurried up the steep iron steps to the gangway above.

As Mason looked down at the vast concourse below, he stopped suddenly, his stomach gripped by an iron hand of fear. Below him, looking straight up at him, was the S.D. Lieutenant he had seen last at Liegntiz station. As he looked down, the officer turned away and strolled alongside the Leipzig train. Hackett and Davis saw him stop, and went back to him.

Mason hesitated for only a moment. 'Quickly. Follow me!' He turned back the way he had come, past the staircase they had taken from the Breslau train, and down the staircase that led to the station exit. He hurried out into the street followed by his two bewildered companions. He crossed the street and turned into a small alleyway. Halfway down the alley he saw an inconspicuous sign: Café.

He led the way inside where it was cool and quiet in contrast to the station hubbub. Two diners, heads close together, conversed in low voices at a table near the window. The clatter of crockery could be heard from the back. Mason led the way to a table on the opposite side of the room.

Davis was puzzled, Hackett furious. 'What the hell do you think you're doing, pal? Let's get the hell out of here and on to that train. We've got exactly two minutes.'

Davis nodded. 'Dammit, Bob, Tom's right. We have to get that train. God knows when there'll be another.'

'Shut up and listen to me! On Liegnitz station I saw an officer of the S.D. with two of his henchmen. They watched us leave, and now they're here, nearly a hundred miles away from where I last saw them. They weren't on the train, because they watched it pull out, so they must have driven here. And what's more, he looked straight at me each time I saw him.'

Hackett was not convinced. 'Don't be a bloody great idiot! The S.D. are everywhere. Even though you saw the same man twice, it doesn't mean anything. This may be part of his patrol. If they were on to us they would pull us in.' He grabbed the case. 'Come on. We'll miss that train.'

At that moment, a thin elderly woman came through the curtain from the back. 'You wish to order, gentlemen?' She wiped the table with a spotless white cloth.

Mason smiled at her. 'Three beers, please.' Hackett shrugged resignedly. Mason glanced at his companions. 'And some food. Whatever you have that is not rationed.'

'I have some ham and potato cakes.'

'Good. Good.' As the woman turned away he stopped her. 'Do you know the time of the next train for Dresden?'

'There is one that leaves at twelve-thirty.' She looked up at the clock on the wall. 'You have nearly an hour to enjoy your food.' She stood contemplating them, her hands tucked under her apron. 'You are going to Dresden?'

Mason was aware of his companions glowering at him uncomprehendingly. 'Yes. As you see, we are French. I regret that my friends do not speak German well, but they are nevertheless patriotic workers for the Reich.'

She smiled and went through the curtain to the back.

Hackett said angrily: 'What the hell was that all about? Do you realise we've missed that damned train?'

Davis shook his head in bewilderment. 'Bob, I – '

At that moment the street door was flung open, and a man strode swiftly through the café towards the kitchen. The three men looked at him, startled, and as he saw them he hesitated. Then he pushed aside the curtain and went into the back. As he disappeared he took a blue cap from his head.

Mason looked at each of them in turn. 'He seemed to recognise us. I don't like it. There's something going on here, I know it.'

Davis frowned. 'What's got into you, Bob? This is a hell of a time to lose your nerve. It's not like you to panic.'

'I haven't lost my nerve. I know what I saw back there at the station. I don't know what it means, but the only way to outfox the Gestapo is to do the unexpected. Germans are so used to order and method that they come unstuck if you break the rules. Well, from now on, I'm breaking them. I'm going to assume that everything I see that I can't fathom, that hasn't got a rational explanation, is suspect. A hunted animal doesn't ask why a hunter does this or that. He smells the danger and runs. Well, that's me from now on.' He looked at each of them in turn. 'There is no rational explanation for that officer being in two different towns on the same day. He isn't a policeman on a beat, and he wasn't doing anything positive. So I'm suspicious. Don't ask me to explain it, because I can't.'

Davis stared at him for a long moment. Then he shrugged. 'O.K. I've trusted your instincts before. I'm with you, but I'm not going in blind. You have to keep us genned up.'

'I don't expect you to go in blind. All I ask is that you trust my judgement.'

Hackett struck the table angrily. 'Dammit, that isn't good enough! We had a well-prepared plan that's all shot to hell, and you want me to trust your judgement. Who the devil do you think you are making decisions on a go-to-hell basis.'

Mason looked at him grimly. 'Whatever you say, it *is* on a go-to-hell basis. Back at camp you agreed I was in charge, and that's how it's going to stay. So make up your mind. You've got exactly –' he looked up at the clock – 'thirty minutes before the Dresden train leaves.'

The two men looked at him, undecided. Diplomatically Mason outlined his conversation with the woman. 'And that's another thing,' he said. 'This could be a lucky break for us. We know now that some food is off-ration, so we look for a café when we're hungry, and see what we can get. Now we stoke up here, and then get tickets for Dresden. Our papers are good enough; we know that. From Dresden, we can still get to Leipzig and Nuremberg.' He smiled. 'So all we've done is switch the route. If the Gestapo are really on to us, this will throw them off the scent.'

Hackett smiled grudgingly. 'O.K., so you're smarter than we thought. I still don't know what you think they're up to. Surely, if they had the slightest idea where we were, it would be back to camp with us. I can't see them playing cat and mouse at this stage of the war.'

Mason said: 'I'm not so sure. You remember –'

At that moment the woman appeared with their beer. She stood for a moment, her head on one side. 'You will be a long time on the train. If you wish I can wrap some bread and sausage for the journey.'

Mason said regretfully: 'You are very kind, but our ration books are with our luggage at the station.'

She smiled. 'These things are not rationed. The bread and sausages are made here in my kitchen.'

'We are deeply grateful.'

'You are only a short while in Germany not to know these things.' She went back to the kitchen, smiling. Mason watched her go, wondering if they were being too naïve. They would have to watch themselves, testing every important move before they made it. He was conscious of the other two watching him expectantly.

'Well?' Davis said.

'Well, what?' Mason was perplexed.

'What do you remember?'

'Oh, that. Yes. I remember the C.O. back at camp telling us what a flap there was amongst high-ranking German officers when the Gestapo killed fifty of those who tunnelled out in March. He said that Colonel Lindeiner told him privately that many of the officers were beginning to believe that Hitler was insane.'

Davis looked at him speculatively. 'That bomb under Hitler on 20th July?'

'Yes. That has a bearing, I suppose. But I was thinking of something else. What if Anthony Eden's statement in the house about "exemplary justice" has scared the hell out of some of them now that the writing is on the wall; that defeat for Germany is only a matter of time? Perhaps the high command doesn't want any more prisoner executions. Perhaps something else is being planned for us.'

Hackett looked sceptical. 'Like what?'

'Hell, I don't know. Like seeing we get pushed off a train or shoved under a bus, or something equally nasty.'

Hackett shook his head. 'Too far-fetched. All they have to do is pick us up and get us back to camp.'

Mason rubbed his tired eyes. 'Maybe you're right.' He yawned and swallowed the last of his beer. 'I'm too tired to think.'

The ham when it came was thick and filling, and the potato cakes were crisp and well-spiced. They ate hungrily, and cleaned the plates with warm black bread that had recently come from the oven. When they were ready to leave, the woman handed them three parcels of bread and sausage. They paid her gratefully.

She watched them leave, then went back to the kitchen where the man with the blue cap waited.

He looked out through the curtain. 'Have they gone?'

'Yes.' She watched him as he went to the telephone and dialled six digits. A deep masculine voice answered him.

He said: 'You'll have to change the plan. They left the train here.' He listened for a moment and then smiled wolfishly. 'They came here. Here to the café.' He paused. 'Yes. They are taking the Dresden train at twelve-thirty.' He listened once more. Then he said: 'No, that won't do. They saw me when I came in here. It's too dangerous. They may see me again. The fair-haired one is as wary as a cat. Someone else will have to take over.' He nodded. 'Right. I'll meet you at the house in Nuremberg. Good.' Gently he replaced the receiver and smiled at the woman.

She said: 'Joachim will know what to do. He will see that we do not fail.'

'Yes.' The man sat down at the kitchen table. 'Let me have some coffee.' He drummed his fingers on the table. 'Joachim is putting the whole group on the Dresden train.'

Mason, Davis and Hackett found the station less crowded when they returned. They separated at the entrance, bought their tickets and walked warily, one at a time, to the platform where the Dresden train already awaited them.

Mason looked around carefully, but could see no sign of the S.D. officer. There were black- and grey-uniformed men everywhere, but all of them appeared to be engrossed in their respective duties, some inspecting documents, others just standing guard and looking as bored as soldiers often are. No one appeared to be paying them any attention. He saw Hackett board the train, followed by Davis, and with a last casual look around the concourse, he followed them.

The coach was less crowded than the one from Breslau.

They even managed to get compartment seats, each in a different part of the carriage. Mason leaned back, grateful for the relative softness of the leather behind him.

Far up ahead, they heard the whistle from the engine and the train slid out of the station. Two men sitting at the window seats began to play cards on a suitcase set up as a makeshift table. Two others joined them. Mason put his head back and began to doze.

'Ausweis bitte!' The shout woke Mason from a deep sleep. Quickly he looked out into the corridor. At the end of the coach, the conductor, accompanied by an obvious Gestapo type, was examining papers and taking tickets. They spent a few minutes in each compartment, then they were in front of him. He handed over his ticket, and then his polizeiliche erlaubnis – his permit to travel. The conductor glanced at his ticket, handed his permit to the Gestapo man, and collected tickets and papers from the other passengers.

The Gestapo man made a note in his daybook and looked down at Mason. 'It says here that you have special skills. What are they?'

'I am a milling machinist.' Mason saw the thick nose and stubby chin. He felt his heart pounding. 'I make equipment for aircraft.'

The man grunted and handed back the permit. He snapped his fingers impatiently, and the conductor handed him the papers from the four card-players. Mason struggled to appear calm. When all the papers were returned, the two men disappeared into the corridor. He was suddenly aware that the card players were watching him curiously.

'The Gestapo worries you, friend?' It was the player in the green coat.

'Yes, they worry me. I am here in Germany because of the Gestapo. They hold me responsible for the safety of my family. If I work well, they are safe. If I do not . . .' He stopped. Mason realised from the sympathetic looks that he had convinced them. Since they were civilians, it was likely that they too were foreigners, workers recruited from the occupied countries to boost factory production. The four men went back to their game.

Mason stood up and pushed past the few passengers in the

corridor. On his way to the toilet, he glanced in first at Hackett and then at Davis. Both appeared to be dozing. Everything appeared to be under control. On his way back to his seat, he looked out of the corridor window. The train was passing through fields of beet, and on the horizon he could see clouds darkening the western sky. Here and there he could see farmhouses, their windows reflecting sunlight like molten gold. It could have been any peacetime English country scene. Mason remembered the picnics at home; the friends, the girls and the companions of his youth. He remembered too, the days at Oxford, punting on the Cherwell on Sundays, or strolling through the ancient gates of the Botanic Gardens to sit on the grassy banks and watch the swans, with the tower of Magdalen rising ancient, weathered and magnificent on the skyline.

They had been sure, all of them, that the future would always be as secure as it was then. Well, it had been a near thing. The tide was turning, the Allies were back in Europe, and it was only a matter of time. Far ahead he heard the triumphant scream of the train whistle. He went back to his compartment.

Chapter Three

Monday, 7th August, 1944. 11.30 a.m.

Lieutenant Schäfer watched the three men walk across the iron gangway towards the steps that led down to the Leipzig train. In a few minutes they would be on their way, and he could get out of this crowded steamy hole and into the car that would take him to Rietschen, where he would meet this same train.

As he turned away, he was unaware of the tall, fair-haired one looking down at him. Had he noticed it, he would have seen the hasty conversation, and the quick change of direction. But Lieutenant Schäfer, a member of the elite corps, was impatient to be on his way, and he went quickly to the car parked outside the station.

The Lieutenant was confident of his ability to carry out his part of the operation. It was simple enough. All he had to do was to see that these three sub-humans boarded their train, and then meet them at the next stop. The train was an express, and there was no way to leave it before Rietschen, where he and his corporals would make the arrest.

But Lieutenant Schäfer's confidence was even greater than his common sense. What he did not realise was that although he had seen the three men making for the Leipzig train, that did not necessarily mean that they had boarded it. In fact, Lieutenant Schäfer was soon to learn that a smart black uniform was no substitute for brains, a commodity in which he was woefully deficient.

The Lieutenant was aware of none of this as he lounged

comfortably in his car as it rolled through the green countryside towards Rietschen. So confident was he, in fact, that he even instructed his driver to stop at a small country inn, where he demanded and got some fine veal, a bowl of freshly cooked vegetables and a bottle of the finest wine available.

Well-satisfied, he returned to his car and was soon on his way, arriving at Rietschen several minutes before the train was due in spite of being held up at a minor traffic jam in the Ludwigsplatz, where one of the army vehicles bound for the front had smashed into the Saint Johannes bridge.

He strolled through the station doors to the platform where he was to meet the Kripo officer who was to assist him with the arrest. The officer and his men had been instructed to block all exits and examine the papers of every one on the Leipzig train. The Lieutenant thought that this was a completely unnecessary manoeuvre since he was confident of recognising the three men instantly, but since those were Brunner's orders, he would have to humour the good Major.

The train was only four minutes late, and the Kripo men took up their positions as they had been instructed. It was fortunate that the Kripo officer was extremely efficient, otherwise the Lieutenant might have tried to blame him for his failure to find the three men. But the officer had stationed three men at every gangway, so that not even a rabbit could slip through the cordon. The Lieutenant himself had gone through the train, first casually, then frantically, searching every coach and every compartment. Even the baggage car and the guard's van were searched in case their quarry had somehow managed to conceal themselves there.

It was after the fourth fruitless search of the train that Lieutenant Schäfer realised his predicament. He had jeopardised an important operation, one that had been launched from the very highest level, and he had no doubt that his failure would have a greater influence on his future than anything he had ever done before. Reluctantly, he went to the Railway Police office, where he asked to use their telephone.

As soon as Major Brunner heard the news, he left his plush red and gold office in the Breslau Headquarters building of the Kriminalpolizei in Bismarckstrasse, called for his car, and drove the short distance to the office of his chief, Colonel Wiessen.

As his driver slammed the door behind him, he took the wide steps two at a time, strode swiftly past the saluting sentry, and along the colonnaded passage to a door on the second floor. He went straight into an antechamber occupied by two corporal-clerks and a typist. The men snapped to attention.

'Will you kindly inform the Colonel that I am here, and that I request permission to see him?' He strolled to the window as the corporal knocked on the thick door and entered. He was back in a moment.

'The Colonel will see you, Herr Major. Will you go in.'

The Colonel stared at Major Brunner through gold-rimmed glasses as he approached the desk and saluted.

'Sit down, Major. I take it there has been a balls-up somewhere or you would not have come to see me. I don't know whether you realise it, but your visits coincide with bad news, and your telephone calls herald the good.'

The Major sat opposite the thin greying man behind the desk, and wondered for the thousandth time why he let the old bastard get under his skin. Perhaps, he thought ruefully, it was because the Colonel always appeared to have an uncanny foresight into any situation.

He sighed. 'Correct, Herr Colonel. Lieutenant Schäfer informs me that he has lost our three hares. He says he saw them on the Leipzig train, but at Rietschen they had vanished.'

'Schäfer is lying, of course.'

'Of course, Colonel. If they had boarded the Leipzig train, it is fatuous to suppose they would leave it before the next stop.'

'It's obvious he could not have seen them board that train. They must have slipped past him somehow, and boarded another. The idiot probably made them suspicious, and they panicked.'

'That is my view precisely, Colonel.'

'Well, what is your next move?'

'The situation is still under control, Herr Colonel. Before the operation began, I requested Sturmbannführer Scharpwinkel to instruct all Gestapo agents on duty on westbound trains to record in their daybooks the names of all French artisans they encounter in the next five days. The information is coming into our offices minute by minute.'

'Excellent. The S.D. drop the box, and we pick it up. Obviously you would not have told them why we wanted the information.'

'I forgot to enlighten them, Herr Colonel.' He smiled. 'I didn't think it would be in our interests to connect one operation with another. It would have been too confusing for them. That is why I did not name the men we wanted.' He shrugged. 'I mentioned that it was a Führerbefehl, and gave them the code number in case they wished to confirm it with Berlin.'

Colonel Wiessen smiled back at him. Major Brunner thought he had never seen anything so wolfish.

'Major Brunner, you have my compliments. That is, of course, if you manage to find our three hares.' The smile disappeared. 'Otherwise you will find yourself in the same predicament as the good Lieutenant Schäfer.'

'There is no question of failure, Colonel. These men will be found. The only problem at the moment is the question of security. Only four people in the Breslau office have been fully briefed. You Herr Colonel, myself, Captain Schmidt of my office, and Colonel Baatz of the Reichenberg Gestapo. Schäfer, of course, will be on his way to the eastern front within a week.'

'Well?' Colonel Wiessen was impatient.

'You will agree that it is important that these men be taken with the utmost secrecy. But Schäfer's blunder has forced us to widen the area of search.'

'Get to the point, man!'

Major Brunner took a deep breath. 'It is essential, Herr Colonel, that I be vested with the full authority to act without having to give reasons to area commanders.'

Colonel Wiessen looked thoughtful. He stared at Brunner for a full minute, then he stood up and walked to the window overlooking the Kaiserplatz and the fountains of the square beyond.

He spoke without turning. 'You want the full authority of

a Gauleiter merely to recapture three prisoners-of-war?' There was no trace of sarcasm in his voice. 'You have been fully briefed on the goal of the project. You have been told that one of the three prisoners is working for us; that when they are returned here, we will substitute two of our men for the other two, and the third man will lead them through the underground route – a route which our masters tell us can then be smashed by the Gestapo.' Brunner remained silent. The Colonel turned from the window and stared at him. 'You do not contradict me? Perhaps you believe this unlikely story?'

'No, Herr Colonel. I never believed it for a moment, but if our masters wished to give us that story to cover the real object of the mission, then who am I to question them?' He shrugged. 'Whatever the real reason for the mission, it does not affect our strategy.'

'Ah!' The Colonel walked swiftly back to his desk and sat down. 'No one knows what General Müller has in store for these three men. Keep in mind the essential details of the operation, and carry it out to my satisfaction, and the satisfaction of Gestapo headquarters and General Müller. If you fail, or if I thought for one moment you were speculating on the true goals of the mission, I am sure Oberstgruppenführer Muller would be very disappointed to hear of it.'

Major Brunner inclined his head without speaking. There was no mistaking the threat behind the mild tone.

Colonel Wiessen rubbed his cheek with a stiff forefinger. It was the only sign of the stress he was under. 'This full authority to act that you ask for . . . it is extremely difficult and dangerous for both of us. A request for this kind of authority suggests we know more than we should. We would not ask for it just to catch a few miserable escapees.' He was silent for a moment. 'However, I will see whether Berlin won't suggest such a course of action to me when I explain the difficulties Lieutenant Schäfer has caused us.'

Brunner had no doubt that his Colonel would succeed in getting the order. 'Thank you, Herr Colonel.'

The Colonel leaned back in his chair. 'Don't thank me yet, Major. If this gets out of hand, I will see that you answer to Berlin personally, and you know what that means. Don't let us have a grossfahndung for these men. If we eventually have to launch a full-scale manhunt, then the whole operation is blown.'

'I realise that, Herr Colonel.'

'Good. See me tomorrow morning.'

Major Brunner realised he was being dismissed. He stood up, saluted, and left the room.

As soon as he had gone, Colonel Wiessen picked up the telephone. 'Get me the Reichssicherheitshauptamt in Berlin. I wish to speak to General Müller.' He replaced the handset and strolled to the window. He saw Major Brunner's car drawing away from the kerb. He had time to smoke a long cigar before his telephone rang.

Back in his own office, Brunner rang for his assistant, Captain Werner Schmidt. Schmidt was a tall Kripo officer whose career went back to the days of Hindenberg. He loved his job, but sometimes he wondered whether he could continue to go on watching the Gestapo excesses that he was compelled to condone. He was a policeman trained under a benevolent regime, and Germany under Hitler made him wonder about himself and his career.

Brunner smiled at him. 'For heaven's sake, Werner, sit down. You look like a damned S.S. officer. You make me nervous.' Schmidt smiled and sat down. The two men had been colleagues for several years. They liked and respected one another, and had learned that their mutual heresies had never left these four walls.

Schmidt leaned back in his chair. 'Word came a few minutes ago. They definitely took the Dresden train.'

Brunner nodded. 'I would have staked my life on it.' He smiled ruefully. 'Perhaps I have already.'

Schmidt looked puzzled. Brunner shook his head. 'It's nothing. Anyway, the next train out was the Dresden train at twelve-thirty. If they had panicked, it had to be the next train. It would have been too nerve-racking to wait about.'

Schmidt swivelled in his chair and stared out of the window. He glanced at the watch on his wrist. 'In two hours our three minnows arrive at Dresden. I wonder if they know how important they are to us. To you, to me, to all of us.'

'Highly unlikely. You have an adequate force at Dresden?'

'Of course.' Schmidt swung his chair back to face Brunner. He smiled as though pleased with himself. 'I have men on the train. They will be watched through to Dresden. Schwartz has been briefed on the importance of this operation. As soon as the three men are in custody, they will be rushed back here. Then they will be separated and the operation can begin.'

'Good. Keep me informed. Let me know the moment Schwartz has them.'

Schmidt stood up and straightened his jacket. 'I'll be glad when this is over.' He clicked his heels without saluting, and went out of the door, closing it gently behind him.

S.S. Oberführer Hermann Becker, head of the Gestapo in the Breslau District Office, was puzzled. He was also a little angry, and when S.S. Oberführer Becker was angry, his subordinates trembled, for the head of a district as large as Breslau had the power of life and death over everyone in it. The Oberführer usually transferred those who displeased him to places where death was a preferable alternative.

S.S. Oberführer Becker also killed people. Indeed, it was an order from the head of the Reichssicherheitshauptamt to execute a prisoner that was the cause of his puzzlement. Becker was also angry because he had been ordered by S.S. Obergruppenführer Kaltenbrunner to carry out the execution without being told why. This was a discourtesy that would never have been allowed under Kaltenbrunner's predecessor, S.S. Obergruppenführer Reinhard Heydrich. But Heydrich had been dead two years now, assassinated near the village of Lidice, and it had been Becker who had been entrusted by the Führer himself to raze the village in retaliation, execute all the men and send the women and children to concentration camps. Lidice no longer existed, and now Heydrich's successor was treating him like a lackey.

Becker allowed himself a glimmer of satisfaction when he remembered what he had done to Lidice two years ago. He had been decorated for that. The Führer had thanked him personally.

He studied the document on his desk. The man to be executed was being held in a prison just outside the city. Becker remembered him well. He had been taken prisoner ten months ago, together with another man from the same unit. Both men had been removed from his jurisdiction before he had had time to interrogate them. When he had protested to Berlin, he was told that the national interest was involved. Later the two men were returned to the prison. After a short while one of them had been sent to Stalag Luft III, the POW camp near Sagan.

The other was the subject of the order on the desk before him.

Becker drummed his fingers on the arm of his chair. On the other side of his desk S.S. Obersturmführer Ziegler stood stiffly to attention, black cap under his right arm, his eyes staring straight ahead. Becker ignored him as he read the order through for the second time. There was no doubt about it, something strange was going on in his district, and his attempts to discover the nature of that something had been frustrated at every turn. He remembered his commanding officer's cold gaze as he rejected Becker's request for information. S.S. Gruppenführer Pohl had reminded him of the previous reply to his request for further details, and Becker had been dismissed with a warning to stay away from the matter of the two prisoners. It was obvious to Becker that Pohl had been warned off as well, probably at the highest level.

Well, it wasn't good enough. He would have to take the matter further even if it meant an unofficial investigation, but he would have to move carefully, for he knew the dreadful consequences of discovery.

He looked up at the waiting officer, then signed the document with a flourish.

'Take this across to the prison and see that Major Jacobs has everything ready for me at twelve o'clock.'

The Lieutenant took the paper, and saluted. 'At once, Herr Oberführer.' He turned and left the room.

At precisely twelve o'clock, the prisoner stood with his back to the pock-marked wall, his hands manacled, facing a firing squad of eight S.S. men. He felt no fear, only a deep sadness for what might have been. There was so much he had wanted from life, and so much he had wanted to do. He breathed deeply and stared straight ahead at the black uniformed men before him. As he looked at the officer in the shadow of the wall, a bitter hatred overwhelmed him. He felt a momentary satisfaction as he saw the man avoid his stare and turn to the firing squad. The prisoner lifted his head defiantly as he heard the S.S. Oberführer give the order to fire.

Back in his office, Becker began his enquiries into the whereabouts of the second man. He knew he had not been executed, for once having been sent to Stalag Luft III and attained official prisoner-of-war status, it was unlikely that the authorities would have risked more prisoner executions. The man he had shot today had never been processed as a prisoner-of-war after his capture, and his fate would be known only to those with access to the right documents.

He pressed the bell-push attached to the right of his desk. Within seconds an orderly appeared at his door, marched down the long red carpet to the front of his desk, and saluted.

Becker looked up from the file in front of him. 'Bring me all the top-secret files received in this office in the last month, particularly those that refer to Allied prisoners.' He looked back at the file, ignoring the orderly's salute, and continued reading the documents before him.

At that moment, nearly two hundred kilometres away on the Dresden train, a man dressed as a French artisan sat in a compartment and stared at the scenery drifting past the window. He knew nothing of the S.S. Oberführer's interest in him; he knew only that he was part of Operation Geld, and the thought sickened him, but there was nothing he could do about it. If he did not do as he was ordered, another man, a man being held in a Breslau prison, would be killed.

It was perhaps as well that he did not know that the man was already dead. The Gestapo had achieved their object. Operation Geld was under way, and they had no further use for the prisoner at Breslau.

Chapter Four

Monday, 7th August, 1944. 2 p.m.

Mason heard the rhythm of the wheels change before he heard the sing of the brakeshoes. The train jerked slightly and began to slow. The wheels clattered over points, and then they were passing warehouses and factories. They passed under several footbridges, crossed a wide river, and began to glide into a station. As they jerked to a stop, Mason saw a sign: BAUTZEN. This was the longest stop on the route. He remembered from the timetable that they would be in Bautzen for at least three-quarters of an hour.

Tensely he waited for the inevitable document inspection. Alighting passengers pushed through the mobs waiting to board, and soon the corridor outside the compartment was a confusion of luggage, people and parcels. Gradually some sort of order was created out of the chaos as passengers settled down, some on their luggage, and others more fortunate in compartments. Apart from the card-players, his fellow passengers in the compartment were two little girls and a slightly built peasant woman. The girls sat quietly, their hands passively palm-up in their laps. Both wore blue knitted hoods, thick woollen jerseys and blue skirts. He smiled at them. The elder sister smiled back, but the younger girl looked up shyly at the woman before giving him a tentative smile in return. Their mother, a woman with her hair in a bun, and her feet in thick sensible shoes, smiled too, and soon he was listening to her complaints about bringing up two little girls in wartime. The card-players continued their game, oblivious of everything but the slap of cards and the calculation of wins and losses.

People peered into carriage windows, while latecomers pushed through the corridor seeking non-existent compartment space, shouting to friends or relatives, adding to the din of imminent departure.

Over the chatter of the woman opposite him, Mason listened tensely for the shouts that would mean another document inspection. The whistle of the engine when it sounded went almost unheard, so sure was he that an inspection was inevitable. He was only shocked into awareness by the jerk of the extended coach couplings and the slow movement of the buildings past the window.

Twice as the train picked up speed through the outskirts of the town, uniformed Kripo officers passed along the corridor, glancing briefly into the compartment before pushing brusquely through the crowd.

Mason suddenly felt stifled. He stood up and picked his way through the corridor to where he had last seen Hackett. He looked in to motion the American to follow him, and stared into the cold gaze of another uniformed policeman. Mason backed out as casually as he could, but his head was pounding. He pushed blindly down the corridor, past several seated men, and encountered Davis emerging from the toilet.

'Where's Hackett?' Mason was hoarse with fear.

'He's in my compartment. We decided to sit together just before the train left Bautzen. Handy to have someone to keep a place, like.'

'Damn! You could have let me know. I bloody nearly walked slap into a German copper. You should have let me know.' Mason was shaking with rage.

'Calm down. What the hell's the matter with you!' Davis took Mason's shoulder and shook him roughly. 'There's nothing to get upset about. We're on our way, and as you said, we've only changed the route a little.'

Mason was not mollified. Headache pounded his temples and tension churned his stomach. 'The train's crawling with policemen; I don't like it.' He rubbed his forehead. 'There's one at each end of the coach, and one in every second compartment. Get Hackett.'

Davis shrugged. 'You'd better come to the compartment.'

In spite of the discontented rumblings from the other passengers, Hackett had managed to save enough space for the three of them to squeeze together on the seat. Quickly, in whispered French, Mason imparted his uneasy assessment of their position to the two men.

'One other thing,' he said. 'Tell me exactly what you saw when the conductor came through the train.'

Davis looked puzzled. 'When? Before the last stop, you mean?'

'Yes. When the Gestapo man looked at your papers.'

Hackett looked thoughtful. 'As I remember it, he looked at them and gave them back. Yeah, and he wrote something in a book.'

Mason pounced. 'Right. That's what he did when he looked at my papers too. But he didn't do the same for any other passengers; at least that I could see. Something's up, I'm sure of it.'

Davis looked at him with astonishment. 'Don't be bloody daft. You say they're all bloody sitting there, knowing we're escaped prisoners and not doing a damned thing about it?' Unconsciously he had lapsed into English. Hackett nudged him. Mason looked around, but no one had heard the whispered altercation.

He rubbed his forehead again. 'Look, I know it sounds crazy, but why should the Gestapo man only make notes when he looked at our papers? It doesn't make sense.'

Hackett shook his head. 'You can't know it was only our papers he noted. It could be that some passengers sharing a common factor are routinely recorded. Like French males, or non-Germans. Something like that.'

Mason felt some of the fear recede, but he was not completely reassured. 'It sounds convincing when you put it like that, but I'm spooked just the same.'

Davis looked uncomfortable. 'I've trusted your instinct up to now, Bob, and it's usually been right – like that time in the desert when no one else heard that German patrol – but I think you're worrying unnecessarily this time.'

'Instinct!' Hackett was scathing. 'How the hell can we run on instinct? You've already thrown the whole timetable out the window, fer Pete's sake, and now you talk of instinct. Why don't we just get off this train and walk back to camp? We can tell them back there that the moon wasn't right, or maybe your birth sign wasn't in the right orbit. Shit!'

'Keep your voice down.' Mason glanced at the other passengers. One of them, a homburg-hatted man by the window, was watching them curiously. He felt a momentary resurgence of alarm. 'Look, humour me. Let's go forward to the next coach I think we're attracting too much attention here.'

Davis nodded his agreement. 'Right, and we can do a quick recce to see just how the Kripo are arranged.'

The three men made their way to the front of the coach, where a uniformed man stood staring out of the window. He appeared to be completely unaware of their presence as they passed him through the connecting door. Mason began to feel a little easier. Slowly they walked along the swaying corridors to the front of the train. All the coaches were equally crowded, but it was at the second coach from the engine that Mason became aware that he had not seen another policeman since they had left their coach. In growing alarm, he led the way through the last connecting door.

He turned back to the other two men. 'No police. Did you notice? The only police were in our coach.'

Hackett looked thoughtful. 'I'm way ahead of you, and if you look back now, which I hope you won't be stupid enough to do right this minute, you would see that in the coach behind us, there is a cop where there wasn't one before.'

All at once, Mason felt his tension slip away from him. He felt calm and relaxed. He recognised the symptoms that presaged his moments of decision, when all the logical faculties of his mind sorted, disgarded and retained facts that contributed to the decision-making process; when his fears dissolved in the relief of having to act, even if action might invite disaster.

'Right. Are you both with me? If not, say so now, because I'm going to make decisions I haven't time to justify.' The officer in him was the only characteristic evident at this moment. His resolute attitude was in startling contrast to his consternation of a few moments before. 'At present, there are no Kripo ahead of us. We still don't know if they are on to us or if this one is just suspicious for some reason. But we must assume the worst.' He looked out of the window at the flashing telegraph poles and the fields beyond. 'I don't know how long it will be before there is another stop, but I don't think it is going to come soon enough for our purpose. We have to improvise. We've got to keep them away from the front of the train. We'll go a short way back, and see if Charlie-boy there follows us.'

He turned casually and began to stroll back the way he had come.

Chapter Five

Monday, 7th August, 1944. 3.30 p.m.

Lieutenant Schwartz watched the American leave his seat and make for the compartment occupied by the short Englishman. Thankfully he took the vacant seat in the compartment. He was tired, his legs ached, and his eyes felt as though they had been sand-papered. He had been on duty for twelve hours and had been about to put his feet up in his tiny two-roomed apartment in Gorlitz, when the call came to rush twenty men to Bautzen to board the Dresden train there. From the descriptions he had been given, he had had no difficulty in identifying the wanted men. He had ordered a strategic disposition of his men, and resigned himself to a two-hour trip to Dresden.

His instructions were clear, though puzzling. He was not to alert the men, nor interfere in any way with their movements. He was to maintain close surveillance and the arrest was to be made discreetly as the men attempted to leave the train at Dresden. They were to be taken to the Kripo office, and Captain Schmidt was to be notified. There, they were to be isolated, and no one, not even the Gestapo, was to have access to them. If there was any difficulty, he was to quote Führerbefehl 44/VIII and refer anyone disputing his authority to Major Brunner.

This was the most puzzling part of his instructions. He was well aware that in February the German High Command had issued the Stufe Romisch III order, which laid down procedures by which captured escapees were to be dealt with by the Gestapo. Then in March S.S. Oberstgruppenführer Muller, head of the Gestapo in Berlin, had signed the Aktion Kugel order, giving the Gestapo unlimited powers when dealing with recaptured prisoners; yet here was an order in direct contradiction to standing instructions. Ah well, that was Major Brunner's problem, not his.

He rested his head on the cushion, and was about to close his eyes when suddenly the tall Englishman was in the doorway in front of him, his startled eyes staring straight at the policeman. The Englishman stood for a moment, frozen in surprise, then turned and hurried down the corridor.

Schwartz stood up and looked out of the doorway, and with a movement of his head sent a young constable after the Englishman. Strolling casually as though he were on his way to the toilet, the policeman kept him in sight until he joined the short man. The two disappeared into a compartment. The constable went back the way he had come, nodded briefly to the Lieutenant and returned to his post at the rear of the coach. The Lieutenant had every exit covered, and men in every second compartment. He put his head back and prepared himself for a moment of relaxation. Just before he closed his eyes, a man in a green jacket carrying a battered cardboard case passed by his compartment. He was closely followed by an elderly woman with a lined face. The woman, dressed in a bilious green head-shawl and faded full-length peasant dress, stopped at his compartment door.

'Ah, Herr Conductor, there you are.' Schwartz realised she was speaking to him. He heard a snigger from one of the passengers.

'Go away, you silly woman!' Schwartz was amused in spite of himself. 'The conductor is at the other end of the train.'

Confused, the old woman shuffled away down the corridor. By craning his neck slightly, the Lieutenant could see the woman as she staggered to the swaying of the coach. He smiled to himself as he saw her accost the constable at the end of the corridor. He could imagine her ultimate confusion at the sight of twenty conductors spread over three coaches. At that moment, a woman in a macintosh, carrying a basket and parcel, pushed through the passengers in the corridor. There would be a stop shortly. The knowledgeable ones were always first at the exits. He had learned from the railway officials at Bautzen that they would make three stops before Dresden.

It was a nuisance. A non-stop trip would have avoided the complication of having to deploy his men to prevent the three men leaving the train before Dresden. As it was the deployment would have to be a highly discreet manoeuvre if the quarry was not to be alerted. He had detailed four men to stroll along the platform; the exit men would alight as though stretching their legs, but would stay close to the coach door. He had arranged for papers to be examined at the exits.

He felt edgy and restless, and went to the rear of the coach to find his sergeant. The man was standing at the rear coach door, staring out at the sunlit fields drifting by the window.

'We're stopping soon, Sergeant. See the men are ready. I'll be at the front of the coach.'

'The men are ready, Lieutenant. Albrecht reports that the three men went to the front of the train, but they came straight back.'

'Where are they now?'

'At the end of the coach, Lieutenant. One is in the toilet. The other two are in the second compartment.'

'Good! Keep an eye on them.'

Schwartz pushed through the crowded corridor to the end of the coach where several passengers leant against the walls, or sat on their luggage and dozed. Most of them were women and children, but a small group of men stood at the toilet door. At that moment, a woman in a yellow coat came out, and the woman in the sickly green shawl took her place. Schwartz smiled and wondered if she had found the conductor. He saw the American in the group and went back to the end of the coach, satisfied that his men were placed strategically close to his quarry.

As soon as he had taken his seat again, lethargy spread through his body. He pushed up his cap and rubbed his forehead. He closed his eyes and put his head back. The rhythm of the wheels forged a monotonous beat in his weary brain, and in spite of himself, he slipped into a half-world of lassitude where all his energy was drained into a single dark ball under his eyelids. To keep himself awake, he thought of his wife and their small baby daughter alone in their apartment.

He was one of the lucky ones. After the hell of the desert campaign, he had managed to have himself transferred back to the police. He was even lucky enough to get back to his own headquarters in Gorlitz, and as soon as he had arranged an apartment through his departmental chief, he had married a girl he had known since his schooldays. As an officer he was entitled to many privileges undreamt of by other ranks.

Unlike most of his countrymen, he had no illusions about Germany's chances of victory. He had seen too much of the power and strike capabilities of the Allies in the desert to believe that Germany alone could defeat the world. In his heart he was appalled at Hitler's attack on Russia, but he was too wary of the Gestapo to comment, even to his family. He kept his thoughts to himself, but with the landings in Normandy was increasingly concerned about his future and that of his family. He could even envy the three hunted men on this train with him. At least they would be going home to a victorious future. It was the fools who had never been at the front who still believed in the miracle of a glorious German victory.

He yawned and sighed deeply. At that moment he felt the light touch of the brakeshoes on the wheels as the driver began his approach to the next station. He felt the coach sway and jolt against the couplings, and looked out of the window to see where they were. They appeared to be approaching a small town, and he guessed it was Bischofswerda. His duties had taken him there in the past, but although he had never approached it by train, he remembered that the station was the open type with a single passenger exit to the road. It was a double-sided platform and the trains in the opposite direction took the other half of the loop. Passengers left the island platform through a subway. High fences protected both sides of the permanent way.

They were running into the station now, and Schwartz left his seat in the compartment. He went to the end of the corridor and motioned his sergeant to join him.

'I want both sides of the train watched. I'll be on the platform; see the other side is covered.'

'Right, Lieutenant.'

The men parted, and Schwartz pushed his way through the crowds who sullenly made way for him and his men to alight first. The train stopped with a slight jerk, and Schwartz could hear the roar of steam as he opened the coach door. He looked along the train. All along the platform, his men were the first to alight, and he saw that there were two men at each door.

Not many passengers were disembarking at this small country town, and at the far end he saw the familiar green shawl and red dress being helped down by the young woman in yellow. He saw but could not hear an altercation between the young woman and his constable. He strolled towards them, and heard the policeman demanding her identification. He saw her produce her papers which the policeman examined briefly and then handed back.

'Check the men first, Brandt. Don't waste time on the women.'

The two women shuffled away, and he turned to see a man helping two small girls from the train. He saw their knitted blue hoods and skirts, and then he saw the woman in blue, with a blue shawl over her head, following them to the platform. The man's papers were examined, and he was allowed to go. There was no sign of the three men. The Lieutenant was not surprised. His information was that they were bound for Dresden, and that is where he would have to be extra cautious.

A few men began alighting behind the women, and he saw that each one of them was stopped and papers examined. At the end of the coach, he saw the last passenger leave the train; a thick-set man in a green jacket, he appeared to resent the attentions of the police. Schwartz heard his protests at having to produce his papers, but as the constable unclipped his holster flap, the movement appeared to subdue the belligerent man. Sullenly he presented his papers for inspection.

The platform was almost deserted now, and Schwartz saw the guard rise his flag. The driver blew a long impatient blast on his whistle, and the policemen climbed aboard the train. Doors slammed, and the Lieutenant stood on the coach step as the train slid imperceptibly forward. He watched the station buildings disappear behind him, and then went forward to the compartment he had left a few minutes before.

As he sat back, the Sergeant appeared in the doorway.

'All correct, Lieutenant. No one got off on the wrong side of the train.'

Schwartz nodded. When he spoke, his voice was so soft that the Sergeant had to bend forward to hear him. 'Our men are still on the train. A few women and about five men got off. No one else. Three men got on the train.' He flipped the side pocket of his tunic and took out a packet of thin brown cigarettes. 'It's time to close in a little.' He lit his cigarette with a silver lighter. 'Maintain continuous surveillance from now on. I hardly think they would have been unaware of the activity at the last station. They may try something. The important thing is that no one should see us take them at Dresden.'

The Sergeant saluted. 'I'll arrange the surveillance at once, Herr Lieutenant.'

He pushed his way through the crowded corridor. The lieutenant watched him go, then leaned his head back and blew a thin stream of smoke through his nostrils. He closed his eyes and dozed through the soft murmuring of the three women in the compartment. The fifth passenger, an elderly man wrapped in a patched overcoat, snored heavily in the corner seat.

He felt the rhythm of the wheels quicken as the train picked up speed. They were descending into the valley. He heard the sound of wheels echoing back at them as they flew into a forest of tall pines, and the setting sun threw flashing shadows at them. He heard the sing of the flanges on the track as they began the long turn at the bottom of the incline.

He sighed and stood up. At that moment, the Sergeant appeared at the door of the compartment. Schwartz saw the concern in his face, and knew at once that something was seriously wrong.

'There's no sign of them, Lieutenant. We've searched the train from end to end. Nothing.'

'It's impossible! Have you looked in the guard's van – the baggage coach?'

'We looked there first, Lieutenant.'

'Come with me.'

As the train sped through the tiny villages and began to approach the next stop, Lieutenant Schwartz went frantically through the train, covering all the possibilities that had already occurred to the sergeant.

At last, he was forced to admit the unpalatable fact that, somehow, the impossible had happened: his quarry had eluded him. Somehow they had slipped off the train, either at Bischofswerda or when the train had slowed before a stop. He was not looking forward to his imminent conversation with Captain Schmidt.

Twenty minutes later in Breslau, Captain Schmidt slammed down the telephone and walked swiftly down the corridor to the office two doors away. He knocked and went in. Major Brunner looked up as Schmidt walked in and saluted.

'Well? Schwartz has them, I take it?'

'No. They've slipped through the net.' Quickly he summarised Schwartz's report. 'I can't criticise his strategy, Herr Major. The consequences may be serious, but he did everything by the book.'

The Major leaned back and placed his pen carefully on the blotter, lining it up meticulously with the edge. Then he took a cigar from the humidor on his desk, and lit it with practised care. Neither man spoke. Brunner stood up and walked to the long window overlooking the square two floors below.

The sun had set, the long twilight softening the shadows of the tall trees, and the lights were beginning to glow in shops and offices all over the city. Schmidt watched him uneasily as he turned and walked back to his desk.

He sat and looked at the Captain. 'Are you a gambling man, Werner?' He flicked his wrist impatiently. 'No, of course you're not. But I am. I am going to gamble today, my friend, and if I lose – well, in a year or two, I don't think it will matter anyway.'

Schmidt looked puzzled. 'I don't think I understand you, Herr Major.'

'Werner, my good friend, I am going to gamble on our man.' He puffed at his cigar, his granite face relaxing slightly. 'With every move the other two make, he must be getting more and more worried. He can't do much about it at the moment, but it is against his own interests to make an irrevocable escape. He must go through the motions, but inevitably he must deliver the other two to us. He is part of the operation whether he likes it or not; and like it or not, he must get in touch with us soon.' He puffed at his cigar once more. 'Keep your men in the Bischofswerda area. Maintain the road blocks. I'm positive we will find them there. I am also positive that our man will eventually call us on that emergency number we gave him at the start of the operation.'

When Schmidt left him, Brunner sat for a long time staring at the wall opposite. Something bothered him. At his briefing in Berlin, the details of the operation were set out for him, and out of the comprehensive planning, one factor did not fit. That factor was one which required him to have three men ready to travel by 14th August. The date was stressed over and over and he was warned that it was imperative for the success of the operation that the date be adhered to. Why? The operation as it stood appeared to be independent of any timetable. Why the 14th? He knew there was much they hadn't told him, but no amount of analysis produced a reason for the fixed timetable.

He sighed, pushed his chair back and went to the window. He stared out at the busy street, hands behind his back, his body sagging with weariness. He looked across the square at the darkened window of his apartment. Its only convenience was its proximity to his office. For the rest it was austere and almost bare. He had never been one for luxury, though he could have had all he demanded. He preferred to live an uncluttered, unfettered existence.

It had always been so. Product of the harsh discipling of the Naval Gymnasium, his only relative was his father's brother who had given him all the necessities of life, but very little more – and never affection. He had never known his parents. Just after he was born, both had succumbed to cholera.

He was not yet forty, but the harsh lines in his face, and his greying hair made him appear much older. He had no friends, only acquaintances, and his colleagues knew him as a fair, yet hard man who never displayed the slightest sign of sociability to either sex.

He turned from the window and went back to his desk.

That same night, Lieutenant Schwartz returned to Bischofswerda and set up his headquarters at the Kripo headquarters there. His instructions were explicit. He was to set up road blocks, conduct searches of hotels, boarding houses, railway stations and forced labour hostels. The hostels were an ideal hideout, because there they were among friends and could easily be hidden and fed, lost amongst the hundreds of inmates.

Now and then, the Lieutenant escaped to his apartment in Gorlitz for a few hours' relaxation with his family. In his own mind he was certain that the fugitives were well away from the area by this time. Bischofswerda was less than twenty kilometres from the Czech border, and although it was part of the Reich, the Underground was more active in Sudetenland than in Germany.

He reported daily to the Breslau office, and Captain Schmidt never varied his instructions. Refer all Gestapo questions to Breslau, and keep your mouth shut. Keep up the roadblocks and be discreet.

Captain Schmidt was not as sanguine as Major Brunner, however, and he too had his private doubts about the outcome of the mission. He too believed that they had lost their fugitives for good. It was just not feasible that the men were still in the area of search.

On the morning of the 10th, his usual call came from Bischofswerda. Expecting the usual negative report, he was completely unprepared for what he heard.

He left his desk in a daze, and almost in a state of shock, walked the few metres to Major Brunner's office.

The Major looked up as he entered.

'Herr Major, I am pleased to report that our man has walked into our office at Bautzen and given himself up.'

'He's what?'

'Given himself up.'

'Alone?'

'That is what I understand.'

'And what of his compatriots? The other two?'

'He says they are dead, Herr Major.'

Chapter Six

Monday, 7th August, 1944. 5 p.m.

Mason took out his fob watch and glanced at it. Five o'clock. Five hours ago they were being served ham and potato cakes by the woman in the café in Gorlitz. It was only four and a half hours since they had boarded this train for Dresden, yet it seemed the Kripo had found them already. Their change of plan had had no effect. It was clear to Mason that the abnormal number of Kripo boarding the train at Bautzen was more than coincidence, and when he and his two companions walked to the front of the train and found a policeman close behind them, he was sure of it.

He looked out at the flashing telegraph poles and the field beyond. 'I don't know how long it will be before there is another stop, but I don't think it is going to be soon enough for our purpose, so we have to improvise. We have to keep them away from the front of the train. We'll go back a little way, and see if Charlie-boy there follows us.'

He turned casually and began to stroll back the way he had come. As he got to the communicating door of their coach, he stood aside to allow a man in a green coat to pass but instead the man stopped beside him. Behind the first man, three more men crowded the corridor, apparently waiting to pass. Mason recognised the card players from his compartment.

The first man spoke, his tone low and urgent. 'You are in trouble. You cannot get off this train without our help.'

Mason began to speak. The man cut him off. 'Don't talk. Just listen. Take this case.' He thrust a suitcase into Mason's hand. 'Go into the toilet and change into the clothes you will find inside. Your friends must follow my comrades.'

Mason looked at the other three men, who were gazing out of the window as though they were waiting to use the toilet, but he noticed that they had spread themselves so that their actions were hidden from anyone in the corridor. Davis and Hackett were watching, surprise and suspicion mingled in their expressions.

'Who are you? Why – '

'Enough. Do you want to get off the train, or don't you? There is no time for talk. Trust me. You have four minutes to change before the next stop. Wilhelm here will wait for you to come out. Trust him, and do as he says.'

Mason hesitated for a moment. He looked at his companions and shrugged. 'I think he's right. We're done for if we don't do as he says. We've no choice.' He picked up the case and disappeared into the toilet.

The man motioned to Davis. 'You go with Gunther here. The American will come with me.'

Inside the toilet, Mason opened the case, his heart pounding with hope and excitement. In the case was a full length peasant dress and a sickly green shawl. Female clothing. He held them up in bewilderment. How the hell was he supposed to look like a woman? On the other hand, why not? There was no reason at all why he should not look like any other peasant woman in these clothes, with this shawl over his head. Many rural women wore full-length dresses. But what about papers? He would have to trust Green Coat. There was nothing else he could do. He realised now, that he had been blinded by hope, refusing to admit to himself and the others that they were under surveillance. But why were they not arrested at once?

Hastily he stripped off his clothes and packed them into the case. He pulled the dress over his head and over his hips, then wrapped the shawl about his shoulders and over his head. He looked at his reflection in the mirror. By clutching the shawl at his chin, most of his face was hidden. All at once, the image reminded him of the woman in the red dress and a green shawl, searching for the conductor. She must have accosted ten policemen. He pondered on the meaning of what he had seen.

An impatient knocking roused him from his speculation, and he slid the door across. Outside, the man called Wilhelm took the case from him and indicated that he should follow. Keeping his head down, he kept the black boots in sight. At the end of the coach, waiting near the exit door, a man stood holding two little girls by the hand, while next to him, holding the other hand of the bigger girl, was a woman in blue. It was certainly not the mother of the children, The eyes were those of his Welsh companion. The shawl was clutched at the chin, and the rest of the face almost hidden.

Mason looked back surreptitiously to see if he could recognise Hackett, but at that moment a young woman in yellow took his arm and indicated that he should follow her. With her leading and Wilhelm behind, they went forward to the next coach. There were policemen everywhere, all of them watching silently as the passengers eased forward to the exits. The policemen had placed themselves strategically so that they would be the first to alight. Suddenly Mason felt conspicuous in his ill-fitting clothes, and was certain that at any moment hands would grab him, his ridiculous disguise be torn from him, and he would be marched back to the prison camp. Momentarily he was almost paralysed with fear, but he was one of those people on whom fear acts as a catalyst to fuse together the processes of logic and reasoning. He took a deep breath and felt the fear evaporating.

The beat of the wheels slowed imperceptibly, and the babble of voices around him increased as the passengers began edging towards the exits. With a long scream of brakes, the coach stopped in front of a dilapidated station building. Mason saw policemen step off the train, and he felt his arm being held by the woman in yellow. He realised that she was acting out the charade of helping an elderly woman off the train, and remembered to make his movements as slow as possible.

Suddenly he was certain of disaster. The policeman was demanding their papers, and the woman was arguing volubly, producing her papers and waving her bag at him. Mason felt a resurgence of fear as he saw an officer walking towards them from the rear of the train, but all at once a miracle happened. At a word from the officer, the policeman handed the papers back to the woman and they were allowed to go. As they shuffled with agonising slowness across the platform towards the subway, Mason saw the man with the two little girls. They were in a group crossing the platform about ten metres away, and Mason noticed that Davis walked slightly ahead as though anxious to reach the subway. There was no sign of Hackett.

A shout froze him for a moment, but as the young woman pulled at him, he realised it had come from the guard. He saw the policemen boarding and as the platform emptied, the train slid slowly past them out of the station.

At the subway, he had to suppress a wild impulse to run, but the woman kept a firm grip on his arm. For the first time he took a covert look at her face, and almost stopped in surprise. He did not know what he had expected, but he certainly did not expect to see anyone so young. She was no more than twenty, with a generous mouth and a soft complexion, but her fairish hair was pulled back in a bun, and her eyes were hard and uncompromising. As they walked, she was aware of him looking at her. She looked quickly right and left.

'Pull yourself together.' Her German was slightly accented, and he thought perhaps she was Polish. 'Act as though you've known me for years; not as though you are seeing me for the first time.' She spoke softly but with impatience, and he realised he had been acting like an idiot. This was a serious situation; perhaps a life and death one for both of them.

They came out of the dimness of the subway into a late afternoon sunlight. The road that ran alongside the station was lined with trees, and beyond the few houses he could see, were fields and woods. A sign opposite said: BISCHOFSWERDA 2 Km. He looked at her questioningly.

She looked at the sign and back at him. 'The railway does not run through the town.'

He looked around for his companions. She saw his concern. 'Your friends will come. Trust me.'

He smiled wryly. 'Trust' was all he had done for the past twenty minutes. Events had moved with astonishing swiftness, and he had had no other option. If anyone had told him this morning that he would place his life in the hands of perfect strangers as he had done, he would have thought them insane.

The girl led the way across the street and down a lane that led past a small café. He could hear the voices of men and the clatter of crockery. He heard footsteps behind them, and he looked back to find that they were being followed by the two little girls, their two chaperones, and further back the man in the green coat accompanied by two women. Mason saw with relief that the second one was tall and walked with a slight limp.

They turned into another lane where an ancient Reo truck was parked on the verge. A man was standing by the front mudguard, smoking a short stub of cigarette which he discarded as soon as he saw them. The girl spoke briefly to him and he swung into the cab and started the engine. Mason heard the man in the green coat say something to her.

She motioned to the back of the truck. 'Quickly. All of you. Get on the back and sit down.' Mason was astonished to hear her speaking English.

The three men in skirts struggled to get their legs over the backboard, while still retaining some dignity in their embarrassing clothes. The girl and the three men followed quickly, but there was no sign of the mother and two little girls. Mason assumed they had gone into the café.

Mason heard Hackett chuckle, and then begin to laugh. His two companions joined him, and in a few moments seven people on the back of a Reo truck in the middle of the Third Reich, being sought by the Gestapo, the S.S., the S.D., and the criminal police, were shrieking with mirth, and slapping one another on the back. The relief of tension tore the laughter from them, and it was minutes before they subsided, wiping the tears from their eyes.

'What the hell are you laughing at?' Mason wiped his eyes with the shawl.

Hackett almost exploded once more. 'I was – was wondering what I was going to get for Mother's Day.' He went off into another paroxym until Mason slapped him on the back.

'You'd better start wondering what we're getting for Christmas – if we're still around to celebrate. We'd also better start wondering about these characters that have hi'jacked us.'

The man in the green coat put out his hand. He said in English, 'I know it is foolish to say you have no reason to fear us. You don't know who we are, but I assure you, you are amongst friends.' He clutched the side of the truck as it swayed around a sharp bend and entered a forest road. 'Call me Joachim. That is not my real name but it will do for now. Wilhelm and Gunther have other names too, and Pauline there is my daughter.'

Mason took his hand and shook it gratefully. 'We are indebted to you. We were in great danger back there on the train.' He frowned. 'But why are they playing cat and mouse with us? It is obvious to me now that all those policemen were on that train on account of us.'

'Yes. They were.'

'And you risked your lives to get us away. Why?' He glanced at Wilhelm and Gunther, but the two men stared ahead at the winding forest road.

Joachim shrugged. 'We have been living on borrowed time since we broke out of the ghetto. And now this is how we use that time.'

Hackett said: 'You are Jewish?'

'We all are.'

'We would not have known.'

'Perhaps that is what saved us. We now have authentic papers to prove that we are good Polish catholics.' His voice was expressionless.

'Authentic papers?' Davis spoke for the first time since leaving the train.

Joachim looked at him. 'I talk too much. We are nearly there.'

As the truck began to labour, the driver changed down to take a short hill, and the old motor clattered like castanets, but soon they were running down a long slope deep into the forest, where they stopped at last in front of a small hut.

At a word from Joachim, they all descended from the truck which immediately made a three point turn and disappeared into the trees.

Joachim pushed open the door of the hut. 'Quickly.

Change into the clothes you will find inside. You will find several sizes of each garment. But hurry. We are not entirely safe here. These woods are patrolled by the Home Guard and the Youth Brigade.'

Mason looked around at the quiet trees. 'How could you be sure this place wasn't compromised? We drove straight up here. Wasn't that dangerous?'

Joachim smiled. 'We would have known. We would have seen a signal. Now hurry.'

The clothes they found in the hut were rough working clothes of the kind worn by woodsmen; thick woollen jerseys, corduroy trousers and cloth caps. Mason looked out of the small window as he changed. He saw the girl, Pauline, stroll a few metres into the trees, and in the other direction he saw Wilhelm keeping watch some way up the road. He had no doubt that Joachim and Gunther were somewhere else, equally vigilant.

When they emerged from the hut, the three men looked no different from their hosts. Wilhelm and Gunther, two silent powerful men who were alike enough to be relatives, were dressed in blue woollen shirts and thick trousers, with the bottoms tucked into high boots.

When the group was ready to move, Joachim led the way to a path almost hidden from the hut.

The twilight was deepening into evening and the night insects were clamorous in their secret places. The tall firs whispered in the slight breeze that had sprung up out of the still day, and from somewhere nearby could be heard the gurgling ripple of a small brook.

They climbed a steep path that led to a prominent rock, out of which flowed a small spring.

'Drink deeply. We have a long way to go.'

They all took their turn at the spring, and because they were thirstier than they realised, the ice-cold water was like nectar.

They continued upwards for about five hundred metres before the path began to descend. About ten minutes walking brought them to a dirt road that went off to their left up a steep hill, and to their right to some dark structures that appeared to be a dilapidated and deserted sawmill.

'Only I will go on with you from here. My friends have business elsewhere.'

Joachim turned and spoke briefly to his daughter. After hasty farewells, they watched the two men and the girl out of sight before Joachim led the way across the road to a path that skirted the sawmill and went on upwards through the forest. It was getting colder and dark clouds drifted across the sky. Soon, heavy raindrops were splattering the trees, and the storm which had been threatening all day from the west, broke upon them with a fury that caught them unawares.

Joachim began to walk faster but his three companions, who had been surviving on prison food for so many months, began to feel the effects of their inadequate diet. Wet, miserable and exhausted, they struggled through the night, slipping in rivulets and walking into trees in the dark. Soon hunger was the least of their discomforts, and it was almost with disbelief that they heard Joachim call a halt.

'We rest up here for tonight. Give me your hands, one at a time, and I will guide you. We're going into a cave with an opening only one metre high, so keep low.'

In the pitch dark, completely blind, the three men allowed themselves to be guided and pushed through a tiny aperture in the mountainside that opened into a warm dry grotto.

Joachim lit a kerosene lamp that hung from the roof. In the yellow light, they saw that the cave was a chamber about ten metres square.

'Welcome to our underground,' he said and laughed out loud. All at once they saw the joke, and within seconds they were laughing like crazy men. Wet, tired, hungry and cold, they laughed until they could laugh no more.

S.S. Oberführer Becker stared at the man standing on the opposite side of his desk.

'Why wasn't I told of this development?'

'I thought you knew, Herr Oberführer.' The man heard the tremor in his own voice, and was ashamed. Yet how could one not fear this man, the destroyer of Lidice; the man who had personally directed the execution squads at Kovno where one hundred and ten thousand Jews died?

'How am I to know things if I am not told?'

'I received the instruction by telex, Herr Oberführer. I understood that it had come through this office. The instruction was most insistent on absolute secrecy, Herr Oberführer. Therefore I did no more than I was instructed, and burnt the documents.'

'The order did not come via this office.' Becker's voice was like ice. 'It must have gone directly to you from Berlin.'

'I did not know that, Herr Oberführer. I apologise if it has been an inconvenience.'

'Inconvenience? You call this inconvenience!' Becker spoke with cold rage. 'It is more than that. It is an insult!' His voice dropped to almost a whisper. 'Give me in accurate detail what your orders were.'

'I was instructed to see that a Major Brunner of the Kriminalpolizei received every cooperation, and to second one of my Lieutenants to his section.'

'And what cooperation did this Major Brunner ask for?' Becker's voice was thick with sarcasm.

'He required only one piece of information – a composite list of all the prisoner-of-war escapes from my area.'

'Nothing else?'

'Nothing, Herr Oberführer. I ordered Schäfer to assist him.'

'Did Brunner say why he wanted the lists?'

'No, Herr Oberführer. I did not ask, because the instructions were explicit. Only three other people were to be briefed fully on the operation. I was not one of them. I concluded that you had been fully informed, Herr Oberführer.'

'Where is this Schäfer now?'

'Berlin instructed me to transfer him. He is confined to barracks. Apparently he blundered and is being punished.'

'Berlin? Who signed that order?

'S.S. Obergruppenführer Kaltenbrunner, Herr Oberführer.'

'And the first order?'

'The same, Herr Oberführer. S.S. Obergruppenführer Kaltenbrunner signed both orders.'

'I see.' He thought for a moment. 'I want to see this Lieutenant Schäfer. Get him here and bring him to me.'

'At once, Herr Oberführer.'

'And you will tell no one that I have discussed this matter. No one. You understand.'

'I understand, Herr Oberführer.' With that Colonel Baatz of the Sicherheitsdienst left his superior, thankful that his name was not Schäfer.

After he had gone. Becker sat staring into space. He was on dangerous ground, and he knew it. Berlin, in the form of the head of the Gestapo, had given orders that none but those designated were to know of the operation. If it were to become known that he was fishing in waters protected by Kaltenbrunner, his life would be instantly forfeit, but Becker was arrogant and obdurate. He was also wily. He was determined to discover why this Major Brunner was entrusted with this operation, and why the head of the Breslau District of the S.S. was not told of it. More important, he was determined to discover the nature of the operation, and how prisoners-of-war were involved.

Chapter Seven

Monday, 7th August, 1944. 8 p.m.

The hard drumming of the rain sounded oddly muted inside the cave, and although they could hear the gurgling of the runnels coursing through the rocks and down the fissures, there was no sign of damp or seepage in the warm dry cavern. The ceiling was domed, about three metres at its highest point, and the floor, though uneven, was clean and free of dust. Several mattresses were piled against one wall, and stacked on top of them were folded blankets. Apart from a table, the only other object in the cave was a large square box measuring about two metres long by half a metre wide and half a metre high. It had a hinged lid which Joachim opened to reveal canned food, utensils, and some small red tins of what appeared to be sealing wax. Joachim lit a match and held it to the wax which burst into flame. He saw their surprise at the sight of American supplies marked with PX labels.

'Camp cookers,' he said. 'First used in the Spanish war, and adopted by the Americans, whom we have to thank for our present supplies.' Mason forbore to ask how American equipment found its way into this remote cave. He was sure Joachim's explanation would be as evasive as his replies to questions about his identity documents.

Joachim took a two litre pot from the box, opened three tins with a Swiss army knife, and poured the contents into the pot. He set up a small tripod over the cooker on to which he placed the pot.

'I'm sure you'd prefer a tournedos chasseur, but what

you're going to get is baked beans.' He grinned at them, puckish lines creasing his face. Mason realised that the man he had first assessed as a rough labourer was in reality both cultured and educated. 'While this is warming, make up beds for yourselves.'

The three men dragged mattresses on to the floor and covered them with blankets. Davis sat with his back to the wall while Hackett stretched full-length on his back.

Mason looked at the small Welshman. Davis seemed tired. His normally neat black hair had grown and hung over his ears and neck. With eyes closed, head tilted back and his round face lined with fatigue, he appeared to be close to collapse. Mason realised guiltily that he hadn't asked whether the little man had slept the night before. In any event they would all sleep well tonight.

Mason sat back on his mattress and watched Joachim pouring water into a coffee-pot which he rinsed with a deft swirl. He went to the cave entrance, pulled aside the canvas hanging in front of the doorway, and tossed the water out into the night.

'How safe is this place?' He watched the Pole walk back to the box, his face shadowed in the dim light of the lamp.

'As safe as Trafalgar Square.'

'How can you be sure?'

'When I lead you out of here tomorrow, you will never find your way back. It is on protected property, it is in thick bush and difficult to find, and is so well camouflaged, you won't see it from five metres.' He grinned. 'Besides, on a night like this, who's looking?' In the flickering light, his features cast satanic shadows on the wall behind him. He poured water into the pot and placed it on the second burner.

Mason looked at him quizzically. 'Protected property?'

Joachim did not answer, but turned an impassive face to him. He looked at Mason for a moment and then at the other two. When he spoke, his voice was hard. 'There is really nothing more I am prepared to tell you. Would you trust your lives to me if you knew I talked too much?' He turned back to the stove. 'Although I think it is unlikely, there is no way you can prove to me that you are not agents of the Reich.' Mason started to protest. Joachim held up his hand. 'No, I don't really think you are, but there have been three attempts to infiltrate our organisation, and I've no doubt that the Gestapo will try again.'

Hackett sat up and took a stub of cigarette from his pocket. Silently Joachim tossed him a pack of Chesterfields. Hackett looked at them in awe.

'I tell you, man, Christmas *does* come every day. Where the hell did these come from?' He held up his hand. 'Sorry, I won't ask again.'

Joachim just grinned at him. Hackett lit three cigarettes, one for each of his companions. The men smoked silently, content for a moment with the unaccustomed luxury.

Eventually Joachim filled four plates with food. They ate hungrily, and when the coffee came, it was real coffee. They had been drinking ersatz for so long that they had forgotten the heavenly smell of the deep brown brew.

Davis swallowed the last of the coffee in his cup and looked up at their benefactor. 'Would it be giving anything away if you told us why you helped us? How did you know we were POW's? What mistakes did we make?'

Joachim grinned at them all, and Mason realised how much they had come to like this big Polish Jew: not only because he had helped them, but for his kindness and obvious good humour.

Davis persisted. 'What did we do wrong? We don't want to make the same mistakes again.' The Welsh lilt was in his voice again. It always was when he was worried.

'Mistakes?' Joachim was jocular, but not cruel.

'My young friend, there wasn't a thing you did right. It's a wonder you lasted as long as you did. For a start, you should never go from one coach class to another. It's the surest way to antagonise the conductor and get him calling for the Gestapo. You were lucky the conductor was otherwise engaged.'

'Of course, how stupid! If we were found in a first class coach with second class tickets, we would have been arrested at once.'

Joachim nodded. 'And then you spoke English. If you are going to play a part, you must be alert every second. Not just nervous all the time, but alert.' He grinned again. 'And you were so nervous, it was obvious.'

'But how did you arrange for a change of clothing on the train? And all those people – ' Mason stopped, wondering if he was being too inquisitive.

Joachism dismissed his hesitation with a smile. 'That team is always geared up for that ploy. We've used it many times with different variations. It's a variation of the old magic trick where you get your audience to concentrate on one action while you're busy with something else.' He nodded to Mason. 'When you went past the policemen in that red and green outfit, he immediately associated it with the silly old woman asking for the conductor, so in his mind you became that silly old woman.' He laughed out loud. 'That silly old woman was once a lecturer in law at a university, and Wilhelm and Gunther were partners in a building firm started by their grandfather. The woman with the bun in her hair with the two little girls? That was Johan, my nephew. He would have been in his final year at university.' He stopped, overcome, and turned and fiddled in the big box.

Davis shook his head. 'All those talented people, wasting their lives because a generation of Germans has such hatred for the Jewish people.'

Joachim turned swiftly to him. 'No. Not wasting their lives. They are living for a purpose. Each according to what the Almighty has designed for them. And why blame only the Germans?' He saw their looks of surprise. 'Oh no, my friends. Anti-Semitism has been with us for centuries. Hitlerian racism only appeared on ground which previous centuries had prepared for it.' He sat on the box and leaned forward earnestly. 'Do you imagine that Hitler invented the yellow patch?' He shook his head slowly. 'No, it was Pope Paul IV who decreed that Jews should live in ghettoes, own no land and wear yellow hats. And in Seville, during the Spanish Inquisition, the synagogues were destroyed and forty thousand Jews murdered.' He sighed. 'And the Crusaders. They began their pilgrimage to the Holy Land by killing hundreds and thousands of Jews at Cologne, Mayence, Treves, Worms, Speyer and other places along the Rhine.' He waved a hand impatiently. 'But I could go on for hours.'

'But surely this must be the worst period in the history of the Jewish people?' Mason stopped as Joachim turned on him.

'Jew-baiters have appeared in every generation since the Crucifixion. When the war is over, there are those whose duty it will be to find the perpetrators of these crimes and see that they are all punished. But beware you do not punish the innocent.' He rubbed his forehead. 'There is a man, Anton Schmidt by name. He was a Wehrmacht sergeant who helped the Jews in the ghetto at Vilnyus. He warned them when the raids were coming. He smuggled the condemned out of the ghetto, and whenever he could, he brought milk in bottles in his pocket for the babies. He was a devout Catholic who suffered when others suffered. He knew he was going to die, because there was no way to avoid discovery, but he carried on until they caught him.'

Joachim leaned wearily back against the wall. 'When finally they took him, they dragged his mangled remains out of the Gestapo headquarters at Bialystok, threw him on to a cart, and dragged the cart to the gates of the ghetto. In front of the Jews he had helped, they tied him to a post and shot him. He could not stand up against the post before he died, because he had no skin on his feet where the beasts had tortured him.' There was a long silence. Then Joachim continued. 'The Jews waited all that week to find out if he had given the Gestapo the names of the resistance leaders before he died. But he had not. The non-Jew, Anton Schmidt, kept faith with the Jews of the Bialystok ghetto.' He looked at each of them in turn. 'There are many like him, Jew and Gentile, heroes who are prepared to stand against the beasts of this world.'

Hackett said softly, 'But when this is over, who will tell about them?'

Joachim shrugged. 'There are those who will never forget. And on the guilty, they will take retribution.' He took his papers from his pocket. 'The man who made these possible, and helped us to escape the degradation that others suffered, is one of those we will remember. He is dead, so he can no longer be harmed, but we must be careful to distinguish the innocent from the guilty. Hate the guilty if you must, but do not hate a whole race for what members of that race have done.' He looked at the three men for a moment and then chuckled. 'I must stop lecturing. You look as bemused as some of my students used to.'

Mason shook his head. 'After what those people have done, you can still be magnanimous?'

Joachim lifted his hands and dropped them. 'I see you've missed the point. No matter.' He sipped at his coffee.

Davis said, 'If the man who arranged your papers is dead, what happens when they have to be renewed?'

Joachim smiled. 'The chain wasn't broken with his death. The conspiracy against Hitler's gangsters wasn't killed with the death of the July bomb plotters.' He leaned forward and lifted his finger. 'Think: if I hated the German race, I would have to hate Anton Schmidt; I would have to hate all those amongst them who have helped us. No, racial hatred is the expression of backward and ignorant people.'

Mason marvelled at the compassion in this kindly man. 'But who will know the difference when this war is over?'

'I don't know the answer to that. For the moment it is enough to survive.' He looked at Davis, whose head had slipped forward on his chest, and whose soft snores betrayed his absolute exhaustion. 'We had better join him. We have much to do in the morning.'

Joachim snuffed out the lamp and lay back on his mattress. In the dark, he heard the restless movements of the others in the cave with him. He felt wide awake, and sleep would not come easily. It was always so when he remembered the ghetto years; those dark times of living in constant fear, not for himself but for the loved ones whose helplessness was a burden that his own impotence made more intolerable. The beast walked with armed fangs, and in all the ghetto there were no more than three weapons, and perhaps two people who knew how to use them. Those who could get there were in the forests with the Jewish partisans. He remembered the nightly journeys through the fetid slime of the sewers to bring back the food dumped by the partisans at rendezvous points. He had wanted to join the roving bands in the forests, but he had obeyed the Jewish Council who decreed that the strong ones should be the couriers.

The day they caught him at the rendezvous point, he had fifteen loaves in a sack, a crime which would have merited instant execution. But because of his size, he was put to work digging up bodies buried by the man known as The Butcher.

This man had been responsible for the thousands buried in the pit, and now either because of fear of retribution or because of orders from higher up, the bodies were to be exhumed and burnt.

The stink of putrefaction would be forever in his nostils.

One day, Joachim discovered a body that was intact – and, more important, was his own size and colouring. Because the guards kept well back from the stinking pit, he was able to clothe the body unobserved, and while his comrades reported to the guards that he had died, he lay naked under the thin layer of earth they spread over him. That night, after the guards had marched the detail back to the camp, he had slipped away naked into the forests. He stole clothes and food, and within a week was a part of the band of partisans operating out of the Augustow Forest. He went back in the spring, back to the reeking ghetto, and brought out the only surviving member of his family. Together they returned to the forest. He and Pauline had been together ever since.

The route from the Augustow Forest to this cave was a long and tortuous one, embracing conspirators from the Wehrmacht, the Abwehr, and even from the Reichssicherheidshauptamt (RSHA). But with the ill-advised and bungled attempt on the Führer's life on 20th July, the conspirators were now scattered and disorganised.

Joachim still had his contacts in the Abwehr, but he knew that even these would, in time, be lost to him.

He settled himself comfortably, and before sleep claimed him, saw once more the face of The Butcher hovering at the edge of his consciousness. It was a face he would remember all his life, the focus of all the hatred remaining to him.

They woke while it was still dark. The rain had stopped, but a raw wind knifed through the forest, rattling and bending the trees whose wild branches swung frighteningly overhead. After a full body wash and shave, they ate a meal of tinned meat, bread and coffee.

Joachim reached into the box and produced three knives. 'You must take these with you. They will come in useful both as a weapon and a utensil.'

Mason examined the weapons with practised eye. He noted that, like Commando knives, they had a double-edged tip and slim, razor-sharp tapering blades. These, however, were made in Germany, and unlike the Sykes-Fairbairn, the grip was not shaped. Joachim handed them scabbards with four leather straps on each. 'Wear them on the forearm, hilt-down. That way, they're easier to get at in a hurry.'

They left the cave in single file, Joachim leading the way down a steep incline to a level path that wound left and right through the firebreaks. The morning was pitch-dark, and they travelled almost by instinct, the men in front just visible a metre away. Several times Joachim stopped and listened, once for at least five minutes. It was getting lighter, and finally, through the trees, they saw a small hut much like the one they had seen when they had first entered the forest. Joachim signalled that they should conceal themselves, and when they had done so to his satisfaction, he approached the hut warily, using every bit of cover to get close unobserved. When he was at the rotting window-frame, he peered cautiously into the dim interior. They saw him retreat and stand for a full minute watching the path below, then he went swiftly to the door and opened it. He signalled for them to go into the hut, while he disappeared into the trees.

It was a relief to get out of the wind, and Mason hoped they would be able to shelter for a while. Up to now, he and his companions had followed blindly, but he felt it was time for the big man to answer questions about their future. While he had no reason to believe that he was not what he appeared to be, Mason though it was time for Joachim to reveal what was in store for them.

As though he had read Mason's thoughts, Hackett said: 'I figure about now is question time. I for one wanna know what these guys've got in store for us. It's clear the others have been out gettin' things organised.'

Davis nodded. 'It's what I've been thinking. It's time we got back to the original plan, even if we are a day late.'

Mason shook his head. 'The original plan must go by the board. It seems that somewhere along the line, that plan included a bunch of Kripo. No, I think it's safer to change direction entirely, and take our chances with what this lot have planned.'

'I don't agree.' Hackett was emphatic. 'If we pick up the

original route a little further along the line, we can still get to Nuremberg.'

'What if the Kripo knew our whole route? Then they could find us at whichever stage we were. It's funny they were so quick to get on to us when we changed trains at Gorlitz.' He frowned. 'What the hell are they playing at? Why didn't they arrest us?'

Davis nodded. 'Yes. It's very odd.' His face lit up suddenly. 'Could they have been watching us to see us make contact with the Underground? Then they could sweep the whole lot into the net.'

Mason nodded. 'It's feasible.'

Hackett looked thoughtful. 'Yeah. I never thought of that, yet it's so obvious. Yeah.'

The three men were quiet for a long moment. Mason eased himself down on the bench against the wall. Hackett and Davis, squatting on two logs fashioned as stools, shared a cigarette between them.

Finally, they heard voices, and Joachim returned to the hut followed by Wilhelm, rubbing his hands and stamping his feet. The man's trousers and jacket were soaked and his eyes were bloodshot from lack of sleep.

Joachim said: 'Pauline and Gunther will be here shortly. They have made arrangements for new papers for you. You will no longer be French, but Dutch. You will have to get used to your new names as quickly as you can. From here you will be taken to a station west of Tetschen where you will get a train for Bayreuth.'

'Tetschen!' Mason was appalled. 'That's in Czechoslovakia. We're right off our route.'

'Not really. We are a little south of Dresden now. The line from Dresden, and the one from Tetschen, converge at Bayreuth. From there you go on to Nuremberg as you planned, but it is best that you avoid Dresden now.'

Davis was agitated. 'I don't agree. I think we should get back to our route as soon as possible. In Nuremberg we have to make contact with the people who will get us to Switzerland.'

'In Lorenzerstrasse? Near the cathedral?' Joachim's voice was sardonic.

'Why yes, do you know it?' Davis could not keep the surprise from his voice.

'Only too well. Since 20th July, that cell has been compromised. They went down with those arrested after the bomb plot. No, you must do as we advise.' He looked out of the window. 'Here is Pauline now.'

Whatever task Pauline and Gunther had been given, it was obvious that it had not kept them awake. They were dressed in different clothes, and Pauline's hair was groomed and tidy. She looked more relaxed, and the hard look was gone from her eyes. Mason thought she looked almost pretty.

She smiled. 'We can move almost immediately. Here are your new papers.' She handed them each a set of documents which included a polizeiliche erlaubenis – a permit to travel. Mason studied them carefully. They appeared to be authentic enough; far better forgeries, if that's what they were, than their own. The rubber stamp impressions were clear-cut and more official-looking. He looked up and saw her watching him.

'All right?'

Mason shrugged. 'They look all right.'

'You need not worry about their authenticity. Just be sure that your performance is as authentic. It won't be the papers that let you down.' Her English was stilted, as Joachim's was. Her voice became sharper. 'Come, we must start. We have a long way to go.'

Gunther handed them a small parcel. It was the first time they had seen him smiling. He looked friendly and affable.

'You will need this. It is bread and sausage.' He put out his hand, and Mason took it, strangely pleased to see another side to the taciturn brothers. They shook hands all round.

Hackett looked at Joachim. 'Who will be coming with us?'

'Only Pauline. We three have other things to do.'

As Joachim watched from the hut, Pauline led the way down the path and out of sight.

Wilhelm saw his leader's deep preoccupation. 'Well? Is it the right group?'

Joachim nodded. 'I never had any doubt.'

'Which one is the traitor? The American? The short Englishman?'

Joachim shook his head. 'I don't know. I just don't know. My instinct tells me it is the American, but I am not sure.'

Wilhelm sighed deeply, his weariness etched in his face. 'Then we had better find out soon if we want the plan to succeed.'

Joachim looked at him. 'I will know by tonight.' He leaned back in his chair, easing the knot of tension in his shoulders. 'That is not bothering me as much as the deadline. There is something we do not know.'

'Oh? What is that?'

'Why the 14th? What is to happen on that date that makes it so important?'

'Didn't our Berlin friend know?'

'Only two people know besides the two men who are to be substituted for our friends.'

'What about the man in charge? The Breslau man?'

Joachim shrugged. 'He may know, but I doubt it. Everyone concerned has been told only as much as he needs to know, to carry out his part of the operation.' He stood up. 'Come, we have to get back to Dresden.'

They walked out of the hut and into the trees.

Chapter Eight

Tuesday, 8th August, 1944. 9.30 a.m.

The bleak wind blew unceasingly from the peaks of the mountains in the south, whipping at their clothes and penetrating deep into tired bones. They leaned into the icy gusts, heads down, following the path that led upwards through the forest to the mountain pass.

Ahead of them, the trees topped the towering shape of the Elbsandstein, its dark stone hidden under a cloak of green pines. Here and there naked rock stood out, barren surfaces of crumbling scree and sheer cliffs, that defied the skill of the foresters. Mason wondered how much of the forbidding slope they would have to climb, but he was too winded to speak. He followed the girl ahead of him, head down against the freezing wind, conscious only of the need to place one foot after the other. He felt as though they had been walking forever, yet it was only twenty-four hours since they had boarded the train at Liegnitz. So much had happened since then, he found it hard to comprehend the reality of his situation. It seemed like a dream world peopled by phantoms: Joachim, Wilhelm, Gunther, the young man he had thought was a woman, and the two children.

All at once he was aware of the girl standing still in front of him, her back rigid, one arm raised warningly. Mason listened intently, but he could hear nothing above the whine of the wind and the swaying of the trees above them.

She turned to them swiftly. 'Get under cover. Quickly!' She made for a copse just off the path and motioned them to crawl into the undergrowth. They wriggled into the bush, and pulled branches and leaves over themselves. When she was sure they were securely hidden, she followed them into hiding.

Mason lay on the damp earth, his heart beating uncomfortably quickly, yet thankful for the respite from the wind and the fatigue. The scent of pines and the damp smell of the earth was in his nostrils, and in front of his eyes the fronds of a large fern waved frantically in the wind. He wondered what the girl had heard. From his position he could see the path stretching away from them to a bend under an overhanging rock. Nothing.

Then suddenly they were there, three of them in black and khaki uniforms, shoulder straps and belts highly polished, and sub-machine guns at the ready. They came out of the trees not twenty metres away, looked right and left, crossed the path, and disappeared into the firebreak. Mason lay there, heart thudding fiercely, the sour taste of fear in his throat. He was aware of the girl lying near him, her green overcoat covering her slim figure, her head covered with a silk scarf. She lay there, still and silent, watching the path ahead. The minutes dragged by, and Mason was conscious of a numbness beginning in his fingers and the start of cramp in his feet. He realised he had been lying as still as a hunted animal.

Beyond her prone body he could see Davis and Hackett lying as still as he was. He saw Hackett's head moving slowly from right to left, eyes intent on the terrain he could see through the gaps in the leaves. Davis began to move his arm, and Mason saw the girl reach out and clamp his wrist with strong fingers.

They stared, fascinated, at the path ahead of them. Minutes crept by; minutes during which their perception of time was lost in the heart-wrenching knowledge that the hunters suspected something. Perhaps the soldiers' suspicion was ephemeral, but the feel of it was strong enough to twitch their warning senses.

When they reappeared, they were shockingly close. If they had taken one more tree line, they would have stumbled over the hidden watchers. The soldiers moved cautiously, in single file, close enough for Hackett to see the weave of their trousers. They were experienced men, young with hard faces under their peaked caps. Hackett had seen them before in many places and in many guises. He had seen them in Yugoslavia, in Albania and in France. They were of a pattern, moulded by the same discipline as millions of others like them. Hackett, the professional, knew them and their kind. These three moved silently across the carpet of leaves. They crossed the path, and the American let out a soft, slow breath.

They lay there in the undergrowth, not daring to move, fear and uncertainty beating at them. Mason turned his head slowly toward Hackett and Davis, and as he did so, was alarmed to find that Pauline was no longer with them. Without a sound, she had disappeared from the thicket, and he saw from the surprise on the faces of his companions that they too had neither seen nor heard her leave.

Mason saw a slight flicker of movement beyond the path, and the soldiers were again moving silently past them, returning the way they had come. He saw the polished boots, and the stiff creases in the trousers, then they were gone, vanishing behind him through the tree line.

The three men lay there, knowing the power of decision was beyond them, that all control had been taken out of their hands. They just lay there and waited. It was at least twenty minutes since they had hidden themselves, and Mason turned his head from side to side, willing the girl to reappear, wondering for a fleeting moment if she had deserted them.

The sudden feel of cold metal on the back of his head was like a touch of ice.

A voice said in German: 'Get up.'

He turned his head. Behind him was one of the three soldiers, his sub-machine gun muzzle three inches from Mason's forehead. The other two stood well back, covering their colleague. The man motioned for the three fugitives to rise.

As Mason stood up, despair filled him. Was it to end like this? After coming so far, were they to be marched back to the prison camp for another year or more of incarceration? In spite of himself, he felt the tears of frustration and rage welling behind his eyelids. He wanted to curse and shout and break things. Then he took a deep breath. The moment of childishness passed, and he felt the familiar calmness sweep over him.

'Raise your hands. Turn around.' The man pushed the muzzle of the gun into Mason's rib to reinforce his command, and Mason saw the other two lift their guns perceptibly. He felt probing hands patting his body, then sweep down his trouser leg. When he turned to search Davis and Hackett, Mason realised that the man had missed the knife strapped to his arm.

'Papers.'

Mason took his papers from his pocket and placed them in the hand just visible at his shoulder. He saw his companions hand over their papers, then he heard his captor move back. He heard the rustling of paper as their documents were examined.

'Who are you? Why are you hiding in these bushes?'

Mason shrugged. 'You have our papers. You can see we are Dutch artisans. We lost our way, and we were afraid we would be arrested if we were in the wrong zone.'

A vicious blow stunned him and he fell to his knees. His head throbbed painfully. He staggered to his feet.

'Lies. Speak the truth or I will kill you here. You are escaped prisoners-of-war.' Another blow sent him reeling. He felt the warm trickle of blood on his neck.

Mason stood up painfully. As he did so, he saw the concern on the faces of his companions. He wiped the back of his head with his hand. The blood was warm on his palm.

'You!' The soldier was motioning to Davis. 'Who are you? I want the truth.'

Davis looked at him uncomprehendingly. Mason said quickly: 'We are telling you the truth, but what is the use you do not believe what we say.'

'Quiet!' He prodded Mason with his gun. 'Brandt, go and fetch the Lieutenant. He will know what to do with this scum.'

They heard the men walking away, and Mason wondered whether they had time to concoct a plan of escape. At least the odds were slightly better. He started to turn, but the corporal prodded him once more.

'Still! You will not move until the Lieutenant gets here. Lie down all of you.'

The three man lay on the ground, listening to the two soldiers speaking in low voices. Mason tried desperately to hear what they were saying, but their voices were too soft.

At that moment, from somewhere deep in the copse, Pauline's voice was heard. 'You two, stand quite still. You are covered by machine guns and if there is the slightest move, you will both die. And don't bank on the Lieutenant. He and

Brandt are both dead.' She raised her voice and spoke in English. 'Mason. Davis. Hackett. Stay where you are. Keep lying flat on the ground.' Mason turned his head to watch the soldiers. He was sure Pauline was bluffing, and he was certain that unless she took the initiative quickly, the Lieutenant would appear to expose the ruse.

The uniformed men were equally sure she was bluffing. They stood quite still, but he could see their eyes searching for some sign of where the girl's voice had come from. The tension was heightened by the fact that the three men on the ground were, in fact, hostages of the two soldiers. Their weapons were pointing straight at the three, and a split second was all it needed to send death crashing into their helpless bodies.

The stalemate was broken by one of the soldiers. He was the one who had been doing all the talking, and he must have seen some sign of the girl, for he swung his machine gun upwards and across, but before he could fire, another machine gun chattered from the opposite side of the copse. The soldier's head exploded in a crimson spray, and the second man, in the swift reflex action of a trained soldier, swung around to face the new danger, his weapon swinging upwards into the firing position. As he did so, the weapon in the bush chattered once more, and he too died, his gun still silent.

The three lay where they were, shocked by the frightful appearance of sudden death. Even the sound of the wind was like silence after the chattering sounds of the machine gun. Mason looked at the two men lying in grotesque parodies of foetal slumber. The shattered heads and the blood were an obscene blasphemy in this peaceful glade.

Davis stood up first, followed by his two companions. At that moment, Pauline and Gunther appeared from the side of the copse, both carrying machine guns.

Mason quickly recovered his composure. 'Gunther – it's good to see you. It seems you have been with us all the time.'

The big man nodded dourly. 'Joachim insists on a backup, he does not like Pauline working alone.'

Mason glanced quickly at the girl, but far from being mortified, it was a measure of the discipline of the cell that she nodded in agreement. She said: 'It is good to know that help is always near at hand. It prevents errors of judgement. I realised that the soldiers had seen one of us though they tried not to show it. They weren't sure if we were armed, and were being cautious. That gave me time to disappear. I wasn't sure whether Gunther was close enough to see the danger, and if he was, whether he could help. But he had already dealt with the officer.'

Gunther nodded. 'They had seen you some way back. They were seasoned men, these. I knew I had to destroy their back-up, so I got to their headquarters hut first. It is only four hundred metres from here. Brandt was not expecting me to be there.' He sighed. 'I have a big job ahead of me. The bodies must disappear so that the authorities don't know where to start looking. Fortunately desertions from the Wehrmacht are becoming more numerous.' His picked up the identity documents from where the soldier had dropped them. 'Here. You'd better have these back.'

Davis picked up the machine gun. The girl spoke sharply. 'Leave that. No weapons.'

The Welshman shrugged. 'I wasn't going to take it with me. I just wanted to look at it.'

Hackett said: 'You seen one, you seen them all.' He lit a cigarette, and Mason saw that the American seemed unshaken by the violent deaths of the two men.

Gunther spoke briskly. 'Now you must move on. Leave everything to me. I will deal with it. I have twenty-four hours before this patrol is relieved, but you have only six hours to catch your train.' He turned to the girl. 'I will take the identity papers from the dead men. They will come in useful. The food in their hut, too. I will see it gets to our cache. We must make the authorities think they have deserted.'

Pauline nodded. She was pale and tense. She handed the weapon to Gunther and said to Mason: 'We have no time to waste, but we should eat first anyway.' She took her parcel of food from her pocket, and then saw Mason's involuntary glance at the dead men. 'One must do what has to be done. I am not indifferent, but you will learn that survival comes first. If you are nauseous, you must force yourself to eat, because if you don't, when the nausea has gone you are still left with hunger and hunger brings weakness.' She led the way down the path.

Hackett said: 'Makes sense to me.' He followed the girl to a grassy patch a hundred metres away. Mason and Davis went with him. Hackett opened his packet, and as he ate watched the girl covertly. Pale though she was, he knew she was always in command of her emotions. She was another whose kind he had seen before. He had led women like her in France; hard and uncompromising in their determination to stay alive and destroy as many of the enemy as possible.

To his experienced eye, she was obviously a product of a partisan group. He wondered where she had been trained. Certainly not in any orthodox training school. He remembered his training for the Office of Strategic Services. He had been sent first to the evaluation centre, and soon found himself on Catalina, going through the tough eight weeks of orientation followed by courses in hand-to-hand combat, the use of all kinds of firearms, cryptography, lock picking, demolition and all the myriad skills the brass thought he might need in combat. And then finally, when push came to shove, it was women like this who ended up more professional than the professionals.

And Mason? To the American, the man was an enigma. Well-trained, obviously, and apparently from an upper class family. He was a big athletic man, and Hackett remembered his fleeting comments about his family back in England, his childhood years when they lived alongside a canal. Hackett thought he was a good leader, quick to make decisions that were invariably the right ones, and the American was sometimes awed by his unerring instinct. A good man to be with in a crisis.

Davis was a type he knew well. Small, hard and tough, his kind was unbreakable. He was always good-humoured, never doubting the fact that his life would end in old age. Product of a Welsh mining village, he had won a scholarship to Jesus College, Oxford, and had told Hackett of his plans for his family after the war.

When they were ready to move, they said their farewells to Gunther who was already busy on his gruesome task.

The path turned west beyond the overhanging rock, and for another hour their trail led uphill. Then imperceptibly their way became easier, and they were descending through green meadows and pastures, and here and there farmhouses were visible in the distance.

Towards afternoon, they skirted a small village. Pauline slowed the pace a little. She kept glancing back at Mason, whose throbbing head was causing him to slow down considerably. She wondered if he was concussed, and twice she stopped to examine his wound and look at the pupils of his eyes. Mason felt strangely warmed by her concern.

Soon they left the hills behind them, and finally as they topped a small rise, they saw a small wayside station, roughly five hundred metres away. There was one small hut locked with a padlock, a waiting room, and at the far end, a water tower. At the end nearest to them, two spur lines ended in buffers, one on each side of the main line. Both points were set to the main line and locked with a steel bar. Thick grass and weeds flourished at the edge of the permanent way, and as the wind whipped at the grey ash between the rails, a fine cloud of dust rose above the dilapidated buildings.

Pauline led them to a small wooded plateau about two hundred metres away from the station. A screen of shrubs hid them from anyone below.

'We will wait here. We have to check to see if patrols come.' She settled herself on the turf, and the men lay back, thankful for the chance to rest. 'It is unlikely that a patrol will come, but we cannot be too careful.'

It was still cold but the wind had abated a little. Small patches of sky appeared in the broken clouds, and now and then the sunlight warmed them for a moment before disappearing behind a new cloud. High overhead, a flight of white storks flapped and soared, their necks straight out, long legs trailing behind. Occasionally a farmer crossed his fields, and cattle grazed in a distant meadow.

From a distance they heard the long cry of the train whistle. Davis began to stand up, but Mason grabbed his arm.

'Look.' They turned to where he pointed. Along the dusty road, four soldiers had emerged from the trees flanking a small farmhouse. They could see the Schmeisser MP 40 machine guns hanging from slings on their shoulders. They were dressed in the same uniform style as those they had met in the forest. The fugitives watched the soldiers stroll to the station and take up strategic positions along the platform. They saw the train come into view around the bend two kilometres away.

Mason watched in growing consternation. 'Do the soldiers come out for every train?'

'No. Only for the ones bound for the concentration camps. They will not come out for the ordinary passenger trains. The partisans have sometimes attacked the trains bound for the death camps and freed the prisoners.' She said sadly: 'Sometimes the prisoners don't want to come out of the trains. They have been told they are to be resettled on farms.'

'But this is an ordinary passenger train.' Mason was still perturbed.

'It only goes as far as Teplitz. The one we want goes to Eger, where we change for Bayreuth. The soldiers are here because there must be another train coming.'

They watched the train come to a stop. An elderly couple alighted, and they saw the guard walk along the platform towards the engine. The driver swung down from the footplate and strolled to meet him. They heard the sound of conversation, but the men were too far away for the watchers to distinguish the words. Then the driver climbed back into the engine, and slowly the train began to reverse the way it had come. They saw the guard unlock the points and swing the lever over.

Pauline answered their unspoken question. 'This train will wait in the spur for the eastbound train to pass.'

The minutes dragged by. The soldiers paced along the platform, and from the stationary train, passengers craned their heads out of the window, impatient at the delay.

Then they heard a long whistle in the distance, and an engine pulling a long line of cattle trucks emerged from the trees a kilometre away. It slowed for its approach to the station, and as it stopped, the driver released a cloud of steam. The soldiers went along the freight train, banging the sides and testing the heavy bolts. The two guards met for a brief moment and then returned to their respective vans. The freight train began shunting back and forth, eventually fly-shunting a cattle truck on to the second empty spur. The van was coupled to the end of the train, and then, with a prolonged whistle, it rumbled away to the east. The westbound train reversed on to the main line, and finally it pulled out of the station. They watched it disappear into the trees in the distance. The soldiers strolled back to the farmhouse.

Hackett stood up and stared to the east where the freight train had gone. 'There were people in those cattle trucks.' He turned to Pauline. 'I tell you, there were people on that train.'

The girl looked at him with hard eyes. 'East of here the line branches to Krakow and Auschwitz or north to Breslau. The death camps to the east receive three trainloads of prisoners every day. That was one more load.'

There was silence for a moment. Pauline looked at the three men and shrugged. 'We have grown used to our helplessness, but we never become accustomed to the pain.' She turned toward the station. 'There is a timetable stuck to the board in the waiting room. If we are lucky it may be fairly new.' They followed her down the incline, watching warily for any sign that the soldiers might return. The whole countryside appeared to be deserted. The elderly couple had already disappeared in the direction of the distant farmhouses. They came alongside the permanent way, their footsteps crunching on the ash beside the line. The wind had dropped to a slight breeze, and the countryside was silent and deserted. A hundred metres away, the shunted cattle truck stood where it had slammed into the spur buffer.

Just before they approached the waiting room, Pauline, who was leading them, stopped suddenly. 'Listen.'

The three men listened intently. Nothing. Mason looked at her. 'What is it?'

'I'm certain I heard something. Sobbing. There it is again. Do you hear it?'

They all heard it then, a drawn out moan followed by soft sobbing. Mason began to run. 'That coach.'

'Wait.' Pauline stood still, turning her head in the direction of the farmhouse. 'If there are people in that truck, they may post a guard.'

Mason said impatiently: 'Well, they haven't yet. Come on! Let's see what this is about.'

He ran towards the truck, the others following close behind. It was only when they were a few metres away that they noticed the smell, a stench of urine and human waste.

'Bloody hell! There are people in there.' Mason picked up

a stone and banged the side of the truck. 'Who are you? Where are you from?'

Silence.

Hackett tugged at the bolt sealing the door. Pauline grabbed at his arm. 'Wait! We must be careful. There may – '

'Wait for what?' Hackett was furious. 'Goddam it to hell! There are people in there, and by the stink, they've been there for days. We gotta get them out.'

Pauline shook his arm impatiently. 'Do you think I don't know that? I want to help these people as much as you do, but we have to be sure they know we are friends or they may become hysterical and alert the guards.' She banged softly on the door, and said in German: 'Do not be afraid. We are friends. Where are you from?' There was no sound from the truck, and the girl tapped again. Then she said in French: 'Do not be afraid. We are here to help you.'

There was a moan then, followed by a high-pitched wail. They heard a voice from inside the truck. 'Francine! Be silent. Do you hear? Be quiet!' A girl was speaking in French.

Davis was outraged. He grabbed at the bolt across the door. 'Some of them are children! For God's sake, let's move and get them out of there. Here! Help me!'

He pushed at the heavy bar, and Mason added his weight. They felt it begin to lift. It came away suddenly, and the door, released from its tension against the frame, swung open rapidly, revealing bodies crowded against one another, sitting, sprawled, and lying in a bed of wet filthy straw. The four stood there, transfixed by the horror, appalled by the smell, and then Davis turned and vomited behind the truck.

Mason spoke first. 'Holy Mother of God! They're all children!'

Pauline clutched at the hand-rail at the side of the door, and pulled herself into the truck. Gaunt faces stared at her, fear in every one. Children, perhaps fifty of them, some mere babies, others nearer twelve or thirteen, dressed in thin rags and covered in the filth of their own excrement, whimpered and sobbed with fear. Anger stirred in her, and then rage swept over her at the monsters who could perpetrate this horrifying act of desecration against her God. She stood and stared, tears coursing down her face. She felt Mason standing in the truck beside her, and she turned to him and buried her face in his shoulder. He held her, staring numbly at the weeping children.

Hackett climbed into the truck and stepped gingerly amongst the children, comforting one here, touching a face there. He felt he was in the presence of a nightmare, a horror from which he would surely wake, sweating with fear.

Davis, recovered from his nausea, was the first to speak. 'We've got to get them out of there.' His voice shook. 'For God's sake, let's get them out.'

A girl no more than fourteen years old, looked at them with fearful eyes. 'I tried to keep quiet. I really did. You won't let the soldiers take us again? Please. We'll be good, we promise. We've been good a long time now.'

Mason felt the hot tears burn his eyelids. 'No,' he said softly. 'We won't let the soldiers take you.' And he hoped with all his heart he knew what he was saying. 'Come. You must all stay very quiet, and come with us.'

There was a general movement of children towards the door, Pauline put out a restraining arm. 'Slowly now. We will pass you down one at a time.'

The four adults formed a chain, with Davis and Hackett in the truck and Mason and Pauline on the ground. At last she had them all seated on the grass alongside the track. When she realised that no more were coming down to her she looked up at the two men on the truck who were staring down at her from the door.

'Is that all of them?'

'Not quite.' Hackett's voice cracked with emotion. Davis just looked at her, his eyes hard.

'Well, where are the rest?'

Hackett jumped down from the truck and Davis followed him. They pushed the truck door closed. Pauline stared at them in horror. Mason took her arm and turned her so that her back was to the closed door.

He said: 'There is nothing we can do for them. We haven't time to bury them, even if we had the implements. It's better to leave them there.'

'How many?'

'Six.'

Mason felt her back stiffen with shock. He wondered if there was anything he could say, and then he knew that there wasn't.

He said: 'We must get away from here. The guards may come back.'

They looked down at the faces staring up at them, some fearful, some curious, and all of them unkempt and dirty. Somehow they would have to clean them up, find food for them and get them to safety. All at once the enormity of their mission dawned on them. If it was difficult escaping from Germany on their own, to do it with fifty children was an enterprise that presented insuperable difficulties. Once the Gestapo discovered that fifty children were missing from a consignment bound for the gas ovens, the countryside would be overrun with S.S.

The appalling extent of their undertaking had escaped them until this moment. Their actions had been prompted entirely by emotion, and now they were faced with the practical consequences of their quixotic impulse.

The children stared up at them, fear and hope mingled in their faces. Most of them were girls, but there were a few boys amongst the younger children. None of the boys appeared to be above eight years old, but the girls ranged from about seven to one girl who could have been fourteen. Mason guessed it was she who had admonished Francine. He wondered if he would be with them long enough to learn their names. It was a daunting prospect.

Pauline clapped her hands to get their attention. She spoke in French. 'Do you all understand me?' Mason saw the expectant faces and nodding heads. He was reminded of his infant school teacher. Pauline looked them over carefully. 'Does anyone know of a child that does not speak French.'

The fourteen-year-old girl stood up. 'I am Lisette,' she said politely. 'We are all French. We are all from Lyon.' She sat down.

Pauline looked at Mason, her eyes glistening. Then, her emotions under control, she said: 'Now if you wish to go back to France, you must do exactly as we say. You must be obedient every moment, or the soldiers will come again.'

A small child began to wail. Lisette cuffed her lightly.

'Quiet, Francine.' The child subsided into intermittent sniffles.

Pauline looked up at the lowering sky. 'Now we must go. Follow me, the youngest in front.' She turned to the men. 'You three follow behind to help the laggards.' She led the way up the slope.

Suddenly Hackett stopped. 'Do you hear that?'

Mason lifted his head and listened. He looked at Davis. The Welshman nodded. 'A train.' From the distance came the sound of a deep rumbling, then a long whistle.

Mason called to the girl: 'A train! Get under cover. Hide in the brush. Hurry!' He jumped on to the buffer to see how far away the train was. Davis, Pauline and Hackett were shepherding the children into the field, pushing some into the long grass, others behind shrubs.

At that moment a lone soldier appeared from the other side of the truck. 'Stop where you are.' He raised his machine gun. 'Get back here, all of you.'

Still on the buffer, hidden by the side of the truck, Mason saw the fear in the faces of the children. The soldier had his back to him, unaware of a third man behind him. Mason felt for the knife Joachim had given him. He saw Pauline's eyes on him for a moment and he nodded to her. She interpreted his signal correctly, and began to usher the children down the slope, the sound of their movement covering any noise he might make. Swiftly he moved behind the man with the gun. His arm went over the man's shoulder, throat held in a throttling grip. For a moment the soldier was surprised into immobility. It was just time enough for the knife to do its work. All the anger, frustration and hatred he had felt during the past few hours went into a single vicious knife thrust. Moments later the jerking stopped, and Mason let his victim slump to the ground, eyes staring upwards.

'Tom, help me get him into the truck.' As they lifted the man into the stinking truck, Pauline sent the children back into hiding. She moved amongst them quickly, pushing one down, and sending another to better cover.

Their task done, the men joined the children in the field. Mason lay behind a small shrub, his anger spent, his body trembling. It was not the first man he had killed, but it was the first that he had translated into the object of his personal revenge. It was an uncomfortable moment for him. The men of the Underground killed like that, but they had learned out of necessity. He recognised the goads that had spurred him to such savagery, but he knew that, unlike the hardened ones, he would always have to reject the ultimate requirements of survival as a way of life.

He heard the wheels rumbling on the permanent way, and a long eastbound train rolled into the station. After a short hiatus the engine began shunting back and forth as it collected the truck on the spur, and as he peered through the leaves of the shrub, he could see faces at the high barred opening of the trucks. He could not see the armed guards, but finally, as the train drew out of the station, he saw them leaning indolently outside the waiting room. He heard them talking loudly, apparently puzzled by the non-appearance of one of their quartet. One of the trio pointed to a nearby farmhouse, and said something to the others. There was general laughter, and it appeared to Mason that they suspected the missing man of taking time off to visit one of the local girls. The fact that the dead man had arrived at the station a few minutes before the others was the only thing that had saved them. Mason watched with relief as the three men disappeared into the farmhouse at the end of the road.

Pauline stood up and urged her charges up the incline towards the trees. She was almost frantic with anxiety. 'We must get the children away from here and into the forest. Those men will start looking for their comrade when he does not go back for his next meal.'

Hackett stared after the train disappearing into the distant trees. 'Someone is in for a hell of a surprise when they open that truck.'

Davis said: 'Yes, but they've still got another thousand in the other trucks. And more coming every day.'

They began the long climb up the hill.

Chapter Nine

Wednesday, 9th August, 1944. 9 a.m.

S.S. Oberführer Becker studied the Lieutenant carefully. He looked down at the dossier on the desk in front of him. All the facts indicated that the man was a bloody fool, but it wasn't a genius he wanted right now. What he wanted was someone who would carry out his orders and keep his mouth shut, and the officer standing to attention in front of his desk was the ideal candidate. Becker evaluated men, not according to how capable they were but by how much they were indebted to him, and in that respect, this man ranked high. He had been in trouble, and Becker had extricated him from his difficulties. Instead of being transferred to the Russian front, he would join a Waffen S.S. unit in Breslau, and he would be sufficiently grateful to the Oberführer to do as he was told. Yes, Schäfer was definitely the man.

Becker leaned back in his chair. 'What do you think happened to the three men at Gorlitz?'

'I thought they had caught the Leipzig train, Herr Oberführer. I now realise that they must have doubled back and caught some other train. Perhaps the Dresden train. The twelve-thirty.'

'That was the next express leaving Gorlitz?'

'Yes, Herr Oberführer.'

Becker looked thoughtful. He stood up and went to the window behind his chair. The Dresden train? That meant that at that stage they were still within his district. He turned and, with a quick gesture, dismissed the Lieutenant. He pressed the buzzer on his desk.

To the orderly that hurried into his office, he said: 'Look up the duty rosters for – ' he looked down at the calender on his desk – 'Monday the 7th. I want to know who was on the Dresden train that left Gorlitz at twelve-thirty. Have them relieved wherever they are, and send them to me.'

Later that afternoon, a small man in civilian clothes arrived at the Breslau District Office and was sent in to see his superior.

Becker looked at the raincoated figure standing before him. 'You were on duty on the Dresden train on Monday?'

'Yes, Herr Oberführer.'

'Did you see anything unusual happening on that train.'

'Yes, Herr Oberführer. But it did not concern us. It was a matter for the Kripo so I did not report it.'

'Tell me exactly what happened.'

'About twenty Kripo boarded the train at Bautzen. They appeared to concentrate in one carriage. I asked the conductor if he knew why they were there, and he informed me that he was instructed to ignore them and carry on with his duties as though they weren't there. The officer quoted a Führerbefehl and said it was a highly sensitive operation.' He looked nervously at his commanding officer. 'In view of the Führerbefehl, I decided not to intervene.'

'You were quite right.' The Gestapo man looked relieved. Becker went on, 'I want you to tell me what happened after that.'

'The train made a short stop. The Kripo carried out a strict check of the papers of all the men leaving the train. No one was detained, and the train continued. But about five minutes after leaving the station, there appeared to be some sort of alarm. There was a thorough search of the train, and all the Kripo left the train at the next stop.'

'And what are your conclusions?'

A fleeting expression almost like contempt crossed the man's face, then impassively he said: 'My conclusion was that they had allowed a fugitive or fugitives to escape them.'

'At Bautzen.'

'No, Herr Oberführer. At Bischofswerda.'

Becker went to the map that hung on the east wall. His

finger touched Bischofswerda, and his finger moved first to Kamenz to the north, then slowly to Radeburg in the west, and finally, decisively, he tapped the darker green to the south. 'Elbsandstein. That's where they would go. Of course, Elbsandstein. The place is reported to be a hideout for all sorts of criminals.'

'I understand that the patrols have been increased in that sector, Herr Oberführer.'

Becker looked preoccupied. 'Yes. There is a railway line running just south of the Czech frontier. It passes through Tetschen.' He touched the map. He looked up and realised the Gestapo man was still there. 'You may go. You have done very well. I will remember it.' The man turned to leave, but stopped as Becker spoke. 'And remember, you will discuss this with no one. No one, you understand.'

'No one, Herr Oberführer.'

After the man had gone, Becker pressed the buzzer on his desk. An orderly appeared. 'Find me a large scale map of the area covering the Elbsandstein. One that shows the forest and the roads crossing it.'

Joachim lit a cigarette, waved the match to extinction, puffed out a stream of smoke, and looked at each of them in turn. Mason sat upright in the hard chair, his eyes flicking to Joachim and back to Davis and Hackett who sat slumped on the long bench against the wall of the small log cabin. The cabin, the third one they had seen since they had escaped from the train, was deep in the forest.

Gunther leaned against the door jamb, his huge frame filling the doorway. Wilhelm sat on the sill of the open window, and Pauline was at the table with Joachim. They sat side by side with their backs to the wall opposite the doorway.

The silence stretched interminably, heightening the tension in the little room. Hackett cleared his throat, twice appeared about to speak, and then subsided into silence. Davis picked his teeth with a small splinter.

The silence stretched on. Mason was suddenly aware of the fact that if anyone wanted to leave the cabin, it would be impossible with Gunther and Wilhelm to prevent them. He realised too, that Joachim's attitude towards them had changed. He was no longer jocular and good-natured, but grim and uncompromising. The metamorphosis was sudden, and somehow a little sinsiter. It wasn't only the sight of the children that had caused the change. Mason was certain that it had something to do with him, Davis and Hackett, but if he were asked to say how he knew, he would have to admit that it was nothing but his overworked intuition.

He wondered how the children were. The young man, Johan, had joined them just as they had entered the forest. Mason had expected a new arrival when he had seen Pauline change her head scarf from the blue one she habitually wore to a bright yellow one she kept in her overcoat pocket. He knew they had a procedure for every eventuality, and the extent of their efficiency never ceased to amaze him. Every operative had a back-up, and the knowledge comforted Mason.

That Johan had been following within signalling distance was indicated by his lack of surprise when he saw the children. Their limited options must have been evident to him too, for he had had no comment to make on their drastic change of plan. The young man had led them away from the path they had been following to a deep ravine hidden by tall trees and shrubs. A small brook rippled between the walls of the ravine. Johan had left them then, and when he returned, had been carrying a sack of provisions over his shoulder. Gunther had arrived shortly afterwards with a similar sack.

The children had been fed then, and while they were eating, Pauline had listed their names and ages. There were four seven year olds, twelve were eight, twenty-two were ten, five were twelve, three were thirteen and there were two fourteen year olds. Forty eight children; ten boys and thirty-eight girls. The two oldest were both girls. Matters were complicated by the fact that there were several pairs with the same name. Pauline had elicited from the oldest one that they had been put on the train five days before they had been found.

Gunther had gone away again, and later had returned with blankets, and when the children had been washed in the small brook, he led them to a large grotto near a waterfall.

A short while later, Wilhelm had come for the three fugitives and had led them through firebreaks and little-used paths to this cabin where the others had joined them. Joachim had told them that they were waiting for Johan to come with information they needed to plan their next moves. He had said that the children would be safe where they were until a plan was made to return them to France. He did not tell them who was supervising the children in the meanwhile, but Mason was sure that they would be in good hands.

There was a movement at the cabin door, and Gunther stood aside to allow Johan to enter. Mason smiled inwardly. When they had met on the train, this slim fair-haired young man had been disguised as a young mother with two girls, complaining about bringing up children in wartime. Mason had been completely deceived.

Johan placed a long envelope on the table and sat beside Davis on the bench. Joachim slit one end of the envelope with a knife, and extracted a page of typescript. Mason could see a printed letterhead and two paragraphs of typing on the letter. Joachim read it through, and looked up at them. His eyes were hard. When he spoke his voice was soft, but no one could mistake the menace in his tone.

'One of you three has been sentenced to death,' he said. He looked at each of them in turn. He held up the paper in his hand. 'This letter, which outwardly appears to be a quotation for building repairs, is in fact a communication from the Abwehr, the German military intelligence.' He smiled grimly at the shock on their faces. 'It is now time to put our cards on the table.'

Mason looked at his two companions. Davis was frowning. Hackett stared impassively at Joachim. He seemed completely disinterested, and Mason knew that the American was probably the most self-possessed of all in this little cabin. Mason admired the man's courage and professionalism.

Joachim went on. 'I believe it is important to attack from strength, and in the present circumstances I think it is important for the enemy – the traitor amongst you – to know our strength. So, some explanation is called for.' He stubbed out his cigarette. 'A year after we joined the Jewish partisans in the Polish forests, we were sent on a mission to Breslau, where we were picked up by the Gestapo. Dietrich Bonhoeffer, a young theologian, heard of our plight, and passed the word along to friends of his in the Abwehr – the German Counter-Intelligence. There Major General Hans Oster went to Admiral Canaris, who realised we could be useful to him in the conspiracy against Hitler.' The smile flickered on his face. 'I see you are impressed. So you should be.' His voice became softer. 'Admiral Canaris went to Himmler and complained that the Reichführer's men were arresting his agents – us. The result was that we were released into his custody, and ever since then, we have been working for German Counter-Intelligence, but in our own way. With the divisions between the Abwehr, the Sicherheitsdienst, the Gestapo and the Wehrmacht, no one knew who was who, and the interdepartmental rivalry and jealousies enabled us virtually to run our own organisation.'

Mason stood up angrily. 'I don't know what the bloody hell your game is, but why didn't you send us straight back to Sagan?' His fury mounted. 'If this is why we are under sentence of death – '

'Sit down. I haven't finished.' Joachim's voice was like steel. 'I said *one* of you is under sentence.' He paused and looked at each of them in turn. 'Yes, we have been working for the Abwehr, but as I said, in our own way. Our work has actually been for Admiral Canaris, but since his arrest and the takeover of the Abwehr by the RSHA in Berlin, our protection has been taken over by others who are still at their posts. They remain unsuspected of complicity, and it is to them that we are answerable.'

Davis looked puzzled. 'You said one of us is a traitor. That can't be so. We were all prisoners in the same camp. We've been together since . . .' His voice died away.

Joachim smiled sardonically. 'I see that it has occurred to you that you can't vouch for anybody.'

Mason looked at Hackett. Joachim continued. 'Our job was to gather intelligence for the war against the Reich, see that it went to the right quarters, sabotage Gestapo intentions wherever we could, and help Jews and others to escape. We had a period of intensive training with the Abwehr, and were told to concentrate on this sector. We studied the terrain, mapped the forests so that we knew every path and trail, and set up caches of arms and food. We have contacts in a section that can get us any kind of papers in twelve hours. It is this kind of efficiency that keeps us alive. Outside this sector we'd be vulnerable.' His voice grew hard. 'So you see why it is necessary to destroy traitors wherever we find them.'

Mason snapped angrily, 'Get to the point.'

'Have patience. I will get to the point soon enough.' He lit another cigarette. 'In January, we got word that the RSHA were mounting an operation that required three prisoners to escape. They had taken two brothers prisoner at about the same time. One was captured in North Africa. The other was an officer in the OSS. By sheer coincidence they were thrown together into the compound at Hartheim. When their relationship was discovered by the Germans, it was a simple matter to compel the OSS man to do what they wanted by threatening to shoot his brother. Of course we did not know that the traitor was an OSS man until we got this letter.' Mason and Davis glanced involuntarily at Hackett, who stared impassively at Joachim.

He stubbed out his cigarette. 'They introduced their reluctant traitor into Sagan as an American flyer, and primed him with the escape plan. Of course, it helped that the man was a flyer before transferring to the OSS.'

Hackett spoke, his voice cold and hard. 'You sit there like a bloody god, and make judgements. If my brother dies, you're dead.' He looked around the cabin. 'All of you. And you'd better believe it. I'm no half-assed rookie.' He turned back to Joachim, his face like stone. 'If Mac dies, I'll kill every mother's son of you.'

Joachim looked at him for a long moment. He said sadly: 'I'm sorry. Do you think for one moment the Gestapo kept their side of the bargain.'

Hackett stood up suddenly. 'You're lying! He's still alive.' His voice was hoarse. 'You're lying.'

Mason and Davis watched, their emotions a mixture of confusion and anger. Mason said: 'Then it's true. But what was he going to do? Who was he going to betray?'

Joachim ignored him. He was still looking at Hackett, sympathy in his eyes. 'No, I'm not lying. It's best you know now, while you can still help our cause. He was shot three days ago. They could not risk leaving anyone alive who could expose the operation.'

Mason almost shouted. 'Who the hell was he going to betray?'

Joachim turned to him. 'You.'

Mason shook his head wonderingly. 'But what was the point? We were already prisoners. What was the point in letting us go and then have someone betray us?'

Davis said: 'I don't believe a word of it. This lot is up to something.'

Hackett sat down slowly. He stared at the ground, head down, stunned by the enormity of his loss.

Mason said angrily, 'Taff's right. It doesn't make sense.'

'Oh yes it does.' Joachim tapped the letter on the table. 'It makes sense if you are used to the kind of convoluted thinking these gangsters employ.' His craggy face looked at Hackett sympathetically. 'I said one of you is under sentence of death, but I'm sure Hackett is no longer ready to betray you.'

All at once, Mason realised the terrible dilemma the American had been facing in having to choose between his brother and his comrades in arms. To the cynical it would appear no contest, but in the time he had known Thomas Hackett, the one quality that had impressed him was the man's integrity.

Hackett looked up. 'How do I know you're not lying? You'd say anything if the motivation was strong enough.'

'I can't prove it to you if that's what you want.' Joachim stubbed out his third cigarette. It was his only indication of stress. 'But from what little you know of us, do you think it likely we would be cruel enough to use those tactics?'

Hackett shook his head reluctantly. 'No. I believe you.'

Mason looked at Pauline. She had remained so still throughout, he had forgotten she was there. Her face was an impassive mask. If she felt anything, it was not evident. He guessed she had willed herself not to feel, to keep herself under control at all times. He realised that the only moment he had seen her betray emotion was when she had looked at the children. Then she had recovered her composure, and it was as though it had never happened.

Joachim said: 'Then if you believe me, you are no longer bound to the operation. Will you help us instead?'

Hackett looked at him with surprise. 'What can I do?'

'Continue with Operation Geld. With slight changes, of course.' He smiled sardonically. 'Their plan is similar to the one we had been contemplating. When Major General Oster stumbled across the operation, he realised that with slight modifications, it would suit our purpose. Two days before he was arrested with Canaris, he briefed us on what he wanted us to do.'

Mason frowned. 'How were we involved in Operation Geld? What good were Taff and I to them?'

'No good at all.'

'Well then?'

'You personally were of no value to them, but the plan was to estabish that three Allied airmen had escaped. Then, when three escaped prisoners are returned through the Underground, who is going to question their bona-fides, especially if they are vouched for by a member of the OSS?' He lit another cigarette. 'The plan was for the three of you to be discreetly recaptured, and two of you replaced by two S.S. officers who have been educated in England, and who speak English perfectly.' He smiled briefly. 'Naturally it would have been impossible to duplicate the accents of our friend Mr Davis, but exact duplication wasn't necessary since they would never get to England; they only want to get as far as Switzerland.'

'And what was going to happen to us?' Mason asked the question, knowing what the answer would be.

'You would have disappeared without trace.'

Still he was sceptical. 'Do you mean they went to all this trouble just to infiltrate the Underground?'

'Good heavens, no! I never said that. Their plan was much more devious. Hackett was to lead the two substitutes through Allied control. Once they had established themselves as returned prisoners, and before the usual debriefing enquiry was mounted, they would disappear – how, we haven't yet established, but their final destination is an Italian monastery in Allied hands. There they will make contact with someone who controls a vast sum of money on behalf of a high-ranking German, whom we believe to be either Bormann or Muller.' He blew a cloud of smoke. 'We believe this is the first move to organise a route for the removal of vast fortunes held by the Nazi brass.' His voice betrayed his contempt. 'The rats begin to make for the bolt-holes, and they need the money now. They know that the Allies will block Swiss funds once the war is over.'

Davis looked first at Mason and then at Joachim. 'How does all this fit in with your plan, whatever it is?'

'If Mr Hackett agrees, we would like him to walk into the Kripo office in Bautzen and give himself up.'

Mason said: 'You're crazy!'

Davis stood up quickly. 'They'll kill him.'

Joachim shook his head. 'They won't. The plan is too important to them. I am certain they are waiting for him to make contact with them in some way. They are confident their hold over him is enough to make him do that. They will jump at the opportunity to go on with it, since the plan is being run by subordinates and they won't want the brass to know how close to failure they were. Mr Hackett will be given his two substitutes and be allowed to continue, only now his escape will be so much easier. The two men are sure to have some safe conduct document to ensure they are not hindered.' He turned to the American. 'We have something we want you to take back to Allied Intelligence.'

Hackett looked at Mason and Davis. 'I'm prepared to go along with that, but how am I to account for my missing friends here?'

'Your story is that you were asleep in a barn – one we will take you to – and it caught alight. Before you could wake your friends and get them out, they were burnt to death. You will be able to show them the barn, and the bodies will be there to prove it.'

Mason was sceptical. 'It will never work. As soon as the bodies are examined, they'll know it isn't us. And where are the bodies coming from?'

'It will work.' Joachim was supremely confident. 'This is wartime. The forensic labs are overworked, and the bodies will be so badly burnt that identification will be impossible. In any case, my superiors will ensure that the bodies will be identified to our advantage.'

Mason persisted. 'You still haven't told us where you will get the bodies.'

'There are four bodies hidden in the forest?'

'The soldiers . . . of course!'

'Two of them we will bury. The two that are strangled will go into the barn.'

Davis leaned back against the wall. 'And what happens to us?'

For the first time Joachim looked at Pauline. Mason saw the agony of decision in his eyes. 'Pauline is determined to take the children to safety in France.' He looked at Mason. 'I want you two to go with her.'

Mason looked at the girl. She stared back at him steadily as though challenging him to dissuade her. He guessed that she had already been through it all with her father. He said: 'What do you think of our chances?'

She paused for a moment then said: 'Not very good. The problems are tremendous but not insurmountable. Feeding will be the most difficult part.' She shrugged. 'I've worked out a route that will give us the best chance of success.'

'Where do we take them – in France, I mean?'

'We have been told of a small village near Lyon called Le Chambon where a protestant minister will take them in. His name is Trocmé.'

Mason looked at Davis. 'Well, Taff?'

Davis shrugged. 'It's not the way I meant to go. I've always wanted to fly Imperial Airways, but what the hell – there's fifty young 'uns waiting to get home, too.'

Mason smiled. 'I always suspected you were simple-minded. That's why I let you decide.' He turned to Pauline. 'When do we go?'

'The earliest we can move is Friday morning. We have to get food cards for them. The arrangements will take time.'

While they were speaking, Davis looked at Joachim, a puzzled frown on his face. 'I wonder why the German plan was so elaborate. They didn't need us. Why not have Tom take off with two ersatz prisoners?'

Joachim shook his head. 'The names of all escaped prisoners are communicated to London. They needed a genuine escape, so that when two people with your names turn up behind Allied lines, a check with London will prove positive.'

Mason frowned. 'You said the operation is being run by subordinates. How many of them know what the final objective is?'

'Only two. The two who are to replace you. The rest know only what is necessary to carry out their part of the plan. It is possible that even the man running the operation is ignorant of the eventual objective.'

There was silence for a moment in the tiny cabin. Then Davis looked at the American. He said softly: 'You will never make me believe that you would've gone through with it, Tom.'

Hackett looked up. 'I'm glad you're not pushing it, Taff. I don't think you'd have been comfortable with my answer.' He paused for a moment. 'Anyway, fortunately it's a dilemma that doesn't have to be resolved.'

Mason looked at Joachim. 'I take it you don't want us to know what Tom is taking back – besides two ersatz prisoners, I mean.'

Joachim shook his head. 'You know better than to expect an answer to that. It's better you don't know.' He stood up. 'Come, we must go and burn a barn.'

Chapter Ten

Thursday, 10th August, 1944

They called him 'the ferret'. Sometimes 'that bastard, the ferret', or even 'that bloody bastard, the ferret', but whenever they spoke of him, the listener was in no doubt that the man was heartily disliked, and in some quarters even feared.

He was small, no more than five feet seven inches, with jet black hair and the type of face that attracted no more attention than a single leaf on a tree. His eyes were close-set, and his voice was higher than most men were comfortable with.

His reputation in the Gestapo was fearsome, even in an organisation where ninety percent of its members had reputations for sadistic cruelty. He was tenacious and unforgiving, and had an enviable record amongst his colleagues for his success rate in tracking down enemies of the state; which in fact was the task he was engaged upon at the moment.

He was in the corner of a small café in Bischofswerda with a glass of red wine before him. He hated red wine, but in his guise of a labourer, a double whisky would have been incongruous. His colleagues said that he was no fool, but the cliché was a gross understatement for his intellect was superior to that of most men in his calibre.

He could blend with any background, and he could be charming and affable, and those people who had been apprehended by him could never believe that the likeable little man they had bought a schnapps for in the bar around the corner, was the same man who wielded the implements of torture with which they were being interrogated.

His superiors avowed that the word 'ferret' had been coined for him. They also remarked sardonically that a ferret was a domesticated European polecat of the genus *Putorious,* and they would invariably add that you could make whatever you liked out of that.

The sole exception to the intense dislike which he engendered among his superiors, was S.S. Oberführer Becker. He considered that The Ferret was the best man he had, and because of his record, allowed him more latitude than he did more senior officers.

Thus it was that when Becker discussed with him the question of appointing an assistant, and mooted that the luckless Lieutenant Schäfer would be a possibility, the Gestapo man had been allowed to be more undiplomatic than usual.

'Pardon me, Herr Oberführer, but the man is an asshole, and will never amount to anything. If he is told what kind of information you require, I wouldn't put it past him to rush into Bischofswerda and ask the local innkeeper. No, sir, the man is a halfwit.'

'What do you suggest?'

'Let me work alone for three days. If I haven't found the escaped prisoners in that time, then I will ask for assistance.'

'Very well, but I want results.'

The Ferret set up his headquarters in a small abandoned hut outside the village. In the guise of a farmer displaced by the battles on the eastern front, he was received with a certain amount of sympathy that was, however, mixed with the usual suspicion country people felt for strangers.

Nevertheless, to his gratification and that of his superior, he soon learned that the area around Bischofswerda had been the scene of an intense manhunt on the afternoon of the 7th. Several garbled stories were repeated at the inn, especially in the hours around closing time when the wine has flowed and tongues are loosened.

In the dark, timbered room, the Gestapo man sat close to the regulars, and when he had thrown out a judicious comment, was attentive when the discussion took the turn he wanted. He heard about the men dressed as women, and about a mysterious group of people whisked away by a truck that had waited two hours for them near the station.

And the driver of the truck? No one knew who he was. He wasn't from hereabouts. The truck? No one had even seen it before, but it looked like one of those old French models they used to see before the war.

And then it was time to be quiet, because the questioning had gone on too long, and soon someone would begin to suspect that it was more than idle gossip that he wanted to hear. And so he went back to his little cabin, put out the light and waited in the dark until he was fetched by a driver from the pool. By five o'clock the next morning he was back in the cabin, ready to resume his intense ferretting into the matter of the missing prisoners-of-war.

He had asked for three days, but it was in fact only eighteen hours after he arrived that he got the information he wanted.

A farmer near Rutberg had had his barn burnt down by a trio of vagrants who had sheltered there in the night. Two were burnt to death, and the third had disappeared in the confusion. Now the Gestapo man knew that vagrants in wartime Germany were rare enough, but the coincidence in the number was too much for him to swallow.

The next morning he reported to S.S. Oberführer Becker. 'All three are definitely alive, Herr Oberführer.'

'How can you be certain?'

'There can never be certainty in this type of investigation. Only conviction based on deduction.'

'Explain.'

'Firstly, the men escaped from the train in women's clothes on Monday. Three days later, a barn burns down near Rutberg, less than fifty kilometres from Bischofswerda. Assuming it is the same three men, and the assumption is not far-fetched, why aren't they in Switzerland by now?'

'I agree. If it was a conventional escape, they would have been well away.'

'Secondly, by remaining in the area, the organisers of the operation indicate that something is to happen here, or at least somewhere close by.'

'That makes sense.' Becker stood up and walked to his favourite spot in front of the window. 'And what's more, I think it will happen very close to the offices of the Kripo in Breslau. In fact, not five hundred metres from here.'

The Ferret looked thoughtful. 'If this were an ordinary Gestapo investigation, Herr Oberführer, I could have the information you want in two hours. I would haul them all into the basement, and tell them about the meat hooks.'

Becker said sharply, 'This is not an ordinary investigation. You will watch yourself.' He sat at the desk. 'Just remember what I told you. This is dangerous ground we are on. We can't afford to make a single mistake.'

'I was merely wishing I had a free hand, Herr Oberführer.'

'What do you think happened to the two men who were reported dead.'

'I believe they are superfluous, Herr Oberführer. If they were part of a project initiated in Berlin, they would have been reported alive.' He stroked the top of his head. 'I think the third man is the key to the project. I am sure he is the one they will use.'

Becker grunted. 'Mmm, I agree entirely.' He thought for a moment. 'I think he was compelled to cooperate with them by threatening the man in prison. When he was under control, they ordered the hostage killed.' His face brightened. 'Now we're getting somewhere. We have to find the other two men. They were helped to escape from the train. Whoever helped them is responsible for faking their deaths. We must find them quickly, and the scum who helped them.'

'I think I can do that, Herr Oberführer.' The Ferret smiled toothily. 'In fact, I think I know just where I can find them – and where they found two bodies to burn.'

'Then get to it, man. I want results.' He waved dismissal. 'Oh – and I don't have to tell you to be careful.'

'No, Herr Oberführer.'

After the Gestapo man left the office, Becker sat for a long while contemplating the wall opposite. He stared unseeing at the picture of the Führer, musing on developments, considering all the possibilities.

'One thing I know,' he said softly. 'There's money involved here. Lots of it.' He smiled to himself. 'Heil Hitler.'

The bomb damage was evident from at least three kilometres outside Bautzen, where a collection of warehouses stood roofless in the driving rain. As the ancient truck jounced along the potholed streets, Hackett rubbed the mist from the inside of the windscreen and peered out, but the windscreen wipers hissed inefficiently across the glass, leaving a distorted vision of the world outside.

The driver, an ageing farmer with a bristly chin and grey hair, swung right to circle the main square, and pulled hard on the handbrake to stop the truck in front of the civic offices housing the Kriminalpolizei. Hackett paused for a moment before opening the passenger door. He turned to look at the driver. The man was watching him with something like pity in his eyes.

He said: 'I hope Joachim knows what he is doing.'

Hackett frowned. 'So do I.' He put out his hand. 'Thank you. I'm sorry about your barn.'

The man clasped his hand. 'It's nothing. It was falling down anyway. And if it helps to do those swine –' He shrugged. 'Be careful.'

Hackett watched the truck pulling away from the kerb and thought he had never felt so alone in his life. The vanishing vehicle was the last link with his friends. He wondered if he would ever see them again. He doubted it. Their task was virtually impossible. He could see no way for anyone to get fifty children through Germany to France, and the thought depressed him. Not since his imprisonment eight months ago had he ever felt so depressed and lonely.

He looked around him. The square was deserted, and the only traffic in the circle was an occasional military vehicle splashing through the puddles in the cobbled street. Oak trees edged the sidewalk every thirty metres, and under every second one was a concrete bench. He looked up at the grimy portico of the civic buildings, then his eye caught the small sign above the entrance of the building a short way along the street: BIER. Why not? Why the hell not?

It was dark in the café. Two of the tables at the rear were occupied by couples, but several near the window were empty. Both the couples looked up as he entered, then looked away, engrossed in each other. Hackett noticed that both men were in the uniform of the Waffen S.S., and both wore the dark blue piping of the medical units on their shoulder straps. The girls were both wearing the field grey uniforms of the Army

Signals Auxiliary, with the lightning flash patch on the sleeve.

Hackett signalled for attention, and the proprietor, a small elderly man with wire-rimmed spectacles, shuffled over to his table to take his order. While he waited for his beer, it dawned on him that he had subconsciously noted the uniform details, a skill he had acquired in the OSS. He wondered what the hell he was doing, walking into a police station to give himself up. He, Tom Hackett, a man who had successfully eluded the Gestapo for two long years while he roamed the countryside behind the lines with his band of partisans, was about to give himself up to his enemies.

He was filled suddenly with a surge of burning anger. To hell with the lot of them! Mac was dead, and he had no obligation to anyone. For months he had been jumping whenever anyone called the tune, dangling like a puppet with no volition of his own. He was good. He knew it. He had proved that he was as good an agent as any in the field, and if he walked out into the street and kept on going, he knew they would never find him again. He had a bloody good mind to do it.

Slowly his anger subsided as he remembered the mission he had been entrusted with by Joachim. This was far more important than his personal freedom. It was important enough for Joachim to send three agents on identical missions in the hope that at least one would be successful. He hadn't been told about the other two, only that they existed; and he had only been told so that he would realise the urgency of the mission, and the importance of the information he was carrying.

He lifted his glass to his lips, and felt again the pain of the burns on his wrist where Joachim had touched the hot iron. If he was to tell the Kripo that he had tried to save his friends, then it was essential that he could show some evidence of it. He hoped like hell they bought it.

He drained the glass and stood up to go. The rain was easing up a little. The couples ignored him as he turned up the collar of his coat and trudged the few steps to the municipal building next door. At the portico he hesitated for a moment, and then went up the steps into the building.

* * *

From the high window above the square Colonel Wiessen watched the workmen clearing the rubble from the bomb-damaged building. Behind him, seated in the chair opposite the heavy desk, Major Brunner tapped monotonously at the file cover on his lap, his granite features showing no sign of the satisfaction he was feeling.

The Colonel watched one more beam crash down from the damaged roof, and then returned to his chair. He sighed. 'I don't like it. Here we have one of a trio of escaped prisoners who walks into the police station and gives himself up. Moreover, it just so happens that it is the two prisoners he is to deliver to us that are burnt to death.' He leaned forward and pointed with his cigar. 'It is all just too facile. I repeat – I just don't like it.'

The Major shrugged. 'You will recall, Herr Colonel, that I predicted that the American would have to come back to us, and that – '

'Ah!' The Colonel slapped the top of the desk with the palm of his hand. 'But you did not predict that he would report that his friends were dead. I agree that if he wants to keep his brother alive, he must come back to us, but it is just too convenient that his friends happen to be burnt to death.' His mouth twisted in a sardonic smile. 'If they were still alive, don't you think this is exactly how they would have planned it?'

'We have the bodies of the two Englishmen.'

'Correction. You have the bodies of two males. You have not yet established who they are.' He leaned back and sighed once more. 'No. I don't believe one word of his unlikely tale – not without a thorough check.' He stood up and walked to the window. The workmen were levering another beam from its supports. 'I want the autopsy report. I want his story checked in every detail. I want you to put him through the wringer until he is flatter than his mother's pancakes.' He paused as the beam moved, slid from its supports and crashed to the ground in a heap of rubble. A cloud of dust floated slowly upwards. 'If there is the remotest possibility that the Englishmen are still alive, then I want them back.'

'Of course, Herr Colonel. However, am I to understand that the operation still takes priority?' There was no hint of challenge in his voice, but the Colonel was aware that it was there.

He turned from the window. He stared at the Major for a long moment, his expression cold. 'You will understand nothing of the kind. If the Englishmen are still alive, their recapture is part of the operation.' He sat. 'The original plan called for them to be returned to the Gestapo office at Reichenberg.' He leaned forward and pointed his cigar at the Major. 'I have no desire to explain to S.S. Obergruppenführer Kaltenbrunner or to S.S. Gruppenführer Müller why we have not done so. Do I make myself clear?'

'Perfectly, Herr Colonel.'

'Then if the autopsy proves unsuccessful, you have twenty-four hours to find them. If they are not found, I will send you to the Reichssicherheitshauptamt in Berlin to explain personally why you have not done so.'

'I understand, Colonel. If they are alive, they will be found.'

The Colonel was silent for a long moment. He stood up and went back to the window. The Major sensed his uneasiness. The Colonel said: 'We have lost too much time already. The group must be put together by tomorrow night at the latest. The substitutes should join the American as soon as you have confirmed his story.' He turned to look at the Major. 'Grant and Patterson are ready?'

'They are ready, Herr Colonel.' Brunner smiled inwardly at the Colonel's pronunciation of the English names the substitute prisoners were using. He realised too that the Colonel half believed the American's story in spite of his professed doubts. He wondered why his superior was so uneasy. A moment later his question was answered.

'Have you any information concerning the brother of the American?'

'No, Herr Colonel.' He hesitated. 'In view of the Gestapo's preoccupation with secrecy, I would suggest that he is no longer a threat to them.'

'In spite of the slaughter of thousands every day, you still have time for euphemisms.' The Colonel's voice was bitter. Major Brunner realised for the first time that it was possible that the Colonel cared what happened to people the Gestapo had no further use for.

'I'm sorry, Herr Colonel. You are quite right. Some of us are not yet used to it.'

'After ten years!' The Colonel's bitterness deepened. 'By now you should be accustomed to it.' He sighed and shrugged and went back to his chair. 'I digress. The Englishmen are our concern only as long as it is necessary to prove whether they are dead or alive. Our concern is centred on the American.'

Brunner wondered if the Colonel realised that he had just contradicted himself. The operation was priority after all. He said: 'Captain Schmidt of my office has made a suggestion, Herr Colonel. He suggests we call in the services of Doctor Hertzinger.'

'Hertzinger?'

'He was assistant to Kockel in the thirties. You will recall the Green Opel murder? Both Kockel and Hertzinger are recognised authorities on death by burning.'

'Is Hertzinger here? In this city?'

'Yes, Herr Colonel. He is on a short vacation from Berlin. Schmidt was fortunate enough to see him in the foyer of his hotel.'

'Use him by all means if he is prepared to give up some of his vacation.' He paused. 'What about Doctor Harmann?'

'He and Harmann are old friends. Harmann will be delighted.'

'Good. You have my permission to make the necessary special payment. Impress on them that the matter is urgent.' He picked up his pen to signify that the interview was over. Brunner closed the file on his lap and stood up. The Colonel looked up. 'I want that autopsy report the minute it is prepared.'

'You will have it, Herr Colonel.' Major Brunner saluted and went from the office. As soon as he had gone, Colonel Wiessen sighed, stood up and went back to the window to watch the workmen of the Todt Organisation send another beam crashing to the ground. It was, he thought, a symbolic presage of the fate of his beloved Germany.

Back in his office, Major Brunner pressed the bell on his desk. A girl appeared in the doorway. 'Ask Captain Schmidt to come to my office.'

A few moments later Captain Werner Schmidt knocked on

the door and came into the office. Major Brunner looked up at his junior officer. 'Sit down, Werner.' He went on turning the pages of the file until he found the document he was looking for. He eased it out of its binding and placed it in front of Captain Schmidt, face up so that the junior officer could read it. Schmidt glanced at it briefly and looked at Brunner expectantly.

Brunner said: 'You've been through the file; you've seen that document. Didn't you feel there was something odd about it?'

Schmidt frowned. 'Odd?'

'Odd. Peculiar.'

Schmidt pulled the paper towards him with one finger. He read it through carefully. Brunner watched him. Finally the Captain looked up, bewilderment in his eyes.

Brunner smiled. 'You see it?'

Schmidt nodded slowly. 'We are instructed to deliver the three men to a house in Friedrichshafen.'

'Exactly. Which is only a few kilometres across the lake from Switzerland. Which means they will bypass every Underground cell in Germany. Yet it was orignally hinted that the objective was the Underground.'

'Hinted, yes. But we were never given that as an objective in so many words. And as you have said before, we are not so naïve as to believe so inane a plan.'

Brunner tapped the paper with his forefinger. 'Before this arrived two days ago, it seemed clear that we were infiltrating agents into Allied territory. With this instruction our masters have abandoned that excuse. It would appear that Italy is the objective.'

'Then why not fly them straight to Italy?'

'What if they have to pay a call somewhere on the way? Say, in Switzerland? What if that call is so secret that no one besides Müller or Kaltenbrunner must know of it?' He leaned back and looked at Schmidt quizzically. 'Isn't that the reason why this has been entrusted to the Kripo instead of the Gestapo? So that Reichsführer Himmler never gets to hear of it? Why is it that the Gestapo know nothing of the operation except the things that concern them under the Stufe Romisch III Order – the order that all recaptured prisoners must be dealt with by the Gestapo?'

Captain Schmidt shifted uneasily. In spite of his long friendship with Brunner, or perhaps because of it, he was not happy about the trend of the discussion. The concentration camps were full of people who had been indiscreet.

Major Brunner sensed his discomfiture. When he spoke his tone was faintly derisive. 'Come, Werner, has your fear of the Gestapo paralysed your deductive faculties? You profess to be a good policeman, yet you are afraid to be one when you suspect a crime is being committed by a head of the RSHA.'

Schmidt was derisive in his turn. 'Of what use is suspicion? For that matter, of what use if proof? Even if you had proof, could you go to Berlin, arrest the man, and bring him back to Breslau in handcuffs? This whole discussion is childish.' His fingers drummed nervously on the arms of his chair. 'If you had the proof right here, you know as well as I do that there is nothing you could do about it.'

Major Brunner laughed out loud. 'Don't be indignant, my friend. As you say, there are people who are above the law.' He sobered. 'What I'm saying is that we keep the facts in mind; that we don't commit errors of judgement through ignorance.'

Schmidt shrugged. 'We may need an escape route ourselves one of these days.'

'So!' Brunner was delighted. 'You believe exactly as I do. Someone is probing the prison walls. Someone is definitely getting ready to run for it – and not empty-handed either, if our guess is right.'

'Isn't it obvious?' Schmidt cut the air with his hand. 'The Allies are going to demand heavy retribution when this is over.' He stared at Brunner, his eyes hard. 'What are we going to do about it?'

Brunner got up from his chair and paced once, twice, across the carpet, his head down, his hands behind his back. Schmidt watched him. He had seen the Major in this mood before – many times when they had been close to the solution of a difficult case.

The Major stopped. 'See what you can get on the head of the Kripo office at Friedrichshafen. Hesselman, isn't it? Find out it if he is a member of the Party. Get anything you can.' He went to the window and stared unseeing at the trucks rumbling through Bismarchstrasse on their way to the Eastern Front.

Schmidt pushed back his cap and rubbed his hairline. 'We'll have to be careful. With the services in disarray after the arrests, we don't know who to trust.'

Brunner turned from the window and went back to his chair. 'Did we ever know who to trust? Now that the Reichsführer Himmler has assumed responsibility for the Abwehr, in place of Canaris, we don't know who our friends are.' He swivelled his chair and stared out of the window. 'This operation could only have been mounted in a climate of confusion. The time has been well-chosen.' He swivelled back to face the Captain. 'What puzzles me is how they came to choose an American from the OSS to be part of the operation. Was it deliberate or a happy coincidence?'

'Is it important?'

'Very important. An agent of a free-wheeling organisation like the OSS is an ideal choice for the success of the scheme. Their clandestine sections even confuse each other sometimes. If someone says he is an agent of the OSS and has papers to prove it, no one questions it.'

'Then it must have been deliberate.' The Captain stood up and adjusted his cap. 'I'll have that information on Hesselman by tonight at the latest.' He went to the door and opened it. He looked back at the Major who had swivelled his chair to look out at the window once more, then went out, shutting the door softly behind him.

Major Brunner sighed and turned his attention to the reports from the Central Distribution Office, reports of all crimes, which came to him as a formality. Many of them did not concern the Kripo, they were dealt with by other services, but he had to sift out those that did and hand them on to his staff for attention. The first one he put aside. That one dealt with the desertion of four Waffen S.S. men on patrol in the Elbsandstein. They had gone, taking their rations and blankets. The Feldgendarmerie – the orange patches – would deal with that one. He pressed the bell on his desk.

Chapter Eleven

Friday, 11th August, 1944. 7 a.m.

Rosamund Bedaux was very tired. She had been awake since five o'clock, and she had been walking for nearly an hour and a half. True, all the other children were walking too; all those who had been with her on the train. But an hour and a half is a long time for a little girl of seven to keep walking. Her shoes weren't the best kind for walking either. It seemed, however, that they were the only ones that could be found for her at such short notice. Like the clothes she wore. This pale, faded blue dress was the only one that fitted her from the pile that the lady had brought to the forest last night. She would rather have had one like her sister Lise had on. It was an elegant pink dress with bows; but Lise was ten years old and big enough to get into it. Still, she was one of the lucky ones. Some of the children could not get anything to fit them, and their old dirty clothing had to be washed and ironed. Rosamund did not say anything but she noticed that Francine's dress still smelt a little from the train journey, even after it had been washed twice.

No, Rosamund and her sister had been among the lucky ones. Lise was at this moment holding her left hand and occasionally helping her over the rough bits on the forest track. Well, Lise was half helping her, that is. Holding her other hand was the nice fair-haired man. Her eldest sister Agnes was helping the other seven-year-old children. Agnes was thirteen, and her mother used to say that Agnes could always 'be relied upon'.

She wondered where her mother was now. Her father, of course, had been gone a long time. She remembered distinctly the day the two men had come to fetch him. They were wearing light raincoats, and had interrupted their music lesson. Her mother had cried a lot after that. Mother used to teach them the piano, violin and singing. Rosamund liked the singing best of all, especially when they sang in harmony. They still sang together sometimes, Lise, Agnes and herself, together with their cousin André Bedaux, who was with them now walking in the forest. They sang together when the soldiers put them in the train. They sang whenever they were frightened.

They were never frightened before the two men came for her father. They lived in an apartment in Lyon, and there were always friends calling, and dinner parties, and when they celebrated the Jewish holy days, her father and mother taught them the significance of the festivals and what they meant to the Jews. There was always laughter and happiness at mealtimes, and when friends came to call, there was joy in the house.

Rosamund was very tired. She wondered how much longer they had to go. The lady in the blue head scarf said they would have to travel for several days before they got back to France. She had never seen her mother wearing a head scarf. She had beautiful long black hair that used to sway when she laughed. People said she, Rosamund, had hair like her mother. Her hair too was black and silky.

The path was becoming steeper, and her steps were getting slower. She tried to walk faster, but her legs ached, and she dragged against the pull of the two hands holding hers.

All at once, she felt herself being lifted up and cradled in two strong arms. It was a relief to rest her head against the rough wool of his jacket. Gently she slid into a deep sleep, unaware of the soft chatter of the voices around her.

At the head of the column, Pauline called a halt for a brief rest. Mason placed the sleeping child on the carpet of leaves by the side of the trail, and sat beside her. The girl shifted restlessly and then settled down, her hands clasped under her chin. Mason looked at the small serene face framed by a halo of lustrous black hair.

The night before, Joachim had directed them to a barn in a beet field owned by an elderly couple. It was there that he had become acquainted with the children and learnt some of their names. There were the Dreyfuss children, Sarah, Isaac and Ruth, eight, ten and fourteen respectively. Then there were the Galland girls, Elsa and Maria. They were eight and ten, and perhaps the most lively of the group.

But the ones to whom Mason was most drawn were the Bedaux children, three sisters and a cousin. The four children had performed for them last night, singing a lovely French ballad in a beautiful four-part harmony. They were children whose superior education was evident, but it was not because of that Mason was drawn to them. They were natural and engaging, and their chatter was touched with a sense of humour that was unaffected by their terrible experience. They had a resilience that amazed him.

The night before, with the children asleep in the barn, they had studied the route Pauline had suggested, and could find no fault with it. Indeed, how could they since they were looking at a pencil line drawn on a map? When she explained the logic of her decisions, it was obvious that only time would tell whether her confidence was justified.

This path in the forest led to Liebstadt, a small village south of Dresden. From there, Gunther had arranged for a bus to take them as far as Komotau, a town in Sudetenland. The bus was one of three owned by an elderly Czech who had managed to prevent his buses from being commandeered by offering them to the local District Director for outings. The shortage of fuel was overcome by the Director's friendship with the commander of the local Home Guard unit.

Mason had been sceptical of their ability to account for fifty children and three adults travelling from a village in Germany to a town in Czechoslovakia, a hundred kilometres away. Joachim explained that Gunther had prevailed on his Czech friend to give him an expired permit for a school tour. It had been a simple matter to turn it into a permit for a current excursion. He explained to Mason and Davis that the timing had to be perfect, for the permit was valid for one day only. Outside the limits of the permit, they risked the attention of the Gestapo.

After Komotau, they were on their own. Joachim's cell did not operate beyond that, but he had arranged for a contact with someone to direct them on from Komotau. He stressed that this was the area of greatest danger, since many of the cells had been penetrated, and they would have to exercise the greatest caution in making contact.

Mason looked around him at the children chattering amongst themselves. He saw that they had remained in their groups, as Pauline had arranged them. She had organised a system of monitors consisting of the five oldest girls, who were responsible for eight or nine children each.

The column moved on once more, Pauline at the head, Mason in the middle, and Davis in the rear to watch for stragglers. The trail wound upwards through the tall firs. The air was bright and clear, and the forest was alive with the sound of birds. Above them, through the wide arms of the conifers, they could see the clouds drifting across the sky, and now and then they caught a glimpse of jagged peaks in the distant haze. Although at times they could hear the muffled crack of axe strokes, they saw no sign of the foresters, and Mason wondered how it was that in all their time in the forest, they had not encountered any. Now and then, they saw signs of an encampment – a damped down fire or a bed of fir branches – but not once did they encounter even a single peasant.

Soon the trail began to descend, and as they skirted a deep ravine, they could hear the sound of water rushing below. A few minutes later they came to the bank of a river, where the white water skittered over rocky shallows. They stopped then, and the children splashed and played, and drank their fill. Mason could not help contrasting their attitudes now to the terror stricken faces they had seen in the cattle truck.

Mason flopped on the grass next to Davis. 'You need some fast French lessons with this lot, Taff.'

'Aye. Some of the little ones jabber away like a machine gun, and look at me as if I was daft when I don't answer.'

Mason laughed. 'It won't be long before you learn.'

'If they speak slow like, I can get most of it.' He shook his head. 'But when they rattle it off, then I'm lost.' He looked at Mason soberly. 'D'ye think we're going to make it?'

Mason looked around them at the children. 'I pray we will, Taff. I just pray that we will.'

'I'm not much on praying, Bob.' Davis stared unseeing at the water bubbling over the stones. Then he looked up and said quickly, 'Don't get me wrong. My folks were God-fearing right enough, but there never seemed to be enough time for church and praying, what with the time we spent on the coal face.' He looked at his friend. 'My Da were dead against me going down the mine, but I wanted to do what he did. Stupid bugger that I was.'

Mason held his shoulder. 'Every boy wants to follow his father's trade. Especially if he loved him.'

Davis said softly: 'Aye, I loved him right enough. We all loved him. He was good to us, and kind, and I never heard him say a harsh word to my mother. To the day he died.' He looked up at Mason. 'Before he died, there never seemed enough food in the house for six of us, but after he died, God help us, it was worse.'

There was silence for a long while, and Mason was conscious of the voices of the children, the sound of the river, and the hiss of the breeze in the tall trees.

Davis went on, 'I swear to God, when I get home, I'll get all of them out of that stinking village. No one has to live like we did.'

'But you got out, Taff.'

'Aye, on a scholarship, but that's no help to the others. How do they get out, tell me?' His voice was soft and without emotion, but the bitterness was in every word he spoke.

Mason realised that there were many benevolent owners, but he knew too that there were some who were as Taff described them. He sighed. He wondered if the war would bring any changes to the people of his country.

He looked up and saw Pauline watching him. He smiled and she smiled back, indicating that they should move on.

Once out of the gorge they saw below them, across a field of purple bell-like flowers, a village that could have come straight from the Brothers Grimm. A road wound through the valley to pass between houses of weathered stone and slate roofs, and above the village was a church with two circular towers. In the distance, Mason could see several men wielding scythes, while the women raked the hay into stacks. A hay-wagon was being loaded by men with forks. On the higher slopes were timbered houses with steep pitched roofs while beyond the valley, the dark green of the forest swept upwards to the distant hills.

Where their path joined the rutted road, they found Gunther waiting for them. He nodded silently, and then turned and led the way into the village. Alongside the road a post and rail fence of weathered timber enclosed a meadow where cattle grazed. Beyond the meadow stood the first row of houses. In front of the second house an old man sat dozing in the sun, but apart from him and a woman at the window of the house opposite, the village was deserted. As the first group of children were passing the cobbled street that followed a short steep slope to the church above, a man appeared at the end of the village and walked swiftly towards them. He stopped to speak to Gunther, fifty metres away from them. The two men turned and walked back to Pauline at the head of the column of children. Mason sensed the urgency of their movements.

Pauline looked up the path to the church. Mason saw the man nodding and pointing as Pauline motioned the children up the path.

As Mason approached, she said: 'A motorised patrol is on the way. We must get the children into the church.'

'But the permit – '

The man interrupted brusquely. 'A precaution. It is safer not to invite questions. They rarely look in the church, but if they do, they will not question a choir rehearsal.'

Gunther nodded. 'We must do as Lazero says. He has had a signal that they will be here in five minutes.'

'A signal?'

Lazero nodded. 'This region is the headquarters of the Lidice unit of the Czech partisans. They keep us informed.' He looked across the road at the woman in the window. 'But we have to be careful. Many Germans moved into Sudetenland after the Nazis came.' He looked at Mason significantly. 'We keep a record of them. After the war . . .' He passed his finger across his throat.

The men followed the children up the steep path. Inside, the church was bigger than it appeared from the road. There were twenty pews on either side of the aisle, and the heavily timbered pulpit was a good three metres above the worshippers. Two large ornate chandeliers hung from the vaulted roof.

Pauline hustled the children to the front of the church and sat them in the first three pews on either side of the aisle. Lazero led the three men to a door at the back of the church which led to a passage. At the end of the passage was a steep staircase. He led the way up the stairs to the first landing where, to their surprise, he moved a section of wooden wall disclosing a short flight of steps. The men found themselves in a small closet. At head height were slots in the timber through which they could see the entire church. They heard Pauline's voice coming up to them from below, as she instructed the children in the parts they should play.

Mason whispered. 'We should be down there with her. We can't do anything for her up here.'

'No.' Lazero was vehement. 'The Germans would be suspicious if they saw four men hanging about during choir practice. It is safer for her this way.' In the dim light from the slots, Mason saw the Czech listening, his head to one side. 'Quiet. They are coming.'

Mason heard the low hum of a truck as it entered the village. A few moments later they heard the drop of the engine note as it came to a stop.

'They've stopped at the café. It is unlikely that they will search, but we may have to stay here at least an hour.'

An hour! Mason looked down at the group below them. Every minute would make them that much later at their destination. They had hoped to be in Komotau by nightfall, and in the normal course of events the time they had allowed for the journey would have been ample, but if they were held up for an hour in this village, they would still be travelling after dark.

Mason turned to Davis who had been listening to the German words uncomprehendingly. 'We might have to stay here for an hour. The krauts are at the café.'

'An hour, bloody hell! Those kids will never get through it.'

Almost as though she had heard them, Pauline said in

French: 'Now we may have to wait here for some time, so we will go over what we learnt yesterday.' She looked at the expectant faces. 'Remember "Die Fahnhoch! Die Riehen Dicht Geslossen". Does anyone remember what it means?'

A boy of about eight shot up his hand.

'Isaac Besnard. Tell us what it means.'

'Raise the flag! Close the ranks!'

'Very good. And where do those words come from?'

A chorus of voices cried out. 'The Horst Wessel Song!'

Mason looked at Lazero. 'The Horst Wessel Song? The Nazi anthem?'

The Czech shrugged. 'What song do you think a German schoolchild would learn?'

Pauline went on. 'I want the children who speak German to come out and stand on my left.'

Mason saw six girls move into position. They were Elsa and Marie Galland, Elena and Henriette Wiskamann, and Francine and Paulette Delaroux.

Pauline moved them into a orderly group. 'Henriette and Marie, I want you to listen to me carefully. Whenever I ask anyone – anyone at all – to tell me the date of Horst Wessel's birth, you must be eager to tell me. Can you remember that?'

The two girls nodded vigorously. 'Let us rehearse that then.'

Mason looked at Lazero in bewilderment. The Czech shrugged once more. 'She's a clever girl. She knows what she's doing.'

Pauline walked slowly along the front pew. 'Giselle Florens. Tell us please the date of Horst Wessel's birth.'

Before Giselle could open her mouth, both Henriette and Marie burst into a chorus of entreaty. 'Let me tell them, Fraulein. Please, Fraulein.'

'Marie, you tell us then.'

'The 9th October, 1907, in Bielefeld.'

'And when did he die tragically for the Führer?'

'On the 23rd February, 1930.'

'That's very good. Remember, from now on we speak only German. Those who cannot must be still and quiet. Only in that way can we stop the soldiers from taking us back to the train.'

Elsa Galland raised her hand. 'What is it, Elsa?'

'My father said we should not sing that song.' The child's German was faultless.

'Whyever not? You and your sister were the only ones who knew it when we practised it yesterday.'

The child nodded. 'Yes, but Papa told us that we should know evil if we wish to avoid it.' The child looked up solemnly at Pauline.

'Quite right, Elsa.' She suppressed a smile. 'But we must be careful not to say things like that to the Germans. It would only annoy them.' Elsa looked chastened. 'We must go on with our lessons.' She held out her hand, one finger raised. 'Who brings the bread to our tables?'

With one voice, the children shouted in German: 'Our beloved Führer!'

Mason looked at Gunther. 'When did she teach them that?'

'Yesterday at the barn. She said they had to be prepared for anything.'

Pauline's voice floated up to them from below. Her hand was still raised, this time with two fingers showing. 'What do we love and fight for?'

The chorus cried: 'Our beloved Germany.'

Mason was puzzled. 'Do they understand her?'

'No. They watch her fingers.'

Pauline walked quickly to the organ. She struck a note and turned to the children. She raised her hand to give them the beat, and when her arm fell, forty-eight voices were raised in harmony. The notes of the song resounded through the church, and Mason was aware that, evil or not, Elsa and Marie Galland sang as lustily as the others. When they came to the end and the last notes died away, Pauline walked back to the organ.

'That was wonderful. Now once more.'

She struck a note, but before she could give them the beat, Mason saw her look beyond the children to the doorway of the church. Slowly forty-eight heads turned to see what held her attention. In the doorway, stood a man in civilian clothes, while slightly behind him, and on either side, were two soldiers of the Waffen S.S., their sub-machine guns cradled in their arms. Mason watched the tableau, the moment frozen in time. No one moved, and the civilian stood there, hands in the pockets of his raincoat, hard eyes staring at the girl at the other end of the church. Then his eyes swept over the children, and he walked slowly up the aisle. Mason recognised the Gestapo tactic of intimidation. He saw two more soldiers join the two at the door.

The civilian spoke. 'Who are these children?'

'These are children from Liebstadt, Glashutte and Niederfrauendorf. We are rehearsing for a concert, Herr – ' Pauline hesitated.

'Preiss. From the Teplitz Division. I haven't seen you in this area before. Who are you?'

'Anna Strauss,' she said, giving the name she was travelling under. 'I have been asked by the three communities to teach the children songs for the concert.'

'Where are you from?'

'Dresden. I have a music school there.'

'Have you a permit to be here in the Sudetenland?'

'Of course, Herr Preiss. It was arranged for me by S.S. Oberführer Franz Schauschutz of the Prague office.'

The Gestapo man looked at Pauline for a long moment. The children looked from one to the other as they spoke, fear in every face. Mason held his breath. She would never get away with it. As soon as he asked to see the permit, they were done for – and so were they. They could not let the soldiers drag the children away without trying to do something about it.

Preiss put out his hand and snapped his fingers. 'The permit! Let me see it.'

'Certainly, Herr Preiss.' She walked to where she had thrown her coat over the back of the first pew. She said over her shoulder, 'I hope you will attend the concert, Herr Preiss. It will be most instructive.'

'Instructive?'

'It is the Horst Wessel Memorial Concert.' She walked back to him, a document in her hand. Mason released a slow breath. By heaven, she had a permit. He saw her place the paper in the outstretched hand. 'It was suggested by my good friend S.S. Oberführer Schauschutz. He thought that not enough was being done to immortalise our National Socialist Party heroes.'

'You know Oberführer Schauschutz personally?'

Pauline waved a deprecating hand. She smiled. 'I suppose I should say he is a friend of my father. But he has known me since I was a little child.' Mason hoped Herr Schauschutz was over forty. But somehow he knew he would be. Mason's respect for the girl deepened. In spite of the tension, he saw she was beginning to convince the Gestapo man. He was examining the document carefully. The soldiers watched, boredom in their faces, and Mason realised that this drama being played out meant nothing to them. If they had to drag the girl out and shoot her, they would do it without compunction; then go back to their beer in the café without another thought.

'This concert. It is the first I have heard of it.'

'Then you must allow us to give you a sample, Herr Preiss. It will take place on the anniversary of the birth of our great hero. You know the date, of course?'

Preiss looked uncomfortable. 'The date?'

'Won't you tell the children the date to show that a good Nazi knows all about the heroes of the Reich? It will be a good example for them.'

'The heroes of the Reich? Of course. I suppose – ' Mason realised that Preiss was at a loss for words. 'Horst Wessel's birthday – '

At that moment two voices cried out in unison. 'Let me, Fraulein. Please, Fraulein.' Henriette and Marie were waving their hands in the air, both apparently eager to show what good Nazis they were.

'No children.' Pauline was firm. 'Herr Preiss must have the privilege of – '

'No. No. Let the children tell us. Constant repetition will fix it in their heads.' Herr Preiss was plainly relieved. The prospect of displaying his ignorance of Nationalist Socialist history to a church full of children and soldiers was disconcerting. Mason realised how cleverly Pauline had taken the initiative and gained psychological ascendency over the Gestapo man. What made it more astonishing was that she had obviously planned for just such an eventuality.

'Very well then, children. What is Horst Wessel's birth date?'

Henriette spoke up. 'He was born in Bielefeld on 9th October, 1907, Fraulein.'

Pauline looked at Herr Preiss. He picked up his cue. 'Quite correct. Very good.' Mason realised that Pauline, by inviting his participation, had forced on the man a subconscious acceptance of their position.

'And now, Marie. When did he die tragically for the Führer?'

'On 23rd February, 1930.'

'Excellent. And now everyone.' She lifted her hand, one finger raised. 'Who brings the bread to our tables?'

'Our beloved Führer.' The shout was deafening. Herr Preiss was gratified.

'What do we love and fight for?' Two fingers raised.

'Our beloved Germany.'

Herr Preiss was overwhelmed. 'I must congratulate you, Fraulein Strauss. You are instilling into these children a love of all that we revere in our glorious Reich.' Mason could almost hear the fanfare.

Pauline smiled. 'And now, Herr Preiss, you must hear how much we have learned of our song.'

'You are most kind, Fraulein.' Mason couldn't believe it. Preiss was almost simpering. 'However, I must decline your generous offer. It is getting late, and I have a large area to patrol.' He lifted her hand and pressed it to her lips. For a fleeting moment, while his head was over her hand, an expression of revulsion crossed the girl's face. Then it was gone, and she was smiling at the Gestapo man as though he was the most charming she had ever met. He looked at the children. 'Very good. Very good. You must sing well at the concert.' He went down the aisle, turning to give an arch little wave at the girl. She smiled and lifted her hand. Preiss went out, and the soldiers followed him.

For a long moment there was dead silence in the church. The girl stood where Preiss had left her, her head up, her back stiff. Then slowly she relaxed and slumped into a pew, head down, arms limp at her sides. Mason moved to go to her.

Lazero held his arm. 'No. I'll go. They may come back.' He moved the panel and went out. A few seconds later he appeared below them, walking towards the girl in the pew. He touched her lightly on the shoulder. She looked up at him, smiling wanly through her tears, and Mason was poignantly aware of her vulnerability behind the tough façade.

She stood up and walked to the front of the church. 'Ready, children. We will sing one more song.'

As the sounds of the voices filled the church, Lazero went out of the door, returning a few minutes later. He beckoned for the three men still in the priest's hole to come down.

'They've gone,' he called.

The three men went down into the church.

Herr Harster, the Gestapo agent known as The Ferret, looked carefully through the papers on his desk, reading each one thoroughly before putting it aside and picking up the next. He wasn't sure what he was looking for, but he knew he would recognise it when he saw it.

Every now and then, he would nod with satisfaction as he read something that interested him, and that paper he would place on a separate pile on his left. Finally, when the last document was picked up and put aside, three reports had been separated from the others. He bundled the discarded papers together and placed them in his Out tray to be filed by his clerk, and then pulled the three documents towards him. Swiftly he reread them.

The reports from the Central Distribution Office were circulated daily to all offices involved with crime, and represented everything from murder or treason to circumstances which were merely suspicious.

Harster went through them again. The first dealt with the disappearance of an entire patrol of four men from the Elbsandstein sector. They had taken their blankets, food and weapons. Their unit commander had reported it as desertion. The second report had also been reported as desertion, but in this case the man had left all his possessions with his comrades, and had not been seen since. The man had disappeared from a patrol of four whose sector covered a small siding west of Tetschen.

The report that interested him the most, however, was one from the Ostrava Office which reported that a truck which should have contained fifty Jews had arrived at Auschwitz with six dead children and a dead soldier. None of the bodies had been identified but identification would be made, and an amended report forwarded in due course.

Herr Harster went through to the communications office, and activated the telex. His message was brief. It read:

> '40513/8 Ostrava. Reference CDO 241/12.
> Suspect dead man is Gefreiter Albert Smital.
> Please investigate and confirm. Urgent.
> Harster. Breslau.'

He went back to his office and unrolled a set of charts after which he spent the next five mintes studying a map of the Elbsandstein, paying particular attention to a thin line representing a track between Bishofswerda and Tetschen. Finally he rolled up the maps, locked up his office and went through to the office of S.S. Oberführer Becker. He felt sure that Becker would be pleased with what he would hear.

Chapter Twelve

Friday, 11th August, 1944. 11.30 a.m.

Opposite the café, Wilhelm leaned against a lamp post, hands deep in his pockets, his cap low on his forehead. Johan stood beside him, holding the bar of a street-sweeper's cart and leaning on his broom. They smoked incessantly, watching the silent street. This was their third foray along the road since Joachim disappeared into the café. They had no reason to suspect that the rendezvous had been compromised, but they were taking no chances, providing double back-up whenever possible.

Inside the café, Joachim sat waiting beside the telephone, looking now and then at the watch on his wrist. Finally as the hands showed precisely eleven-thirty, he picked up the handset and dialled. One hundred kilometres away, an officer in one of the services of the Third Reich stopped near a telephone kiosk on the corner he invariably passed when he walked the short distance from his office to the Gestapo headquarters in the city. He lit a cigarette and surveyed the quiet street. He saw a street sweeper near the intersection, and an elderly woman with her basket trudging towards the local market. The sweeper looked right and left, then swung his broom over his shoulder in a signal the officer recognised. Safe.

At that moment the telephone rang in the kiosk. He went to it quickly and picked it up, pressing the receiver to his ear.

He heard Joachim's voice. 'Karl?'

'Yes.'

'The bus left ten minutes ago.'

'Good. No problems?'

'They were intercepted at Liebstadt. A random patrol. The plan worked as she said it would. There is nothing to worry about.'

'Good. You realise there is no more I can do once they leave Komotau? You'll have to rely on our Berlin friend.'

'You've done enough already. The children were an unexpected complication. We had no right to involve you.'

'You know how I feel about that.'

'Yes. Thank you again.' Joachim heard the silence hum on the line. 'What of your end?'

'The report went to Kripo headquarters this morning. Satisfactory. The bodies have been identified on the basis of identifying scars.'

'And?'

'There is no doubt that the bodies are those of two men known to have escaped from a certain prisoner-of-war camp on the fourth of August.'

'Astonishing! I don't know how you did it.'

'Don't ask.'

Joachim smiled at the Jewish idiom. 'If I didn't know you better, I'd suspect your Aryan background.'

Karl smiled then grew serious. 'Joachim, be careful.'

'I know.'

'Things are getting worse. There will be more arrests tomorrow. I'm told Goerdeler is on the list. And Nebe.'

'Nebe! S.S. Oberführer Nebe.'

'Yes. Even the Kripo head in Berlin isn't safe.'

'No one is safe any more.'

'No. No one is safe.' Karl looked across at the street-sweeper. The broom was down. 'I must go.'

'Take care.'

'You too.' Karl replaced the receiver, and continued his walk to Gestapo headquarters.

In Gorlitz, Joachim stood up and called to the elderly woman in the kitchen. It was she who had served the escaped prisoners when they had visited the café between trains. She came in, wiping her hands on her apron.

He said: 'This is the last time I will call here for a while. I don't want to compromise you or this place. You are too valuable to us, but if you have any information, telephone the emergency number.' She nodded silently. 'The cell will close temporarily.' She nodded again. He touched her cheek and left the café.

The Gestapo man they called The Ferret puffed slightly as he climbed the path towards the overhanging rock. It was noon, but the sun was hidden behind thick grey cloud. The Elbsandstein was at its most lowering, though the wind had dropped to a soft breeze. The two men with him were dressed in bright shirts and lederhosen, and carried heavy packs.

As they walked, the Gestapo man's eyes searched the ground in every direction. Suddenly he stopped, and pointed at a small glade on the left of the path.

'Begin here.' He looked around him. 'The ground is disturbed as though it has been raked.'

The older of the two men looked to where he was pointing, 'It seems you are right, Herr Harster.'

The Gestapo man shrugged. 'I am always right.'

'How did you know?'

'It was obvious.' He sneered. 'These people are so stupid. They leave a trail a blind man can follow.'

'A trail?'

'They leave Bischofswerda in a French truck of an unusual make, a vehicle that is rare enough to be noticed by the farmers we questioned. They tell us it took this road over the mountain.' He turned his hand palm up. 'There is only one place they could head for – the Tetschen line. From there they can travel south-west to Karlsbad and Nuremberg.' He smiled thinly. 'And what do we find?' A soldier deserts from his post at a railway siding near Tetschen; and he leaves behind all his belongings, including his identity documents and letters from home.' He sneered once more. 'And his bungling commanding officer reports it as desertion!'

The two guides laughed. The younger man looked around the glade. 'And you think we may find something here?'

Herr Harster spoke with heavy irony. 'What we have here, I think, is another coincidence. Not twenty kilometres from the other desertion, four more men desert their post taking their rations and blankets. Yet no one has seen them from the moment they disappeared. Not their families, nor their friends – and above all not their girl friends.' He smiled as the guides laughed at his heavy wit. 'I think we will find at least two of them buried somewhere near here.'

'And the other two?' The older one looked puzzled.

'Burnt in a barn to give someone an alibi.' He shrugged impatiently. 'Come, we must find them before dark.'

'If they really are here.'

'Oh, they're somewhere here, all right. I'll stake my life on it.'

The two guides began following the faint trail through the forest to a small ravine. They saw footprints heavily embedded in the soil as though a heavy weight was being carried, and finally two hours later they found the bodies where Gunther had buried them in the shallow grave.

As they scraped away the dirt and uncovered the uniformed figures, Herr Harster looked down at the grave with grim satisfaction.

'Now I can go by the book. This is no longer a stupid operation about missing prisoners. This is an official investigation into the murder of soldiers of the Reich.' He smiled wolfishly. 'And if I happen to uncover things no one is supposed to know about – ' he spread his arms wide – 'how can I help that?'

He saw the older man looking at him, bewilderment in his face. 'A stupid operation, Herr Harster? What operation.'

'That is no concern of yours. Just get those bodies uncovered.'

The bus lurched along the dusty, rutted road, skirted the village of Glashutte, climbed once more into the forest, and topped the ridge above Geising, a village on the old German-Czech frontier. Since the war, Geising had become just another farming community.

Mason sat next to Pauline on the seat behind the driver. Davis sat at the back of the bus. The children were chattering animatedly their fears forgotten in the heady excitement of their journey.

The road emerged from the forest once more and wound

through a valley of wild crocuses, their pale violet blooms a breathtaking complement to the blue of the sky and the dark green of the forest. Beyond the valley, they saw a chata, a nobleman's chalet now silent and deserted, but in the fields above the valley the country folk were at their inevitable haymaking. Now and then they passed close enough to a farmhouse to see the grey stone of the walls and the flowers in the garden.

As they travelled further and further away from Liebstadt, Mason began to feel more and more vulnerable. He was aware of the fact that for the first time, they were travelling without the comforting though unseen presence of the cell back-up. They had left Gunther at Liebstadt to make his way back to Gorlitz, and Wilhelm and Johan were with Joachim.

Mason looked at the girl. She had her head back, and her eyes were closed. Lazero was engrossed in his driving, his hands tight on the wheel of the old Mercedes-Benz. It was warm in the bus. The children had grown quieter, and Mason looked back to see that Davis had succumbed to the general lethargy. His eyes were closed and his chin was down on his chest.

Pauline opened her eyes and looked out of the window.

Mason said: 'We should be in Komotau by five o'clock at this rate. The direct route would have been two hours less.'

'We have to avoid the checkpoint at Leutensdorf.'

Mason nodded, remembering the thick cross on the map. 'The train? Do we board it tonight.'

Pauline shook her head. 'No. The night trains are checked more thoroughly. So many refugees have been caught travelling at night without permits.' She rubbed her forehead. 'We board at seven in the morning at Schöneck, a small village outside Komotau.'

They were silent as Lazero negotiated a small stream, and climbed a short hill on the other side. Mason said: 'What happens when you get to France. How will you get back to Gorlitz?'

'Didn't Joachim tell you our plans?'

'What plans?'

'I suppose he didn't have time. I am to stay in France. The others will join me there eventually. The cell is finished in

Gorlitz. We have been fortunate. The other cells have been arrested. Leipzig. Dresden. Prague. Nuremberg. They're all in concentration camps or dead.'

'And you have survived.

'Only because of my father. Because of his insistence on absolute security, his refusal to move until every detail is accounted for. Above all, his planning was meticulous, and this is what kept us alive.' She frowned. 'But he was upset about the four soldiers in the forest. He knew it was necessary, but he felt it had compromised us. He said it was evidence of our existence.'

'But won't they be posted as deserters?'

'For a while, but the small questionable factors will arouse suspicion. There may be questions from their families; unfinished business one of them may have had to do. One can never tell. These are things he would have taken into account if he was in control.'

'But it was unavoidable!'

'Yes, but it does not alter the fact that – as he put it – we left footprints.'

'I see.' Mason looked at her. 'And now we are on our own entirely?'

Lazero looked at Mason briefly and smiled. Pauline said: 'No, not entirely.' She smiled. 'We never have been alone.'

'No. Who is with us now. Gunther went back to Gorlitz.'

'Since we have been in the forest we have had the Lidice Vengeance Group of Czech partisans with us all the time. They covered our march through the forest, and since Liebstadt they have been responsible for our reconnaissance.'

'I never saw anyone in the forest.'

'You would not have seen them. They are experienced woodsmen. They are used to fighting a silent war. I knew they were there, yet I never saw them either.'

'What would have happened if a German patrol had seen us?'

'Their job was to intercept and wipe out any patrols before they got to us. That was how my father planned it.' The pride in her voice was unmistakable. This was only the second time Mason had heard her call him anything but Joachim. He realised with a shock that he did not even know their real names.

At that moment Lazero waved to a man standing in the shadow of a red spruce at the edge of the forest. The man lifted his hand briefly, and then the bus went past him and into the next corner.

Pauline said: 'This group has been assigned to cover the road to Komotau. They will warn us of danger. There are not many of them left. More than a hundred of their unit have left to join the uprising in the south. They will join the corps in the Carpathians who are supporting the Russians.'

'And after Komotau?'

She shrugged. 'Then we will finally be alone.' She smiled. 'Does that make you nervous?' There was no malice in her tone.

'Nervous!' He smiled back. 'It frightens the hell out of me. But then, I don't know when I'm not nervous.'

She was suddenly serious. 'It is wise to be afraid – always. Fear heightens the senses.' She put her hand on his. 'I have never seen your fear.'

The small intimacy warmed him. He covered her hand with his and said quickly: 'I know of no one with more courage than you. It has been a great privilege to be with you these last few days.'

She coloured and withdrew her hand. She turned quickly as Lazero braked hard, and brought the bus to a sliding stop in the loose sand. In front of them, in the middle of the road, stood a civilian with hand raised. He came towards them. Lazero stepped down from the bus with Pauline and Mason close behind him.

The man spoke in a dialect Mason could not understand. Lazero translated for them. 'He says that word has come back that a motorised patrol is on its way down this road. He has been assigned to get us off the road.'

'Off the road?' Mason looked around him. On either side of the road were deep woods stretching for hundreds of metres.

The man spoke again, his words coming with rapid urgency as he pointed to a break in the trees. Lazero said quickly, 'You must leave the bus and follow him into the trees. He will show you where to hide until they are past. I will stay with the bus as though it has broken down.'

Mason looked at the children craning their heads out of the windows. Davis stepped down and came towards them. 'Trouble?'

Mason nodded. 'Another patrol.'

Pauline said: 'We must get the children out of the bus.'

Davis grinned. 'Nothing easier.' He raised his voice, and in his Welsh-accented French, called out: 'Come on now. All out. Last one out is a green monkey.' Shrieking and laughing, the children scrambled for the exits. 'Right. Line up with your monitors.' Pauline ushered them briskly towards the break in the trees. The partisan led the way, while Mason and Davis swept away their footprints with branches. Lazero opened the hood of the bus and removed a small link from the injector. Mason went quickly down the aisle of the bus to check for signs of the children. He picked up a cap and followed Davis into the trees.

The children were already a hundred metres into the woods, following a trail that went down into a hollow. The partisan stopped and indicated to Pauline that they should go a little further down and take cover in the ravine. Then he left them and went back into the bus. Mason and Davis helped the monitors to settle the younger ones into hollows and behind fallen logs, cautioning them to remain silent. When they were satisfied that the children were safely hidden, the two men went back to the bus. They found Lazero sitting on the bumper, puffing nervously at a thick brown-paper cigarette. Its mouth end was flat where his lips had held it.

The two Czechs spoke rapidly together, then the partisan went to a shrub just inside the woods, dug out a cloth-wrapped bundle, and opened it to reveal a squat M3 sub-machine gun. He slung it over his shoulder, directed a remark at Lazero who replied with a monosyllable, and disappeared into the trees.

Lazero said: 'He and the other three will spread out on either side of the road. You had better take cover.'

'The other three?' Mason looked around him at the silent forest. 'What other three?'

Lazero shrugged and waved vaguely at the trees. 'They are there somewhere.' He flicked the cigarette on to the road and stamped it out.

Mason and Davis retreated about fifty metres into the woods where they found a small dry gully. They lay down and threw a few handfuls of leaves over their bodies in an attempt at camouflage rather than concealment. They did not expect the Germans to leave the road to search the woods, even if they stopped.

From his position, Mason could just see the bus through the leaves of the shrub in front of him. There was no sign of Lazero. In the silence, he felt he could hear his heart beating. He lay there for a long while, tension growing within him, while overhead birds fluttered through the branches and once a small furry animal scurried along a dead branch and into a hollow tree.

Wild bees hummed in the still air. All at once, out of the sound of the bees grew the ugly drone of a truck motor, its note changing with the rise and fall of the uneven road. They heard it for a full five minutes before its mud-green shape slowed alongside the bus. They heard the shouted questions and the answers, and they saw the helmeted soldiers, weapons slung over their shoulders alighting from over the tailboard at the back of the truck. Mason felt the tension rising within him as he thought of Pauline and the children behind him. If one of them should move or cry out, they were done for. Help – the kind they had known until now – was no longer with them, and exposure would be disastrous.

Mason counted the soldiers as they appeared and reappeared from the bus and the truck. He counted five, but he couldn't be sure there weren't two more. He heard a demand for papers, and glimpsed Lazero as he walked to the bus.

Mason caught a hint of the disaster to come when he saw one of the soldiers leave the road and walk a short distance into the trees. The man began unbuttoning the front of his trousers when something on the ground held his attention. He bent slightly to look more closely, his scrutiny following some pattern he had seen in the soft earth. Mason thought it must be a child's footprint, but whatever it was, he watched in growing alarm as the man buttoned himself up and walked towards the hollow where the children lay hidden.

He passed within three metres of the gully and the hidden men, oblivious of everything but the sign he was following.

Mason saw Davis lift his head silently to watch the man moving away from them. Mason knew he had no choice. He had to stop the German discovering the children. There was no time to plan beyond the immediate decision, no time to consider the consequences. He rose to his feet, and moved with infinte caution. All the skills he had learnt as a soldier became reflexes conditioned by years of experience. Silently he stalked the man a few feet ahead of him, feeling for the knife strapped to his sleeve.

Suddenly the man stopped, head to one side as though listening, and it was at that moment that a child whimpered. It was just a tiny sound, but to Mason it was as loud as a scream so intent was he on the man ahead of him. He hesitated for a second, and then with every nerve tensed, took one pace to bring him within reach of the unsuspecting man. His arm went over the shoulder and under the chin in one quick movement, and the knife was rammed home. To his horror, the man began to struggle, his throat rattling hoarsely as he kicked backwards. All at once Davis was in front of them, his knife unsheathed to end the unequal struggle.

Davis held the man for a moment and then let him slump to the ground. He looked up at Mason. 'What now?'

'We must draw them off – away from the children. Here, help me to carry him to the road.'

'To the road?'

'We must draw them to the other side of the road. Give me his gun.'

Davis picked up the Schmeisser MP 40. Mason saw that the nine millimetre magazine was full. He slung it across his chest and lifted the man by his arms as Davis took the feet. They could hear the Germans laughing and shouting on the road. They carried the dead soldier at an angle to the road, towards it and about fifty metres ahead of the truck.

Panting with exertion, they half carried, half dragged their grisly burden to a large bush at the edge of the road where they were effectively screened from the soldiers fifty metres away. Mason moved a branch carefully to enable him to see the activity alongside the truck. Lazero was still inside the bus, searching his coat pockets. A soldier, his machine gun unslung, was watching him from the bottom step.

Mason let the branch fall back quietly, and indicated to Davis that they should lift the soldier between them.

'Let him fall into the road the moment I fire a shot. Then we run like hell for the other side of the road.'

They hoisted the man between them and with the gun on his right arm, Mason pulled the trigger. A deafening burst of gunfire echoed through the woods, and Mason swore as he remembered that the Schmeisser had no single shot mode. The German tumbled into the road, and the effect on the patrol was electrifying. As the two men made a fast zig-zag dash for the trees on the other side of the road, the Germans dived for cover and opened up with their weapons. Mason slid into the gully on the edge of the trees and brought up the machine gun. He fired a burst at a prone man beside the truck and saw him half-rise and slump back, his weapon clattering to the ground. Mason swung to the left and fired at one of the soldiers sprinting for the trees on their side of the road. The man threw up his arms and collapsed at the edge of the trees, not ten metres from where they lay.

'Run for it, Taff. Keep moving away from the children,' he bellowed over the bursts of machine gun fire.

Bullets cut the branches above their heads. Davis was about to run when a new note suddenly burst upon them. The harsh bark of heavy calibre bullets echoed through the trees, and soldiers caught in a crossfire on both sides of the truck, thrashed about wildly as point four-five calibre slugs tore into them from their unprotected flanks. Within ten seconds, silence descended on the woods and the battle was over. Mason looked at Davis blankly, and the Welshman grinned at him.

'The Czechs. Those grease guns they use make a bit of a mess.'

The two men stood up, and keeping a watchful eye on the sprawled soldiers, moved warily towards the bus. From the trees opposite, four men carrying M3 machine guns emerged cautiously from the bushes. At that moment, Lazero stood up from the floor of the bus where he had thrown himself at the sound of the first shots.

The Czechs quickly gathered up the German weapons and stacked them in the truck. Mason dumped his with the others.

One of the Czechs shouted something at Lazero.

Lazero laughed. 'He says you are either mad or stupid. He wants to know why you ran across the road.'

Briefly, Mason described what had happened from the moment the soldier discovered the children. Lazero translated for his compatriot. The man made a brief comment and Lazero roared with laughter.

'He says it is as he thought. You are crazy.' He began to help the others as they dragged the soldiers off the road.

Mason watched them, puzzled. 'What are they doing?'

Lazero looked up. 'They will strip the soldiers and leave them in the woods. Soon, ten men will come from the village and bury them. In the meanwhile they will take the truck to the partisan headquarters, and the weapons will be distributed amongst them.' He looked at one of the men covering the blood with sand. 'We must get the children here and out of the area. Another patrol will start searching for this lot before tonight. These men will collect the bullet cases and remove all sign of the Germans.'

Suddenly Mason felt desperately tired. After the exhilaration of the past few minutes, doing what he had been trained to do and making decisions for himself, instead of being moved about by the machinations of others, the aftermath was a tremendous anti-climax.

A faint haze hung in the air, and all about them was the smell of cordite. Mason looked at the Czechs as they began removing the uniforms from the corpses, and knew he would remember this moment for the rest of his life.

Chapter Thirteen

Friday, 11th August, 1944. 3 p.m.

Major Brunner stared for a moment at the three men sitting at the bare wooden table, then turned away and walked to the dirty uncurtained window overlooking the ruins of the bombed tenement.

Without turning around, he said: 'I can't agree to your proposals, gentlemen.' He turned and pointed his cane at the swarthy man on the left of Hackett. 'Do you think I am going to deliver you to Friedrichshafen, and send you into limbo without knowing where the hell you've disappeared to?' He smile frostily. 'I'm afraid my superiors would hardly entrust me with the control of this operation if they thought I was simple-minded.' He tapped his calf gently. 'I am afraid there is no alternative to my decision. Kuhn will go with you, and stay with you until you make contact.'

The swarthy man looked up. 'On one condition.'

Brunner struck the table with his cane. 'There are no conditions.' His voice grew softer. 'Kuhn will be your unseen escort whether you like it or not.'

The third man stood up. He was fair and well-built, and his light blue eyes reflected an inner core of ruthless cunning. He said: 'Just as long as he keeps clear of us, he can do what he likes.' He cracked his huge knuckles and paced to the window and back. 'We have a job to do, and we don't want anyone getting in our way. We were thoroughly briefed in Berlin.'

'Then you were told about Kuhn. He was Kaltenbrunner's choice as your escort.' Brunner looked at the two men. His eyes were cold. 'Did you tell him you objected to being nursemaided?'

'We don't object to Kuhn being there, as long as he stays out of sight.'

Hackett watched them silently, looking from face to face as they spoke. He had been brought to this room two hours ago to meet the men who were to replace Mason and Davis. From the beginning he had been intrigued by the two men. Grant, the swarthy man, was obviously the leader, but Patterson soon let it be known that he was not to be trifled with. Hackett thought they must be men of consequence in the Nazi hierarchy, probably Gestapo, since they were not overawed by the Major's rank. He in turn was imbued with the confidence of his mandate from Berlin, and was in no mood for compromise. His insistence on the plan being followed to the letter had caused some difficulty. Hackett was puzzled by his persistence. To him it seemed an unnecessary refinement that Brunner should require their agreement, but he finally had it, and the apparently empty victory gave the Major some sort of satisfaction.

The three men were similarly dressed. Corduroy trousers and roll-necked jerseys, covered by jackets of a rough woollen material had been issued to them when they arrived. Each had been issued with identity documents and travel permits, and Grant had been given a map with their route marked on it. Hackett had no way of knowing if the others had been issued with any special documents as Joachim had suggested they would be. He wasn't about to ask.

Since they had arrived, they had spoken only English, Major Brunner in his stilted German phrasing, and the other two in a way that was indistinguishable from anyone from the south of England. Hackett was not sufficiently familiar with accents to pinpoint their dialect, but to his ear they sounded authentic. He was even prepared to consider the possibility that they were Englishmen, perhaps members of the ill-fated British Free Corps, raised by Hitler from about a dozen misguided prisoners-of-war. But most mystifying of all to Hackett was their choice of rendezvous. This bare office in an abandoned building in the middle of Gorlitz, appeared to be an inappropriate place to begin an operation of this nature.

Hackett suspected that Brunner had some ulterior motive of his own in planning it this way.

He was aware that the Major was speaking to him. 'Here are your ration cards for the next eight days.' He drew two large pages of stamps from a folder on the table. Hackett looked at them curiously. In the middle of the cards was a large square without stamps. The square was headed 'Reichskarte für Urlauber', and on the left of the card was a large '4' with the word 'Tage' below it. Hackett presumed that each card was valid for four days' rations. He realised that the Major was still speaking. 'Those are Wehrmacht ration stamps. You will have no difficulty with them since your papers describe you as a member of the Feldgendarmerie who sometimes work in civilian clothes. You have been fully briefed on what you have to do. It is essential that you meet with the Underground group in Kempten. They don't know yet that they have been penetrated. We have left them in place for this operation. We need them to pass the word on that you are coming.' He tapped his boot once more with his cane, and looked hard at Hackett. 'Remember the penalty for failure, so don't be foolish.'

Hackett thought of his brother and a hot anger surged through him. With an effort he controlled the urge to lash out at the supercilious bastard on the other side of the table. His time would come. He comforted himself with the thought of the shock awaiting the two agents once they were in Allied hands. In the meanwhile it was important that they should have no suspicion that he knew Mac was dead.

Brunner handed ration cards to the other two men. He looked at Hackett once more. 'Is there anything you wish to know? Any question you wish to ask me?'

Hackett thought for a moment. Was there anything he should ask? Anything he would ask if he thought Mac was still alive? He looked up at the Major. 'You are certain that one month from now, my brother will be handed over to the British consulate in Sweden?'

Brunner turned away from him and walked to the window. 'Providing you keep your side of the bargain, and we receive the signal from Grant.'

'What if something happens to Grant? Something that has

nothing to do with me?' Hackett felt a grim satisfaction in the game he was playing.

'Then in six weeks we will hand him over to the consulate anyway.'

The reply was so preposterous that Hackett was momentarily silenced. Then anger stirred in him once more. You bastard! You lying bastard! The thought was so vehement, it was almost as though he had spoken aloud. He suppressed his anger once more. He looked at Patterson and caught a look of contempt on the man's face. Good. As long as the man thought he believed their lies, the less he would be on his guard.

He nodded. 'See you stick to your side of the bargain.'

Brunner ignored the thrust and said: 'You will wait until you are told that your car is waiting downstairs. Don't move until then. You will be taken to the station where someone from my department will give you your tickets and take you to your compartment which will be sealed off by my agents. You will have no difficulty in getting to Friedrichshafen unhindered. From there you will be on your own.'

'Except for Kuhn.' Patterson smiled mockingly.

Major Brunner inclined his head a fraction. 'Except for Kuhn.' He went on. 'Once in Switzerland, your difficulties will begin. If you are obstructed in any way, ring the number written on the top of the map. You will get immediate assistance, even if you are held up at the border. Once in Switzerland, you should have no difficulty in completing your assignment. Even Italy will be simple after that.'

There was a sudden silence in the room. Hackett saw Grant and Patterson look at one another and then at Brunner. The tension in the room was palpable. Hackett was astonished. He doesn't know, he thought. Not even the great Major Brunner knows what this operation is all about. He doesn't know! He is only the chauffeur, he thought, unconsciously dropping into the OSS idiom. He's only driving the bus.

Patterson's hard eyes stared unblinkingly at Major Brunner. 'You wouldn't be trying to trap us into some indiscreet comments, would you, Major?' His voice was soft, but the menace was evident.

Major Brunner smiled blandly. 'Come now, gentlemen.

Whatever the S.S. Obergruppenführer Müller has not told me, a simpleton could deduce. I am the custodian of many more important state matters than this little episode.' He turned and went to the window. 'Hackett here will soon become aware of your ultimate destination, if he has not guessed it already. He is certainly no simpleton.'

Grant stood up angrily. 'What you have said amounts to treason. When we report back to Obergruppenführer Müller, you can be sure he will be informed of your comments.'

Major Brunner inclined his head once more. 'I trust you will do so. I'm sure he will be most interested in how much you were indiscreet enough to let slip.'

Hackett watched the thrust and parry with silent amusement. These two thugs were no match for this cunning bastard. The trouble was they didn't know the difference between brawn and brains. The knowledge comforted him. He knew what he had to deal with.

At the window, Brunner saw that the end of the broken beam in the courtyard was now covered by a small square of yellow cloth. Good. His man was in position. He turned to go.

'Remember, you will wait until your car arrives. If you have any last minute questions, ask them now.' He looked at each of them in turn. 'None. Right. Good luck, gentlemen.' He opened the door, returned the salute to the man standing at the door outside, and picking his way through the litter on the stairs, went down to the hall and left the building.

Back at his own office, Major Brunner rang the bell for his second in command. Schmidt arrived, looking pleased with himself.

He said: 'We got it all. You were right. It is Italy.'

Brunner smiled. 'You heard their reaction when I threw in Italy.' His smiled broadened. 'They're pathetic. They even accepted Kuhn finally.' He frowned. 'For a while I couldn't understand why they baulked at having him along. Kaltenbrunner chose him personally. He is the most efficient killer in the Gestapo. Then I realised that they didn't trust anyone else to kill the American. They want to do it themselves and make sure he isn't around to double-cross them.'

'Do they know about Hansen – Kuhn's backup?'

'They suspect there is one. They will look for him. You can

be sure they will lose both Kuhn and Hansen. But they won't lose Ohlendorf so easily, even if they do suspect there is a third man.' He leaned back in his chair. 'They will never suspect that we would be devious enough to send in a fourth man – and he will be waiting for them at Friedrichshafen.'

'Who will that be. Rowecki?'

'Yes. Are you certain that Hesselmann is cooperating?'

Schmidt nodded. 'He has placed the Kripo office at our disposal. Rowecki will have everything he needs.' He turned to go, then looked back at Major Brunner. 'As a matter of interest, Hesselmann is not a member of the party.' He smiled and went out.

Brunner went to the filing cabinet, took a key from his pocket, opened the top drawer and took a file from the back. He went back to his desk and studied the contents of the file then stood up after a few minutes and paced the floor in front of his desk.

What facts did he have?

Firstly, the two men were definitely bound for Italy.

Secondly, they were going via Switzerland, where the only objective could be money, or documents that represented money.

Thirdly, they were bound for a monastery.

A monastery?

Now what was the name of that pro-Nazi Bishop the Sicherheitsdienst had used in Rome last year . . . Huber? Huder? Hudal! That was it. Bishop Hudal.

Brunner went to a bookcase and took down a volume. The item he wanted wasn't there. He dialled a number that gave him access to the archives, and in five minutes he had the information he was looking for. Bishop Alois Hudal, born in 1885, graduated from the University of Graz and became Procurator General of the order of German knights and a member of the Consistorial Councils of several dioceses. When he was called to Rome, he became Coadjutant of the Instituto Santa Maria dell'Anima. Author of the books *Introduction to the Old Testament* and *Missa Papalis,* Hudal became widely respected for his knowledge of Papal matters through his study of the liturgy of the Papal Mass. However, his unrelenting opposition to communism led him to Nazism.

He was known to be associated with Prior Hermann Keller, a Benedictine monk who spied on Rome for the Sicherheitsdienst. Not so widely known was Hudal's work *The Foundations of National Socialism,* which espoused the Nazi cause. Most important of all, he was a good friend of S.S. Obergruppenführer Müller. This then was the man Grant and Patterson would be hoping to see in Italy.

Brunner closed the file on his desk. He sat back, quietly satisfied. He didn't know at this moment how far he dared go in using the knowledge he had, but use it he certainly would. First he had to make two calls. One to Major Hesselmann in Friedrichshafen to assure the Kriminalpolizei man in that city that Major Brunner had the backing of the authorities in Berlin, and to give him the Führerbefehl code number. The second was to a man who knew more about matters in Rome and the Vatican than anyone in the Third Reich. From this man he wanted one simple piece of information – the exact whereabouts of Bishop Hudal.

When his two calls were made, he sat back, satisfied. He looked at the notation on his file, and shook his head wonderingly. Everything was beginning to make sense. Bishop Hudal had been in Switzerland as recently as July but now he was back in Italy. It was time to report.

He shrugged his topcoat over his shoulders – it was beginning to turn cold – and pulled his gloves over his hands. A few minutes later, he was striding along the familiar colonnaded passage to the office on the second floor. There he found the Colonel sitting with his back to the door, glasses swinging in his right hand, staring out of the window at the workmen opposite. At his entrance, Colonel Wiessen swivelled his chair to face him.

Brunner saluted. The Colonel nodded briefly and waved to a chair. When he was seated, the Major opened the file. He took a page of typescript and passed it to his superior officer.

'My report, Herr Colonel. I have summarised the most important facts and brought the summary up to date. The three men have been briefed. They will leave the rendezvous point tonight.'

The Colonel looked at the report briefly. 'Kuhn was there?'

'He was there, Herr Colonel.'

'He knows what he has to do? He knows he has to kill the American?'

'Of course.'

The Colonel was silent for a long moment. 'It was necessary, I suppose?'

'Obergruppenführer Müller's instructions were explicit, Herr Colonel.'

The Colonel sighed. 'Yes, they were explicit. Herr Müller has left nothing to chance.' His voice was bitter. 'No one must be left alive after their usefulness has ended.' He looked directly at Brunner. 'Whatever happened to the days when we were nothing more than policemen?'

Brunner looked steadily at the Colonel. 'Those times are past, Herr Colonel.'

Colonel Wiessen appeared to brace himself. 'Yes. And God knows what times are coming.'

The Major remained silent. His superior officer stood up and went to a cabinet against the wall and took out a bottle. When he spoke, his voice was almost cheerful again. 'Come, Major. Drink a toast with me. A toast to the success of the operation. After all,' he continued mockingly, 'we are only obeying orders, aren't we, Major?'

Just before dark, three men in an abandoned building were led to a car waiting for them at the front entrance. Patterson scanned the quiet street as they drove off. He saw a motor-cyclist kick his bike into life and pull away from the kerb. He looked back as they turned the first corner. The motor-cyclist turned a hundred metres behind them.

Patterson looked at Grant. 'Kuhn. We'll have to sort that bastard out before we leave the train.

Grant nodded. 'Watch out for the other one. We'll have to get him too. We'll soon spot him on the train.'

Hackett listened to the quiet words without interest. He realised that his strategy would have to depend on circumstances. At least they had confirmed Joachim's briefing; that Italy was their destination. If only he were armed. He suspected that Grant was. In the meantime he would have to devise an overall strategy, one that was adaptable to most conditions. He had no doubt that he was to be killed when his usefulness was ended, but he would have something to say about that.

He was aware of the other two looking at him, and that Patterson had spoken. The man's ice blue eyes shifted to Grant and back to the American. 'Are you bloody deaf? I said, don't think of trying anything stupid. One of us will be watching you every inch of the way.'

'Why should I try anything? We both want the same thing; to get you to wherever you're going, and let you make that call to Brunner.'

Patterson grunted. 'Just remember that.'

Hackett wondered whether there had been any other candidates for the job besides these two. It appeared strange to Hackett that these were the best on offer. He surmised that Patterson was a man who pushed his blustering authority at every opportunity, and he considered Grant to be lazy and only marginally less stupid than his partner. Perhaps they were creatures of the men who had originated the operation, so choice was not a factor in their appointment for the assignment.

He turned to face the front and watched the uniformed driver guide the car skilfully through the streets towards the station. Behind them roared the motor-cyclist, his face and head grotesque under the helmet and goggles, while the man named Kuhn lay in the basement of the abandoned house, staring upwards through sightless eyes, a small bullet hole in his temple. It would be a month before he was found.

At exactly nine o'clock that same evening, an officer in one of the services of the Third Reich stopped at another call box in the same town. He looked up and down the deserted street, but apart from the music from a distant beer hall, nothing stirred. He looked up at the window on the fourth floor of the building opposite, where the light was on and the curtains drawn on one side. As he watched, the other curtain was drawn over the window. Good. They had seen him. He waited, glancing now and then at his watch. At last the telephone in the box rang. He picked it up before it rang again.

The officer held the receiver to his ear without speaking. He heard the familiar voice. 'Karl?'

'Yes. You are prompt.'

'Didn't we say it would always have to be like this?'

'Yes, forgive me. People sneer at the trappings of subterfuge, but this is what keeps us alive.'

'You sound depressed.'

'A little. I'm worried about you – Pauline – the others.'

'It's good of you to think of is, but it isn't necessary, believe me.'

'No. You are right. I am depressed. Have you heard anything?'

Karl caught the slight hesitation before the other man answered. 'The same patrol caught up with them on the other side of Geising. They – '

Karl caught his breath. 'The children?'

'No one was hurt, but the Czechs helped them to wipe out the patrol.'

For a moment, Karl felt infinitely sad. Although some would have been German, others would have been soldiers of his own land, Austria. Then he remembered he had accepted the consequences long ago. Nazism was the destroyer, not he.

'Karl?'

'Yes.'

'You still there? I'm sorry. I know how you must feel.'

'I can't grieve for the whole world.'

'No. No one can.' There was silence for a moment. 'One thing puzzles me. Preiss was not with the patrol.'

'Preiss?'

'The Gestapo man. He questioned Pauline in the church in Liebstadt.'

'Strange.' Karl thought for a moment. 'He could have gone back to Prague. No matter, it doesn't affect the situation.'

'No. Anyhow, we have disposed of Kuhn. It was necessary. We have replaced him with our own man.'

'Good. I have no regrets about Kuhn. He was a sadistic killer.' Silence for a moment. 'Will your man stay with them all the way?'

'Yes. He can go to ground in Switzerland after he completes his mission. It is one more of the cell safe.' Another pause. 'You are certain Kuhn was instructed to kill the American?'

'Absolutely certain. You were quite right to eliminate him.'

'Why Kuhn? Why not Grant or Patterson?'

Karl was mocking. 'German efficiency. The principle of one man for one job. The other two have to concentrate on their task. There must be no possibility of them being compromised.'

'Of course.'

'I hope you are right about your man. Grant will try to eliminate him.

'My man is good. They won't get to him. I'll stake my life on that.'

'You may be staking his.'

'He knows the risks. If it wasn't this job, it could have been another even more dangerous.'

'Of course. Forgive me. I'm not thinking straight tonight.'

'I wasn't cavilling. I wanted to put your mind at rest.'

'Of course.' He paused and looked up at the window which commanded a view of the streets in both directions. It was still curtained. 'Tell your man that the American's knife has been taken from him. He is unarmed.'

'I'll tell him. He would have expected it, but it is nice to be sure.'

'I must go.'

'I will keep to the contact schedule.'

'The next one as planned.' Karl was emphatic.

'Good. Take care.'

'You too.'

Karl replaced the receiver gently. He walked slowly away from the call box. Above him the light went out on the fourth floor.

On the other side of the city, Joachim replaced the receiver, stood up and stretched. It was time for him to move. He longed to rest, but for him, rest was a long forgotten luxury. He went to the window and looked down at the streets below. Then he sighed and went downstairs.

S.S. Oberführer Becker picked at his praline, and looked down the dinner table at his guests. Silver and crystal gleamed under the opulent chandelier overhead, and waiters hovered discreetly at the edges of the vast dining room.

Becker watched the scene with satisfaction. Lisa had done it again. Amongst the guests his wife had invited to his birthday party was a wealthy industrialist, a banker, an opera star and his own senior, S.S. Gruppenführer August Pohl. Becker was especially pleased by the presence of the head of the south-eastern region. Becker knew that Pohl liked him, and it would do no harm for him to see how elegant and accomplished Lisa was. Later Becker would give a modest but proficient violin solo, and then accompanied on the piano by Frau Pohl, he would play two or three little pieces by Schumann.

Since they were completely unaware of it, Becker's guests would not be particularly concerned that the rich trappings in this house had been paid for by thousands of Jews who had been murdered for their possessions. Becker's tour of duty in Poland had provided numerous opportunities for the acquisition of wealth undreamed of by this son of a puddler's assistant at the Aplerbeck Smelting works.

The conversation was light and animated, and Becker was gratified to see that Pohl monopolised Lisa, who had placed Pohl on her right at the other end of the table. For his part, he knew that Frau Pohl, seated on his left, was charmed by him. He had that effect on women, and Gerda Pohl, still slim and attractive at fifty, responded to him. At that moment one of the servants appeared at his side and bowed respectfully.

'A Herr Harster sends his compliments and requests permission to await your convenience. He apologises for the intrusion and says it is important that he speak to you tonight.'

Becker had a flash of irritation. Then it passed as he realised that The Ferret must have discovered something significant to interrupt an important occasion.

'Put him in my study. See that he has food and drink. I'll be with him later.'

'I'll tell him immediately, Herr Oberführer.'

He apologised to Frau Pohl, who dismissed the interruption with a smile. The evening continued without incident; the recital was a huge success and at last S.S. Oberführer Becker saw his guests to their cars as they rolled up in turn at the portico. The last to go was the opera singer, who left with the industrialist. It was after midnight.

He found Herr Harster in his study, nodding over Becker's

copy of the morning newspaper. The Gestapo man stood up as Becker entered.

'My apologies, Herr Oberführer. I –'

'It's quite all right, man.' Becker selected a cigar from a box on his desk. 'What is it?'

Briefly Harster reported the finding of the two bodies, and the connection between the missing soldier and the bodies in the truck at Auschwitz.

'I have confirmed that the body of the soldier is that of Gefreiter Albert Smital, the soldier who was posted as a deserter. I also believe that the bodies of two of the men murdered in the forest were burnt on a farm near Rutberg, and misrepresented as the bodies of two prisoners-of-war.'

Becker, his cigar forgotten, stared at the Gestapo agent. Then finally he reached for the desk lighter, flicked the wheel and touched the flame to the end of his cigar.

He took several puffs before he spoke. 'And the children? What on earth do they have to do with this operation?'

'Nothing, Herr Oberführer. I believe that the three men were being guided to that siding. They were intercepted on the way by a Home Guard patrol, and the patrol was killed by partisans. At the railway siding, they found the children in the truck which was waiting to be picked up, and released them. They must have been discovered by Gefreiter Smital, who was killed and his body placed in the truck with six already dead children.'

Harster watched in silence as his superior officer paced the study, puffing at his cigar, his brow wrinkled with thought. At last Becker returned to his easy chiar.

'So this top secret operation only required one of the prisoners. The others were expendable, so Brunner accepted the deaths of the other two which made no difference to his plans.' He paused. 'But what is this prisoner needed for?'

Harster coughed deprecatingly. 'I have a theory, Herr Oberführer. I offer it only tentatively, but I think it fits the facts.'

'Well, what is this theory?'

'I believe that the two supposedly dead prisoners have been substituted by two Germans, and that the prisoner is required to vouch for them when they reach Allied control.' He coughed again, plainly nervous at putting forward his theory. 'I believe the two substitutes are either setting up an escape route for someone, or moving valuables for that someone.'

Becker smiled broadly, and pointed with his cigar. 'Money. I felt it in my bones. I'm positive it concerns money, and the extent of the operation means that there must be a fortune involved.'

Harster sat back, relieved that Becker had accepted his theory so readily. 'I agree,' he said. 'I too felt more strongly about the money theory than the other.'

Becker began pacing once more. 'The other two, and the children, is there any sign of them?'

'They have disappeared from sight, Herr Oberführer. But it will be a simple matter to track them down. We should have them in custody in a day or two.'

'How does that affect the operation?'

'It doesn't. We can open a docket to investigate the murder of the soldiers, and since it is linked to the escape of fifty children, it will have no bearing on the operation.'

'I don't agree. If we arrest two prisoners-of-war who were originally part of the operation, it might prove an embarrassment for someone.'

Harster said blandly: 'Only if they are taken alive.' He smiled. 'After all, since they have already been burnt to death, it would be ridiculous to suppose that they would come back to life.'

Becker laughed out loud. 'I congratulate you, Herr Harster. You have an answer for everything.' He grew serious. 'What of the third man? Have you found any sign of him – or of the two who are now with him?'

'No, Herr Oberführer. But in this case, too, it will only take a short while to pick up their trail.'

'Pick up the group with the children first. Do it quickly. Then find the men involved in the operation.'

'And when I have found them?'

'Do nothing, but report back to me immediately.' He looked at Harster quickly and looked away. 'You realise we are on extremely dangerous ground? Don't do anything rash.'

'No, Herr Oberführer. Thank you for seeing me at so late an hour, but I felt it necessary to report at once.'

Becker showed his visitor to the door, and went up to bed feeling that the night had been one long success. The fact that Lisa was still waiting up for him didn't dampen his spirits one little bit. It was, he thought happily, the cherry on the top.

Chapter Fourteen

Friday, 11th August, 1944. 7 p.m.

The little Sudeten town of Komotau lies south of the Erzbirge range, and about eighty kilometres southwest of the city of Teplitz. The road from Teplitz climbs steadily after leaving the town of Brux, and within sight of Komotau the elevation is high enough for mist to settle in the hollows and chill the night air.

The yellow lights of the bus searched out the potholes in the rough dirt road, and behind the battered vehicle rose a swirling cloud of yellow dust. The children huddled together on the narrow seats, and now and then tired eyes closed and cramped limbs stretched against the enveloping fatigue.

Pauline sat in the seat next to Lazero and peered with reddened eyes through the dirty windscreen, searching for landmarks described to her by Wilhelm two days before. Suddenly she raised her arm, and Lazero slowed to a crawl, and then stopped alongside a massive rock just off the road.

'Wait here for a moment.' She jumped down from the bus and disappeared into the darkness. Some of the children, woken by the cessation of movement, peered sleepy-eyed through the window. Mason stretched and stood up. He stepped down into the road, looking anxiously into the dark. He felt irritable, and not only through weariness. Her habit of acting without consulting anyone seemed to him to invite unnecessary dangers, risking the safety of the whole expedition. It was a legacy of the secrecy of the Underground, but he felt it was time for her to take him into her confidence.

He heard Davis's voice from the dark. 'Where's she gone now?'

'She didn't say, and I wish she bloody well would.'

'I think I hear her coming back.' They both listened intently, but apart from the night sounds and the spit and hiss of the engine noises, they heard nothing.

'I don't hear her.' Mason began to walk back and forth as the cold began to seep through his clothes. 'We'd better get the children out for a short break.'

Together they herded the group from the bus, enjoining the monitors to watch the smaller children and to help them with their clothing. They had scarcely settled the children back in their seats, and counted heads, when they heard footsteps on the road. Pauline appeared out of the dark.

'The lay-by is two hundred metres ahead. It's empty, but Wilhelm told me that military vehicles arrive at all hours and stop there for a break.'

Mason nodded. 'Then we can't stay there. It would look too suspicious if fifty children were seen out at this time of night.'

'There is a side road just a little further on, with a gap in the trees. We can drive the bus in there, and leave it until I come back.'

Mason's irritation surfaced. 'Hold it! Until you come back from where?'

Pauline looked surprised. 'I have to make contact with the cell here. Joachim arranged for a friend to use all her bread coupons, and we will return them to her. Then we don't have to search for an open shop at this time of night.'

'That makes sense, but you appear to think we can guess what your plans are.'

Pauline sensed his anger. 'I'm sorry. I know I've been secretive, but it has become second nature.' She took his arm, 'Come. Get on the bus and I'll brief you.' She nodded to Lazero. The Czech started the engine, and with Pauline guiding him, steered the bus along the dark road into a gap in the trees. He went in as far as he could and stopped the engine. Davis went through the bus talking to the children in his broken French, soothing and reassuring them, and settling them down. Mason watched, wondering at the Welshman's way with children. They trusted him and Mason could see that some of them even loved him, and in turn the Welshman was warm and friendly towards them.

Pauline sat beside Mason. 'I have a rendezvous at nine o'clock, with this friend in Komotau. If the signal is set at safe, I will go in and fetch the bread. If not I will go back every hour until it is.'

Mason frowned. 'What is the signal?'

'A piece of ribbon tied to a railing in front of the building. The third vertical railing from the left as you face the building.'

'And what of tomorrow? What happens on the train? What are we supposed to be? A choir? A party on a picnic? What other permits do you have?' He suppressed his irritation. 'Forgive me for sounding off, but you have told us nothing. If anything happens to you, we'll be stranded with no plan.'

She took his hand and smiled. 'Nothing will happen to me.' She laughed out loud. 'There is a saying in English: "The devil looks after his own." I have my very own private devil.'

He laughed with her. 'And what have you got beside your very own devil? Do you have other permits?'

'I have the permit I used in the church. Then I have one for the train. On that we are described as an excursion party bound for the Horst Wessel Memorial concert in Bayreuth.'

'Then there really is a memorial concert?'

'Of course. There is the regional concert in Bayreuth, and then the final concert in Berlin on the anniversary of his birth. We must use what actually exists. It is so easy to get caught out otherwise.' She smiled. 'But I don't think we will bother to go to Berlin in October.'

Mason laughed. 'You are quite a different person from what you were in the forest – so withdrawn and angry.'

'Was I really like that?'

'Ferocious.'

Pauline laughed once more. 'I am sure I was not.'

Mason grew serious. 'When I saw you on the train, I thought you were very lovely. Now I think you are beautiful.'

Pauline took her hand away quickly, and looked away from him. In the dark Mason thought she was frowning.

He said: 'I'm sorry. Have I offended you?'

'No.' She turned back to him. 'No, I am not offended. It was the nicest thing anyone has said to me, and I was afraid.'

'Afraid?' Mason was startled. 'I would have expected you to be offended, but why afraid?'

She was silent for a long while. 'Perhaps I am afraid my very own devil will stop looking after me if something wonderful happens to me.' Her voice was soft. She paused, then suddenly she laughed, as though she wished she had not spoken her thoughts aloud. 'No. Berlin is out. After Bayreuth – '

Mason felt he had to match her tone. He said facetiously: 'Then we are a party returning to France from the Memorial Concert.'

Pauline looked at him with surprise. 'How did you know that?'

Mason looked startled. 'You mean we are?'

'Not to France exactly, but to Kempten, which is about fifty kilometres from the Swiss border.'

'And you have all these permits with you? What if Herr Preiss had decided to search you, and found three or four permits on you?'

She smiled secretively. 'But I have no permits on me?'

'You haven't. Then where are they?'

'Agnes Bedaux has them – in her bloomers.'

'In her – ' Mason laughed out loud.

'We sewed a pocket in her bloomers. They're tucked in there. She is very proud of her new role – custodian of the documents.' She chuckled. 'She was quite indignant when I referred to her bloomers. She said modern girls called them panties.'

Mason said: 'What if she – '

'Don't ask! When I teased her, she pouted and said that only happened to little girls like her sister.' She grew serious. 'We joke, but it is a serious business to a young girl her age. She made the suggestion, and she has become more responsible – if that were possible.'

At that moment Davis joined them. 'If that is Agnes you are talking about, I agree. She is a very brave girl. From what the children told me, it seems that Agnes kept them going in that stinking truck. She made them sing and taught songs to those who didn't know them. She shared out the food, and showed them how to keep warm. I believe more would have died but for her.'

Pauline said quietly. 'We have to get them to France. If we fail now, I don't know how I could face it.'

'By heaven, woman!' Davis feigned anger. 'Don't you dare talk of failure. Not while we have life in our bodies, and Agnes Bedaux's bloomers.'

Mason laughed. 'You heard, Taff?'

'Agnes told me about it.'

Pauline, who was about to become tearful, smiled and pressed Davis's hand. 'You're very good with the children, Taff.' She frowned. 'I've heard Bob call you that, but it isn't your real name, is it?'

He held up his hand. 'For you I will make the supreme sacrifice and bare my hidden secret.' He threw his arms wide in mock tragedy. 'I cannot tell a lie. My name is Gwillam Aloysius Davis.'

Pauline stifled her laughter. 'Aloysius! I swear I'm not laughing. It's a beautiful name.'

Mason said: 'Aloysius!' He laughed. 'Now you'll feel much better. Confession is good for the soul, and you can't confess to worse than that.'

They all laughed, and for a short while, the real world seemed far away. They talked desultorily, while the time passed and the sound of the night came to them from the forest. Lazero had begun to snore softly, his head on his chest, his legs stretched out on the seat.

Pauline looked at her watch. 'You must take down the address of my friend with the bread. If I haven't returned by morning . . .'

Mason stopped her. 'I'm coming with you.'

'No. It is too dangerous for both of us to go into the house.'

'I'll stay a hundred metres behind you. You can't go alone.'

'No closer than a hundred metres.'

'What is the address.'

'Six Shönaustrasse. Apartment fourteen.'

'What time will you go?'

'In half an hour. It is no more than twenty minutes from here.'

'Then rest a while. I'll call you if you sleep.'

Half an hour later, the girl walked along the quiet streets of Komotau, taking careful note of the street names, and remembering the map Wilhelm had shown her. She crossed the bridge over the Komotau river, a stream which eventually flowed into one of the many tributaries of the Elbe. Below her, the dark water rushed past the bridge supports, and swept in a wide wake over the stony shallows. She crossed the park and turned into a narrow street of tenement buildings, now silent and dark, their windows blacked out against air raids.

Number six was a four-storey block protected from the street by a row of wrought iron palings, which stood two metres from the building. Between the palings and the building was a walkway filled with the litter of years. The palings themselves, set in a metre-high brick wall, were almost two metres high and shaped like spears with twin spikes at the top. There was no way to get over or through them, and Pauline walked to the end of the building where she saw a narrow gap between the palings and the building next door. She went back to the other end of the building and searched for the ribbon. It wasn't there. She looked back along the street, and saw Mason's dark figure against the wall on the corner. She went back to him.

'There's no signal. We'll have to come back in an hour.'

'Are you sure? You looked at both ends just in case.'

'Of course. But these people don't make that kind of mistake. The instructions were explicit.'

'Then we'll come back in an hour.'

They walked swiftly back the way they had come, and twenty minutes later climbed tiredly aboard the bus. Most of the children were asleep, but there were some whose hunger had prevented their weariness from overtaking them. They stared at her hopefully. She just shook her head.

Lazero patted her shoulder. 'The signal will be there this time, you'll see. They are very reliable, these people.' Pauline just nodded.

Thirty minutes later Pauline left the bus, followed within a few minutes by Mason who kept her in view across the bridge and through the park. They moved silently through the deserted streets, their rubber soles making no sound on the cobbled surface.

Mason stopped on the corner of Schönaustrasse and watched the girl walk slowly along the railings in front of the building. She disappeared for a few minutes and then reappeared from across the road on his left.

'It isn't there.' She slipped off her head shawl, tucked it into her pocket and then took off her coat.

She said: 'I'm going in. Something is wrong, I know it.'

Mason was vehement. 'You're not going in. If something is wrong, you could be in danger. You said yourself, you don't take chances.'

'I have to go. Not just for the food – ' She was silent for a moment.

'What are you saying? Is there another reason you have to go in there? For heaven's sake, don't go secretive on me now.'

She hesitated. 'My friend. The one who has the food – ' She paused once more.

'Well?

'She is very important to someone. Someone to whom we owe our lives, and who is keeping us informed of every move the Kripo makes. If she is in danger, I have to do something. We owe him that much.'

Mason stood for a moment in thought. He realised that she had made a purely emotional decision, but he knew, too, the value of loyalty within a cell. It was like platoon loyalty. Without it, men fought as individuals, open to destruction by any cohesive opposing force. In the dark, he saw that she was standing close, looking up at him as thought beseeching him to see it her way.

'Right. You have to go. But I'm going in with you.'

'No. I have a plan. You will complicate things. Keep my coat for me. And, Bob – '

'Yes.'

'Please stay nearby.' He held her shoulders, then pulled her gently towards him. As he held her, he was astonished to feel her trembling.

'You don't have to go in there. Let me go.'

She pulled away abruptly. 'No. I must do it.' She turned and walked towards the building. Mason was uneasy as he watched her disappear into the dark. He wasn't sure whether he should stop her, or if she was right to go in. Cautiously he moved closer to the building.

Pauline found the gap at the end of the palings, and walked along the littered path. She hesitated in the tiny hallway, listening for sounds that might betray the existence of danger. Then she turned to her left, moving softly past the first apartment door. In the passage, she could just make out brass numbers screwed to the doors. Softly she tried each of the doors in turn, but they were all locked. Some of the numbers were missing, but she counted the doors from the last number she saw. It wasn't until she was on the fourth floor that she found what she was looking for. One of the doors opened at her touch, and inside she saw the discarded papers and broken furniture that told her she was in an unoccupied apartment. She went back to the door and looked at the number again. Forty-one. She looked over the low parapet wall to the street below where she could just discern Mason's figure on the corner. He saw her and lifted his hand. They could have been the last two people on earth. Not in the park nor in the streets had they seen a single soul, and the silence and the dark gave her a feeling of enveloping menace. It seemed to her like the silence of a forest when all the feathered creatures are aware of the presence of danger.

Back on the first floor, she braced herself and then tried the handle of number fourteen. The door swung open, and in the room beyond, by the light of a dim unshaded bulb in the ceiling, two women sat at a table embroidering tray-cloths. Both looked up at her with startled eyes.

Pauline recognised the younger one, but the older woman was a stranger to her. She looked around the tiny room, and was conscious of a strange tension in it. There was no doubt that someone was desperately afraid.

She said brightly, 'Haven't you finished that cloth yet?' She shut the door behind her. 'I finished mine today. I should have brought it down for you to see.' She began to improvise. 'You know the tree bit that was so difficult? I did it in stem-stitch, and it worked.' Her voice trembled slightly, and she realised she had been caught up in the pervasive fear in the room.

The younger woman was the first to recover her composure, and followed the girl's lead. 'But I told you twice, it was the only way to do it.' As she spoke, her eyes looked fearfully in the direction of the door on her left. The older woman kept hard eyes on Pauline. Her animosity was as tangible as the younger girl's fear. Pauline pulled out a chair and sat. The girl continued, 'I shouldn't be sewing in this light. Johanna here keeps telling me I'll go blind. But I have to finish this.'

Pauline picked up the cue. 'My husband is the same. "Anna", he says, "why are you so stubborn?" Men are all the same. They're worse than we are for nagging.' Pauline hoped the dialogue made sense. At least she knew the older woman's name was Johanna, and the other two knew that she was calling herself Anna. She continued, 'Now he's complaining because I forgot to do the shopping today. As though he never forgets anything.'

The younger woman gave a perceptible nod, and Pauline sighed with relief. So they had the food. At least that was something.

At that moment the door on the left opened, and in the semi-darkness Pauline saw the outline of a man in the unmistakable dress of a Gestapo agent. His raincoat was the light-coloured regulation wartime issue. He had black hair, full lips and slightly eastern cheekbones and eyes. His wire-rimmed glasses gave his eyes a protuberance which was comical rather than sinister. Pauline knew that he wasn't a bit funny.

It was strange, but her fear had given way to a numbness, and she wondered if she was becoming inured to their intimidation. She watched him, knowing she should show some sign of surprise at his appearance, but the fact of his being there was somehow anti-climactic. She simulated surprise, and then concern.

'I'm sorry.' She smiled at the man. 'I didn't know I was intruding. I wouldn't have barged in if I had known you had a visitor.' She saw the younger girl nod imperceptibly. So there was only one of them.

He came into the room and stood over her. 'Who are you? Have you papers?'

She laughed. 'Good heavens! Must I carry a permit when I come downstairs for a visit?'

'You live in the building?' He began unbuttoning his coat. 'Which apartment?'

'Forty-one.'

When she saw Johanna frown slightly, she knew it was the wrong number. When he took a pad from his inside pocket and flick the pages over, her heart sank.

He stopped at a page of numbers. 'You're lying. Forty-one is empty.' He closed the pad, slipped it into his pocket and buttoned his coat. He studied her carefully, his eyes lingering on her full breasts. 'Who are you?'

'Anna Strauss. I live in the building.'

He swung his arm and the back of his wrist slammed against her cheek, sending her chair crashing over backwards. The blow caused her eyes to water, and for a moment she was blinded. She never saw the kick coming, and it caught her in the side, forcing the air from her body. She lay where she had fallen, struggling for breath, willing her limbs to move.

'Get up.'

She struggled to her feet, and he grabbed her arm, his fingers biting cruelly into her flesh.

'Let us go together and see this apartment forty-one, and you can make a cup of coffee for me.' His lips smiled, but his eyes remained cruel. 'Perhaps you would like to offer me a drink.' He dragged her towards the door. It was then that she realised that he really meant to go up there; but what was the point when he knew that the apartment was empty? He must have searched the building. Then she knew and despair overwhelmed her. When they arrived in front of the door to number forty-one, she knew she had guessed correctly. He stopped her abruptly, and with one wrench tore the front of her dress.

'What have we here?' His mouth began working, and her skin crawled with revulsion. He hooked his fingers in the top of her brassiere to tear it from her body, and her hand flew up to stop him.

She managed a shaky smile. 'Why didn't you tell me what you wanted? You don't have to tear my clothes. I'll take them off for you.' She turned to open the door of the empty apartment.

'Wait. Where do you think you're going?' This wasn't the reaction he expected, and he suspected a trick. 'Don't play games with me.'

'Games? Why do you think that? You're a handsome man. It will be a pleasure to spend an evening with you.' She moved close to him, and put her hand on his lapel. 'Haven't you got a friend? There are two of us. My sister is waiting in the street. She is younger than I am.'

His eyes gleamed behind his spectacles. 'I have no friend. But let's get her up here anyway. Better still, we'll kick those two out of fourteen and use their apartment.'

As soon as she knew there were no other Gestapo agents waiting outside, she acted. She swept downwards and with one movement, grabbed his ankles and heaved upwards. Standing as he was with his back to the low parapet wall, he stood no chance. He toppled backwards and without a sound disappeared over the edge. Pauline heard the sound of his body striking the palings, and looked downwards to see his corpse arched backwards over the iron fence, one of the spears protruding from the middle of his chest. She saw Mason move swiftly towards the body, then look up at her. A moment later he disappeared into the hallway, and she heard his footsteps pounding up the stairs. He appeared at the end of the passage, stopped for a moment to take in her torn dress and shocked face, then in two strides he caught her in his arms. She was hicupping with shock, her body shaking uncontrollably, her eyes blinded by tears.

Incredibly no one appeared from any of the apartments. She felt his arms holding her tightly, and slowly the shaking stopped and she was able to speak once more.

Mason began to release her and she stopped him. 'No. Keep holding me. Just hold me.' Her voice was hoarse with shock. 'You make me feel safe.'

Mason held her for a long while, content just to hold her, to alleviate the shock and fear.

At last she released him. 'We must get away from here. The women have the food downstairs.'

Mason let her go, and she stumbled and almost fell. He

caught her and held her once more. 'Wait. Get your strength back. You're still shaking.'

She looked up at him, her face streaked with tears. 'I'm sorry. I thought I was strong. Strong enough to carry on forever, but the last few months have made me realise that I am like other women.'

'No. You are stronger than other women. You are tired, and that makes everything seem worse.'

'I'm glad you are with me.' She held him, content for a moment to feel his strength against her. It was as though she were drawing on his reserve of courage. At last she moved. 'Taff will be worried. We must go.' She looked up at him. 'We will have to take Inga with us.'

'Inga?'

'My friend. She cannot stay here now. This place will be alive with Gestapo by morning.'

Downstairs in fourteen, the two women stared at Pauline as she opened the door. They saw the torn dress and then looked at Mason, and back at her.

Inga said: 'Where is –'

'Dead. I had to kill him.'

'Where is he?'

'His body is caught on the palings. I pushed him from the fourth floor.'

Inga looked at her wide-eyed. Johanna said: 'Shit! Now we're in trouble.' The word sounded strange in her accented German. 'They got on to us because of the amount of food I bought. They were looking for large purchases, suspecting that someone was supplying the partisans. They planted him here to see if anyone made contact with me.' The woman was plainly angry. 'Why didn't you stay away? There was no signal, and you ignored the basic rule of security.'

Pauline was crying now. Her shock had not entirely dissipated. 'I'm sorry, but I was desperate. I was worried about Inga, and I have fifty children to feed. I didn't know what else to do.'

Mason watched her, feeling immeasurably sorry for her, but knowing the woman was right. Pauline had ignored the very strictures she had so often impressed on him. She had allowed her emotions to sway her judgment and the result was a disaster.

The woman was speaking again. 'Well, it's no use crying over what is done. The cell is finished anyway. They picked up all but three of us yesterday. I'll have to warn the others to get out.' She threw the embroidery aside and rose to her feet. 'The food is in the kitchen. Take it all. We can't come back here.' She glanced around the drab apartment. 'I'll be glad to be rid of the shitty place.' She looked at Pauline. 'It isn't a tragedy; just a setback. Don't stay long. It isn't safe.' She looked down at Inga. 'Look after this one. She is very much in love, and she deserves her time.' She turned to Pauline, tears glistening in her eyes. 'She is brave, this little one. She has more courage than I have.'

Impulsively, Inga stood up and flung her arms around the older woman. She began to sob. 'I will miss you.'

Johanna patted her shoulder. 'Enough. Enough. We don't want these people to think Czechs are less than Jews.' She smiled through her tears at Pauline. 'Look after her for Karl.'

Mason touched her on the shoulder. 'What about the man downstairs? We can't leave him there.'

Johanna nodded and waved a dismissive hand. 'He will be moved before morning. He won't be found again; the men will see to that. We cannot have another massacre like Lidice.' She kissed Inga lightly on the cheek and went out of the apartment.

Mason put out his hand to Inga. She took it in cool fingers. He said: 'I am Bob Mason.'

'Yes. I know. I knew you were coming.' She went to Pauline and hugged her. 'It's good to see you again. Now we must get the food and go.'

Mason stopped her. 'What about travel documents? We are taking a train in the morning.'

Inga laughed. 'It was all arranged. I was leaving tomorrow anyway. I am meeting Karl in Friedrichshafen on Monday at three o'clock.' She saw the astonishment on Pauline's face. 'I was going with you anyway. I wanted to surprise you.'

'Karl – in Friedrichshafen? How? Why?'

'He says he will explain everything to Joachim.'

Pauline put her arm around the girl. 'I'm glad. I really am.'

'I know. Now I must get the food ready.'

Chapter Fifteen

Friday, 11th August, 1944. 11.30 p.m.

As Inga went through to the kitchen, Mason touched Pauline on the cheek. 'Are you all right?'

'I'm fine now. I'll help Inga pack the food.' She shut the apartment door behind him and followed Inga into the kitchen.

The food was in a cupboard beside the tiny stove. There were twelve loaves of bread, a kilogramme of sugar, a kilogramme of powdered milk, coffee, cheese and potatoes. It appeared to be a four week ration for one person. At least the children would be fed tomorrow. They heard Mason returning, and Pauline began loading the food into a large double-handled basket Inga had produced from under the sink.

Mason watched the two girls packing the basket. For the first time, he realised that Inga was a remarkably pretty girl. Karl, whoever he was, was a lucky man. She was small, slim, and her soft brown hair hung to her shoulders. Her eyes were alive and good-humoured. Mason thought she looked about twenty.

When the girls were finished, Inga went to get her attaché case with her meagre belongings. Mason handed Pauline her coat and headscarf. She took her coat, and as she looked down at her dress, remembered that nothing was covering her brassiere.

She smiled at Mason and shrugged on her coat. 'I'm not going to start blushing now. If you heard what I said to that man – ' Abruptly, she remembered the corpse on the palings, and began trembling once more.

Mason pulled her to him. 'Steady. There's nothing to be afraid of now.' Slowly the shaking subsided, and as Inga came back to the kitchen, Pauline bent to take one handle of the basket. Together, she and Mason carried it out of the apartment and into the passage, while Inga put out the lights, put the bolt on lock and pulled the door shut.

Pauline stopped suddenly. 'I forgot to give Johanna the food cards.'

Inga shrugged. 'She doesn't need them. She had a stock of them.'

Outside, the streets were still silent, but there was the glow of a rising moon in the east. They avoided looking at the shape hanging over the palings.

At the bus, only Lazero was still awake. Davis, having succumbed earlier, was stretched full-length across the long back seat with little Gigi Envers in his arms. It was as though they had fallen asleep whilst he was comforting her. Her cheeks were still streaked with the marks of tears.

Lazero took the basket from them. 'You leave this to me. Go rest now.'

Inga followed Pauline into the bus, and stopped, astonished by what she saw. 'When Joachim sent the message about the food, he told me you had fifty children with you. I didn't realise it was as many as this.'

Mason laughed at her logic. 'Fifty children is still fifty children.'

'But it doesn't seem so many when you say, "Fifty children". When you see the reality, it seems so – ' She dropped her arms helplessly.

Pauline smiled. 'You'll get used to it. Now, we must rest.'

Mason woke to the sound of the first bird calls. The weather was still fine, with a light breeze stirring the top branches of the tall pines, and a pale moon just dipping behind the Erzbirge range. He could smell the coffee brewing and went out quickly to where Lazero had made a small fire. He had heated some water he had brought in the cans, and baked some potatoes in the hot ashes. Soon, most of the children were awake and Pauline took them to the stream to wash. They were curious about the newcomer, and Inga chatted to the older ones. All the children were ravenous, but after they had eaten there was still food spare. Pauline gave each child a small piece of extra bread to keep for the journey ahead. Lazero backed the bus into the road, and turning at the park, took a road that skirted the town.

On the other side of Komotau, the road ran alongside the railway line, then climbed a saddle to drop down into a valley of dwarf pines and red spruce. The station they were looking for was amongst the trees at the bottom of the valley. It was here that Lazero left them. He wasted no time in making his farewells. He had to return to Liebstadt by early evening, the time the permit expired. Mason watched him go, feeling almost as though he had lost a good friend.

They rested on a grassy bank under some pine trees about five hundred metres from the station. Mason sat beside Pauline as Inga and Davis talked quietly together amongst a group of children.

They still had forty-five minutes to wait before their train was due. Pauline yawned and leaned back against a tree. Mason felt her hand in his palm. He smiled at her and cupped her hand in both of his. He looked across the railway line to where a meadow sloped gently into a valley of farms and cultivated fields, and sighed. 'It's a long time since I have felt so content.' He looked down to find her dark eyes intent upon him. 'I remember I'd been sitting on the bank of the Isis. It was the day before I had to report to the army. Later that afternoon I walked along the High – that's the main street in Oxford – just to look at it for the last time before I went away. I stood outside Queen's, looking down towards All Souls and St Mary's, and I remember thinking of the dignity and the elegance of those beautiful buildings, and what could happen to them if the Germans bombed our cities.'

They were silent for a long while. Mason was exquisitely conscious of her nearness, and wondered how much of what he felt was due to the heightened tenor of their situation. He had only known her for a week, and yet here he was, wondering if he was in love.

The sun had risen above the hills before they heard the sound of the train in the distance. Swiftly the children were gathered into groups and marched briskly to the station. There, Mason and Davis stood apart from them. It had been decided that the two men would continue as Dutch artisans, but would remain close in case they were needed.

They heard the sound of the whistle just as the train appeared at the bend five hundred metres away. The engine rumbled past them, and Mason saw that most of the train was made up of day coaches, without corridors or toilets. It meant they would be separated from some of the children unless they could find places in one of the three corridor coaches. He looked up at Pauline. She was looking up at the carriages in front of her. She glanced at him and shrugged helplessly.

The train stopped, and Mason and Davis searched quickly along the coaches for empty seats. He saw the curious faces looking down at the row of children, and then he saw the conductor hurrying towards them from the rear of the train. He was a little round man, and his legs moved with officious precision as he marched along the platform. He was a type that Mason disliked intensely, the type that makes everyone a victim of his authority by creating difficulties if no legitimate ones exist.

'What is this? Who are these children?' He started blustering before he was five metres from the girl. 'I wasn't told about a group booking. You know the railway authorities have to be told about large groups, and permits have to be specially arranged.'

Mason decided that boldness was called for with this man. He said in a loud voice, 'I agree with you, Herr Conductor. It's a damned shame when people take advantage of railway staff just because they know people high up.' He was aware of Pauline's startled look. Davis was staring at him, bewildered. He went on, 'Ever since she arrived, she hasn't stopped talking about her friend Oberführer Schauschutz, as if that entitled her to special consideration.'

Mason saw the inquisitive passengers crowding the windows. The conductor looked first at Pauline and then at Mason. He appeared to be temporarily nonplussed. Then he took command once more. 'You keep out of this. It has nothing to do with you.' He turned back to the girl. 'You have a permit to travel with these children?'

'Of course.' Pauline played up to Mason. 'And I did not mention Herr Schauschutz to get special attention. I merely said I knew him, and that he had arranged this excursion for these children.' She handed the permit to the conductor. Mason could not resist a glance at Agnes Bedaux, who was grinning hugely. She saw Mason looking at her, and blushed and averted her eyes. The conductor examined the permit. He appeared to be fascinated by the signature at the bottom which purported to be that of Herr Oberführer Schauschutz, head of the Prague office of the S.S.

The conductor clearly knew where his duty lay. He turned to Mason. 'You, shut up and get aboard if you have a permit to travel.' He turned to Pauline. 'Fraulein, I would be glad if you would come with me, and bring the children.' His tone was decidedly conciliatory. Davis winked at Mason and followed him aboard.

Within minutes, the conductor had moved a dozen passengers from one of the corridor coaches, and bundled the children aboard, seating them ten to a compartment. The two men found themselves seats in the same coach, but at the other end. Inga decided to sit alone, since her document was a separate permit. She took a seat in the next compartment to the men.

Davis said: 'I didn't understand all of it, but I understood enough to know you won't go to heaven.' Mason grinned at him and sat back as he felt the wheels begin to move and the train began to slide past the station buildings.

There were four other passengers in their compartment. Three women and a soldier in the uniform of the Waffen S.S. Mason looked at him warily, hoping he hadn't heard the Welshman's whispered comment. The man appeared to be ignoring them, but Mason noticed that his eyes continually strayed past them, looking at them without seeming to take note of what he saw.

Mason looked carefully at the uniform. The collar emblem looked like a truncated "Z" with a bar across the middle. He wished Hackett was with them still. The American knew the emblems of every German regiment. Mason's eyes strayed to the cuff titles, and he felt a numbing sense of shock. The title on the cuff read "Landstorm Nederland". The soldier was a

Dutch volunteer! This was a danger that had haunted them, the danger that Joachim had warned them about when they had set out. Whilst their papers were as good as Joachim could arrange – Mason was convinced they emanated from an official source – their command of languages was a weakness they could do nothing about.

Mason was oblivious of the clattering wheels beneath them and the landscape flashing past their window. At any moment he expected the conductor to arrive and take their money for tickets to Bayreuth. Since the wayside station had no booking office, the conductor was responsible for writing out a voucher, and he was certain to mention their Dutch citizenship. If he did that, they were in trouble. The soldier would wonder at their inability to speak their home language.

Mason nudged his companion and indicated they should leave their compartment. He stretched, and as casually as he could, moved to the door but at that moment the conductor was heard in the corridor.

'Fahrkarten bitte!' His shout caused a flurry of movement among the passengers, and those who had not already produced their tickets began going through pockets and handbags.

As the conductor appeared in the doorway, he looked up into Mason's face. 'Ah! The man who doesn't think Oberführer Schauschutz important enough to help with the arrangements for the young lady.'

'Excuse me, Herr Conductor, I did not say that. I merely said that it was unfair for people to use influence.' Mason smiled. 'But you are quite right to help the Fraulein if her papers were in order.' Mason felt Davis pressuring him to move out of the compartment, but the conductor was blocking his way.

'Thank you very much.' The conductor was being elaborately sarcastic. 'So you give me your permission. I find that most gratifying. Now, if you please, you will let me see your ticket.' His voice hardened as he held out his hand. 'Unless you have boarded the train without one.'

Mason's heart sank. The bastard was going to be difficult. He knew damn well that they had boarded the train at Schöneck. 'I beg your pardon, Herr Conductor.' Mason decided to be obsequious. It was galling, but safer. 'There is no ticket office at Schöneck. We had no opportunity to buy tickets, and I'm really sorry for the inconvenience I have caused you.'

The conductor was slightly mollified. 'I will have to see your papers.' Mason produced his permits and money from his inside pocket. He glanced at Davis, whose gaze was rivetted on the soldier's cufftitle. Mason handed the papers to the conductor. He nudged Davis, who tore his gaze away from the S.S. man and looked at Mason blankly.

Mason said in German: 'Papers.'

Davis hurriedly fumbled in his pockets and produced his papers and handed them to the conductor who was examining Mason's permit to travel.

The little man said: 'You are Dutch?' Mason held his breath. 'Then you have a compatriot right here.' He gestured to the soldier. 'This man is a gallant soldier who volunteered to fight for the Fatherland.' Mason wondered fleetingly why Germans always spoke in capitals when they became patriotic. Mason glanced at the soldier who was staring idly out of the window, apparently deep in thought, whistling softly under his breath. Gradually Mason became aware of the tune the man was whistling. He couldn't believe his ears. The tune was "Sweet Lass of Richmond Hill", and then he was aware that the conductor was still speaking. 'You three will have much to talk about.'

Mason decided on a bold gamble. He put out his hand and said: 'Ixnay eakspay.'

The man turned to him and smiled. 'Onay. Otnay utchday.'

Davis looked at the two men blankly. He had recognised the school pig-latin at once, but the meaning of it all escaped him. The conductor smiled and nodded as he wrote out the vouchers. The two men understood one another. Good. It was nice to travel with a compatriot when you are away from home. He handed the vouchers to Mason and went down the corridor. They heard him shouting at a new group of victims.

Mason waited until his cries had faded before he went into the corridor. Davis and the soldier followed him. They heard the whistle from the engine and the jerk of the couplings. There would be a stop shortly.

He said quietly, 'How come?' gesturing to the uniform.

The soldier grinned. 'The escape committee got it for me. I just walked out of the camp with it on. No one stopped me. That was yesterday.'

'Was there any special reason why it's a Dutch uniform?'

'I speak Dutch. My mother came from Rotterdam.'

'What about papers?'

'They're working. I've had no trouble up to now.'

'I don't want to tell you your business, but get out of that uniform as soon as you can. If you're caught, you'll be shot as a spy. Our escape committee wouldn't allow anyone to go under the wire in anything but civvies.' He remembered the courtesies. 'I'm Mason, by the way. And this is Davis.'

The other stuck out his hand. 'Hamilton.' He smiled. 'My word! I thought I was for it when you fellows got on. The Gestapo have been dressing their fellows in working clothes and touring the trains. They get into a compartment with someone they suspect, and before you know where you are, you've given yourself away. I thought that's what you were.' He frowned. 'I say – you're not, are you?'

Mason laughed. 'Not guilty.' The man's naiveté was astonishing. He wasn't the type for this kind of subterfuge. Mason felt faint stirrings of uneasiness. The basic rule of prisoner-of-war survival was to stay away from other escaped prisoners who were not involved in your own escape plans. There were elements in their plan that could endanger your own. Then he shook off his fears. This was different. Their own plan had been abandoned long since and they were working on a day to day basis anyway.

'Are you on your own?'

'Yes. The committee didn't think it would be a good idea for two of us to risk it.' Mason thought the escape committee was stupid to let anyone try it.

Hamilton looked from Mason to Davis. 'Are there just the two of you?'

Mason smiled. 'There are another fifty in our party.'

'Fifty! You mean to say – ' The man was speechless.

'Come. I'll show you.'

Mason walked along the swaying corridor and stopped at the compartment where Pauline sat with ten children. She looked up, alarm in her face as she saw the Waffen S.S. uniform.

Mason said quickly: 'He's one of us. He escaped yesterday.'

'In German uniform? Does he know – ?'

'Yes he knows. It doesn't appear to worry him.' Mason made the introductions and smiled at the man's look of disbelief.

'Do you mean to tell me this lot is all yours?'

Mason nodded. 'In a manner of speaking, yes. We are a party of school children on our way to a Horst Wessel Memorial Concert in Bayreuth.' They felt the train jerk. 'We're stopping. Better go back.'

Minutes later the train stopped at another village. The signboard read: SCHLAKENWERTH. They had come more than fifty kilometres. Another hundred to Bayreuth.

The three men dozed, and the train sped across the plains and skirted the lakes at Eger. Passengers boarded and alighted and the ebb and flow continued with each town and village they passed. There was no Gestapo or Bahnhofs Polizei activity and Mason surmised that the more congested routes were receiving most of their attention. No one bothered them and the morning passed uneventfully.

At Eger, the train paused for ten minutes in the main platform, and then they were shunted on to an outer spur to wait for an eastbound train to pass them. Mason was dozing, his head back, when he felt Davis touch his arm. He opened his eyes, and the Welshman nodded towards a group of people being herded into the shunting yard where a freight train stood waiting without its engine. Soldiers with Schmeissers watched the group shuffle along in single file to the waiting trucks. An officer shouted at the older ones to hurry. There must have been about two hundred of them, men, women and children carrying their bundles and suitcases and streaming towards the waiting train. The soldiers filled one truck before allowing the others to make for the next. The whole operation took about fifteen minutes, and when the last truck had been filled and the bars slammed shut, Mason was sick with the memory of the truck in which they had found the children. If ever there had been a justification for war on Germany, this was it.

Mason thought back to the days in the Western Desert when men had spent weeks in idleness and boredom before the big battles; when each in turn asked themselves what the hell it was all about – why bombs were falling on the innocent and rarely on the guilty? He remembered the words of the Victorian philosopher Herbert Spencer who defined morality as an act adjusted to a good end. Did that mean that a declaration of war was a moral act if it was fought to eliminate the cruelty and degradation perpetrated by the Nazi thugs? Mason had no answer.

All at once he thought of Pauline. He went back to her compartment, where he found her staring at the train standing opposite them, tears coursing down her cheeks, and he knew that she had seen it as well. The children stared up at him dumbly, confused by the sight of adult tears.

He went through to the other compartments where he found the children sitting quietly or sleeping, but in Agnes Bedaux's group, the children were singing softly while she spoke the words of the song she had just taught them. Just then, the train began to move and soon they were out of the station and running alongside the lake on the outskirts of Eger.

Mason stayed with the children, spending a little time with each group, talking to them, reassuring them, and repeating the warnings against speaking in the presence of other passengers unless they spoke German. They seemed quiet enough, but Mason was aware that any naïve indiscretion could be overheard and then they would all be faced with disaster. The possibility haunted him.

He went back to Agnes Bedaux's compartment. The children had finished the song and were sitting quietly, some staring out of the window, others playing word games.

'You look tired, Monsieur. You were late back last night.' Her brown eyes were concerned, and her hands fluttered as though she would like to wave away his tension.

'You were awake?' Mason made a space next to her and sat down.

'I could not sleep. I knew you and Mademoiselle Pauline were doing something dangerous.' She smiled. 'I was glad when you returned.'

'Were any of the others awake?'

'Only I.' She was a pretty child with long black hair and a fine-boned oval face, but the source of her beauty lay in a luminous inner quality and an essential purity of spirit. Mason was struck with the thought that it was a quality that was possessed by saints.

'Were you afraid?'

'Not for myself. For you and Mademoiselle.' She shrugged. 'There's no longer any need to be afraid for myself. The Germans have taken everything but our lives, and life is nothing without roots.' She spoke without bitterness but with a dignity that belied her age.

For a moment Mason was unable to speak. Then he said: 'You will find new roots. And time will let you grow into a woman who will love and be loved.'

She smiled. 'If Mademoiselle can find someone like you, then perhaps there is hope for me.'

'I think you are too discerning.' He smiled and touched her shoulder. 'But too premature.'

She shook her head. 'I think not, Monsieur.' She laughed out loud. 'But if I am, then Mademoiselle is sickening for something.'

Mason laughed with her and stood up. 'Go on with you.'

He left her chuckling to herself, and went back to his own compartment, finding Davis alone. There were no other passengers with him.

'Where's Hamilton?'

Davis shrugged. 'He went out saying he wanted to get something to eat, and the last I saw of him he was walking across to the station café at Eger. He didn't come back.'

'The bloody fool! He'll get caught.'

'I tried to reason with him, but he's a stubborn bugger. Said he'd be all right.'

'I hope he is, but I can't see him lasting another day. Did he get back on the train?'

'I don't know. I didn't see him. He may have decided to sit somewhere else.'

'I'll have a look in the other coaches.'

Mason walked through the two second-class corridor coaches without seeing Hamilton in either of them. There weren't many passengers in either coach and after the stop for Waldershof, the train was practically deserted.

Mason stood in the corridor, leaning on the brass rail, staring out at the countryside, so different from his native Oxfordshire.

As the coaches swayed and the wheels played their monotonous rhythm on the track, his reverie turned to his father, that quiet gentle man whose loving and generous soul gave so much comfort to his parishioners. A spare grey man whose voice seldom rose above a soft murmur in polite conversation, but whose pulpit voice resounded through his church with passion and confidence.

Mason loved his father, and wondered how he would feel about welcoming home a son complete with a prospective daughter-in-law; that is, if he could persuade Pauline to accept him. He didn't think the difference in their faiths was a factor in their relationship, though he conceded to himself that there could be difficulties. He knew he loved her, and he knew she felt something for him. He hoped that whatever she felt would be strong enough to overcome any difficulties they had to face.

He went back to this compartment and found Davis alone, stretched out on the seat, fast asleep.

Mason sat down wearily, put his head back and closed his eyes. He was tired, and beginning to feel depressed. At moments like this, he wasn't sure whether they would get beyond the next town; France appeared to be an impossible goal. The problems grew with every milestone. On the other hand, he was thankful that this line carried so little traffic. It meant that it was not nearly as rigidly watched as the trains carrying the big city traffic in the north.

He dozed, and just after noon they began clattering through the forests of Fichtelgebirge. Just beyond Neusorg, they entered the two kilometre tunnel before Speichersdorf.

Just before three o'clock, they began seeing houses and factories, and then they were running alongside the Burgerreutherstrasse and slowing down as they approached the main station in Bayreuth. As soon as the train stopped, Mason jumped down to the platform, and keeping a wary eye out for the conductor, began helping the children down from the train. Quickly they formed up in their groups, and drilled as they were, were at the main entrance of the station before the other passengers had gathered up their luggage.

Inga and Davis brought up the rear, while Pauline and Mason led the children into the street. Pauline had the address of one of her father's friends, who had studied with Joachim in Warsaw and had a house on the Kulmbach road. The house had a large cellar where the children would sleep tonight. She led them along Friedrich von Schillerstrasse to the circle where the public transport stopped. Mason could see soldiers everywhere, and now and then men in civilian clothes passed them; men with an air of authority about them. He and Davis followed the children at a discreet distance.

They were almost at the circle when a middle-aged couple, passing them in the opposite direction, turned back and walked alongside the children, peering into the faces of the two Wiskamann girls. The woman was stout with dark hair and spectacles, and the man was greying, well-dressed and carrying a cane. The woman looked at Pauline who had stopped a short way ahead.

'Fraulein.' She waved. 'Fraulein! Surely these are the Wiskamann children?' She turned to her husband. 'Look, Simon! It's the Wiskamann girls.' The two girls were staring at her in astonishment, delight slowly spreading across their faces. 'Look, Simon. They recognise us. It *is* them.'

The two girls threw themselves at the woman. Mason was aware they were attracting a small crowd.

The man said: 'Fraulein, what are you doing with these girls?'

Pauline looked at the two children holding the woman's hands. 'Are you relatives?'

Elena said quickly: 'This is Maman's friend.'

The man looked at Pauline over his spectacles. 'These children are very dear to us. They stayed with us during their holidays. Their parents are our dear friends. Please tell us what they are doing here. Where are their parents?'

Mason edged closer, alarmed at the turn of events. He saw Inga, despair on her face, looking at Pauline, hoping for a miracle. The crowd was growing, and at that moment, a civilian in a light raincoat appeared at the edge of the throng and began pushing his way through. Mason looked at him in despair. Just then, a man in identical dress stepped off the sidewalk on the other side of the street and strolled towards them. He remembered his commanding officer's words back at the prison.

'Watch out for the Gestapo. Remember, if you see one, look for the other. They usually hunt in pairs.'

Chapter Sixteen

Saturday, 12th August, 1944. 3 p.m.

Herr Harster stopped the car below the church. Liebstadt was asleep in the afternoon sunshine, and in the meadows cattle stood ruminating in sleep-eyed somnolence. He looked up towards the church but the doors were closed and the building had a deserted air, in keeping with the uninhabited character of the whole village.

He turned towards the house on his left, and saw the curtain in the window twitch. He left the car, walked to the door and knocked. There was a long silence, and he knocked once more. Finally the door opened a fraction. The woman who peered through the opening looked about fifty, with grey hair, a stout figure, and on her face a look of apprehension – a familiar sight to the Gestapo man.

The Ferret lifted his hand, indicating the village street. 'Where is everyone?'

'Most of them are in the fields.'

'Open up. I want some information.'

The woman stood there, terror building in her eyes. 'They will kill me. Already I have been threatened. There is nothing I can tell you.'

'Open up, woman. You will talk to me here, or I can show you another place where you will answer my questions.'

Reluctantly the woman opened the door sufficiently to allow the man to enter. He walked inside and looked around.

'Who will kill you?'

'The Czechs.'

'You are not one of them?'

She sneered. 'One of that lot – certainly not! My husband and I came here in 1938. I am a German.'

'Where is your husband now?'

'He was killed in Normandy.'

'And now you are being threatened.'

The woman remained silent, looking fearfully at the Gestapo man, her fingers twisting endlessly about themselves.

'Well, are you?'

'The man who used to have this farm has told everyone he will kill me when the war is over.'

The Ferret grunted. 'We have to lose the war first. That won't happen.' He looked around the neat sitting room at the furnishings, the white cloths and antimacassars, and the black-draped picture on the mantelpiece. 'Are there many children in the village?'

Her mouth twisted, and her eyes reflected a moment of cunning, then she smiled. 'I know what you want. It's the children, isn't it? I thought something was going on when they came here yesterday.'

'Who came here yesterday?'

'Three men, a woman and about forty children. It could have been more.' She pointed through the window. 'They went up to the church when the patrol came.'

Harster smiled. 'When did they leave?'

'About an hour later. Zigcek took them in a bus.'

'Zigcek?'

'Lazero Zigcek. He runs a bus company. He took them.'

'Where did they go?'

'I can't tell you. I don't know. They went that way.' She pointed westwards.

'Where will I find this Zigcek?'

'He lives in Glashutte.'

Harster turned to go, then he stopped. 'What is the name of this man who is threatening you?'

'Zigcek.' She saw his surprise and said quickly: 'Not the bus man. His cousin.'

'And where does this cousin live?'

'He lives in Glashutte too.'

Harster left the house, looking right and left as he walked

back to his car. He picked up the men he had posted at the entrance to the village, and twenty minutes later drove cautiously into Glashutte. An old man sitting on a bench outside the café directed him to the home of Lazero Zigcek. The Ferret couldn't believe his luck. He found the man and his cousin together, playing cards in the small back room behind the bus shed. Harster took them into custody, and drove out towards Teplitz. On the way, in a remote wood, Lazero's cousin was shot 'while attempting to escape'.

Lazero was taken to the basement of the Gestapo office in Teplitz, where he held out for half an hour before he admitted that he had taken four adults and fifty children to Schöneck, where they had boarded a train for Bayreuth.

As he stared down at the naked and bloodied body lying on the floor of the cellar, Harster came to a swift decision. 'Clean him up. Get his clothes on him, and keep him here until I come back.' He looked at his watch. Four-thirty. The train should have arrived in Bayreuth an hour ago. He would have to move quickly. However, he did not think they would be difficult to find.

He was unable to locate S.S. Oberführer Becker that night, but early on Sunday morning, Becker gave him permisson to contact the Bayreuth office. He left the Oberführer, and an hour later the Bayreuth office of the Gestapo was being advised of the arrival of fifty children and four adults in their town and that they were to be apprehended and held, pending the arrival of four Gestapo agents from the Breslau Office. Herr Harster was not one of them. He had other orders; orders that concerned Operation Geld.

The man named Karl pulled up the collar of his overcoat against the icy wind gusting along the Kanalstrasse. The blackout was complete. There was no automatic blackout in this Silesian town, but an air-raid alarm had sounded half an hour ago, and already Karl could hear the dull thunder of the falling bombs over the whine of the wind. He had been waiting almost five minutes, but he knew he was early and felt no impatience. Useless emotions were never part of his character, but his empathy with human suffering was sometimes the cause of acute anguish.

The death of his wife from cancer early in the war left him entirely alone. They had had no children and in the circumstances in which he found himself, it was just as well. He could see no conclusion to his covert operations other than exposure and death. Most of his friends and colleagues were in prison or dead. Today they had arrested Carl Gordeler, a former mayor of Leipzig, and one of the key men in the underground war against Hitler. Karl sighed and pulled his coat closer and tucked his hands deep into his pockets. There were so few of them left. He couldn't help feeling that the July bomb plot could have been better planned and executed.

For his own part, he was fortunate that he had had so much longer to bury himself in covert operations than his colleagues. His secret war had begun in 1940, when he realised the extent of Hitler's final solution. When he realised that Canaris was behind Operation 7, the scheme to save Jews from death, Karl used his office to direct those he could to the Abwehr, where some were given clearance to go to Switzerland on the pretext of being Abwehr agents.

He had worked anonymously for four years, and not one of his co-conspirators knew his identity. He had buried himself so deeply, and his precautions were so thorough, that his safety had been assured for four long years. True, the Jews that had been saved in this way were a drop in the ocean, but the rescue of five hundred Dutch Jews by Abwehrstelle den Haag in May 1941 was a source of reassurance. There were other operations, too, about which he felt deep satisfaction.

At that moment the telephone rang twice in the call-box. He lifted the receiver and heard Joachim speaking from two hundred kilometres away.

'Karl?'

'Yes.'

'I have arrived. Our friend – you remember, the man who eliminated Kuhn? – is still with them. He is staying out of sight. They think they've lost him.'

'Have they arrived?'

'The car with the three men arrived in Munich at seven o'clock this evening. The train was held up by an air raid in Nuremberg, so they decided to take a car to Munich, stay there tonight, and then continue their journey tomorrow.'

'I see. And your other man?'

'Wilhelm has taken out Ohlendorf and replaced him. That leaves only Hansen, the second man.'

'Hansen was recalled to Breslau.' Karl was sardonic. 'With Hansen, Kuhn and Ohlendorf neutralised, the Breslau office has only one man left in the field.' He chuckled. 'Erich Rowecki.'

'Yes. Erich Rowecki.' The mention of the name appeared to give them both a great deal of amusement, as though they were sharing a secret joke. 'I won't ask how you managed Hansen.'

'Don't, my dear fellow. Just be thankful it was managed. Hansen was the dangerous one – even more dangerous than Kuhn. And now – '

'We take over the operation.'

'Exactly.'

'You've planned well.'

'Yes.' It was not a compliment and he accepted the statement as one of fact. 'What of Pauline – and Inga?'

'I haven't heard, but I am not unduly worried. Perhaps Johan has not been able to report for some reason.'

'Is he still with them?'

'Yes.'

'Do they know he is there?'

'No. I think it is safer, unless they need him badly.'

'I agree.' He heard footsteps approaching the telephone box, and he paused a moment to listen. The footsteps passed, and he saw a dark shape disappearing into the night. The wind was a lonely reminder of the cold.

'Karl?'

'I'm still here. Just someone passing. I didn't want to be overheard.'

'Will they know it was you?'

'Who destroyed the operation, you mean?' He paused, thinking about it. 'Yes, I suppose they must eventually. It is my fervent wish that it will then be too late for them to do anything about it.'

'Then you must anticipate their enlightenment. Remember Inga will be waiting.'

'Yes. Joachim – '

'Yes.'

'Look after her for me.'

'Of course. And you look after yourself.'

'Don't worry about me, my dear fellow. I don't intend to be a victim. I must go.'

'Take care.'

'You too.'

Karl smiled to himself as he replaced the receiver. The two phrases had become a rite, an almost superstitious talisman for their mutual comfort. He tucked his hands deep into his pockets and put his head down against the icy wind.

The Waldeck Hotel is in Arnulfstrasse, near the main station. Hackett sat in his room on the sixth floor of the building, looking morosely at the lights of the shunting yard opposite. The Waldeck was no different from any other hotel catering for transients who needed accommodation close to the trains. It was clean, but the rooms had no baths, and it was noisy. The sounds of shunting engines clanged across the yards, and the peripheral traffic in the streets around the station added a continuous roar to the general hubbub. He wondered if it ever abated. It was already eleven o'clock, and the noise level wasn't a decibel different from when they had arrived at seven. Even with the windows closed, the sound was still a dull rumble.

His two travelling companions had checked in with him and were sharing a room down the hall. He still hadn't been able to discover whether they were armed, but he would act as though they were. He was determined to take a look at their luggage before the night was over.

Hackett was beginning to revel in the position he found himself. For too long, he had been manipulated, and like Mason, as soon as he had an opportunity to reassert himself, he seized it gratefully. He was certain that there were plans to eliminate him once the two men were safe in Allied territory, and he intended giving the conspirators a rude shock. For the tenth time, he looked at the clock on the station tower. Another hour would do it. Both Grant and Patterson had been drinking from a bottle in the car, and he was sure the effect on them would be helpful from his point of view. He smoked and watched the station clock.

At twelve-thirty, he slipped off his shoes and took off his socks. In his bare feet, he opened his door quietly and looked into the hall. It was empty. He went to the door of the adjoining room, and put his ear to the panel. There was no sound from the other side of the door. This worried him. He was certain he should have heard some sounds of sleep, but there was only silence. He tried the door, and to his alarm it opened at his touch. He slipped inside, and closed the door gently behind him. At that moment a bright light came on; a table lamp was standing on the floor and directed at the door so that anything in the room beyond was invisible.

A voice said: 'Come right in, old man. We've been expecting you.'

The light on the floor went out and the overhead light went on to disclose Grant and Patterson, fully dressed, standing on either side of him. 'So you thought we might have succumbed to the liquid refreshment.' Patterson was eager to show how clever he had been. 'We thought you would think that, so we decided to drink a whole bottle of water to see if we could trust you.' He sneered. 'I can see that we can't trust you an inch.'

Hackett looked from one to the other. He was chagrined. They had got the better of him at their first encounter, and he realised that he had made the fundamental error of underestimating his opponents.

He shrugged. There was nothing he could say. The next move was theirs.

Grant kicked a chair to him. 'Sit down. What were you up to?' His voice was harsh. 'Go on. Convince us.'

Patterson grinned. 'Tell the story about how you were coming to tell us something.'

Hackett was mortified. That was exactly what was going through his mind. He just shrugged. 'No. I wanted to find out if you were armed.'

'And if we were?' Patterson's grin had gone.

Hackett made an instant decision. 'You want to know? I'll tell you.' He turned the chair around and sat. 'I have a feeling I'm expendable. As soon as you two have what you want, I'm through. Right?'

The two men looked at one another. They were suspicious of his frankness. Grant said: 'You may be right, but it's not our problem.'

Grant sat down on the bed. Patterson remained standing. He cocked his finger and pointed it like a gun at Hackett. 'We should beat your head off, but we won't, because we think you're right. We think you're expendable, but that's only my theory. We've got no instructions to kill you, but we suspect that someone has, and that someone is the man named Kuhn who has been with us since we left our arrogant Major Brunner.'

'Why are you telling me all this?'

Grant looked at his companion and back at Hackett. 'Because we suspect that our good friend S.S. Obergruppenführer Müller considers us expendable too.' He looked again at Patterson, who nodded. 'We'll level with you, but remember this – we're in this together. All three of us could be eliminated, if what we think is correct.' He spread his hands wide. 'Why the hell should we be the only ones left alive, when everyone else associated with the operation has been killed?'

Hackett was puzzled. 'There have been others?'

'Of course.' He hesitated and looked at Patterson. Hackett waited for what he knew was coming. He felt as though he was suspended in time; as though he was back in the forest with Joachim. He saw Patterson nod. 'I don't think it will come as a shock to you to know that your brother was amongst the first. There have been others; those who did the preliminary investigation, and who were sent to conduct the first interviews with the interested parties. They lasted just long enough to make their reports.'

'How do you know this?'

'We've been in this since the beginning.'

Hackett was curious. 'Tell me. I'd like to know how you speak English so well.'

Grant glanced at Patterson once more. 'We're both half English. We both lived in England for years, and returned to Germany as war started. We were educated at English schools.' He smiled. 'Now we are both Sturmbannführers in the S.S.'

Patterson walked to the bedside table and picked up a packet of cigarettes. 'We planned this whole thing.' He flicked a silver lighter and puffed a stream of smoke. 'We took it to Herr Müller personally – after we saw that the first German reverses would make him receptive to the whole idea.'

'Wasn't that dangerous? Weren't you afraid he would have you shot for preaching defeatism.'

'No more dangerous than being alive in Germany when the war is over. Do you think the Allies will be merciful to the S.S. who remain in Germany?'

'Then you hope to participate in the operation too?'

'Of course. I am sure that you are not naïve enough to believe we are in this to see that Herr Müller is comfortable after the war.'

No, thought Hackett, and I'm not naïve enough to believe you will let me live after telling me all this. Then he thought of his brother, and anger burned in him. Ten to one, it was this disgusting pair who had had his brother killed.

His face was expressionless when he said: 'Why are you taking me into your confidence? It seems to me that the more you tell me, the more reason there is to kill me when I'm no more use to you.'

Patterson stubbed out his cigarette in the ashtray on the bedside table. 'We're in this together. You need us, and we sure as hell need you. We've conceded that you know of your brother's death. That's a guarantee of our good faith. If you want to, you could hand us over to the Allies as soon as we are in their sector.' He paused and walked to the window, then he turned and looked at Hackett. 'If you come in with us, it's worth ten million dollars to you.'

Now that Hackett knew for sure his brother was dead, Brunner's hold over him no longer existed. Grant and Patterson were holding out a carrot instead of threatening him with a stick. He had no alternative at this stage but to pretend to go along with them, but he knew that it was unwise to appear too eager.

He said: 'I don't know. The whole thing seems to depend on trust. Your trust in me and mine in you.' He saw Patterson's eyes shift to Grant, and knew he had struck the right note. In their view, everything was falling into place. From the moment they had trapped him into this discussion, he had reacted exactly as they expected. He went on, 'As I see it, you have no intention of going back to Herr Müller. You will split the loot – if I am to trust your word – three ways.'

'Why shouldn't you take our word? There's enough for all of us, and there is no need for any more killing.'

Hackett thought for a moment. 'The original plan called for you to be in Allied hands for the shortest possible time. Any longer, and you would be exposed once a check is made. Your Mason and Davis would prove to be bogus.'

'We are going to keep to the original plan.'

'Then why don't you stay in Switzerland after you have access to the money?'

'Because there will be no safe place anywhere in Europe once the war is over.'

'There won't be a safe place anywhere in the world when the war is over.' Hackett was emphatic.

Grant said: 'We think we have found a haven. Anyway, that isn't your affair. Are you prepared to trust us?'

Hackett smiled. 'I think the point is, gentlemen, whether you trust me.'

Patterson's smile was as broad as Hackett's. 'With ten million dollars in a Swiss account, we'll trust you. After all, if the Allies are informed, you will lose everything too.' He cracked his knuckles. 'They won't look too kindly on wealthy ex-OSS officers.'

'And Herr Müller? How will he feel?'

'We will shed a little tear for Herr Müller's misfortune and pray that he never finds us.'

'Surely Müller had some guarantee of your good faith. I can't see him trusting you with his entire fortune.'

Patterson tapped his forehead with his forefinger. 'Smart. I see you're thinking things through.' He smiled. 'Herr Müller has at least three Gestapo killers behind us. The moment we step out of line, they step in. They know that won't happen until we have the money, so if we step out of line after that –' he shrugged – 'well, the most difficult part has already been accomplished, and all they have to do is deliver the money to Italy.'

'Are you sure there are only three?'

Grant stood up impatiently. He looked at Patterson. 'I tell you, Rowecki must be involved. He is definitely the fourth man.'

Hackett looked from one to the other. It was clear that they had had this discussion before. 'Four men?'

Patterson cracked his knuckles once more. Hackett wished he would stop. The habit was beginning to irritate him. 'Grant thinks there are four men. Kuhn, Hansen, Ohlendorf and a man named Rowecki.' He turned to the window and looked out across the shunting yards. 'Of course there is our driver.'

'Our driver?'

'Yes. Good old obsequious Fritz. Always disappearing to telephone his mother – who incidentally hasn't got a telephone. I checked.' He turned from the window. 'We can ignore him. He is only an informer. He rings Brunner once a day, but he is no threat.'

Grant said: 'The real threat is Rowecki.'

Patterson looked at Hackett. 'Grant saw him in Nuremberg. He spotted him as we left the train.' He turned to Grant. 'I'm sure he's not on this operation. Why hasn't his name come up before?'

Grant shook his head. 'I don't believe in coincidences. I believe he's been with us all the way.'

Hackett waved an impatient hand. 'What are you going to do about these men?'

'Nothing.'

Hackett was astonished. 'Nothing?'

Patterson shook his head. 'Think it through. These men can only go as far as the limits of the Allied advance. In other words they can go with us as far as Switzerland, and then see us on our transport to Italy. So, as long as we keep to that part of the plan, we're safe. Brunner knows this, so he goes out of his way to let us know we are being watched. Now, when we get on the plane for Italy, we are trapped until we land, and this is where I think Brunner has someone ready to take over until we make contact with Bishop Hudal.'

'Who's he?'

'The good Bishop has been delegated to organise an escape route for our strong silent men in the Reich hierarchy, in the event of an Allied victory. Everything is planned but dormant. The trigger is German surrender, and in twenty-four hours the route can be operational.'

'When will you make a break?'

'Don't worry about us. We've got it all sewn up.'

'What's the next move?'

'Then you're in?'

'Of course.'

'Right. Then let's get some sleep. We can discuss the whole thing once the money is in our hands.'

And I'm dead. Hackett smiled inwardly. He stood up and went to the door. He hesitated as if to speak, thought better of it and went out.

Back in his room, he lit a cigarette and lay back on his bed. His pride was bruised, but he was feeling better than he had done for a long time. This guy Patterson was smart. He had underestimated the man badly, and was mortified at his error of judgement.

Yet Patterson was not smart enough. His S.S. years had made him callous. He really believed that Hackett would just ignore the murder of his brother and do nothing about it. They believed that they could buy his brother's memory for ten million dollars.

It was now that he needed Joachim and his cell. If only they had arranged a signal of some kind. It seemed that once Joachim had entrusted him with the information he was to take back with him, they had consigned him like a parcel, to be delivered in due course.

Or had they? Hackett picked up his towel and went to the bathroom.

He believed that Joachim was the smartest man he had ever met, and it would be unlike him to make the fundamental error of not keeping a receipt for any parcels he consigned. And if he, Hackett was right, Joachim would not have consigned him without keeping tabs on him . . .

He lay in the tepid bath water, mulling over the intelligence that Joachim had entrusted him with. He knew that no Allied Intelligence team would accept the information without detailed corroboration. What is more, it had to come from a trusted member of the armed forces – an OSS officer like himself, who had carried out a thorough evaluation of the documents Joachim had shown him. It was clear that no one could risk carrying those documents through Germany, for once it was known that the Allies had the information, the OKW, the German High Command, could make alterations to neutralise the value of the intelligence. To Joachim, Hackett the professional was the ideal man to carry back the information.

Hackett knew that Joachim and his cell had another string to their bow, but he had been told that the alternative carriers did not have the force of his qualifications of evaluation. What is more, he had memorised the entire contents of the documents in two hours and passed the test of memory Joachim had given him subsequently.

He began to feel a little less helpless as he towelled himself. In fact, he felt happier than he had for a long time. As he walked down the long corridor from the bathroom to his room, he hummed a little tune, and as he passed Patterson's door he thumbed an obscene gesture. The childish moment made him feel a lot better, and he fell asleep almost as soon as he put out the light.

Chapter Seventeen

Saturday, 12th August, 1944. 3 p.m.

Mason watched in growing alarm as the Gestapo man began to edge through the crowd. He realised that he had no more than seconds to act. Davis was looking at him, willing him to do something. He saw Pauline's frightened face in front of him. The man was looking questioningly at her, waiting for her to answer. Mason was aware of the fear on the faces of the bigger children who had recognised the threat posed by the men in raincoats. They had all seen these men before, men who had come into their houses and taken their parents.

The man repeated the question. 'What are these children doing here, Fraulein?' Pauline drew the Wiskamann girls to her. She looked helplessly at Mason, and then at the man with the cane. Inga stood beside her, her eyes betraying her fear.

The woman looked puzzled. 'Where are the children's parents? I don't understand.'

Mason saw the Gestapo man getting closer. His idle curiosity was turning to suspicion. Mason decided to act. They were doomed anyway if he didn't, and there was a chance if he did.

He held the man's arm tightly. 'For pity's sake don't expose us. These are all Jewish children who were being sent to the death camps.' As he whispered close to the man's ear, a look of horror crossed the man's face. 'Their parents have been imprisoned. We rescued them from a truck in a siding.' The man turned a bewildered face to his wife. She was still looking at Pauline, waiting for an answer.

The man drew a deep breath, 'I think we've made a mistake my dear.' He suddenly became aware of the two Gestapo men approaching. 'But what a wonderful group of children. So well behaved.'

Pauline took her cue. 'They are here for the Horst Wessel Concert. They are all from Kempten.'

'But, Simon – ' The woman was completely baffled.

'Not now, my dear. I'll explain later.'

Mason nudged Pauline. 'Sing.' He saw the Gestapo man standing right behind her, while his companion looked searchingly at the children. Neither of them knew what was happening, but they would certainly find out.

The Gestapo man took Pauline's arm. 'What is going on here? Who are these children?'

Pauline turned to him with her brightest smile. 'These are children from Kempten. Four of them are well-known for their singing there, and this gentlemen wondered if they would give an impromptu concert here.' She looked regretfully at the Gestapo man. 'I told him we have to have police permission to sing in the street.'

The man said quickly: 'I recognised them from a concert I and my wife attended last year.'

'Is that so? Where was the concert?'

The man hesitated. Pauline said quickly: 'Salzburg. They sang at the festival.'

'Indeed?' The man was plainly sceptical. 'Then I think we should hear them sing. But first, your papers.'

'Of course.' Pauline handed the man her documents. He examined them closely.

'Your studio is in Kempten? What street is it in?' He looked at her with a half-smile. Mason held his breath. The man obviously knew Kempten well.

'Illerstrasse. Near the cathedral; by the river.'

The man handed back the documents. 'I used to live in Gerberstrasse. It runs into Illerstrasse.' He looked at the growing crowd. 'One song. For the people here.'

'Thank you.' Pauline lined up the children on the steps of the monument. The crowd gathered in a semi-circle around them. She gave them a note and the children watched her hands. As she conducted, they sang better than they ever had.

The harmonies were perfect, and Mason was sure that the crowd had never heard it sung better.

Davis whispered, 'I would not have believed it possible. I do believe we're going to get away with it.'

Mason said: 'That's just it. No one believes it possible that these children could be the victims of an unholy system. No one believes that these children are wanted by the state so that they can be murdered. So they believe what they see. Fifty healthy children going to a festival.' He looked at Davis. 'And you know what, Taff, I don't think the world will believe it either. If you were in Cardiff, with a crowd like this, would you believe it?'

The song came to an end, and the crowd applauded and demanded an encore. Pauline gave them a new note. As they sang, the man and the woman edged up to Mason.

The man was ashen with shock. 'My wife and I want you to come to our house tonight. We must hear more about this. These people were our dearest friends. We have been wondering why we haven't heard from them.' He shook his head. 'We heard about these things. We were told they were vicious rumours put out by the Allies as propaganda. But evidently it is all true.'

Mason said sadly. 'It is only too true.' He shook his head. 'We cannot come to your house. We have to get these children under cover as soon as possible. We have to get them back to France.' He looked at the woman, face still registering shock. 'I thank you both from the bottom of my heart for not giving us away.'

'But we did. We put you in great danger.'

'Unwittingly, and through your concern for your friends.'

The man looked at Mason questioningly. 'Is it impertinent of me to ask who you are? How you came into this?'

'Not impertinent, but it would be imprudent of me to answer.' Somehow he trusted this man. 'At the moment I am a Dutch artisan travelling through Bayreuth.' He looked towards the children. The song was coming to an end. 'You might say that I am in a similar position to that of your friends.'

'I see.' The man applauded with the rest of the spectators. 'Is there nothing I can do for my friends' children? Can't we take them to live with us? We would do anything for them.' The children were accepting the plaudits of the crowd. Pauline was smiling at the people in front of her, but Mason could see the tension in her eyes.

Mason turned to the elderly couple before him. 'How would you account for them? There would be investigation, document inspection.' He shook his head. 'It would be too dangerous for you.' Pauline was ushering the children towards the transport depot. 'We are taking them to a village in France – Le Chambon. A priest will look after them. Write to him if you wish to help them when the war is over. His name is Trocmé.'

The woman pressed his hand. 'We will pray for all of you.' There were tears in her eyes.

'Thank you. We will need your prayers.' He watched the last child board the bus fifty metres away and saw Pauline looking back anxiously. Davis was already at the stop. Mason shook hands with both of them and sprinted for the bus just as the pneumatic doors began to close. He went to the back, and waved through the rear window. The last he saw of them was a forlorn couple waving to him, then the bus turned a corner and they were out of sight.

As the bus disappeared from view, the elderly couple crossed the square, Johan appeared from the corner café and walked across to the bus stop. His hands were still moist from the tension. It had been a close call. For a moment he had been completely nonplussed. The Englishman had reacted with courage and ingenuity. Pauline was in good hands. He waited for about ten minutes before he caught the next bus to the house on the Kulmbach road.

The two Gestapo men watched the crowd disperse, and turned their footsteps to the regional office, where one of them wrote a brief report on the occurence in the square before he went off duty.

The bus carrying the children passed the hospital on Kulmbacherstrasse, ran under a bridge, and turned north through a pleasant suburb of tree-lined streets and detached houses. The children were entranced by the gardens and they sat silent and enraptured. Pauline and Inga sat together at the front of the bus, and Mason and Davis towards the back. All were on tenterhooks lest an indiscreet word from one of the children should alert one of the other passengers that these were Jewish children. If that happened, he knew that the indulgent smiles at their bright happy chatter would soon turn to ugly hostility. Goebbels had done his work well, and there were few Germans at this time who could withstand the onslaught on their reason.

Just before the end of the line, Pauline indicated that they should get ready to move, and when the bus stopped just before the cemetery, the children followed her into the street. The two men were the last to get off, and Pauline and Inga led them to a gate fifty metres from the bus stop. The gate posts were built of limestone, and the gate itself was of wrought iron, each half of which was about two metres wide and about three metres high. They were chained in the middle. There was a large round bell push set in one of the gate posts. Pauline pushed at it tentatively.

While they waited, Mason looked up the drive which extended for a hundred metres to a large three-storey house set amongst full-grown oaks. Cypresses lined the drive, and the lawns stretched down to the boundary wall which was also of limestone. It appeared to be the home of someone of wealth and position, and he began to have qualms about their reception. He looked around him at the swarm of shabbily dressed children.

At that moment an elderly man with a trim white beard, dressed in the traditional servant's dress of bottle-green trousers and striped waistcoat, appeared at the end of the drive. By the time he arrived at the gate, he was out of breath.

'Herr Zeller is expecting you.' He appeared to be quite unperturbed at the arrival of the ragged group outside the gates. 'One moment while I unlock the gate.'

As soon as the gates swung wide, the children surged forward, almost carrying the old man along with them. Pauline called out sharply, and they began moving in an orderly procession along the drive, following the servant up to the house where Joachim's friend awaited them. He was a tall, friendly man, slightly stooped, with a bald head and a small grey beard. Pauline had described him as one of her father's closest friends, and he came towards her and folded her in his large arms.

'My dear, how wonderful to have you visit my home at long last. If only your father would accept my invitation; I have written often enough.' He turned to Inga, kissed her cheek and shook hands with the two men. 'And these are your travelling companions.' He looked at the children crowding the portico. 'Come in. Come in.'

Pauline was hesitant. 'All of us? Perhaps we should take the children to another entrance.'

'I won't hear of it.' He motioned to the servant. 'Take the children to their quarters. See they have everything they need.' He put his arm around Pauline's shoulders. 'Come, you must all relax for a while.'

Lying in a bath for the first time in three years, Mason revelled in the sumptuous elegance of the furnishings. Even a momentary freedom from the presence of the horde of children was relaxation in itself. Unlike Pauline, who was almost possessive about them, his only motive for being with them was humanitarian, and while he never regretted the impulse that had led him to take them from the train, he would have cheerfully passed the burden on to someone else.

The man Zeller intrigued him. It was clear where his sympathies lay. Pauline had told Mason that when the Nazis had Czechoslovakia on her knees, and had invited Poland and Hungary in to carve themselves a piece of the flesh, Zeller had left Poland in disgust. He had loved his adopted country, and had been responsible for many factors in its industrial development, but after the Nazi invasion he had turned his back on Poland and had never gone back; not even to visit old friends, or to supervise the disposal of his holdings in that country.

Naturally he did not broadcast his motives nor the direction of his sympathies, with the result that he had been left alone to build up his German interests which were indispensable to the Fatherland. He was friends with Speer and Ambassador Hewel, and had been introduced to Hitler who had invited him to Bergesgarten twice for consultations. He was widely respected by the Nazis, who were unaware, however, of his extensive contacts in the Jewish underground.

He was deeply although anonymously involved in the July bomb plot, and had contributed considerable financial assistance. It was he, in fact, who had kept Joachim's group supplied with funds. In spite of his involvement in anti-Nazi conspiracies, however, not a hint of suspicion had touched him, and he still retained the power and influence he enjoyed amongst those at the top of Nazi hierarchy. His hatred of the Party had imbued in him a cavalier, almost contemptuous attitude toward the dangers of the situation in which he had embroiled himself. It was typical that he should offer his home without hesitation to a group of Jewish children, in spite of the grave danger to himself.

Mason eased himself lower into the water, content to let lethargy overtake his weary body. Finally exhaustion caught up with him, and he closed his eyes and slept, waking only when the cooling water began to chill his body. He stood up and towelled himself vigorously. He went through to the bedroom, and found a clean shirt and a pair of grey flannel trousers laid out on the bed. Next to them were clean underwear and a pair of socks. He dressed quickly, and felt for his shoes. To his surprise, he found his disreputable slip-ons replaced by a comfortable pair of brown shoes that fitted perfectly. Everything was new. Mason smiled to himself. With money, you could do anything.

A soft knock on the door interrupted his thoughts.

'Come in.' The door opened, and Pauline walked in, closing it softly behind her. Mason caught his breath. For a moment he couldn't speak. She was lovely, and – what was the word he was seeking? – feminine. That was it! Her hair, which had been released from the confinement of the eternal head scarf, fell in lustrous waves to her shoulders. She looked freshly scrubbed and he caught the hint of a perfume that reminded him of jasmine. She had touched her lips with lipstick, and had changed into a form-revealing dress of a soft material that accentuated her figure. Mason realised he was staring, and waved her to a chair.

She sat down, apparently unaware of the effect she had on him, though he discerned the twitch of a smile at the corners of her mouth.

'We have arrived at the point of greatest danger. We must

plan for tomorrow.' She leaned forward in her chair. 'Herr Zeller feels that we should split into four parties, and each of us take twelve children through four different routes and meet in Friedrichshafen. We can try to cross into Switzerland from there.'

Mason shook his head. 'I don't know. We've been successful up to now. And the permits – what are we going to do about those?'

'Herr Zeller has plans. We are to meet after dinner. I wanted you to know that there may be changes.' She stood up and moved towards the door. 'I didn't want anything to . . .'

'Pauline, listen to me.'

She turned. 'Nothing has been decided yet.'

'I'm not talking about the meeting.' He moved close to her. 'I want to talk about us. You and me.'

'No. Not now. I know what you want to say, and it isn't the time.'

'But it is! We don't know what will happen in the next few days, and I don't want to lose an opportunity I may never have again.' He put his hands on her shoulders. She looked up at him, her expression part apprehensive, part distressed. 'I love you, Pauline. I didn't believe it could happen like this after so short a time, but I've thought this through, and I know this is real.' He walked away from her, feeling he couldn't trust himself not to take her in his arms, but realising this was not the moment. 'I know you feel something for me, and I know you must have time to decide whether it is as real for you, as it is for me.'

'No, you're wrong.' She went quickly to him. 'It is real for me. I love you, too, but this is not the time.'

Mason felt a surge of joy. 'The moment is unimportant. Whether it is now or next month or after the war, what matters is how we feel.' He held her close. 'All that matters to people like us, is to love and be loved.' He kissed her then, and when he let her go her cheeks were wet with tears.

She looked up at him. 'For the first time in my life, I'm afraid – really afraid.'

'You, afraid?'

'Yes. I'm afraid for you. I love you so much, I'm afraid to lose you.'

For a moment he couldn't speak. Then he said. 'Come. They'll be waiting for us.'

Just after eight o'clock the next morning, Karl left the Gestapo office in Gorlitz, strolled past the station and turned into an alley. At the end of the alley was a small sign: Café. He went in and found a table near the back. He took a folded newspaper from his pocket and began to read while he waited to be served. The elderly woman who came from the kitchen looked at him expressionlessly. She took his order and went to the back. There she went to an alcove and made a telephone call. She heard the ringing tone, and then a deep male voice answered her.

'Yes.'

She spoke softly. 'Tell Joachim he must make a call in half an hour.'

There was a pause, and then the man said: 'He'll make it to point number three.'

'Good. I'll tell him.' She replaced the receiver and went to the kitchen to make up the order.

While he waited, Karl stared unseeingly at the newspaper in front of him. It was rare that he broke cover like this. Although Joachim and the woman knew who he was, no one else did, but this was an emergency, and he needed Joachim at once. In a moment she would give him the address of the call office where he must wait, and the call would come. This was their safeguard. No one knew in advance; not even he knew the call offices or their point numbers.

He wondered how long it would be before the Gestapo got on to him. He was certain they would. It was only a matter of time. More than ever now, he hoped he would finish his work before they came for him.

And then there was Inga. For the first time since his wife's death, he had allowed himself to feel; to accept the fact that his emotional needs could be warmed by the love of another human being. At their first meeting, it was obvious to both of them that they belonged together, and their passion had developed over the months to the point where his need was all-consuming. Yet here he was, an important officer in the Third Reich, jeopardising everything for a cause he believed in more than life itself. He was beginning to feel the return of his old depression.

The proprietress appeared in front of him. 'Ebelstrasse. Where it meets Wieseckstrasse.' She put the tray down in front of him and went back to the kitchen.

As soon as he had drunk his coffee, he left the café and walked the few kilometres to his destination. He reflected acidly on his driver's prying. He had been more and more concerned at the amount of walking his superior had been doing recently, and had commented on it that morning. Karl had passed it off by saying that he felt a need to walk off some of his increasing waistline.

The streets were crowded with Sunday strollers, but as he got nearer to Wieseckstrasse, he realised he was entering a quarter where few people went, an area of shuttered shops and deserted warehouses. He was a few minutes early, and walked past the box and back again. He stood for only a moment before the telephone rang.

'Karl?' It was Joachim's voice.

'Yes.' Karl hesitated. 'I have bad news. My office has been sent a general alert. It appears that a group of forty-eight children are missing from a truck consigned to Auschwitz. The report says that the truck arrived with six dead children and one dead soldier. The soldier's posting was traced to a small siding near Tetschen. His patrol commander reported him as a deserter, but it now appears he was murdered, and all offices as far as Nuremberg have been warned to watch for them.'

'I had hoped for more time.' There was silence for a moment. 'It certainly is bad news.'

'There is more. Lazero and his brother were taken by the Gestapo yesterday. They must know by now that Lazero drove them to Schöneck to catch the Bayreuth train.'

'Which office made the arrest?'

'They were taken to Teplitz, but the Breslau office was involved.'

'Breslau?'

'Yes. Are you able to warn them? Right away, I mean?'

'Johan will call me soon. His last call was yesterday when they arrived at Zeller's house. His next scheduled call is due.'

Karl looked at his watch. 'It's past nine now.' Joachim heard his agitation. 'We may be too late. Is there nothing I can do to help?'

'My dear fellow, there is no more you can do. That operation must be handled in Bayreuth. I cannot allow you to be endangered any further. The other matter is too important to us.'

'Surely – '

'No, Karl. I am not unfeeling. The children are important, true, but emotion must not be allowed to intervene. I know how important the Bayreuth matter is to you, but we will handle it.' Joachim listened to the silence for a moment, anticipating the other's objections. He said gently: 'There is no need for you to become involved. You must trust me. We knew we would have to face this problem some time. We knew we were placing people at risk, but we agreed we would accept it without becoming more emotionally involved. Now, more than ever, is the time for reason.'

Karl sighed. 'Of course. The need for action is making me indiscreet.'

Joachim smiled. 'You, indiscreet? Never! I have never known a more cautious man.'

Karl knew that Joachim was talking to remind him of his obligations, and to curb his anxiety. He realised that he was becoming more and more concerned about events beyond his control. In his own office, he forced himself to be the brusque officer, the man who was in control, who had the affairs of his section at his finger-tips. But it was at times like this, that he knew he was suffering from the effects of the daily tensions. The effort of being two different people was destroying him.

He took a deep breath. 'You are right, of course.' It was hot in the call box. He wiped his brow. 'I'll leave everything to you.'

'It should be soon now. Another few days at the most, and it will all be over.'

'Yes.' He watched a man passing on the other side of the street. 'I have had no word from Friedrichshafen. The three men left Munich at seven o'clock this morning.'

'Wilhelm will be waiting. He has been told which hotel they are going to.'

'Good.' The receiver was slippery in his palm. 'When will you get there?'

'Tonight. Use the emergency number if you need me. It will be manned constantly.'

'Take care.'

'You too.'

Karl replaced the receiver and strolled slowly back to Bahnhofstrasse, where his driver was still waiting for him. It took him nearly an hour.

Just before noon on that same Sunday morning, four Gestapo officers arrived in Bayreuth on a flight arranged by S.S. Oberführer Becker. The highest priority was given to the search for the children, and the four adults accompanying them. The Gestapo agents who had applauded the children's impromptu performance in the square provided an accurate description of the woman who had passed herself off as the music teacher.

A top-level conference was held at the Gestapo offices in Bayreuth, and it was agreed that the head of the section request assistance from the Sicherheitsdienst. Within twenty minutes, three platoons of S.S. had been despatched to the north of the city, where they fanned out to make a house to house search throughout the suburb. Still later that day, a bus driver was found who confirmed that a group of children had alighted from his bus at a stop just before the cemetery.

Four Gestapo agents converged on the house closest to the bus stop, a house belonging to the well-known industrialist Herr Josef Zeller.

In the meantime, Herr Harster, who had not accompanied the four men to Bayreuth, sat with S.S. Oberführer Becker in a car travelling between Munich and Friedrichschafen. The aircraft which had carried the four Gestapo men to Bayreuth had flown on to Munich, carrying Herr Harster and Oberführer Becker. Ostensibly, their reason for the journey to the Bavarian city, was to coordinate the activities of the Gestapo office there should the children escape the net in Bayreuth. Once in Munich, however, a car was provided for the two men and they disappeared in the direction of Furstenfeldbruck, where, they said, they had information about an Underground organisation which was to provide assistance for the children. They declined the help of the Sicherheitsdienst in Munich, since their investigations were only exploratory at this stage. Once out of the city, they took the southerly route, which did not go anywhere near Furstenfeldbruck, but which strangely enough went towards Friedrichshafen.

Becker looked at the waters of the Ammersee on their left, and then looked down at his watch. 'Two o'clock. We should be there by five.' He glanced at Harster. 'Are you sure about the rendezvous point?'

'Certain.'

'Why was Hansen recalled?'

'I don't know. He doesn't know either. He thinks it is because there is another man available.' Harster shrugged. 'It doesn't matter why he was recalled. It was lucky for us that he was. As soon as I heard he had been involved in a top secret operation, I wondered if it was the one we were interested in.' He smiled. 'With the information I had already, he thought I was also involved. He was quite prepared to talk about it when I dropped a few facts in his ear.'

'And he was certain the rendezvous is at the Handelshof Hotel in Friedrichshafen?'

'Certain. He was very friendly with the driver; one of Brunner's men. The driver heard them talking in the car.'

Becker was silent for a long time. The Ammersee was far behind them when he spoke again. 'You realise that we are on dangerous ground?'

'We've been through all that. I know the risks.'

They crossed the Lech bridge, and the highway eased southwards towards Kaufbeuren. Becker said: 'Everything points to the fact that the operation has been penetrated and taken over.' He glanced at Harster. 'You agree we cannot act officially until we are sure the operation has been subverted. At that stage, we have two choices; either give the money back to Müller and claim credit for preventing its theft, or – if we are still in the clear – take it back to Switzerland and bank it.'

'If we are careful, there is no reason why we should be discovered.'

'I agree. I wonder how much is involved.'

Harster licked his lips. 'It must be millions. At least ten

million dollars. It would not have been worth launching the operation for less than that.'

Becker nodded. 'I have arranged the documents for a frontier crossing into Switzerland. You will have to go alone as a director of Memmingen Castings.'

Harster glanced at Becker. 'You are not coming? You are very trusting.' He laughed. 'You are very sure I will return.'

'Very sure. You need me. You cannot operate alone. In any case, there is more than enough there for both of us. You cross into Switzerland, bank the money, and we can be back in Breslau before Tuesday.'

'If it *is* money. It could be jewellery.'

'It is more likely to be bonds. Millions of dollars in cash would be too bulky. No, I think it is bonds.'

Becker smiled to himself and watched the passing scenery. Harster drove mechanically, visualising millions of dollars.

Chapter Eighteen

Sunday, 13th August, 1944. 8 a.m.

Just seven hours earlier, before the Gestapo men had left Breslau for Bayreuth, Mason woke to the sound of a bell ringing in a distant part of the house. He lay in the warm bed, his eyes open, comfortable in the knowledge that whatever it was, he did not have to attend to it. Outside his window on the second floor, he could see the tops of the oak trees, and a glimpse of a blue sky dusted with flimsy white clouds. He stretched and threw aside the covers. The clothes he had worn on the train had been taken away the night before, and had not yet been returned to him. He wondered if he should dress in the new clothes provided for him.

There was a knock at the door, and he opened it cautiously to find a petite maid holding his freshly ironed clothes on a hanger. He took them from her, watched her curtsy and then closed the door. Just as he closed it, he heard another long peal of the bell. He thought it sounded like the front door bell.

He bathed and dressed, and then found his way downstairs to find that Pauline, Davis, Inga and Zeller had preceded him to the dining room, a vast cavern of a place, gleaming with newly polished furniture and silverware of all kinds. The sideboard held several dishes of bacon, eggs and various kinds of sausage. Zeller greeted him cheerfully, and invited him to help himself. He filled a plate and sat at a vacant place at the table next to Pauline. She looked at him and smiled. He felt her hand touch his under the table.

He smiled back. He heaped his fork but before he put it in

his mouth, he said: 'I won't ask where you've put your babies. I take it they have been properly clothed and fed.'

She laughed. 'While you were sleeping, Taff and I have organised their ablutions.' She looked at Davis frowning. 'Ablutions. That was the word you used, wasn't it?'

Zeller laughed. 'Ablutions! A typically middle-class English word. The kind of word I love the English for.'

Mason grinned. 'You're quite right about it's middle-class origin, but as a word for washing, it has a religious connotation.'

Zeller looked surprised. 'Really!' He forked another piece of sausage. 'I pride myself on my languages, but I must confess the English often have me . . . stumped.' He glanced proudly at Pauline. 'There! Even the idioms are part of my vocabulary.' He frowned. 'But religious? I'm surprised.'

Mason chewed and swallowed. 'The most common use is the act of washing the priest's hands before assuming the sacred vestments.' He waved his fork deprecatingly. 'Forgive me, I didn't mean to lecture.'

Zeller held up his hand. 'No! No! Please. It is most interesting. It is so seldom that I have the opportunity of a sensible discussion.' He sighed, and became serious. 'Even less so now with most of my colleagues gone.' He placed his fork on his plate. 'I have been told that more than four thousand are in prison or have been executed.' He looked up at them. 'Forgive me. I would not have mentioned it at this time, but it weighs on me so.'

Pauline reached out and covered his hand with hers. 'It can only be the beginning of the end. These are the actions of desperate men.'

At that moment, a bell pealed. Mason saw a servant pass the dining room door on his way to answer it. A few minutes later he entered the room and whispered to Zeller, who excused himself and went quickly to the door. Seconds later he came back to the dining room with Johan behind him. The three people in the room sprang to their feet.

'Johan.' Pauline ran to him and embraced him. 'How are you? Have you heard from Joachim?' She saw Zeller looking at them gravely. She was suddenly alarmed. 'Is something the matter?'

Zeller said: 'We are all in danger. We must move quickly.'

Johan took her hand. 'The Gestapo have had a report about the children. They have been traced to this city; perhaps even to this house. They could even now be searching this area.' He had been speaking in German. Davis looked from Johan to Mason, nonplussed. Johan went on, 'We have to get the children away from here.'

Mason saw Davis's bewilderment. Quickly he explained the situation to the Welshman.

Zeller put his arm on Pauline's shoulder. 'You can't go out into the streets without a plan of action. We have to arrange some form of transport. The streets are not safe.'

Pauline looked at him beseechingly. 'We must get them out of the house at once. We should never have endangered you like this.'

Zeller waved the suggestion away impatiently. 'You mustn't think of me at a time like this. The children are more important at this moment.'

Mason went to look out of the window at the street beyond the sweeping lawn. He turned to Zeller. 'What about the servants? Can you trust them?'

Zeller nodded. 'Nothing to fear there. I had to have people I could trust, if I was to carry out some of the assignments from the Underground. They all came with me from Poland, and Hans was my father's valet in the last war.' He walked across the room and back, his brow furrowed. 'Think, man, think.' Suddenly he turned and clapped his palms together. 'The servants! Of course!' They looked at him expectantly. 'How many children are there exactly? I know you said "about fifty".'

Pauline said: 'Forty-eight.'

'Good. There are sixteen servants in the house.' He walked across the room to the bell pull by the fireplace.

Mason was puzzled. 'What about the servants?'

At that moment, Hans, the man who had admitted them the day before, appeared in the doorway. 'Hans, get everyone in here. Everyone. Including the gardeners and the scullery maids.' The man hurried away, and Zeller continued. 'The S.S. will be looking for a group of forty-eight children, not so? But they won't find a group of children if the children are no longer a group.'

Mason began to get a glimmering of the plan, but aspects of it still puzzled him. 'Even if you have numerous little groups, surely they can't stay here?'

Inga cried out: 'The streets! Get them into the streets. Separate them all over the city.'

Zeller smiled. 'Exactly. And the sooner the better. What time is it?' He looked at the grandfather clock. 'It's ten now. We'll have to hurry.' While he had been speaking, servants were filing diffidently into the room. 'Come in. Come in.' He gestured to the centre of the room. 'Spread yourselves around the room. Quickly now.'

A crowd of retainers shuffled into the room; three chauffeurs, several aproned women, gardeners, maids and some whose duties were not obvious from their clothes. Mason looked at the gathering with awe. He wondered fleetingly how much Zeller's payroll was. This was obviously a household of immense influence in wartime Germany, for under normal circumstances some of them would have been in war work or conscripted into the forces.

Zeller began speaking. 'You must all listen carefully. The Gestapo are coming for the children who stayed here last night. They wish to take them away to the concentration camps, and you know what will happen to them there.' There was a chorus of shocked exclamations. 'As you know, these are Jewish children who were saved from death by these people here, so they are all in danger too.' There was another chorus of protesting voices. 'We can save them but I need your help.' Mason saw a variety of expressions cross the faces of the assembled gathering. Some were bewildered, some were eager, and some just waited to hear what Zeller had to say. 'I want volunteers to help us hide them. I want to say – ' he held up his hand to quiet the eager offers to help – 'I want to say that if you are caught, you will be shot. I want you all to think about this carefully.' He looked at each of them in turn.

Hans stepped forward. 'Mein Herr, I am willing to help in any way I can.' There was a sudden babble of voices, and several hands were raised.

Zeller said: 'Let's do this the other way. Is there anyone who, for whatever reason, is unable to help? Please do not be afraid to speak up. No one will blame you.' The group was silent. Zeller said softly. 'It is impossible to convey to you what I feel.'

Mason said: 'You have our heartfelt thanks.'

Hans shuffled his feet, and raised his hand. Zeller looked at him. Hans said: 'Mein Herr, it is we who are grateful. You have helped each one of us in some way, and some of our families are alive only because of what you did.' There were murmurs of assent. 'It is only fitting that we offer you our help now.'

Zeller was silent for a moment. Mason saw that he was overcome, then he said quickly: 'Good. There is no more time to waste. Pauline, get the children and take them into the library.' She hurried out, followed by Inga and Davis. Zeller said to the servants: 'All of you go and put on your street clothes. Martens, how many can we get into the cars?'

As the others filed out, the chauffeur made a quick calculation. 'Six in each of the two smaller cars, and ten in the limousine. That's twenty-two.'

'If we squeeze one more into each of the smaller cars we need only make two complete trips.'

'We can do it if we put the smaller children in the smaller cars.'

'Good. Get them ready – with their drivers.' The man hurried away as Zeller turned to Mason and Johan. 'Come into the library.'

He led the way out of the dining room, across the hall and down a passage lined with oil paintings. He opened the second door off the passage, and went into the library. Mason looked around enviously. The room was about twelve metres by about twenty metres, lined on three sides to the ceiling by bookshelves. Occasional spaces were left amongst the shelves for marble busts. There were ten of them representing scientists, poets and philosophers. The ceiling itself was about six metres high, moulded in various forms; angels surrounded by satyrs, rosettes, and some shapes Mason could not identify in the gloom above the brilliant lights of two crystal chandeliers. There was a long table in the middle of the room, and leather chairs were scattered about. The carpet was a deep maroon pile, and on the wall opposite the door, maroon curtains covered the windows from floor to ceiling to keep out the sunlight and protect the binding of the books. It was a comfortable room, functional yet elegant.

Zeller sat at the table and drew a block of paper towards him. 'First, we will list the names of the servants and then the names of the children who will go with them.'

'Go with them where?'

'Nowhere in particular. The safest place for them is on the buses or in the public gardens and museums. I will give each of them enough to ride the bus routes or visit the museums and art galleries. They must stay out until we make new plans for them today.' He smiled. 'Imagine sixteen small groups accompanied by adults with impeccable papers, criss-crossing – is that the word? – criss-crossing the city as ordinary families do every day. They will never be found.' He scribbled rapidly, chuckling to himself as he did so.

There was a knock at the door, and the children began to file in, led by Pauline and Inga. Mason was astounded . He hardly recognised them; their faces were shining, their clothes were clean and well-pressed, and all the girls had their hair washed and combed. Rosamund Bedaux caught sight of him, with a cry ran to him and threw herself at him. He caught her up and hugged her, deeply moved by her greeting.

'Line up, children. Let me look at you.' Zeller was almost paternal. 'My, what a handsome group.' There were some smiles and some giggles, and Zeller grew serious. 'Now, I think you all know that we are going to take you back to France as soon as we can, but the Gestapo must not know about it.' He paused and looked along the row of faces. 'We have a problem at the moment, and we have to send you out in small groups with the people who work for me here. You know some of them already; the ones who fed and bathed you.' He paused once more to see if they understood him. His French was elementary. Eyes watched him solemnly. 'You will ride around for the rest of the day, but I must put you on your solemn honour that you will not talk to a single soul.'

While he had been speaking, the servants were coming into the library in two's and three's. Zeller waited until they were all present. He said: 'If anyone speaks to the children, they must not answer. You are to say that they are too shy to talk.' He looked at the children and repeated his words in French.

'Do you all understand me?' Several heads nodded. 'Are there any questions?'

Martens, the chauffeur, stepped forward. 'How do the cars come into it; Mein Herr?'

'The three cars will be used to ferry the groups to bus stops, parks and museums all over the city. Drop the groups off at various points, no more than one group to a stop. The groups will either ride on the buses or visit the places assigned to them. Those who are delegated to ride the buses, must be sure that there is no more than one group on any bus. If someone is on the bus already, get off as soon as you can without inviting suspicion.' He picked up the paper on which he had listed the names of the servants. 'We must hurry. As I call your names, pick three children, get their names and give them to me. I will record them so we know who has gone with which servant. Then go out to the cars at once. The drivers must go out and get ready.'

One of the drivers said: 'When do we take our three children?'

'When you take the second group. You can be one of the groups to visit the museums.' He looked around at the assembly. 'One last word. Ring this house at intervals to tell us where you are, and to find out your next instruction.' He looked at Inga. 'You will have to stay by the telephone to take calls. If anyone calls here, you will be my new secretary.'

She nodded. 'Where is the telephone, and what is the number?'

'In my study. The number is on the dial.' He looked around once more. 'No more questions. Good. Hans, you begin. Pick three children.' He took banknotes from a wallet. 'Here is your money.'

Quickly he went through the names, and before he had finally allocated all the children, Mason heard the cars leaving the drive with the first groups.

Pauline looked at Davis and then at Mason. 'What about us? We shouldn't stay here in case I am recognised.'

Zeller grinned. 'No one will recognise you when I've finished with you. Come with me.' He disappeared into the passage with her.

Mason peered out between the curtains. The gates were

closed, but the drive and the street outside were deserted. He paced the big room restlessly, while the waiting servants stood impassively watching him. The children grew restless, and prowled the library, staring at the busts and touching the books. Mason slumped into one of the easy chairs. As he did so, he realised that the three Dreyfuss children were standing beside him.

Sarah, the eldest, gave him a tentative smile. 'We wish to speak to you, Monsieur.' Her big brown eyes looked at him with apprehension.

'What is it, Sarah?'

'We, that is to say, Ruth, Isaac and I, wish to know whether we can remain together when we go out.'

'Of course.' Mason was puzzled. 'Why would you think you would not go together?'

Sarak shook her head. 'The others did not remain together.'

'The others?'

'The Bedauxs and the Gallands. They went in different groups. Not with their sisters.'

Suddenly, Mason realised what they had done. Damn! In their haste to get the children away, they had forgotten to group families together. He looked at little Ruth, and her ten-year-old brother. Both of them would feel more secure with fourteen-year-old Sarah to look after them. He looked at the three children, so similar with their short black hair and brown eyes.

He smiled reassuringly. 'I will see that you remain together.'

The children smiled with relief. Sarah said: 'The journey will soon be over, will it not?'

'It will soon be over.'

'And we will be able to go to our Grandpère. His home is on the road to Vienne. Near Givors.'

'Of course. I am sure the Reverend Trocmé will see that you go to him.'

As he looked into the three expectant faces, Mason realised that it was not the collective tragedies that moved one. The idea of millions being killed was just too big to encompass; it was too impersonal, too incredible. It was the individual grief that brought home the perception of the ineffable suffering of a whole people. The grief of these three children moved him as nothing else had.

There were footsteps in the hall, and Zeller entered followed by Pauline; but it was a Pauline Mason hardly recognised. Her hair was encased in a protective turban, dirty with soot, and she wore a smock which was similarly begrimed. Her face was streaked with dirt, and she was grinning broadly. The servants gaped at her.

Zeller held her at arm's length. 'Doesn't she look wonderful? If the Gestapo come here, she will be tucked away in the fireplace, cleaning for all she is worth.'

At that moment, Martens returned to take the next group, and after he had gone, there were still eight people left; six children and their two chaperones. Mason cautioned one of the servants against separating the Dreyfuss children. Johan took his leave of them, promising to call every hour to get a report. He made arrangements to call Joachim and took a message from Pauline to her father.

Mason went to the curtains once more. Zeller watched him and smiled. 'Relax, my dear fellow. It won't help to be impatient. They will come soon enough if they are coming at all.'

Mason realised that the industrialist was enjoying himself. It was clear that this is what he lived for. Mason thought sardonically: A game for the man who has everything. Then he was ashamed of the thought, and realised that it wasn't in the nature of the man to be afraid. The only other way to meet a crisis was with humour, and this was Zeller's way.

The library door opened, and Martens indicated that he was ready for the last group. The other two chauffeurs had taken their own groups with them. Only Mason, Pauline, Zeller and Davis were left in the library. Inga was in Zeller's study at the telephone. Mason looked at the Welshman, deeply engrossed in a book he had taken from one of the shelves.

'Right, Taff. Put that away and follow me.'

Zeller looked surprised. 'Where are you going?'

'To the nearest bus stop.'

'Oh no, you're not. Your babies as you call them, have left me without help around the house, and that's your job.' He grinned at their surprise. Then he sobered. 'If the Gestapo come and find the house deserted – except for Cinderella here – they'll start to wonder. Your job will be to appear here and there as though there is a crowd somewhere.' He turned to Davis. 'Wherever you are in the house, you can hear the front door bell ringing. Go and answer it. It will look odd if I answer my own front door. I am too well known to the local S.S. It would be out of character.'

'They'll grab me in a minute,' Taff replied. 'I can't speak enough German.'

'Oh, hell! Then you'd better stay away from the door. Bob, you'd better take over that duty.'

At that moment the gate bell pealed. The three men stood, frozen into immobility. In spite of their show of bravado and their jocularity, the moment each of them had been dreading was upon them.

Pauline appeared in the doorway. 'There's a car at the gate with four men in it. Someone had better let them in.'

Maria Krumholz was not a courageous woman. In fact, most of her life had been spent in fear; fear of the partisans, fear of the Russian and German soldiers, and above all, fear of the Gestapo who represented all the phantoms of her childhood nightmares. At thirty, she had the lined face and thick body of a much older woman. Although she had only worked in the Zeller household for three years, those years were the most happy and secure in her entire life.

She was a neat, tidy woman, and dressed now in a severe black dress that was long enough to cover her thick calves, she could have been taken for a governess to the three children following her along this busy street off Kulmbacherstrasse. She had drawn the Bayard children, Vivienne, eleven, Elsa, nine, and Louis, seven.

Maria walked slowly, conscious of the people around her, watching for uniforms, careful all the while to avoid anyone who resembled an agent of the Gestapo. She appeared at ease, but beneath her apparent serenity was a sick, trembling fear that threatened to explode into an all-enveloping panic. She realised that her fear was communicating itself to the children and forced herself to smile and speak calming words.

Although the German words were incomprehensible to the children, they sensed the intention and smiled up at her.

She had come to Bayreuth through the recommendation of her cousin, Albert Martens. When Zeller's chauffeur had told him how the girl had been raped and her parents murdered, the industrialist had sent for her at once. The scars left by her experience had never been erased, and she swore it would never happen again. Before she left her Polish village, she had stolen a Luger from a drunken German officer, and had brought it with her to Bayreuth. Whenever she left the house, she carried the gun in her voluminous handbag. She had it with her now, its weight a comforting bulk under her hand.

She looked down at the three children, and felt a sense of loss for the husband and children she never had. The eldest girl was beautiful, with luminous gold hair and brown eyes. The two younger ones were round-faced with reddish hair and freckles. She wondered which parent had had the red hair.

It was warm in the sunlight, but between the ancient buildings were chasms of cool shadow. She decided she would walk for a few more minutes and then look for a telephone. She ached to get back to the big house, but she knew that terror awaited her there and all at once felt a fierce and protective tenderness for these three little ones.

Vivienne looked up at her and smiled. It was almost as though she felt the sudden outpouring of love from this strange woman, and in spite of her fear, the child seemed comforted somehow. She knew her sister was terrified, and held her hand tightly.

Elsa said: 'When are we going back to Ma'amselle Pauline?'

The woman squeezed her shoulder warningly. 'You must not speak French.'

The child looked at her uncomprehendingly. She was on the point of tears, the weeks of separation from her parents, and the constant bewildering movement from place to place, had confused and frightened her. The boy, too, was terrified, unable to understand why people spoke in strange tongues and commanded him not to speak in the only language he knew.

The three children had been taken from their home when their parents had been seized by the Gestapo. Taken to the bleak headquarters building, they had been thrown into a bare room where they stayed for three days, half-starved, cold and terrified. Finally they had been herded with many others to a station where they had boarded the train that had taken them towards the death camps.

Maria led the children into Hohenzollernring, where she saw a telephone box on the corner. She deposited a coin and dialled swiftly. A soft feminine voice answered her.

Maria said: 'Where must I go?'

Quickly the voice gave her the address of a warehouse west of Bayreuth. 'You must take a bus that goes out on the Hollfeld road and ride to the end of the line. You will see the warehouse on your left.'

As Maria turned from the box, Elsa said: 'Are we going back to Ma'amselle Pauline now?'

The two men in front of her turned quickly, and the woman felt again the devastating clutch of fright. There was no mistaking the Gestapo. Both men stared at her coldly, the one taking hold of the girls by the upper arm, and the other holding Louis in a firm grasp.

The man holding Louis held out his free hand. 'Papers.'

Maria could hardly breathe. The fear in her breast was like a band constricting her lungs. With trembling fingers she took the papers from her purse and handed them to the Gestapo man.

'These children are French.' It was a statement of fact that brooked no denial. 'These are part of the Jewish scum we are looking for.'

Maria looked at him dumbly. Through a mist she heard Elsa sobbing hysterically.

'You will come with us.'

The two men ushered their prisoners towards a black car that stood in the square. As they were hurried through the street, pedestrians glanced at them and averted their eyes.

While one of the men opened the rear car door, the other pushed the children into the back seat, motioning Maria to follow them. The door was slammed behind her, and at once she was held by the two sobbing girls while Louis stared at her, his expression a mixture of fear and bewilderment.

The car pulled away from the kerb, turned into Erlangerstrasse, and made a left and right into Bismarckstrasse before turning towards Eckersdorf. The Gestapo headquarters occupied a large house between Eckersdorf and Eschen.

Slowly Maria controlled her panic, and calmed the children. She looked at the two men in front. Neither was taking any interest in their passengers, and as they reached the outskirts of Bayreuth and left the tarred road, Maria looked around at the deserted countryside. Occasionally they drove through a tunnel of trees, and then they were out in the sunlight, the car raising a swirl of dust behind them.

Slowly, Maria dipped her hand into the large bag on her lap and felt the cold metal of the gun. She was determined that neither she nor the children were going to be taken into the cells below the house on the Eschen road, even if she had to shoot them and then kill herself. Silently she drew the gun from her bag and held it on her lap out of sight of the two men who appeared to be oblivious of the desperate woman behind them.

She felt the car slowing, and looked ahead through the windscreen. They passed a crossroads warning sign, and then she saw a signboard which pointed them left to Eschen. To their left and right the fields were deserted, and she glanced back quickly through the rear window. Nothing. She was aware of the children watching her, and she raised a warning finger.

Suddenly she felt fear welling up inside her, and her hands trembled uncontrollably. Then, as the car rolled to a stop, she raised the gun and fired at the hated figures in front of her. She was dimly aware of the violent explosions, the smell of cordite, and the gun clicking emptily in her hand. Without conscious volition she had emptied the chamber into the two hunched and bleeding bodies in the front seat.

She heard the children screaming, but they were silenced by her harsh command. She scrambled out of the car, opened the front door, and pulled the driver from behind the wheel. The passenger followed the driver into the road, then dropping the gun on to the passenger seat, she dragged the bodies one at a time to the verge and rolled them down the short bank into the ditch. She stood back from the ditch to see if they were visible, but they were hidden from anyone not standing directly above the depression.

She turned to see the three children staring at her mutely from the car window.

'It's all right. Do not be afraid.'

Although the words were meaningless, they appeared to be reassured by her tone.

Maria stood alongside the car for a moment, debating her next move. The road was still deserted, but the trees beyond the ditch looked safe and inviting. She wondered if she should hide the children there and go for help, but she rejected the idea at once. There was no guarantee they would remain where she had hidden them.

She got behind the wheel and looked down at the bewildering array of controls at her feet. If only someone had taught her to drive. She peered at the dashboard for the ignition switch, and as she did so, became aware of a figure at the passenger window. She looked up at a man in the uniform of the S.S. He was holding the revolver she had left on the seat beside her.

Chapter Nineteen

Sunday, 13th August, 1944. Noon

After a night of intensive bombing, the damage to the factories around the old Zepplin works was as bad as Hackett thought it would be. Their car was held up twice while the workmen cleared the rubble from the road ahead of them, and once they had to make a five kilometre detour. They arrived at their hotel just before lunch.

As they went up the steps, Grant looked across the street to where a man sat on a bench under a tree. He wore a hat and his beard was grey and unkempt.

Grant touched Patterson on the shoulder. 'Take a look at the one across the road with the beard.'

'What about him?' Patterson took his bag from Fritz. 'He doesn't look like anyone I know.'

Grant stared hard at the man. 'I wonder what he would look like without the beard.'

Patterson laughed and patted his shoulder. 'Don't tell me you're seeing Erich Rowecki again.' He led the way into the hotel with Hackett close behind him. Patterson lingered on the steps for a moment, then he followed the other two to the reception desk. Fritz drove the car around to the back, where he waited for the man with the beard to cross the yard before he drove the car into one of the slots at the back of the garage. There was only one other car in the park. He got out of the car and shut the door quietly. He saw the bearded man look back across the yard, and then edge himself between two cars where he could drop out of sight if anyone came.

Fritz shook his hand. 'Erich. I'm glad to see you.'

'Trouble?' Erich looked at him quizzically. 'Everything looked fine to me.'

'They know I'm Brunner's man. They plan to lose me after they return from Zurich. The American has agreed to join them in taking over the money.'

'Are you sure. My information is that the American can be trusted.'

'I heard them talking in the hotel in Munich. I saw the American go into their room. I listened at the door.' He glanced towards the main building. 'I may as well go back to Gorlitz. I'm no good on this operation if they know I'm one of the watchdogs.'

The other man was silent for a long moment. 'No. I think you should stay. It will all be over in two days, and one never knows. You may be needed.'

Fritz shook his head. 'I still think I should go back, even if it is to let someone else take over.'

'I'll think about it. I'll see you here tonight at seven.'

'Tonight then.' He locked the car. 'I'd better go in. They'll wonder where I am.'

He watched the man called Rowecki walk through the yard and around the corner of the main building. He took his bag and went into the hotel.

From his window overlooking the street outside, Hackett saw an old man appear from the drive leading to the garages. He shuffled slowly along the sidewalk and disappeared around the corner. All at once his senses were alerted. That was the man Grant thought was the mysterious Rowecki. Then he remembered that Fritz had taken the car to the back, and the whole scene made sense to him. Patterson said that Fritz was a travelling nursemaid, put with them to watch Müller's interests. Then the bearded man had to be Rowecki. Now, more than ever, he wished Joachim had given him some way to communicate with him.

He changed and went downstairs for lunch. Grant and Patterson were already in the dining room and more than halfway through a large chicken pie. An opened bottle of wine was on the table. As he sat down, Patterson poured some into a glass for the American.

'Sorry we've nothing stronger. Neither of us drinks spirits, so if you want some, you'll have to get your own.'

Hackett knew Patterson was mocking him, and he realised how badly he had underestimated this pair. He had taken them for a pair of hard-drinking thugs who were only after what they could get out of the operation for themselves. There was no need to wonder any longer how they came to be chosen for this assignment. He remembered how quickly Grant had made a tentative identification of the bearded man. Although it did not concern them much whether Rowecki was following them, they were constantly watching their back trail.

It occured to him suddenly that they could still be loyal to Müller. Everything they had done and said so far could still be for the benefit and profit of their patron; even the promised bribe to himself of ten million dollars for his silence once they reached Allied territory. Not for one moment did he believe that the offer was made in good faith. He was comforted by the fact that if he had underestimated them, they in turn had underestimated him.

When they had eaten, Grant led the way into the lounge where they sat down at a corner table, remote from the other patrons. Apart from some officers playing cards in the far corner, and an elderly couple by the window, the lounge was deserted.

Patterson lit a cigarette. 'It's time we put you in the picture.' He dropped the match into an ashtray. 'Tonight, Grant and I are going to Meersburg where we will take a ferry to Konstanz. We will spend all day tomorrow in Zurich, and return late tomorrow afternoon. When we come back, we will have a letter of credit drawn on a Swiss bank.'

Hackett lifted his eyebrows sceptically. 'A letter of credit? Surely it didn't need your physical presence in Switzerland to pick up a letter of credit. It could have been done an easier way.'

Patterson smiled. 'The letter of credit is to be drawn on bearer bonds lodged in a safe deposit. It needs our personal intervention, with the key, to draw them and lodge them with the bank before we can draw the letter.'

'And how are you going to split a letter of credit into three?'

'Your share will be banked for you in a numbered account.'

Hackett roared with laughter. 'Hell! Do I look like a raw kid, still wet behind the ears?' He coughed. 'So you're gonna leave ten million dollars in a nice little piggy bank in Zurich? You have to be kidding.'

Patterson watched him blandly. 'It's the only way you'll get it.' He blew a cloud of smoke. 'You're crazy if you think you are going to get it any other way. Where are you going to keep that much while you are on the move? Use your brains.'

'I am using them. What about a small letter of credit for me. Or is that asking too much?'

'No. Your share stays in the bank. You'll get a nice engraved note from the bank to prove it, with a number you'll have to remember.' Patterson stubbed out his cigarette. 'But we will keep a photograph of the document just to keep you honest.' He smiled sarcastically. 'We would hate you to deny having a Swiss bank account.' He shrugged. 'On the other hand, play the game our way, and you have nothing to worry about.'

'What happens after you get back from Zurich?'

'We drive to Wangen airfield where a plane is standing by to take us to Faenza in Italy.'

'Why there?'

'At the moment the Allied troops are in Florence. Just to the north is Kesselring's Gothic Line. That's going to hold up the Allied advance for some time. It could be a stalemate for the whole of winter, so we'll have to find a place the Allied troops will over-run in the next few days.'

'That will take some careful planning, and split-second timing.'

'To the east is a place called Santa Guistina which has a monastery in the hills just above it. There, we meet a gentleman from Spain who will look after the letter of credit until we are through Allied control and it is safe to take it to Rome.'

'How can you be sure the Allies will reach there?'

'Herr Müller has checked with the OKW, the German High Command. Kesselring is going to consolidate his position north of there, and that's where the Eighth Army will end its run.'

'This Spanish gentleman – how can you be sure he won't just disappear?'

Grant shrugged. 'That isn't our business. Müller gave us our instructions and we carry them out.' He looked out across the street. 'But if I were guessing, I'd say that the Spanish gentleman knows what is good for his health.'

'And when do you disappear with your share?'

'That's our affair. Be assured we have everything planned.'

Hackett grunted and said: 'Well, it looks as though you have the whole thing organised.' He stood up, and felt a twinge in his old wound. 'I'm going upstairs for some shut-eye. It's been a long morning, and a short catnap after lunch is great for sharpening up the evening.' He stopped. 'What about Kuhn and the man – what's his name – Rowecki? Are they going with you to Italy?'

Patterson looked at Grant whose face was expressionless. Patterson looked back at Hackett.

'They can't follow us into Allied territory.'

Hackett limped up to his room, deep in thought. It was obvious that the two men had no intention of betraying Müller. The whole charade was to keep him in line. The set-up was as full of holes as a sieve. If only he could make contact with Joachim. There was something fishy about the whole business. He was uneasy, and felt the answer was there, just beyond his understanding.

He went along the corridor, key in hand, and at his door he pushed the key in the lock and pressed the door handle. Before he turned the key in the lock, the door opened and slowly swung wide. He watched it, every nerve alert. He had locked the door before he went downstairs, and now it was unlocked. The hotel staff would not have cleaned yet, since the room had not been used. He moved cautiously over the threshold, and looked around the room. He looked towards the bathroom. The door was open, but he couldn't see anyone there.

Then a voice spoke to him from the curtained shower stall. 'Shut the door and come in. We've got to talk.'

Hackett was overjoyed. 'Joachim! I'd know that voice anywhere.'

A man stepped into the room and Hackett felt a momentary spasm of alarm. It was the bearded man from the bench under the tree. 'Then you must be –'

'Erich Rowecki. Yes, that's my real name. Joachim was my name in the Underground.'

'Hell, I wouldn't have recognised you! That beard looks as real as your arm.' He studied Joachim from both sides and laughed out loud. Then he sobered as he remembered Patterson's remark in the forecourt of the hotel. 'Patterson recognised you. He saw you when he arrived.' Belatedly he remembered the unlocked door, and went and turned the key. 'Sit down. I have a hell of a long briefing for you.'

Joachim sat in the chair opposite the door. 'Yes, we have much to talk about. What is their next move?'

'We drive to Wangen airfield where a plane is standing by to take us to Faenza in Italy. From there we make for a monastery near Santa Justina, east of Florence. A Spaniard will hold the letter of credit while their bona fides are established with Allied Control. They said that Müller has checked with the OKW and was told the Kesselring is going to consolidate just north of there.' He frowned. 'Would he be able to get that kind of information? Müller, I mean?'

Joachim nodded. 'Müller is privy to everything. As head of the Gestapo, he knows how to get what he wants, and as this is an official operation, he would have had no trouble.'

Hackett was impatient. 'How the hell did you get the job of herding this lot?'

'I was brought into it when Brunner wanted bodyguards for them. He asked Oster's office in February to provide a man from the Abwehr. Oster jumped at the chance of putting one of his own men into the operation. We didn't know what the operation was then – they didn't tell us much. Not even Brunner knew everything, but by dint of putting six with five, we discovered it concerned your breakout. That was when we put the whole cell on the alert for you, and it was Nina in the café who finally found you.' He smiled. 'Or you who found her.'

'Surely Patterson and Grant should be pleased to have you around.'

'They were against it from the first briefing. There were four of us there: Brunner, those two and I. They rejected any suggestion that we give them a bodyguard. They insisted that they could take care of themselves, and if it was their honesty

Brunner was worrying about, well, Herr Müller trusted them. That was the first inkling we had that money was involved.'

'And does Müller trust them?'

'Absolutely.' He frowned. 'But the more I thought about it, the more I was puzzled. The whole operation was planned months ago and even when it appeared that everything was set for "go", they still delayed. It seemed as though they were waiting for something; something that had nothing to do with the operation they had outlined.' Joachim paced the floor. 'Finally I found it – it's too long a story to detail now – and the whole thing came together. The deadline – the 14th – finally led us to it.'

Hackett felt a stirring of excitement. 'I knew it! There's something else behind it, isn't there?'

Joachim smiled. 'You're smart. Yes, there is something else.' He turned his palms upward. 'Oh, sure, the money thing is important, but not because Müller is getting money out of the country. No, it's a payoff.'

'A payoff?'

'Yes. Grant and Patterson are two of the most accomplished saboteurs and deadliest killers in the whole of the German Reich.' Joachim paced back to the window and turned. 'They have been waiting for a particular event to take place in Italy; something they knew was inevitable, and now they are ready for it.'

'What is it?'

'They've been waiting for Churchill to tour the Italian Front, so they could set up his assassination. His tour was finally scheduled for 12th–21st August. Now, in fact. He is there now, and everything is waiting; all the conspirators, and all the arrangements. All they are waiting for is the money, and the – what do you Americans call them? – the hit men. The contractors.'

'Churchill! They want to kill Churchill!' Hackett was staggered at the enormity of the concept.

'Yes. What started me off being sceptical about the money business, was that the security wasn't as watertight as it should have been. It was too leaky, as though they didn't really care if you knew what was happening. Everyone was blinded by the spurious objective.'

'Thirty million! That's what it is costing them to kill Churchill.'

'That madman Hitler dreamed this one up. He'd willingly pay a hundred million to eliminate Churchill.' Joachim looked quizzically at Hackett. 'Are you disappointed? Fritz believes you have thrown your lot in with them.'

'I let them believe that. They offered me ten million dollars to go through with it. They even said I'd get a receipt from a bank in Zurich.'

'Obviously it'd be a forgery.' He frowned. 'Did they think you'd turn them in?'

'They guessed I knew about my brother.'

'I see. So they decided to give you a big enough bribe to go in with them. And I bet they told you they were going to run with the money?'

'You don't think they would?'

Joachim smiled and shook his head.

'I got that impression too. Nothing held up if you figured it that way.'

'They wouldn't last a month if they crossed the Sicherheitsdienst, even if they went to the Arctic.' He looked directly at Hackett. 'Nevertheless, ten million dollars is a lot of money.'

Hackett looked back at Joachim, anger stirring in him. 'Is that what Pauline's life is worth to you?' he said brutally.

Joachim smiled. 'No. And I never thought you would join them, but I had to ask.'

Hackett sighed. 'That comes of being around thieves too long.'

Joachim smiled. He lit a cigarette and looked around for an ashtray. Hackett pushed one over to him. Joachim continued. 'Anyway, we decided to do something about the whole scheme, and that's when I brought in the rest of the cell. To begin with, we didn't know who the traitor was, and we had to find out. We couldn't let the other two be murdered in cold blood, but we knew if we gave the three of you enough rope, then the man we wanted would give himself away. That's why we acted out the farce of taking you to the siding near Tetschen. And that's when the spanner went into the works: when you found the children.'

'You mean we weren't catching the train there?'

'You had – what's the American expression? – a snowball's hope in hell. That siding is patrolled every day.'

'How did you know I was the one who –'

'Who had been coerced?'

'Yes. How did you know, if you didn't know eight hours before?'

'Our informant discovered which one of you it was, through the execution of your brother.' He saw the pain in Hackett's face. 'I'm sorry.'

'It's all right.'

'The man discovered the dead man's name was Hackett. He sent a coded letter with Johan.'

'Do you know they are going to a monastery in Italy?'

'Yes. We have learnt that a certain Bishop Hudal is their contact there.'

'They mentioned the Bishop. It's monstrous.'

'No, not monstrous. Misguided, perhaps. Hudal believes Stalin is a greater danger in the long term than the Nazis. So he embraced National Socialism.' Joachim rose to his feet and walked slowly to the window. 'His mistake was believing that either one is better than the other. They are both evil.' He turned and looked at Hackett. 'On the other hand, history may prove him to be right. Communists have never disguised their aim of world domination, and both creeds have anti-semitism as their basis.' He stubbed out his cigarette. 'What are our two hit men doing at the moment?'

'They are waiting for an emissary from their control with documents they will need in Switzerland. They are waiting in the lounge.' Hackett was only half aware that he was answering Joachim's questions. He was appalled by what the other man had told him about the assassination. 'I can't believe that the Vatican is involved in murder.'

Joachim took another cigarette from his pocket and tapped on his thumb. 'Of course not, no. Firstly, I don't believe the Bishop knows about the assassination. I think he believes it is a question of helping his friends.' He lit the cigarette. 'Secondly, the Catholic church helps the hunted, the poor, the weak, and in fact anyone who asks for their help. Their origins are not questioned. The churches are traditional havens of sanctuary.'

'But to –'

'No. Let me finish.' Joachim puffed at his cigarette and paced the floor. 'You see, if a basic tenet of a philosophy is adhered to regardless of the circumstance, then you may find some grey areas in living up to that philosophy, which will be seized on and criticised by those who don't understand.' He went to the window and parted the curtain. 'A society based on this kind of moral consistency is sound, ethical and humanitarian, and these are the qualities by which future generations will judge us.' He stopped and looked sharply at Hackett. 'But I'm boring you.'

Hackett waved his hand impatiently. 'No, no. Go on. This kind of tolerance I find fascinating.' Joachim looked at him suspiciously, but he could detect no sarcasm.

He shrugged and went on. 'But a society based on an evil dogma – militarism, racism or the doctrine of the domination of any one group over another – will eventually disintegrate.' He walked across to the ashtray.

Hackett stared at him. 'Yes. I understand that you have to be consistent.'

Joachim nodded. 'Writers throughout the centuries have pointed out this obvious fact to an uncaring humanity. When Samuel Butler wrote *Erewhon,* he was pointing out the dangers of a society whose moral values are topsy-turvy.' He puffed on his cigarette impatiently and walked back to the window. 'The very fact of Nazis being helped by the Catholic church enrages me, I admit it. After all, I'm on the other side of the fence.' He turned back to face Hackett. 'But I'm not going to be so arrogant as to usurp my maker's function and judge my fellow man by deciding who the church should help.'

'But you'll try and stop them helping Nazis if you can.'

'Of course. I won't judge them or criticise their philosophy, but I sure as hell reserve the right to do something about it.'

Hackett shook his head. 'Now I've heard everything.'

'You should live so long.' Joachim grinned his engaging grin, his eyes sparkling over his beard.

Hackett grinned back. 'Well, what are we going to do about it?'

'Do you know which airfield they're leaving from?'

'Wangen.'

'When do they fly out?'

'Tomorrow night. We move from here to some dump called the Kaiserhof in Wangen. In the Herrenstrasse.'

'As soon as that. We haven't much time. We'll have to work fast.'

'What do you intend doing?'

'First we'll have to neutralise Grant and Patterson. Then Gunther and Wilhelm will replace them. From then on the planned course is followed with the three of you flying to Italy. As soon as you are in Allied hands, you place the information I have given you into the hands of Military Intelligence.'

'What about the pilot? And the Luftwaffe office at Wangen? And the money? All this has to be organised. We haven't time.'

'Leave everything to me.' Joachim grinned. 'The money will go back to Zurich, but in a different account. Perhaps some Jewish refugees will need a stake after the war.' He peered through the gap in the curtain at the deserted street below. 'Fritz wants to go back. I think it's wise to agree. We'll keep the car here.' He went to the door. 'Keep yourself available if you can. I will look for you tomorrow afternoon at the Kaiserhof.'

As he was about to open the door, Hackett said: 'Joachim, what of the others? Pauline and the children?'

Joachim smiled. 'They are safe at present. They are with a friend in Bayreuth.' He opened the door, paused for a moment and said: 'Do you know what kind of plane is waiting?'

'Yes. Grant said something on the way from Munich. He said they had laid on a Junkers-390.'

Joachim's eyes gleamed. He shut the door and came back into the room. 'That makes a world of difference. I wonder if Brunner knows this?'

'Wasn't it he who arranged it?'

'Maybe, but not necessarily.'

'What difference does it make?'

'It means that if I can fix it, the plane can fly anywhere. Not just to Italy.' He went back to the door. 'I'll see you tomorrow.'

Herr Harster hurried back to his hotel where the Oberführer waited in the suite he had reserved for them.

The Gestapo man could hardly contain himself. 'I've found

them. They are at the Handelshof, but they're moving to the Kaiserhof in Wangen.'

'Are you sure?'

'The man at the desk told me. He can't understand why they're moving from the Handelshof to a dump like the Kaiserhof.'

'But is he certain? How does he know?'

'He was told by one of them to ring the Kaiserhof and reserve a room. And only until nine that same night. So they must be moving before then.'

Becker paced back and forth excitedly. 'We must go over there at once and engage a room there. When they get whatever it is they're bringing back from Switzerland we'll be waiting for them.'

Chapter Twenty

Sunday, 13th August, 1944. 1 p.m.

Davis swung the gates wide, and the car swept up the drive, the four men giving him a brief glance as they went by. Davis wondered if he should have tugged his forelock. He smiled to himself as he shut the gate. He wouldn't have known how. Welshmen didn't go in much for tugging forelocks these days. He watched the four men alight in front of the portico and walk up the steps where Zeller was waiting for them. He saw Zeller usher them into the house. Davis went on up the drive to the garages at the back. He hurried through the kitchen and sculleries, and went into the main passage to the library where he found Pauline sitting on the floor in front of the fireplace.

'Where did they go?' He found he was whispering.

Pauline smiled. 'I haven't seen them yet.' She gestured to the fireplace. 'But I'm all ready for them.'

Davis patted her shoulder and went out. He wondered where Mason was. He heard voices coming from the dining room and went through to the kitchen. He looked for something to do; scrub pots or something. He looked around the kitchen, but the place looked as though a battalion of scullery maids had been through the place. Pots, both copper and stainless steel, were hanging in neat rows on hooks along the wall. The huge kitchen range was clean, and polished with something to make the black and silver surfaces gleam in the overhead lights. The curtains over the huge mullioned windows were crisp and clean. He looked about him helplessly. Then he saw the boots on the floor by the heavy oak door, and siezed them eagerly. He picked up the polishing rags from the floor, and began rubbing. He hoped the Gestapo wouldn't be in the house too long. He had always hated cleaning boots.

In the dining room, Mason turned from the window as the Gestapo men followed Zeller into the house. He had been rubbing assiduously at the panes until he thought his arm would break. He greeted them courteously, and they returned the greeting coldly with just a nod of the head. He went back to his rubbing.

Zeller indicated the sideboard. 'Can I offer you a drink, gentlemen? Schnapps, or would you prefer coffee?'

Their leader, a squat powerful man with receding hair, replied for them. 'No, thank you.' He was brusque. Mason realised the man was certain that he would find the children here. He saw one of the younger men give the room a careful scrutiny.

'No?' Zeller was at his most suave. 'I haven't seen you gentlemen before. I know most of the people from the Bayreuth Gestapo.'

'No.' The man was blunt. 'We have come from Breslau.'

'I see. It must be something important to bring you all this way. How can I help you?'

'Herr Zeller, we regret the necessity, but we have to search this house.'

Mason saw the benignity disappear and Zeller the millionaire industrialist, friend of high-ranking Nazis, come to the surface. 'I beg your pardon, Herr – whatever your name is.' He turned and walked to the fireplace, then swung round to face the four men. 'You have the effrontery to walk into my house and tell me you are going to search it, without first telling me what you are looking for. Does S.S. Oberführer Ritter know of this instrusion?' Zeller spoke quietly and with authority, 'What is the purpose of this outrage?'

It was clear that the man had been warned about the influence Zeller wielded, for he was not prepared to be goaded. Nevertheless, he held his ground, and said quietly, 'I said I regretted the necessity, Herr Zeller, but we have reason to believe that some children were seen entering these grounds.'

'Some children were seen coming to this house?' Zeller was

elegantly sarcastic. 'And what, may I ask, is wrong with children coming to this house?' Mason held his breath. 'My grandchildren visit me regularly every Sunday.' He looked at his watch. 'They may in fact arrive in half an hour. So you see, Herr –' He stopped, waiting for the man's name.

'I beg your pardon. Weltzin. And these are Bauer, Neumann and Kretzmer.' Each of them inclined his head as his name was mentioned. Weltzin produced his identity card.

Zeller waved it away contemptuously. 'So you see, Herr Weltzin, you have anticipated them by half an hour.' He waved his hand. 'Once they arrive, you may search this house with pleasure.' His voice hardened. 'After I have telephoned Herr Obergruppenführer Müller and informed him of this intrusion.'

Weltzin glanced briefly at Mason. He wasn't happy at having a servant witness his discomfiture. 'You misunderstand me, Herr Zeller. I –'

'What you have said, I understand perfectly. Correct me if I am wrong. You wish to search this house because you saw children coming here.' He looked at Weltzin quizzically. 'Are you saying that you saw these children yourself?'

'No, Herr Zeller, I did not say that. I said that we have reason to believe some children came here.'

'That is exactly the way I interpreted your statement. You want to search my house because some children came here. I made it clear that my grandchildren have not arrived, and even if they had, I fail to see why I should suffer the indignity of having my house searched.' Mason was suddenly aware of what Zeller was doing. In creating a climate of embarrassment, the Gestapo man would be only too eager to make a perfunctory search and escape. It was a good try, but Mason did not think it would work. Nevertheless any slight victory was an advantage.

The Gestapo man pressed on. 'The children I refer to are forty-eight children who were bound for Auschwitz. They escaped, and when last seen were heading for this area.'

'I see. So they were not seen entering this house. And if I give you my word there are no children in this house, you would search anyway?'

Weltzin looked embarrassed. 'It would still be necessary to search, Herr Zeller.'

'I see. I will, naturally, make mention of this fact when I refer the matter to the Reichssicherheitshauptamt in Berlin.' The Gestapo man inclined his head, but remained unperturbed. Zeller went to a chair and sat. 'You may search all you please, but I assure you it is not my habit to hide criminals in my home.'

'There has been no mention of criminals, Herr Zeller. I have not implied that you harbour criminals.'

'Oh? Surely these people must have been convicted of something heinous to be consigned to Auschwitz.'

Weltzin began to look uncomfortable. 'These were Jewish children. Sub-humans.'

'How old were they?'

'They range from seven years of age to about –'

Zeller was astounded. 'Seven years old, Herr Weltzin! And your office has such confidence in you, that they send only four men to apprehend these desperadoes.' He shook his head. The other three men shuffled their feet self-consciously. Zeller waved his arm elaborately. 'My dear Weltzin, search by all means. See that there are no children in my house. Protect me from these desperate seven-year-old criminals.' He turned to Mason. 'Show these –' he paused and looked at the four men – 'gentlemen through the house while I ring Gestapo headquarters.' He swept from the room.

'Will you come with me, gentlemen?' Mason led the way through the door and into the passage.

Weltzin stopped. 'Wait!' He stopped in the doorway. 'You. You are not German.' Zeller heard him and stopped halfway down the passage.

'No, Mein Herr. I –'

Zeller broke in. 'This man is an artisan in my factory. He earns extra money by working on Sundays in my house. That way I can give my servants Sundays off.'

The man ignored Zeller. 'Papers!'

Zeller stalked back purposefully, joy in his face. Mason realised that the Gestapo man had gone too far. Zeller stormed at him. 'By heaven, Weltzin, I'll have you for this! There is no doubt that you have come here to harass me for some reason. You came here to look for forty-eight children, and now you intimidate my servants.' He pointed to the dining room. 'Herr Himmler and Herr Kaltenbrunner have dined with me in that room. Herr Müller has slept in a bedroom on the first floor, and I am a man trusted by the Führer to be party to the most secret matters.' He pointed his finger in the Gestapo man's face. 'And you have the audacity to harass me!'

'With respect, Herr Zeller, I am not here to harass you. I came to look for forty-eight children – '

'Exactly. That is what you said. And if you are not here to harass me, will you please tell my why you asked for my servant's papers? And why, when I give you an explanation of his presence, you treat me with insolence?'

'I – I – ' Weltzin was at a loss.

'Well, out with it, man! Tell me how you think my servant is involved with forty-eight children?'

'I didn't say he was, Herr – '

'Indeed, you admit he has nothing to do with them, so you asked for his papers to harass him.'

'No, I – '

'Get on with your search.' Zeller's contempt was profound. 'But be sure that I will make a full report about this matter.'

Silently, Mason led the way through the house. In each room, the four men left nothing to chance. They made a thorough search of everything including cupboards, wardrobes, dressing tables and bathrooms. Mason realised they were looking for some sign that the children had been in the house. He was sure they no longer believed the children were hidden there, but if they could establish that Zeller may have been hiding them, they would be vindicated.

He led the way into the cellar. Weltzin stood in the doorway and looked into the huge room with satisfaction. He was no fool. He saw the new mattresses stacked tidily against the wall, and the blankets folded and heaped on the mattresses. Silently, Weltzin counted the mattresses.

He said to Mason. 'What is this room used for?'

Mason shrugged. 'Herr Zeller did not tell me.'

The men began a thorough search, turning the mattresses over and shaking out the blankets. He noticed they refolded everything carefully and smiled inwardly. They still had some respect for Zeller's influence. Suddenly one of the men stooped to pick up something that had fallen out of the blanket he had been shaking. It was a small white sock. The man handed it to Weltzin.

Weltzin took it and looked at Mason. 'What time did you arrive here?'

'At seven o'clock.'

'Did you see anything? Any children?'

'No. If they had been here, I would have seen them.'

Weltzin grunted. 'Where are you from? What country?'

Mason felt the strings of trepidation. He wished Zeller had accompanied them on this search. 'I'm from Holland, Mein Herr. I work in Herr Zeller's factory.' Suddenly he remembered Hamilton. 'I came to join the Landstorm Nederland, but when they heard I was a milling machinist, they made me work in the factory.'

'I see.' He turned and led the way upstairs. 'We will be in the dining room. Please ask Herr Zeller to join us there.'

'Certainly, Mein Herr.'

Mason found Herr Zeller in the library, sitting at the table. He told him about the sock. Zeller just nodded. Mason saw that he was quite unperturbed, apparently rifling through a pile of correspondence.

He looked up when Mason walked in. 'Bring Weltzin in here. I have something to show him.'

Mason sighed and went back to the dining room. 'Herr Zeller wants to see you in the library, Mein Herr. He has something to show you.'

Weltzin looked at his assistants, shrugged, and followed Mason into the library.

Zeller looked up. 'Well, gentlemen, did you find the children? Your seven-year-old criminals?'

Weltzin ignored the thrust. 'Can you tell me who has been sleeping in the basement, Herr Zeller?'

'Of course. The basement.' Zeller smiled sarcastically. 'You found sixty – no, is it seventy? – mattresses, and jumped to the conclusion that I had been harbouring your desperate criminals.' He took a letter from the files in front of him. 'Be so good as to read this, Herr Weltzin.'

Weltzin took a pair of spectacles from his pocket and held them up to his eyes as he read the document. Then he handed it back to Zeller.

Zeller smiled. 'Does that answer your question? As you can see, my good friend Reich Youth Leader Artur Axman asked me for a contribution for his camp at Leutensdorf. I ordered five hundred mattresses and two thousand blankets. Some were delivered after the main consignment had been delivered. Those are the remainder which will be delivered this week.'

Weltzin produced the sock. 'Then this must be one of your grandchildren's socks. It was amongst the blankets.' There was no trace of sarcasm, but the implication was obvious.

Zeller was unperturbed. 'Ah, you found it. Good. The children were playing on the mattresses in the cellar – you know what children are – and she lost it. Her mother will be most grateful.' He placed the sock on the table. 'Now, is that all, Herr Weltzin? Have you completed your search?'

Weltzin was silent, but he subjected Zeller to a long hard look. Then he motioned to his assistants and led the way from the room. Mason saw them to the door, and shut it behind them.

When he returned to the library, he found Zeller at the window, looking through the slightly parted curtains. Zeller said: 'That man's no fool. He knew the children had been here.'

'But what can he do about it now?'

'He has a choice. He can have me taken in and subjected to the cellar treatment.'

'Torture?'

Zeller nodded. 'Or, if he is as astute as I think he is, he'll leave someone to watch the place.'

'Would he dare arrest you?'

'Certainly. I'm no more important than the others in Gestapo hands. My only trump card is my importance to the war industry, and my friendship with Albert Speer, the War Minister. Ah! As I thought. He's left one man across the road. He'll stay there until Weltzin can set up a full surveillance operation.'

Pauline sank into the easy chair by the fireplace. 'What are we going to do? The groups will be telephoning soon. What will we tell them?'

Zeller paced the floor. Then he stopped. 'I've got it!' He went to the telephone and dialled swiftly. 'Ben? Zeller. Have you a driver on duty today? Good. Send him to my home with a vehicle big enough to load fifty mattresses and some blankets. I'll give him the destination when he gets here. He should leave at once.' He put the receiver back and looked up a number in the Bayreuth directory.

Mason and Pauline watched him intently. Mason said: 'Is there anything we can do?'

Zeller shook his head. 'Later.' He found the number and dialled. He heard the ringing tone. 'I'm going to get them out in a milk tanker.'

'A milk tanker!'

'It's the only vehicle available, and it is a reasonably safe way to transport people. Everyone expects a milk tanker to contain milk.' Zeller heard the phone being lifted at the other end. 'Jakob? Zeller. I want to ask a great favour of you. I want a clean, empty tanker for two days. It must be one of the big ones – the inter-city kind.' He listened for a moment. 'Something like that. Yes. Thank you. I'll tell you one day how grateful I am. My driver will fetch it in an hour.' He replaced the receiver, and grabbing hold of Pauline, waltzed delightedly around the room. 'We'll make those overgrown bullies look like idiots before I'm finished with them.'

Mason smiled. The man was enjoying himself; and why not, as long as his enjoyment resulted in the safety of the children? He shook his head. A milk tanker!!

Zeller stopped, winded, and said to Pauline: 'Take this address through to Inga. When the groups report, they must go there at once.' He scribbled quickly. 'It's one of my empty warehouses. There is an old caretaker there. Ring him at this number and let him know some people are coming. When the tanker arrives there, he must open the main doors and direct the vehicle to one of the loading bays. I will be there shortly to supervise everything.' He went swiftly out of the library, then stopped and put his head in the door. 'A truck from my factory will arrive here within ten minutes. Please watch for it while I change my clothes.' His head disappeared.

Ten minutes later the truck arrived, and Mason went out to guide the driver to the garages at the back. He told the driver to wait, and went in through the kitchen. He came upon Davis feverishly polishing a pair of boots.

'What the hell are you doing?'

Davis stopped rubbing. 'Have they gone?'

'Gone? They went ages ago. Haven't you anything better to do than indulge in your hobbies?' He ducked as a boot came flying at his head. 'Come and help me load the mattresses.' Quickly he told Davis about the milk tanker.

Before they had finished the loading Zeller arrived, dressed in an old pair of trousers and a blue shirt. He helped them load the last of the mattresses. There were four piles, each one and a half metres high, which they tied down with rope that came with the truck.

'You men get up front with the driver. Pauline will come with me in the car.' He looked at her soot-begrimed face. 'For heaven's sake, can't you keep yourself clean!' She aimed a kick at his shins, and ran out to wash and change.

Mason looked out through the chink in the curtain. 'What about our watcher at the gate?'

'He'll be watching for forty-eight children coming in or going out.' He went over to the driver of the truck. 'Take this load to the Bayreuth Milk Processing Company out on the Kulmbach road. The foreman will give you the keys of a milk tanker. Throw all the mattresses and blankets into the tanker, leave the truck at the plant, and drive the tanker to my Burgoffstrasse warehouse. Wait there until I come.' He turned to Mason. 'I'll wait here until I know all the groups have reported and received their instructions, then I'll join you at the warehouse.'

Mason and Davis joined the driver in the cab. As they passed the watcher across the road, he stared hard at them and then turned away and looked back at the house. They turned the corner at the cemetery, and saw Johan walking towards the Zeller mansion. They stopped and he leapt aboard, Mason explaining the situation to him.

'Where will Zeller take them?'

'He'll explain when we get to the warehouse. Ultimately we must get to Konstanz or Friedrichshafen.'

At the milk processing plant the tanker was ready for them. Mason studied it carefully. It was a Mercedes-Benz chassis with a steel tank built on to it. The tank was oval with a reasonably flat top and bottom. It was about two metres wide and about ten metres long. It had a square trap at the top with one metre sides. Mason climbed up the steel ladder fixed to the frame and looked into the tank. It was clean, but a faint smell of old milk was evident. With mattresses and blankets on the bottom, it would take all the children easily. They might even be comfortable.

The plant was empty. The foreman handed the keys to Mason without comment and went back to his office on the far side of the building. The four men pushed the mattresses through the trap, and closed the hinged top. Mason saw that it was sealed at the edges with rubber. He made a mental note that they would have to leave the trap slightly open.

The warehouse was fifteen kilometres away on the Hollfeld road. When they arrived, they found some of the groups there already. The driver took the tanker through the big doors to the last loading bay, where Mason found a piece of wood to fix to the trap to keep it wedged open. The ten centimetre gap was sufficient for adequate ventilation.

The driver swung down from the cab, and Mason felt the man nudge him with his elbow. He saw the man staring towards the big doors to where a black car blocked the entrance. The driver was a man in S.S. uniform.

For a long moment no one moved. Mason stood there, the familiar sensation of despair sweeping over him. Against the light he could see at least three other people in the car. He wondered how they had been discovered, and then realised that it didn't matter.

Slowly the door of the sedan swung open, and the S.S. man stepped down from the car. He stood there, peering into the gloom of the big warehouse, then walked slowly towards the tanker.

'Mason, is that you?'

Mason recognised the voice at once. 'Dammit, Hamilton! Is that you? What the hell are you doing here?'

'It's a long story.'

Hamilton went back to the car and helped Maria from the passenger seat. He motioned to the three children to alight, and Maria led them to the other groups at the back of the warehouse.

Hamilton walked across to the tanker. 'It was the damnedest thing I've ever seen. There I was hiding in a ditch by the side of the Eschen road when this Gestapo car pulls up at the cross-roads. Suddenly there's a damned awful noise of shooting, and I look over the top of the bank to see that woman blazing away at the two men in the front seat. Then she drags the two men and dumps the bodies in the ditch – almost on top of me.' He grinned. 'You should have seen her in the driver's seat of that car. She hadn't the faintest idea what to do next.' He shrugged. 'So I took a hand and brought her here.'

Mason looked at him wonderingly. 'What the hell were you doing on the Eschen road?'

'I was making for Nuremberg. I hid when I saw this car coming. It was obviously a Gestapo car.'

At that moment Martens arrived with Zeller and Pauline.

'Come on. Let me introduce you to the boss of this operation.' Mason led the way into the sunlight where Zeller was examining the Gestapo car with a great deal of interest. Quickly Mason told him what had happened.

Zeller frowned. 'The car can't stay here. It has to be dumped.'

Hamilton nodded. 'Of course. I anticipated that.'

Zeller looked at Hamilton thoughtfully. 'And what are you going to do afterwards.'

'Get back on the road to Nuremberg.'

Zeller nodded. 'That's where we're going. You'd better come with us.'

Hamilton shook his head. 'No. I think I'm better off alone.' He grinned at Mason. 'Only a crazy sod like this would travel with dozens of children.'

Zeller nodded 'So be it. Thank you for your help.' He shook Hamilton's hand. 'Good luck.'

Hamilton went back to the car and drove out of the yard. At the gate, he turned and waved.

Mason shook his head wonderingly. 'He has the damnedest luck. I never thought he would last a day.' He smiled. 'Now I'm convinced he'll make it.'

Within an hour all the groups had arrived. Martens organised the servants into groups and began to ferry them back to the bus stop.

Zeller went to Maria and put his arms about her. 'Thank you. You are a courageous woman.'

She looked at him. 'I killed two men. God will never forgive me.' Tears spilled on to her cheeks.

Zeller shook his head. 'You are forgiven already. You were doing God's work – protecting the innocents.'

Maria smiled wanly and joined the group at the second car.

Mason went over to Zeller. 'Who will drive the tanker?'

'I will. I've driven one of these many times. Not with a tank, of course, but with twenty ton loads.'

Mason shook his head. 'You don't care if you get caught, do you?'

'Of course I care. I care because being caught under these circumstances endangers others.'

'Yes, I see. I'm sorry.'

'There's no need to be.' They watched as Pauline and Inga guided the children to the tanker. Johan looked down at them from the top of the trap.

Mason looked up. 'How does it look? Any problems?'

Johan looked concerned. 'Some of the smaller girls are a little apprehensive, but Davis is settling them down in there.'

Zeller said: 'I suggest Mason and Inga sit up front with me, and Pauline and Davis stay with the children.' He felt under the cab seat where he found a length of rope Ben had left for him. 'Make this fast up there, and we'll tie the other end to the driver's seat. If you want us, just tug on the rope.' He put the key in the ignition. 'We'll drop Johan off at the station when we stop for bread.'

Ten minutes later the rig ground out the warehouse in bottom gear. Zeller put it through its eight gears, and soon they were running in to Munckerstrasse towards the station. They turned into von Schillerstrasse, rounded the circle where the Wiskamann children had been recognised the day before, and Zeller slowed the big rig in front of the station entrance where Johan jumped down from the cab. A few minutes later he returned from the bakery.

He said to Mason: 'Don't forget the instructions. It's essential that you go to the Jakobplatz in Nuremberg. See Father Hubert at the church there, and ask him if he has any messages for you. If he asks your name, you give him the correct time. That's the code for this week.' He passed the bread up to them.

'Jakobplatz. Father Hubert. Got it.'

Johan waved and the rig pulled away from the kerb. They ran alongside the railway line for a few kilometres, and then turned south. They passed a sign – NÜRNBERG 85 km – and then they began to swing towards the southwest.

Mason looked at the fuel gauge. The tanks were full. 'How far will that lot take us?'

'About a thousand kilometres.'

'What are the country's operating limits? Its boundaries?'

'My friend Jakob has milk processing plants in most of the big cities. His co-partners expanded the business by closing down his opposition companies. Jakob was upset, but there was nothing he could do about it. He had to hand over fifty-one percent of his company without one mark compensation.'

'I think I can guess –'

'Who his partners are?'

'Yes.'

'You'd be right. Reichsführer Himmler and his gang now own half of Jakob's business.' He laughed out loud. 'Pauline's babies are travelling with the compliments of the S.S. And we can taken them anywhere in Germany, as long as no one looks inside the tank.'

Chapter Twenty-One

Sunday, 13th August, 1944. 11 p.m.

Joachim sat in front of the telephone in his shabby room at the Pensione Krone, and spun the dial. He heard the ringing tone, and then the woman in the café in Gorlitz answered.

'Yes?'

'I need Karl urgently.' He gave her the number of the call box a hundred metres away from the pension. 'The phone I'm speaking from goes through the board downstairs, so give me ten minutes.'

He replaced the receiver and went downstairs into the street. It was a bright moonlit night, and for the first time in weeks, the people of Friedrichshafen were given some respite from the bombers overhead. The traffic was light, their headlights dimmed by blackout regulations, and there were few pedestrians.

Joachim waited at the call box, becoming more and more impatient as the minutes ticked by. At last the bell rang.

He grabbed the receiver. 'Karl?'

'Yes. Is something wrong?'

'No danger. I wanted to find out whether you knew who authorised the Junkers-390 for the flight.'

'The Berlin office. I heard about it before the Breslau Office was notified officially.'

'Why a long-range aeroplane?'

'No one has been told. I expect it is because a large group is expected back from Italy.' He paused. 'There may be a large group in the assassination conspiracy.' He thought for a moment. 'I'm sure that's it. They will need some kind of contingency plan for the evacuation of those involved.'

'What about the forward journey? Who else is going to Italy?'

'No one. Those instructions were explicit. Müller will not allow anyone near the two men after they collect the parcel from Zurich.'

'Can the flight plan be changed?'

'Changed?' Karl was mystified. 'To go somewhere else, you mean?'

'Yes.'

'Impossible. The orders were signed by Müller personally, and only he or Kaltenbrunner can change them.'

'I am going to change them.'

'You're out of your mind. No one can change those orders.'

'I can, and I will.'

'Joachim, be careful. Don't get reckless at this stage.'

'We're near the end of the road, Karl. This is when risks are justified. In any case, the risk is a small one.'

'Where do you want the plane to go?'

'Sweden.'

'Why there?'

Joachim hesitated and Karl caught the momentary pause. 'Bear with me a little longer. Once my plan is finalised, I will lay it out for you.'

'Very well. Keep in touch.'

'When will you be here?'

'Tomorrow at three o'clock.'

'The plane is due out at eight o'clock.' Joachim waited until the roar of a heavy truck had passed. 'Meet me at the Hofbrauhaus in Wangen.'

'At three as planned?'

'Yes.'

'Strange, I –'

'What is it?'

'Foolish thoughts. Tomorrow is my last day in my office.'

'Not foolish. It's a traumatic step, to give up your whole world.'

'I'm deserting my country.'

'You are leaving Germany. Not Austria. And it is important that you are not there when the war is over.'

'No.' He paused. 'I know what I must do. Yet it is still difficult.'

Joachim hesitated. 'You will both be happier in Switzerland. And you said yourself, it can only be a matter of days before they discover what you have done.'

'I hope we will find peace in Switzerland.'

'I know you will. The Dulles Office is expecting you. They have a complete dossier on your work since 1940.'

'I hope they will believe it.'

'They will. Their own operatives will vouch for you.' Joachim looked at his watch. 'I must go.'

'Take care.'

'You too.'

Joachim walked back to his hotel. There he unpacked his bags and laid out the parts of three Sturmgewehr 44 assault rifles. They were the newest weapons in the German armoury, and he had used all his guile to get them. It was a weapon designed to replace the rifle, machine gun and sub-machine gun. It was fitted with a thirty round magazine, and he carried six spares in his satchel. It was a selective fire weapon, and Joachim thought it would do very nicely for the purpose he had in mind.

Zeller swung the wheel of the big Mercedes, and the truck took the right arm of the junction in Josephplatz, continued along Adlerstrasse past the Police Headquarters and into Jakobplatz. At that moment the clock above them struck one.

Zeller stopped the big truck, and he and Mason looked blankly at one another. There was a church on either side of the square.

'It must be the Catholic church. Johan distinctly said Father Hubert.'

Zeller nodded. 'I agree. Then it must be that one.' He pointed to the one occupying the part of the block on which the Police Headquarters stood.

Mason jumped down from the cab. 'Let's see how our passengers have travelled.' He climbed the ladder and looked down into the tanker. He could see nothing in the darkness, and he whispered: 'Is anyone awake?'

He heard Davis say. 'Yes, I am.'

'How was it down there?'

'Not too bad. Like travelling in a train that's in a permanent tunnel. It wasn't so bad while it was still light.'

'Is everyone else asleep.'

'I can't hear anyone else.'

'We'll be moving again soon.'

'Right.'

Mason climbed down the ladder, and as soon as he was back in the cab, Zeller gently rolled the giant rig to the church entrance.

Zeller looked at the massive door and shook his head. 'I don't know how you'll find Father Hubert at this time of the night. I suggest we come back in the morning.'

'No. We must press on. Now that we're on the move, we should keep going. I'll go inside and look for him. You stay here.'

Mason glanced into the bunk at the back of the cab where Inga lay fast asleep, and then he dropped down into the street and went over to the massive door of the church. He pushed against it and felt it give. He pushed harder, and found he could get through the gap.

Inside the huge vaulted nave, dim lights pushed back the darkness in isolated corners, but in the transepts, the lights were brighter, and Mason walked towards them, looking for the door that led to the priests' quarters.

A voice behind him said: 'Is there some way I can help you?'

Mason spun round and peered into the gloom. At first he could see nothing, then in the south transept, he saw a small round man in a priest's habit.

'I'm looking for Father Hubert. He has a message for me.'

'What name should I give him?'

'Tell him it's one o'clock.'

'You must be Herr Zeller.'

'No, Father. I'm Mason. Herr Zeller is outside in the truck.' He looked hard at the little man. 'Are you Father Hubert?'

'No. Father Hubert had to visit a family in Karolinenstrasse. They have a daughter who is very ill, but in case you called, he gave me your name.' The priest came towards him. 'I am Father Lorenz.'

'My name is Mason. Then there was a message for me?'

'You are to go to the Kaiserhof, Herrenstrasse, in Wangen at six-thirty tomorrow night. You are to arrive at that time precisely; no sooner.'

'Is that all? No more? No reason, or what we are to do when we get there?'

'That is all.'

'Thank you, Father. We are grateful.'

'Go with God.'

'Good night, Father.'

In the truck, Mason found Zeller nodding over the wheel. He gave him the message as it had been given to him. 'Where the hell is Wangen?'

Zeller yawned. 'Fifteen kilometres east of Friedrichshafen. It isn't much of a place. There is a Luftwaffe base there.' He yawned again. 'What the hell are we going to do in the meanwhile? It's only four hours from here.'

'We'd better get some sleep. We have to find a place to park this thing and stretch out.'

Zeller started the engine. 'I know the very place.' He swung the truck into Jakobstrasse and rolled past the Kornmarkt. In ten minutes they were on the outskirts of the city on their way south.'

Thirty kilometres south of Nuremberg, where the Altmühl winds it's tortuous way through the hills above Eichstatt, forests of fir and pine stand alongside valleys of natural bush, and here and there, giant oaks throw their shadows over grassy parkland.

Zeller drove on to a little-used road, watching all the while for signs of Home Guard patrols. It was almost dawn when he found a break in the wooded roadside and drove the truck into the trees. They slept then, Zeller under the tanker and Mason in a patch of thick grass beside a tree trunk, each of them rolled tightly in a single blanket against the dew which would search them out before morning.

Mason woke when he heard the children's voices around him. They had been awake since sunrise when Inga and

Pauline had taken the girls to the valley where the river tumbled over a waterfall and into a pool of clear cold water. Davis and the boys went a little way downstream where they bathed in the shallows.

When all the children returned, Zeller seated them in a circle, and broke the bread into portions sufficient for each child. It was dry and filling, and would assuage their hunger for the meantime.

Mason walked down to the stream to bathe, and when he returned, saw Pauline standing alone, looking across the grassland to the wooded valley below.

'What do you see?'

'Nothing. I was thinking.'

He stood close to her. 'About us?'

'Yes. I know nothing about you. I love you, but I love in a vacuum.' She looked up at him. 'I know the things you have done, and you have told me about Oxford and about your parents. But of you, I know nothing. What things you like, what you think when you are alone, and what plans you have for the future.' He began to speak, but she stopped him with a finger on his lips. 'I know you are kind and sensitive, but twice I have seen you kill, and I think you can be cruel too.'

Mason took her hand, and together they walked further into the woods. He said quietly: 'I know almost nothing about you either, but what I do know is that I love you and that is enough for me for now.' He stopped and took her in his arms, feeling her warm body stirring him. He looked at her upturned face. 'I don't know what the future holds. I haven't had time to think about that for the last five years, but I know this: without you I have no future.' A slight breeze ruffled the leaves over them. He looked up and tilted her chin so that she was looking up with him to a blue sky that was lightly streaked with cloud. 'Wherever we are, that same sky will be above us, and the same sun will be overhead. That is the only certainty I know. If people refused to love because of an uncertain future, there would be no lovers.'

She smiled. 'I know you are right, but the ghetto years have made me afraid to believe in the future.' She pulled his head down and kissed him. 'I will try not to be afraid.'

'And when I go back, will you come with me – to England?'

'Yes. Joachim will be unhappy, but he will want me to do what is best for me.' She held him then, and he felt the passion growing within her. At that moment they heard Inga call from the edge of the trees.

'Come. They must be ready to go.' Reluctantly, she released him.

'Wait.' He held on to her. 'I want to say this: My love for you is unconditional. It does not depend on how much you love me, or whether we will be poor or wealthy. You must always remember that.'

She kissed him again, and together they went back to the others.

They left the clearing at about nine o'clock, and an hour later they turned on to the highway south of Donauworth, and it was then that they noticed that the traffic was moving haltingly, a few metres at a time.

Zeller looked at Mason. 'This looks like a road block.'

'Pull over if you get a gap. I'll walk on ahead.' Mason alighted from the slow-moving vehicle, walking swiftly along the verge, passing stationary trucks and cars. He came to a slight rise, and looking downhill, saw the striped barrier and guard huts on either side of the road. Civilian vehicles were being diverted off the road and searched with professional thoroughness. Even the covers of some loads were being stripped off.

He went back along the line of vehicles, and found that Zeller had driven the tanker off the road and had lifted the engine cowling.

Mason said: 'You were right. It's a fully-manned road block, and we'll never get away without a thorough search.' He looked back along the line of vehicles. 'Isn't there an alternative route?'

'There are many, but there'll be road blocks there too. They're looking for something going south. It may even be us.'

'How much time do we have?'

'Jakob is going to report his truck stolen at six o'clock tonight. We have to get rid of it by eight o'clock at the latest.'

'We have to be in Wangen by six-thirty anyway.'

Thoughtfully, they watched the traffic moving slowly past them. Gradually it dawned on Mason that the traffic was thinning out. First the gap was fifty metres, then a hundred, and then vehicles were only coming at rare intervals.

Zeller said: 'This is our chance. Get the children out. They can bypass the road block through the woods. I'll pick them up further down the road. Inga can come with me.'

'Wait beyond the first bend after the road block.'

Within minutes they had the children out of the tanker and into the woods. Zeller put the vehicle into gear and disappeared over the hill. Mason climbed a small knoll, and screened by shrubs, watched the tanker roll to a stop at the road block where a soldier motioned to Zeller and the girl to alight. As one of the armed men climbed into the cab, the second walked around the truck. Mason breathed deeply, the tension in his body rising as he saw the man on the ground stare up at the hatch. If they should find the mattresses, their suspicions would be aroused and Mason had no doubt that a officer would be on the scene in minutes.

Finally the soldier in the cab reappeared and indicated to Zeller that he could go. Mason heard the engine start up and the vehicle moved slowly out of sight. Quickly he went back to the children where he found them waiting in the trees. He led them deeper into the woods, but as they followed the wire entanglement that ran at right angles to the road, he was alarmed to see that it stretched away from them through the trees and into the distance.

'Stop.' Mason listened intently. 'Quiet everyone.' He looked at Pauline. 'Do you hear it?'

She nodded. 'Dogs. They have a patrol as well. We'll have to go back.'

They made their way back towards the road, and Mason peered through the trees to find that they were no more than a hundred metres from the road block. Just then, they heard the whine of several trucks in the distance.

Davis said: 'That sounds like a convoy. We'd better get under cover.'

Pauline quickly ushered the children into some thick shrubbery. As soon as they were well hidden, the three adults took cover at the edge of the woods. Through the screen of leaves, they could see the guards pacing back and forth at the barrier.

Mason wished he had had more sleep. The few hours he had snatched this morning had sustained him for a while, but his eyes ached and his body cried out for rest.

They heard the faraway rumble of the trucks grinding in bottom gear up the long incline beyond the trees. They watched the top of the rise over which they would come; the sound was growing louder.

He rubbed the rough growth on his chin, and glanced at the girl lying next to him. She appeared to be as calm as ever, no sign on her face of the increasing tension, though her brow was furrowed with concentration as she watched the road. Mason realised that even the birds were still, as though they knew what the approaching convoy represented. Suddenly they were there, breasting the rise, the sounds of their motors increasing in volume as the drivers changed gears. The trucks passed them in an almost endless column, packed with troops on their way to the front. Through the gaps in the undergrowth he could see the uniforms of the Waffen S.S. divisions, and the familiar German helmets. Finally, the last truck passed, but no one moved. They waited, staring cautiously at the road in front of them. Time stretched on, minute by minute, with only the reawakening bird calls to break the stillness.

Suddenly, from behind them came a soft whimpering and they turned to see Giselle Florens standing a few metres away, the knuckles of her hands pressed to her teeth, her body shaking uncontrollably. Incoherent noises were coming from behind her hands.

Pauline stood up and went swiftly to her. 'There, my child.' She held the girl tightly in her arms. 'There is nothing to fear.'

'The – the – sol – sol – soldiers. They have come to take us back.' Her sobbing came from deep within her. 'Please do not let them take me.'

'They won't take you, my child. I promise you. They won't take you.'

Mason saw several faces looking at them from the undergrowth, and from their expressions it was clear that the panic was beginning to spread. Lips were quivering, and some were beginning to sob. At that moment, their fear was as real as it had been in the railway truck, and Mason realised that this was the first real glimpse of the hated uniforms since they had been taken from their homes.

He said loudly: 'Now listen all of you. Those soldiers have nothing to do with us. They will not harm us because they are not looking for us. Tomorrow you will be safe in France.'

Slowly the fear began to fade, and some even smiled through their tears. Davis went amongst them, touching them one by one, and it seemed to allay their fears.

The Welshman looked back at Mason. 'We'd better work out a way to get past that road block.'

Pauline went back to the edge of the trees. 'I have an idea.' She motioned to the children to gather round her. 'We are going past the soldiers, and we want them to think we are faithful children of Germany, so we are going to play our beloved Führer game.' She held up one finger. 'Do you all remember this?'

Heads nodded mutely. Mason was astounded. 'You are going to walk past that road block in full view of the guards, shouting "Our beloved Führer", and you imagine they will just stand there and watch?' He shook his head. 'I can't let you do it.'

'I take it you have an alternative plan?'

'Of course I haven't, but no plan at all is better than that.'

Pauline suppressed a growing irritation. 'If we go through that barrier as a school nature study party, they will accept it.'

'Why should they?'

'Because the alternatives are too bizarre. What are they anyway? That we are escaped concentration camp prisoners?' She shook her head impatiently. 'They will accept what they see.'

'What if they have been warned to watch for fifty children and three adults?'

'We have to take that chance.'

'No. At this stage we take no chances. We had a well planned route. We can't introduce any spur-of-the-moment actions that could bury us.' He thought for a moment, then snapped his fingers. 'I know how we can find out if they are watching for us.'

'How?'

'I'll go and ask them.' He grinned at their consternation. 'Not in so many words. Wait here.'

He went back about five hundred metres along the road, so that when he appeared, it would be a more gradual approach to the barrier. As he walked, he peered into the trees, first to the left and then to the right. As he approached to within ten metres of the barrier, and it was clear that he was about to go through, the two soldiers brought their weapons to the ready.

Mason touched his cap obsequiously. 'Pardon, Herr Sturmmann, I am in deep trouble, and I would like you help.'

'You will be in deeper trouble if your papers are not in order.' The Lance-corporal pushed his Schmeisser forward aggressively.

'Shut up, Kersten.' The Sergeant waved the man away. He turned to Mason. 'What is it you want?'

'Thank you, Herr Unterscharführer.' Mason kept his eye on the ground. 'I was sent out as a guide for a teacher and her pupils on a nature study tour. I stopped for a moment to relieve myself, and I lost them.' He looked up at the Sergeant, his face showing apparent distress. 'If I do not find them, the Fraulein will report me. She accuses me of being drunk.'

The soldiers roared with laughter. 'Which, no doubt, you are most of the time.' The Sergeant was enjoying himself.

Mason looked suitably crestfallen. 'They have not passed this way? There are about forty children.' As he spoke, Mason watched the men closely. There appeared to be no reaction.

'No children have passed this way.' The Lance-Corporal was emphatic.

Mason took off his cap, and backed away. 'Thank you. Thank you.' He went back the way he had come, walked until he was out of sight of the barrier, then went into the trees and made for the others.

'They aren't watching for us. It looks as though we can get away with it.' Quickly, Mason described his interview with the soldiers. 'To make it more authentic, get really impatient with Taff and me. Shout at us and insult us.'

Pauline smiled. 'Just the opportunity I've been waiting for. I take it you won't answer back.'

Mason smiled at her. He wasn't deceived. Under the levity,

the tension was clearly apparent, but in front of the children, she made light of the ordeal facing her. She looked at the children once more, and ordered them into a double file crocodile.

'Right. Ready everyone?' She lifted her head. 'Let's go.'

She walked out into the road, followed by the children. The two men stayed well back. She began talking loudly as soon as she knew the soldiers had seen them. 'You will notice, children, that in this particular area, we haven't seen any bright coloured birds like those in the pictures in your books. That is because gaily coloured birds are only found in the tropics.' As she continued her lecture, Mason watched the soldiers covertly. They registered surprise at first and then interest. Pauline walked closer to the barrier. 'You two idiots at the back, keep up. And Blom – if you get lost again, I'll have you discharged.'

Mason saw the soldiers grinning at him and managed to look embarrassed.

Pauline continued. 'Who is it that gives us the wonderful forests around us?' Her one finger was raised.

The shout was deafening. 'Our beloved Führer.'

Pauline smiled at the two soldiers watching her curiously. 'Are we permitted to pass, Herr Unterscharführer? We wish to continue our studies.'

The Sergeant looked at the children and back at the girl. He was young and no more impervious to the sight of a lovely woman than any other young man.

He straightened his shoulders. 'Of course, Fraulein.'

The barrier was lifted and the children filed through. As he approached the barrier, Mason felt the tension grow within him, and knew from the set expression on the Welshman's face that he felt the same. He kept his eyes to the ground.

The soldiers laughed uproariously when they saw his crestfallen demeanour. The Sergeant slapped the Lance-Corporal on the shoulder. 'Perhaps the two idiots can learn something from the children.' They grinned and went back to a contemplative appreciation of the girl's figure as she walked away from them.

Pauline raised two fingers. 'Which is the finest country in the universe?'

'Our beloved Germany.'

The file went slowly down the road, further and further away from the road block, their shouts echoing through the trees. They turned the corner, and there was the truck, with an anxious Zeller standing beside it. Inga, at the cab window, began to wave furiously.

Mason couldn't resist the moment. He called out in French, one finger held high: 'Who is the biggest shithouse in Germany?'

And the joyous cry came from fifty voices: 'Our beloved Führer.'

Chapter Twenty-Two

Monday, 14th August, 1944. 6 p.m.

The entrance to the Kaiserhof in Herrenstrasse was two grubby steps up from the street. The vestibule was covered by a carpet which once had a pattern, but now had a patina of dirt that obscured all but a lonely flower in the one corner that had been missed by the thousands of feet to have passed over it in the years since the hotel welcomed its first guests.

The rooms no longer had carpets. Bare linoleum of unknown design covered creaking floors, and the bathrooms were makeshift affairs, one to a landing. The hotel was built in the days when ladies and gentlemen bathed in steaming tubs in their bedrooms.

Hackett watched Joachim as he sat on the bed, sketching a plan of the Luftwaffe installations at Wangen airfield. He had been at the airfield all afternoon, ostensibly conferring with the officer in charge about the flight. From the officer he had learned that the field was completely surrounded by barbed wire. The entrance was opposite the tower, and accompanied by the guard commander, he was permitted to drive around the perimeter of the field. Having inspected Joachim's documents which appointed him as security officer for the take-off, the guard commander told him that the flight had the highest priority. The plane was scheduled to take off at eight sharp, taxi-ing to the north end of the field, leaving the hangar with the three men aboard, five minutes before take-off.

The officer had warned Joachim that he had been given a code word by Berlin, and unless that code word was given to him by the operation control officer, the flight would not be allowed to take off. In fact he would prohibit anyone entering the hangar where the passengers were to board. Joachim was confident that Karl, as operation control officer, would have the code word before the flight was due to leave.

Joachim finished what he was doing and looked at his watch.

'We've got ten minutes before Grant and Patterson arrive from Meersburg. We must be ready for them.' He opened the satchel and took out a small semi-automatic pistol which he cocked. He took out another and handed it to the American. Hackett saw that it was a Walther PPK, the Polizei Pistole Kriminal which was issued to all Kripo officers. Unlike the Walther P38 which used nine millimetre ammunition, this used the smaller seven point six-five bullets. He tucked it into his right hand jacket pocket. Joachim stood up and went to the door. 'Don't make a move until I come back. They'll be on their guard. Remember, they'll have the equivalent of more than thirty million dollars with them, and they'll be watching for treachery. Don't do anything foolish.' He went out.

Hackett sat in the big chair, completely relaxed. He had slept for a few hours after lunch, and was no longer tense and irritable. He turned over the pages of the old magazine he had found in the battered dressing table. The German-language copy was useless to him, but there were pictures of pre-war rallys and smiling girls, and he whiled away the tedium by turning the yellowed pages.

Down the hall, in a room overlooking the street, S.S. Oberführer Becker turned in front of the fly-blown mirror and studied his immaculate uniformed figure. Against his better judgement, he had decided to make the arrest official. Of course people would have to die resisting arrest, and the money would have to disappear without trace. From their vantage point behind their curtained bedroom window, he and Herr Harster had watched the arrivals that afternoon, and it was Harster who, after puzzling over the various people involved, had shrewdly placed the actors into their different roles.

'It has all the appearance of a robbery.' He dropped the

binoculars on the bed and looked at Becker. 'The bearded one has visited the American twice in his room.' He went back to the window. 'Then he confers with two others down here in the street. That makes it too many people that are involved.'

'Could they not be security?'

'With respect, Herr Oberführer, if he was, he would not have needed to confer with the American – at least that is how I see it.'

Becker thought for a moment. 'It is unusual, I agree, but we must move cautiously. I will continue to watch the street from here while you try and find out what the others are doing downstairs.'

'Good, Herr Oberführer. If I see –' Harster stopped speaking and stared out across the street.

'What is it?'

'Two men have taken up observation positions; one in the street and one at a window in the abandoned building opposite.'

'Bullseye! You were right. Good. We will make the arrest after they have taken over the loot. Then we have an official reason for interfering.'

'I will go downstairs at once.'

In his room down the hall, Hackett looked up from his magazine as he heard the soft knock on his door. He opened it a few inches, his hand on the gun in his jacket pocket. The elderly reception clerk stood there, a slip of paper in his hand. Hackett took it and the man shuffled away. It was a note from Grant. It read: 'Meet us downstairs in the street'.

He looked out of the window, puzzled by the change of plan. He wondered if they suspected anything, then dismissed the idea immediately. They were zig-zagging, doing the unexpected to keep opponents off-balance. Hackett was sure they weren't suspicious. Merely cautious.

The street was deserted. He wondered where the car was. They were certain to be parked where they would have a strategic advantage if an attack was planned. He smiled ruefully. He no longer underestimated these two. They were wily and smart, hardened by their years in the S.S.

He went down the passage to where Joachim was waiting for the two men to arrive. Hackett knocked at the door, and when the door was opened, handed over the note without comment.

Joachim said: 'Go down, but take your time. Give me five minutes. I have to see whether Wilhelm and Gunther have seen where they are parked.' He went quickly down the passage to the back stairs.

Hackett gave him five minutes, picked up his bag and went down to the reception desk. He fiddled for a moment with his key before handing it over, then he went out into the street. As he appeared on the bottom step, Becker and Harster watched him from the window above.

Patterson was standing across the road beside a lamp standard, and as Hackett appeared, he signalled Grant at the wheel of a car which was out of sight in the alley running alongside the hotel. Their strategy was good; he had to give them that, but they were dealing with men who lived in a world where people who were merely good didn't last long. As the car shot from the alley and slowed for Patterson to jump into the back, Grant swung the wheel to swerve to the kerb where Hackett stood.

At that moment a handcart appeared from the mouth of the alley on the opposite side of the street. It careered across the road, struck the kerb and bounced to land directly in front of the car. At once Patterson was out of the vehicle, gun in hand, moving swiftly to the front of the car. Hackett in a fast reflex action, tugged the pistol from his pocket, and jammed it against Grant's ear. Patterson saw the movement, and dropping into a crouch, brought his gun level with Hackett's chest, but at that moment a sharp burst of gunfire from the window of an apartment opposite threw him tumbling over the handcart. Hackett saw Grant bring his hand up in line with the window, and the muzzle of a pistol was inches away from the American's face. Without hesitation, Hackett pulled the trigger of the pistol in his hand. Grant keeled slowly sideways, his nerveless fingers sweeping the horn button, sending a blast of sound down the deserted street.

Joachim and Wilhelm raced from the alley. Joachim grabbed Patterson's feet and Wilhelm the shoulders and together they heaved the body on to the cart. Joachim said to Hackett: 'Quickly, get him out of the car.'

Hackett pulled Grant's body from the front seat. It

followed Patterson on to the handcart, and as Wilhelm wheeled the cart into the alley, Gunther appeared from the block opposite. He threw the assault rifle into the car and got behind the wheel. As he started the car, he called to Hackett. 'Get back into the hotel.' The car roared away from the kerb, disappearing round the corner as the American ran up the steps and cannoned into the curious receptionist. The frightened man scuttled off to his office.

Back in his room, Hackett took a deep breath and looked down from his window into the street. It seemed incredible, but it was less than four minutes since he had left it, and outside, the few pedestrians in this deserted part of town, didn't even realise what drama had been played out in that quiet street a few minutes before. The door opened, and he swung round, gun levelled. Joachim stepped cautiously into the room, and Hackett put the gun back in his pocket.

'What have you done with the bodies?'

'They're in a yard behind an abandoned outhouse. They won't be found for days. This part of town has almost been abandoned since the bombing destroyed most of the buildings.' He looked at his watch. 'If you feel like relaxing, do so. We have half an hour before we expect Mason to arrive. An hour ago they were at Kaufbeuren. They stopped there for about three minutes, and by now they should be just outside Kempten.'

'How do you know all this?'

'Johan rejoined them at Kaufbeuren.'

'Now I know why your group is still alive.'

Joachim smiled at him, and went out of the room. Hackett lay back on the bed, and suddenly his body began to shake from the reaction. He had killed before, many times, but those killings had been remote. Now he had killed someone he knew, and in whose company he had been for the past three days. He closed his eyes and the trembling stopped.

At that moment, his door opened softly, and a man stepped into the room. He was dressed in full S.S. uniform, but the man behind him was in civilian clothes. Hackett knew at once that he was a Gestapo agent.

The S.S. officer pointed a gun at him. 'You will remain quiet. You will stay right where you are, and not move. We will wait for your friends to come, and when they do, you would be well-advised not to try and warn them.'

Hackett lay there as though turned to stone, but through his confusion of mind had time to realise that the man had spoken to him in English, and that the gun menacing him was fitted with a silencer.

Joachim waited at the call box a hundred metres from the Kaiserhof, and hunched his shoulders against the chill wind blowing along the Herrenstrasse. As he waited, he thought for the first time in many months about the wife he had left somewhere in Warsaw. In the past, each time the memory had intruded, he had thrust it from him, knowing there was no more he could have done.

She had gone out one morning with a permit to leave the ghetto to deliver some chair covers she had made for a customer, the wife of a Nazi civilian in the German Foreign Office. She had never returned. He had searched for months, every time he had been able to leave through the sewers, but apart from the policeman who had seen her leave the house of the Nazi official, no one had set eyes on her. She had disappeared without trace, as though she had never existed.

Later they learnt that there had been a series of mass arrests that day, of people who were picked up for no reason that they knew of. It was this kind of government, he reflected, that had destroyed the Germans as much as the guns of their allies. People who grew desperate, became stronger, their desperation imbuing them with the kind of courage that creates martyrs.

When the telephone bell rang, the sound was muted by the closed door. He opened it and picked up the receiver.

'Karl?'

'Yes. I'm in place.'

'We'll need the code word.'

'Yes. I have it. It is "Winston". It was transmitted to me half an hour ago.'

Joachim chuckled. '"Winston"? Someone has a sense of humour.' He grew serious. 'Do you detect any suspicious activity?'

'None yet. I have seen the base commander, and we have

agreed that it will be necessary to identify the three men when they arrive. I will do it personally.'

'Good. The change of plan means that you will identify the original three. Hackett, Mason and Davis. I will drive them to the air base. The assault party will be Wilhelm, Gunther and Johan.'

'Is that all?'

'It is enough. We will have the advantage of surprise.'

'You know your business best.'

'Yes. When it is over, we will pick you up at the Amtzell Crossroads Inn. Inga is waiting there now.'

'I'll be there.'

'Take care.'

'You too.'

Hackett lay on the bed watching the door, his nerves stretched to breaking point. The S.S. officer sat in a chair, placed so that he would be hidden from anyone entering the room. The Gestapo man stood in the wardrobe, the door opened no more than an inch.

Hackett was determined there would be no arrests. How he would accomplish it, he didn't know, but he knew he could not stand by and watch his friends be marched into a concentration camp.

The minutes dragged by. The S.S. man sat patiently watching him, his eyes intense under the death's-head cap. As far as he knew, the Gestapo man was armed with a conventional weapon; one without a silencer.

Outside the wind had blown heavy black clouds across a leaden sky. It had grown dark inside the room, though it was still over an hour to sunset. Hackett wondered if the S.S. man was as good a shot in the semi-darkness as he was in the light.

As though he had read the American's thoughts, the officer lifted the gun muzzle. 'You are too close for me to miss, even in this light.'

Hackett wondered what had happened to Joachim. It had been nearly half an hour since he had left and it was time for them to get ready to go to the airfield. He would have to return soon.

At that moment the room erupted in a shower of glass as a

burst of machine gun fire shattered the window. The door of the wardrobe disintegrated into wood splinters while at the same moment the S.S. officer crumpled forward like a bloodied rag doll. In slow motion, the body of the Gestapo man tumbled from the wardrobe.

Hackett sat up, stunned. He saw a hand come round the door and switch on the light. What was left of the window was pushed open, and Wilhelm stepped through, cradling an assault rifle. He was grinning at Hackett.

'Where the hell did you come from?' Hackett stood up shakily as Joachim appeared in the doorway.

Wilhelm nodded to the door. 'Ask him.'

'I didn't think you would sit in a darkened room with the light out, and in view of what we learned today, Wilhelm decided to take a look through the window.'

'What did you learn today.'

'People like this S.S. man forget that every terrain is a battlefield, even if it is a hotel. We like to make sure that our rear is cleared of the enemy. We had Johan watching the area for people coming and going, and he reported that two people had come in earlier today.' He smiled sardonically. 'Since one was an S.S. man and the other a Gestapo agent, it seemed as though we would have to make sure they were not part of the game.' He looked down at Wilhelm and Gunther who were rolling Harster in a blanket from the bed. 'Unfortunately for them, they had decided to get involved.'

'But how are they involved?' Hackett asked.

'I don't know yet, but since there is no S.S. troop with them, it must be unofficial. He – ' Joachim stopped.

Hackett realised that the Pole was looking down at the S.S. officer as Wilhelm turned the man's face to the light. Joachim spoke quietly in Polish. The three men looked at one another.

'What is it?' Hackett asked. 'Who is he?'

'In the ghetto he was known as The Butcher,' said Joachim quietly. He tore another blanket from the bed. 'Wrap him up.'

Suddenly there was a commotion outside the room. Hackett heard someone shouting, demanding an explanation for the shooting and the damage to the hotel.

Joachim said: 'This is Gestapo business. Shut up and get out, or you will find yourself in the cellars.' There was a sudden silence, and then the sound of footsteps retreating down the passage.

'Move the bodies into the corner and lock up the room.' Joachim took the key from the inside of the door. 'It's time we were going, and we still have to brief the others.'

Joachim put out his hand and Pauline took it. He could see she was close to tears, but he knew that behind the tears was a determination that matched his own. He had known, as soon as she had arrived with the children, and he had seen Mason helping her down from the tanker, that there was something different about the daughter he loved. He had taken her away from the others to his room, uneasy about the difference in her he could not fathom. Perhaps he suspected, but father-like refused to accept the obvious.

He held her hand tightly. 'Mason?'

'Yes.' She took his other hand and looked up at him. 'I love him, and he loves me. He wants me to go back to England with him.' It was a measure of her love for him that she phrased it as a request; a plea for his permission.

'When? Tonight?'

'Yes.' Suddenly she held him close. 'But I am torn. I don't know how I can leave you.'

He thought for a moment. He knew she had to go with Mason, but he knew also that too quick an acquiescence would hurt her. He released her so that she would not see the pain in his eyes. 'Perhaps this is the answer to something that has been at the back of my mind.' He turned to her. 'The Americans want me to work with them, but I would only do so if I know you are safe. I think you should go to England, and you can't do better than that young man. Yes, I think you should go.'

She went to him and held him.

Joachim said: 'I hear the others coming up. We will talk more later.'

The seven people in the room listened carefully as Joachim set out in detail the part each one of them would play in the hours ahead. They studied the plans, and made their comments and suggestions. At last he was satisfied that they had covered the ground thoroughly.

'How long will it take to get the children out of the tanker?'

Pauline looked at Davis. 'We've been getting them in and out for the past two days.'

Davis nodded. 'At first it was tedious, but we developed a pattern. Two people put an arm in and the child takes them together. Then we swing our arms up and the child comes out. The arms go back in for the next one.' He frowned. 'Of course they can get out unaided, but it takes three times as long.'

'Give me your quickest estimate.'

'Roughly three minutes,' Pauline said.

Joachim shook his head. 'Too long.'

Davis was dubious. 'We can try for less, but it's tough on the arms.'

Mason was thoughtful. 'Is it possible to have some of them out of the tank and sitting on the frame? Perhaps a few of the older ones?'

'That's it,' Joachim said. 'We can get them out just before we move in.' He looked at his watch. 'Three minutes to seven. Time to move.'

'Where's Zeller?' Mason asked. 'Isn't he coming with us?'

Joachim shook his head. 'Definitely not. I have insisted that he returns at once. He will go as soon as we take over the tanker from him.' He went to the door. 'Time to go.'

In the street, Hackett, Davis and Mason climbed into the car. It was a Mercedes-Benz Grosser W150, and its seven-litre engine was supercharged. Major Brunner had demanded the best for the operation, and that is what they got. Zeller alighted from the cab of the tanker, and Pauline took his place. The three Poles sat next to her on the long front seat, while Joachim took the wheel of the Mercedes. He signalled them to move, waved to Zeller, and the big black car pulled away from the kerb.

The Luftwaffe base was give kilometres from the town, down in a valley which opened on to a plain. It was growing dark, and the lights of the town disappeared behind them as they drove past factories battered by the bombs of the Allied air forces.

Joachim drove slowly, keeping the tanker constantly in his rear-view mirror. The men were silent, the tension wire taut within them. They listened to the drone of the truck engine, and watched for the first post of the security fence. Davis saw it first, outlined against the sky at the end of the valley. Silently they left the car, stamping their feet and blowing on fingers against the icy gusts cutting across the airfield.

The truck slowed behind them, and the fifteen older children were brought out of the tanker and positioned along the sides of the frame on which the tank was mounted. Mason went to the bulbous trunk of the car and took out two pairs of wire-cutters, while Gunther loaded and cocked the three assault rifles. As soon as the fence was cut and the wire pulled back for five metres, Pauline edged the truck forward until the bumper was against the single post standing in the centre of the opening. She pressed the accelerator pedal, and the truck eased forward by inches until the pre-stressed concrete post snapped at the base. She switched off the truck motor and, in the silence, they heard the sound of the myriad night insects, and the thud of a stationary engine coming from the distant buildings of the air base.

Joachim returned to the car and signalled for the three men to join him. 'Everything's under control at the base,' he said. 'The main thing is not to show surprise at anything you see or hear.'

Mason smiled. 'The sounds ominous. What can surprise us now?'

'It's just a precaution. Don't let anything you see bother you.' He pressed the starter and the engine purred. Wilhelm waved and the car drew away from the tanker and continued along the northern perimeter of the fence towards the lights of the buildings across the airfield. Joachim switched on his headlights, and the bright beams illuminated the road ahead.

Hackett said: 'Have you got the code word?'

'Yes. It's "Winston", but don't worry, an officer will identify you before you get through the gate. Make sure you have your weapons where you can get at them quickly.'

He swung the wheel to turn the car parallel with the eastern perimeter and in the headlights, they saw the checkpoint three hundred metres away. Joachim drove slowly towards it. He stopped a few metres from the barrier.

An officer walked over to them. 'Out. All of you.'

They climbed out of the car, and while one of the guards searched it, they were taken to a hut where a bright light lit up everything within ten metres, including their faces. They realised that this was the identification that Joachim spoke of. They saw the dark shape of another officer standing on the balcony of a tower sixty metres away. The man appeared to be looking through binoculars. Mason was suddenly tense. He didn't know how Joachim had arranged the identification, but what if he was wrong! What if the officer refused to carry out his part of the plan? What if it was a trap?

The officer on the balcony disappeared from view, and a few seconds later a bell rang in the hut. They heard the muttered words, and the officer came out to them. He was relaxed. It was clear they had been identified.

He pointed to Mason, Davis and Hackett. 'Get your things from the car.' He went over to Joachim. 'The code word please.'

Joachim gave him the word, and the officer nodded. 'Good. You may get back in the car and go.' He handed Joachim an envelope. 'Your instructions are in this letter.'

The three men watched him go with mixed feelings. They felt vulnerable without him. They began to walk towards the brightly-lit hangars, escorted by two armed guards. Hackett was carrying a fascimile of the letter of credit for thirty million dollars. It was a measure of Joachim's efficiency that he insisted that one of them carry proof of the fact that they had it. He thought it was unlikely that anyone would ask to see it, but in the event that someone did, it was available for inspection.

Inside the hangar, the three men found the crew of the plane waiting for them to board, and they went up the steps which immediately hissed upwards to become a pneumatic door. The engines which had been warmed up earlier, roared into life and the big plane began its taxi across the airfield.

Joachim arrived at the tanker just as he heard the roar of the engines. He parked the car on the opposite side of the road, and about fifty metres away. Tensely they all waited for the Junker to approach their position, watching the big light grow larger as it came towards them. It began to swing to point south, and as it completed its turn, Joachim moved.

He jumped on to the step of the cab. 'Now!'

The girl, who had kept the engine idling, pressed her foot down on the pedal and the tanker leapt forward. Swinging in a wide arc it stopped in front of the Junker, and Hackett, who had been standing at the door of the cabin, pressed a pistol against the back of the co-pilot's head.

Davis grabbed the pilot's hair and pulled the man's head back towards him. 'Open the door!'

The man's startled eyes swivelled towards him, and the navigator attempted to rise. Mason pushed him back and showed him his pistol. 'Don't do anything foolish. The tower will want to know what is happening. Tell them you don't know. We need two minutes after you open the door, and if you don't open it now, you're dead.'

The pilot threw a switch, and they heard the hiss of the pneumatic door, and then the bump as it reached the end of its opening. Through the window, they saw Wilhelm and Johan popping children through the trap, while Joachim urged the ones on the frame to hurry. The first children began to climb the stairs. Through the pilot's earphones they heard the muted babbling of voices.

Mason prodded the man with his gun. 'What's he saying?'

'He wants to know what is happening.'

'Just say that everything's all right.' The pilot looked at him. 'Go on. Tell him that.' The man repeated what Mason had told him to say. 'Remember, I'm a bomber pilot, so if you don't do as I say, I'll shoot you and fly this thing myself.' Tension made his voice shake, and he found it difficult to breathe. 'Taff, see how they're getting on.'

As Davis went back, Mason saw the tankers move forward to clear their path, and Wilhelm waved them away. The whole operation had taken just two minutes.

Davis saw that Pauline, who was the last to board, was safe in the cabin. 'All aboard here. Take it away.'

Mason prodded the pilot once more. 'Right. Shut the door and fly. Tell the tower that a tanker crashed through the fence by accident, and everything's fine on the plane.' He prodded the gun again. 'Go on. Tell them.'

The man repeated his words to the tower, but at that moment a truck full of soldiers left the buildings at full speed and headed towards them. They heard the bark of the assault rifles, and the truck swerved away from them in a wide arc.

'Take it up! Go! Now!' Mason was screaming at the pilot, and the man sent the plane surging forward. The sound of the gunfire was drowned in the roar of the engines.

As the plane leapt forward, Joachim shouted to the others and made for the car parked across the road. The three men ran towards Joachim, and as they did so, Wilhelm sent a last burst at the truck which was coming at them at full speed. It swerved once more, and answering fire came from the soldiers. Joachim had the engine running, and before the last door slammed, he had the car moving. They ran without lights for about two kilometres, and then the bright beams were switched on. They knew the soldiers would approach the tanker cautiously, certain that the tanker was where the danger lay. Before he switched on the lights, Joachim peered into the night sky where he was certain he had seen a plane banking towards the north.

Two hours later, the Junker landed in Sweden.

A Mercedes-Benz carrying four men stopped at the Amtzell Crossroads Inn where Karl joined them. He was dressed in civilian clothes, and as he strode towards the car, a girl ran from the doorway of the inn. Karl checked his stride, and waited for her.

She stopped a few feet away from him, savouring the moment.

'Hullo, Czech,' Karl said softly.

'Hullo, Austrian.' Suddenly she was in his arms, tears streaming down her cheeks, and ex-Major Karl Brunner, late head of the Breslau office of the Kripo, held on to his Inga as though he would never let her go. Finally they walked hand in hand to the car.

They left Wilhelm and Gunther at Meersburg, and after they arrived in Konstanz, Johan left them.

Joachim, Karl and Inga went on to Zurich where they banked thirty million dollars and waited for the war to end.

In the meanwhile, on 15th August Mason was debriefed in Sweden by British Military Intelligence, and described fully the plot to assassinate Mr Churchill in Italy. As a result, signals were sent to all those involved in the Prime Minister's security, and special precautions were taken in the event that Hitler and his staff persevered with his mad scheme. However, nothing more was heard of any planned attempts, and it was presumed that the whole matter had been dropped with the failure of Operation Geld.

The following week, Mason, Davis, Hackett, Pauline and the children were flown to England and safety.

Epilogue

By early September, the Allied forces had swept through Lyon, and the people of Le Chambon shared in the joy of liberation. By October it was considered safe enough to send the children back to France to be amongst their own people, and the newly-weds, Bob and Pauline Mason, were asked if they would escort them back. The people of Le Chambon took them in, and the Reverend Trocmé arranged foster homes for them as he had done for so many children during the war.

In June 1945, a Bayreuth couple wrote to the Reverend Trocmé, asking if he knew of two girls, Elena and Henriette Wiskamann, and were relieved to be told that they had been adopted by a Jewish couple from Switzerland. The girls pay regular visits to Herr Loringhoven and his wife in Bayreuth.

In the meanwhile, Tom Hackett reported to the OSS office in London, where he gave the Americans the information entrusted to him by Erich Rowecki of the Gorlitz cell. The information was a contingency plan by Adolph Hitler for a powerful counter-attack by German forces if the Allies reached the German border. The plan, revealed by a prominent member of the Oberkommando der Wehrmacht, the German High Command, proposed that the attack should consist of a thrust by an army group between Monschau and Echternacht with a Panzer division on each flank. The initial objective was a crossing of the Meuse between Liège and Givet, and no less than eighteen divisions were to be committed behind the spearhead. In addition, parties of parachute troops would be dropped along the projected route of advance, while saboteurs in civilian clothes and American army uniforms would be sent in to create havoc behind enemy lines.

The plan was subjected to minute scrutiny, but the intelligence was discounted on the grounds that by the beginning of December 1944, Hitler could not raise five divisions, let alone eighteen.

History records that on 16th December, the counter-attack was launched exactly as planned, and the Ardennes became a graveyard for thousands of Allied troops who were overwhelmed in the initial assault. In two days the Germans had over-run two American divisions and had penetrated twenty-five kilometres to reach Stavelot, Trois Ponts and Vielsalm.

Bastogne and the Battle of the Bulge will never be forgotten.

But by then, Erich Rowecki, Karl Brunner and his wife Inga had taken new identities in Switzerland, and in 1949 made a permanent home in California.

An anonymous donation of thirty million dollars was received by the president of the new state of Israel to be used for the rehabilitation of those Jews who had lost everything in the war.